THE TORTUROUS SCHEME

The Torturous Scheme describes John Graham's rite of passage between the austerity of the Second World War and the excitement of the permissive 'sixties. It focuses on his moral dilemma in equating the ethical code of conduct he applies to his business life with the lack of ethics that marks his personal relationships. It is set in Paris and London.

The thirty years which author Joe Sinclair spent in the transport and export trades industry bring verisimilitude and authenticity to the novel's background.

This is the author's seventh published book but his first full length work of fiction.

Educated in South Wales and London University, Joe Sinclair devotes most of his time to writing and publishing but still maintains his commercial links as non-executive director of a container shipping line and editor of the newsletter published by the container division of the prestigious Sea Containers Group.

He also edits *New Learning* for the NLP-Education Network, a quarterly journal which enjoys a gratifying international reputation for the quality of its material.

Joe Sinclair divides his time between his homes in London and Dorset.

By Joseph Sinclair:

Refrigerated Transportation (Published by ASPEN) - 1988
Refrigerated Containers (Published by the World Bank, Washington, DC, USA) - 1989
An ABC of NLP (Published by ASPEN) - 1992
Arteries of War (Published by Airlife) - 1992
An ABC of NLP (Expanded second edition published by ASPEN with additional material by Stephen Bray) - 1998
Peace of Mind is a Piece of Cake (Published by Crown House) - 1998 (Co-authored by Michael Mallows)

THE TORTUROUS SCHEME

Joseph Sinclair

ASPEN
London, England

Published by Container Marketing Ltd
106 Holders Hill Road
London NW4 1LL England
Tel: +44 020 8346 3828
Fax: +44 020 8371 0013
Email: aspen@conts.com

First published 2001

ISBN 0-9513660-4-1

Printed in the United Kingdom by
Redwood Books,
Kennet Way,
Trowbridge,
Wiltshire BA14 8RN

To Michael Mallows
The source of much joy
and not a little learning

THE TORTUROUS SCHEME

". . . That thing beyond one's outstretched hands
which greets with chill disdain
All efforts at possession, whether selfishly
inspired
Or amorously motivated, and would stay apart
While body agonized and brain unite in tort'rous
scheme
And drive one to despair . . ."

PART ONE

She turned over on her side until she was facing me.

"It was wonderful," she said. "I'd forgotten how wonderful it could be."

Her face was flushed. Her eyes held a tenderness that was at once a gratefulness and a reproach. Her smile was a knife inserted in my side. I felt sick. My throat was dry and I wanted to look away, but I couldn't. I could only smile back at her and hope my guilt wasn't as visible as it felt.

I stared at the ceiling and wondered how I could have been so crass as to put myself into this situation. How could I have expected to walk back into her life for a few days and seriously believe that it would mean nothing to her? Was there no bottom to the depths of my rottenness?

This then was the end. I knew now that I could never maintain the pretence and mockery of the situation. I would have to tell her. But tomorrow, I thought. I'll tell her tomorrow, when we're both calm and the surroundings are right. She'll understand; she must understand. And even as I thought it I knew I was deceiving myself again.

The irony of it was that it need not have been like this at all. I remembered how different it had been and I knew how differently it could have turned out . . .

My mind winged back to the beginning, considered the present in all its implications, and I found myself wondering about the pattern in the fabric of my life weaving the two together.

She stirred in the bed beside me. My hand reached out, stroked her hair, then her brow, still damp with perspiration. It was as if my hand didn't belong to me. I was the audience at a piece acted by two other players. We were marionettes and someone else was pulling the strings

The script was written for us and we had neither control over our actions nor responsibility for the consequences of our behaviour. How could I, a puppet, be expected to change the plot?

CHAPTER ONE

The breeze blowing up the Boulevard de Magenta carried with it the aroma and pulsation of all Paris. Perfume and Gauloises; and short skirts made still shorter as the gusts caught them.

For John Graham, seated outside the café, sipping his pastis and water, this was Life, this was Adventure. To be in Paris in 1946, in uniform, at a time when the glamour of that uniform had not yet worn off – when he could still be regarded and, more importantly, regard himself as a conquering hero – was, for him, a new dimension in living.

He had been feeling pleased with himself when he sat down and ordered his first drink. Now the atmosphere really took hold of him and he felt almost drugged with eagerness and excitement and – aniseed. The luck of it! The sheer, unaccountable good fortune to be handed a five-day pass to Paris. The stories he had heard about this place! And now here he was, having missed war service, but still with a chance to share in the spoils. He turned to the infantry corporal seated beside him.

"Isn't this a wonderful city!" he effused.

"Take it easy son," the corporal smiled. "You're new here, aren't you?"

"Well, yes."

"A word of advice, then: don't believe half the things you've heard about Paree."

"But . . . but all this." John gestured expansively. "You know . . . booze . . . and women . . . and . . ." his eyes caught a swirling skirt above stockingless but shapely legs and high-heeled shoes, "and women," he repeated appreciatively.

"How old are you son?"

"Nineteen. Why?"

The corporal laughed. "You stick to the booze. Those tarts will suck you in and blow you out in bubbles."

John Graham snorted, his pride hurt by this imagined slur on his manhood. "I can look after myself."

"Didn't say you couldn't." The corporal winked, sagely re-establishing a man-to-man relationship. "But you're new in this town, haven't learned the ropes yet. What do they call you?"

"John."

"Well I'm Herbert for my sins," he gave a mock-salute, "but you can call me Bert. What're you drinking?"

"Pernod – but . . ."

"That's all right." Bert snapped his fingers. "Waiter, pernod and a beer." He grinned. "No, all I'm getting at, you want a bit of fun, don't look for it round here. First off it'll cost you – know what I mean? – maybe in more ways than one. Secondly, if you want a good time, there's lots of better places to find it."

"But this is Pigalle, isn't it?"

"Well, just up the boulevard, sure. Pig'Alley the Yanks call it. And that's the trouble."

"I don't understand."

"The Yanks," Bert explained patiently. "See that café over there? The Dupont?" His finger indicated the opposite corner of the Boulevard de Rochechouart. In contrast to the rather dingy café whose pavement table they were occupying, the opposing café was all chrome, strip-lighting, and gaily painted raffia chairs. "That's where the Yanks hang out. And pay about twice as much for their booze." He gestured again. "See this road? This is No-Man's-Land. You cross it at your peril." He chuckled. "But seriously, son, what sort of tart's going to give you the time of day with that sort of competition in the neighbourhood? Sure, she might let you buy her a few drinks. She might even give you a short time. But for the serious business, she's going to go where the real money is. Know what I mean?"

"I see." It was beginning to sound very depressing, John thought.

Herbert downed his beer and looked around for the waiter. John caught his arm. "This one's on me, Bert."

"That's right decent of you, John." He lit his pipe while John ordered another round. "Cheers! And don't look so glum, son. I told you, there's plenty of other places were a bright lad like you can make out. The other side of the river, for instance."

"The other side of the river?" John echoed morosely.

"Sure. The Latin Quarter they call it. You're an educated chap, aren't you?" John nodded doubtfully. "You'll be right in your element then, in one of them places where the students hang out. Plenty of the other sort too, but you take my tip, steer clear of them." He laid a hand on John's arm. "If I'd had your advantages . . . " He sighed. "How long you been in the Ordnance?"

"About nine months."

"Where're you stationed?

"Transit camp, Calais."

Herbert grinned. "Well I can understand you wanting to cut loose.

But gently does it. Take your time. Go back to Calais with a few happy memories, not a thick head, a rotten stomach, a lousy taste in your mouth, and an empty wallet."

"Why are you telling me all this?" The earlier fevered excitement had gradually been replaced by a vague depression, brought on by the corporal's apparent attempts to discourage him, and aided by the presence of the pernods in his stomach.

"I don't want to see you making a fool of yourself. I've got a boy almost your age. If he was over here, I'd want him to enjoy himself sure, but I'd be glad to have someone steer him on the right course. Know what I mean?"

John nodded glumly. All at once he had lost every scrap of excitement and desire. He knew he would find no pleasure this evening and wished now he had never come to Paris. He should have stayed in Calais. Better still, he could have spent this leave back home. How on earth had he imagined he would find adventure in this place? Adventure should stimulate a person, not depress him; he should feel good, not sick and disgusted. He realized that Herbert was talking to him again and forced himself to concentrate. The corporal appeared unaccountably to have moved away from him and John leaned forward to bring him back into focus.

"Sorry," John said, "I didn't catch that."

"I said: are you feeling all right?"

"All right? Of course I'm . . . " Abruptly he realized that he was far from all right. He had difficulty in swallowing the saliva that was filling his mouth. "Excuse me," he blurted out, and fled into the café.

Minutes later he came back, pale and shaken, but things were in focus again, both physically and mentally.

Herbert looked at him anxiously. "You feeling better now?"

"Yes. I'm sorry. That doesn't often happen to me. I didn't realize pernod was so strong."

"Haven't you drunk it before?" John shook his head. "Christ! And you've just knocked back three of them!"

"Four," John muttered.

The corporal slapped him on the back and burst into uproarious laughter. "You'll do son," he said when he had caught his breath. "Ready to make a move?"

"A move?" John swallowed, and the sweet-sour taste of vomit rose into his mouth. "The only move I'd better make is back to the billet and bed."

"Nonsense! A cup of strong coffee and a hunk of bread and you'll be on the scent hotter than ever. And then we'll make a move." He snapped his fingers again at the waiter.

Herbert had been right, John decided, as they walked down the Boulevard Saint-Michel. The road ran from the River Seine through the heart of the student quarter, and John found himself immediately responsive to its atmosphere. Despite his earlier hot-cheeked desire to sample the sensual pleasures of Pigalle, he felt much more at home here. In many ways he could imagine himself in Chelsea.

And yet it couldn't possibly be Chelsea. The sidewalk cafés; the bookshops still overspilling their wares into the street despite it being early evening; the kiosks growing out of the pavements and dispensing tobacco, newspapers and lottery tickets: this could only be Paris.

They called at *La Source* for a drink and Herbert, eyes twinkling, asked John if he would take another pernod. John, unhesitatingly, elected to go on to beer. He would have preferred to forgo drinking entirely, but felt that Herbert might interpret this as an unfriendly gesture. But when they had drunk their beers, he did not offer to buy the next round and, after a while, Herbert suggested they move on.

Further up the road they passed a shop crowded with young people, many of whom had earphones fitted over their heads. John asked the corporal what they were doing.

"That's *Chanteclair*," said Herbert. He made it rhyme with Aunty Clare. "They're listening to gramophone records."

"Oh? Sounds like fun. Want to try it?"

Herbert grinned. "It's not my cup of tea, son. But you go ahead. I'll push off back to Barbès."

"Oh no. I'll come with you. I can always return here another time."

"Don't be daft. You stay here and enjoy yourself. I've got to get back to barracks and anyway," he punched John's shoulder, "you'll be safer here than up there. Know what I mean?"

"I know what you mean." John smiled. "Will we see each other again, Bert?"

"Any afternoon you're passing the old caff at Barbie, you'll like as not see me outside." He waved a hand. "Enjoy yourself, son."

John walked into Chanteclair. Facing him were rows of bank tables, back to back, separated by high wooden partitions. It looked almost like a large public telephone switchboard, with buttons to push, dials, earphones, directories. The whole set-up seemed mysterious and incomprehensible.

He went up to a pretty, pink-faced young girl, who was busily thumbing a large catalogue, and asked, in hesitant French, how he went about choosing some music.

She looked at his uniform and answered in English that was rather less hesitant than his French. "First you buy a *jeton* from the man over there." She pointed. "You find the number of the music in one of these catalogues." She thumped them. "You put your *jeton* in there." She touched a slot on the partition. "You dial a number." She demonstrated. "And after a few moments you hear your music in the ear-piece." She smiled. Her movements and her smile were very young, eager, unselfconscious.

John smiled back. "I'm very grateful." He purchased a metal disc and rejoined her. "Now perhaps you will show me how to find the music."

She grinned an impish, *gamin* grin. "Should I also listen to the music for you?" Seeing him redden, she added quickly, "*Je vous taquine* . . . er, I'm teasing you. Look! You find the music in this catalogue under the name of the composer, or in this one under the name of the orchestra or soloist. What would you like to hear?"

He considered for a moment. "I think the Chopin Revolutionary Study."

She leafed through the pages. "Chopin . . . *Etude Révolutionaire* . . . ah, here you are. You have a choice of three versions."

He had been following her finger. "Oh yes, I see. I think I'll try the Cortot."

He smiled his thanks and was surprised as a frown suddenly appeared on her face and, to his bewilderment, she turned abruptly away from him. He put his disc in the slot, dialled the number, and put the earphones on his head. While he was waiting for the music to begin he saw the girl turn to a young man on her other side and begin talking and gesticulating fiercely. The young man laughed at her.

Then the music started. It was not the Revolutionary Study he had expected, but a study he knew as Winter Wind. It must have been an old recording, for it was scratched and blurred in places. But Cortot's mastery of the unmistakeable Chopin idiom was evident through all the defects of the record and, for a few minutes, John Graham was lost in a private world where nothing existed but rich chords and patterned figurations of sound. Then it was over and, with a sigh, he took the earphones from his head.

The young woman was still engaged in furious argument with her neighbour, but as John replaced the earphones she turned to him. "I hope you enjoyed your Cortot," she snapped.

The venom in her voice flustered him. "I'm sorry . . . I don't understand. Did I do something wrong?"

The young man grinned at John across the girl. "You must pay no attention to Yvette," he said in faultless English. "She objects to Cortot."

She turned on him. "And so should you. The fascist!"

The young man grinned again. "She thinks everyone is a fascist."

"But he is! He is! He played for the *Boches*."

He caught her arm. "Little Yvette, he is an old man. Yes, he played for the *Boches*, but only because he wanted to play the piano, not because they were Germans. It did not matter to him who he was playing for. He was too old to make the big gesture." He sighed. "All he wanted to do was play the piano."

"But why for them? Those . . . those animals who killed Pierre?"

"And if he had not played for them – would your brother have lived?" He groaned and his expression became troubled. "Listen Yvette, you must forget these childish prejudices. Your passion is highly commendable, but it should be directed where it can do the most good. I have as much reason to hate the Germans as you – did I not also fight with the *Maquis*? – but we must put our hate to more constructive purpose. We must make a world where such things cannot happen again." He had been speaking throughout in good if somewhat stilted English, perhaps in deference to the Englishman who was listening to them, and now he turned to John. "Am I not right, soldier?"

John shrugged his shoulders. "I don't think I should interfere."

The young man laughed. "Oh, you English! The great non-interferers who always end up interfering too much."

"Now hold on," John said angrily.

Once again the youth laughed. "Please don't take my remarks seriously. I should not be so rude as to make them if I thought you would." He held out his hand. "I am Claude Dumard. This angry creature is my cousin, Yvette Beaumont."

"John Graham." He shook their hands.

"Now what do you say we go somewhere for a drink and you can tell me what is wrong with the French." He looked at Yvette and then winked at John. "Unless, of course, you wish to hear more Cortot."

John smiled. It was hard to stay angry with Claude he decided. There was something artless and infectious about his constant good humour. "I'd love to," he said, "but you must be my guests."

Claude held up a hand. "Let us not speak of guests and hosts. We go out as three friends together. What do you say, little Yvette?"

Yvette looked up at him, smiling, clearly unable to resist for long the charm of his personality, but equally – with female obduracy – determined to get in the last word. "Certainly, as long as we do not go to the Dupont."

"The Dupont?" John queried.

Claude said, "It is a café in the *Boul' Miche'*."

"Oh, of course," John said. "I believe there is one at Barbès-Rochechouart, where the Americans drink."

"It is not of the *Amerloques* that Yvette thinks," explained Claude, "but of the Germans who used to drink there during the war." He patted her cheek. "All right, little one, we shall go elsewhere. I don't care for fish anyway." He caught John's puzzled look and explained, "The *Dupont du Quartier* has a large aquarium of tropical fish. I find them very disconcerting. The protruding eyes and open mouths remind me, too, of many people I met during the war."

CHAPTER TWO

He had invited them to have lunch with him the next day, but Claude had begged to be excused because of a prior commitment. Yvette, however, was delighted to accept despite – she had added with her gamin grin – his taste in classical music.

Now he was waiting for her outside *La Source* and found himself recalling the unexpectedly delightful evening he had spent with them. They had shown him a little of the Left Bank student night-life, drinking mainly fruit juices at various student clubs around the Boulevard Saint-Germain, and discussing one subject after another.

Claude was a first-rate companion. Some years older than John, he seemed to be known and liked everywhere they had gone. His second year at the Sorbonne, studying literature, had been interrupted by his military activities which, apart from his one reference in Chanteclair to the Maquis, he was reluctant to discuss.

Claude's cousin Yvette a fifteen-year old schoolgirl in the middle of her summer holidays. She was less at home than Claude in the clubs they had visited but seemed, nevertheless, remarkably self-assured and confident for her age. Certainly there was nothing hesitant about the way she expressed her views and, John felt, she seemed far more adult than girls of her age in England. He wondered if this were the result of living for so many years in an enemy-occupied country, or if it was a normal difference between English and French girls.

What surprised him most was that he had no regret at missing out on the sort of experience he had been anticipating yesterday afternoon. He certainly felt nothing but pleasure at the prospect of again meeting this precocious fifteen year old schoolgirl, and thought fondly for a moment of the corporal – Herbert – but for whom he would probably have made a complete ass of himself.

John Graham, at nineteen, could not be described as handsome, but there was a great deal of charm in his frank, open face, his shock of dark brown hair, and his grey-green eyes. Five feet nine in height, his ten months of army service, with its solid if plain diet and regular hours, had served to fill out his previously rather slender frame. At the same time, his features retained much of the boyish appeal that had served him so usefully in making friends during his schooldays. He was, in fact, one of those people who, unless personal tragedy overtakes them, seem to remain indefinitely on the threshold of manhood and then pass, overnight apparently, into middle age.

His life before his military service had been enjoyable and interesting without being unduly exciting. His childhood had been spent in Nuneaton, in the middle of England. Then, when the German *Luftwaffe* attacks were approaching their peak, particularly on nearby Coventry, he had been evacuated to South Wales. Here he had spent four of the war years – four years which he was afterwards to regard as the most formative of his life, though why this was so he was never able to define clearly. It was simply that he seemed to have arrived in South Wales a boy, and to have left it a man. Shortly before the end of the war his father died and his mother was offered a flat in her sister's house in Earl's Court, London. When he left South Wales, therefore, at the age of seventeen, he went to London and completed his Higher Schools' studies at the Regent Street Polytechnic.

Then followed his conscription into the army when, after six weeks' basic training in Suffolk, and six months spent in clerical duties at an ordnance depot in Hampshire, he was transferred to the transit camp at Calais.

This was his first venture outside the British Isles, and his initial excitement at being in a foreign country was wearing thin with the tedium and routine of his duties, when it was re-kindled by the prospect of five days leave in Paris.

And exciting it was proving to be, though not in any way he could have imagined. He thought of all the places Yvette had promised to show him today and blessed the happy chance that had taken him into Chanteclair.

Then Yvette arrived.

"Hello, Tommy," she greeted him cheekily.

He took her hand and smiled at her. She was dressed in a short, pleated skirt and high-necked blue jumper and carried a matching cardigan. A blue beret perched saucily on the side of her head and flat sandals worn with white ankle socks competed her dress. She looked far younger than she had yesterday evening and, for a moment, he felt a bit embarrassed at being seen with her, at the thought of taking her into a restaurant. It had seemed different when Claude had been with them.

But, as it happened, she said almost at once, "I'm afraid I can't accept your invitation to lunch today."

"Oh? Why not?"

She shrugged and said simply, "My parents."

"You mean they won't let you?"

"They think it would not be right."

"Then you can't show me the sights this afternoon?"

She smiled enigmatically. "Well no – and yes."

"I'm sorry." He shook his head. "I don't understand."

"Well it's up to you. My mother said that if you want me to show you Paris, you must come and have lunch with us." She lifted her shoulders; not quite a shrug, rather a statement that the matters was out of her hands. "Will you come?"

"I'm not sure. It seems a bit brazen."

She grimaced. "I don't know what that means."

"I mean, we only met yesterday and your parents don't know me. And I know how hard it is to make food rations stretch these days."

She tossed her head impatiently. "That's foolish. They would not suggest it if there was not enough food. Anyway," she added coyly, "they will be terribly disappointed if you do not accept."

"Oh come on now, Yvette. Who's being foolish now? How can they be disappointed when they don't even know me?"

She stamped her foot with vexation, all coyness gone. "All right, then. *I'm* the one who will be disappointed. Now you know."

He laughed. "Despite my taste in music?"

"Despite your taste in music." Her pretended anger fought a losing battle with her natural humour and she joined him in laughter.

"Okay," he said, "let's go."

They took the Métro to République then walked along the Quai de Valmy, beside a picturesque canal which bisected the street. She led him into a large apartment house and, in a second-floor apartment overlooking the canal, introduced him to her parents.

Monsieur Beaumont was a large, florid man with drooping white moustaches, apparently well into his sixties. His much younger-looking wife was a wisp of a woman who looked as if the slightest breeze might lift her off her feet and carry her away.

They greeted John correctly but coldly. It was curious; despite all their efforts to put him at his ease, insisting that he sit in an armchair, pressing a drink on him, he sensed an atmosphere almost of hostility. The result was that five minutes after his arrival he was considerably less at ease than when Yvette had made the introductions.

The feeling persisted throughout lunch, and he was surprised by the variety of dishes they produced despite the meagre ration allowance which he presumed they had to endure. A pâté was succeeded by tomato salad, followed by pork cutlets with haricot beans, sauté potatoes served as a separate course, then green salad, a selection of cheeses (most of which he had never seen before), and finally fresh fruit.

The meal left him pleasantly satisfied with no feeling of having overeaten. His own mother, he felt, could take some lessons from these people in a country where food was reputedly in far shorter supply than in his own. The only fault he could find was with the quality of the bread and the coffee. The long, thin loaf, which he had always regarded as a French speciality, proved quite tasteless, the crust hard, the inside almost entirely hollow. He could not believe it had always been like this. As for the coffee – thick and bitter – it tasted as if it had been made from acorns – which, quite possibly, it had.

Towards the end of the lunch he sensed a distinct thaw in the atmosphere. This followed a somewhat strained conversation in French with Monsieur and Madame Beaumont, Yvette translating eagerly whenever it was necessary, and often when it was not. They questioned him discreetly, but skillfully, about his life in England, his family, his work in the army, his impressions of France and the French people, so that by the time Yvette and her mother had vanished to wash the dishes he was astonished to reflect on how much he had disclosed about himself.

Then he offered Monsieur Beaumont a cigarette and accepted, in turn, a glass of cognac.

"I hope you do not mind," said Yvette's father, "that we have asked you here to lunch."

"Not at all," said John. "It was very kind of you."

They each spoke slowly in French; Monsieur Beaumont in order that John would have no trouble following his meaning, John searching for the right words, knowing how easy it is to be misunderstood when speaking a foreign tongue. But John suddenly felt close to this large, compassionate, older man. He felt, too, as if he had in some way been accepted; as though he had been put to some sort of test – and had passed.

Monsieur Beaumont's next words confirmed this impression.

"You understand, Monsieur Graham, now that our son is no longer with us – that we only have our Yvette – we are naturally concerned with the people she meets. We are no longer young, you see, Madame Beaumont and I – but Yvette . . . she is still very young."

His words had a calm sincerity and John nodded, too moved for the moment to speak.

"And she is so impressionable, our Yvette," Monsieur Beaumont continued with a faint smile. "When she came home last night, so excited, and could talk of nothing but the Englishman she had met . . ." He spread his hands. "You see, we simply had to find out for ourselves. I know you will not misconstrue my words when say that, in all armies, there are good men and some who are perhaps not so good."

John cleared his throat. "Of course."

"And then we had not had the opportunity to question Claude, and Yvette was so insistent that she must not disappoint you today."

"I quite understand, Monsieur, and I hope I have reassured you."

Monsieur Beaumont smiled. "Yes, yes indeed, Monsieur Graham. And I know I speak for my wife also."

And then, as if on cue, Yvette and her mother returned to the dining room. Yvette threw herself into her father's lap, her arms around his neck, hugging him.

"*Tu vois, tu vois qu'il est gentil, comme je t'ai dit!* Didn't I tell you how nice he was!"

It had been arranged that he bring her home by nine o'clock that evening. Claude was expected for his weekly game of chess with

Monsieur Beaumont and they would be delighted to have John spend the remainder of the evening with them. That is, if he had nothing better to do.

He asked Yvette if she would mind their going to the Boulevard de Rochechouart first, as he wished to see somebody there.

"But no," she said, "that's perfect. Then we can visit Montmartre and the Sacré Coeur."

They took the Métro from République station and left it at Barbès-Rochechouart where the underground train left its subterranean tunnel and travelled on a viaduct above the centre of the wide boulevard. From the station platform John could see the Dupont café and the café Rousseau – where he had met Herbert – on the opposite corner, but at that distance he could no see if Herbert were there.

However, as Yvette and he approached the café, he could make out the corporal's placid features, his pipe clenched between his teeth, the perpetual beer before him.

"Well John," Herbert smiled, lifting his eyebrows slightly at Yvette, "how's it going?"

"Fine, Bert." He introduced Yvette as they sat down. "This young lady is showing me Paris."

"Pleased to meet you," said Herbert. "What'll you have?"

"I don't think we'll have a drink, thanks Bert." He looked at Yvette and she smiled, leaving it up to him. Then he leaned towards the corporal. "But I'd like to ask a favour of you. Do you think you could get hold of some bread and coffee for me? The sort of bread we get in camp? And some *real* coffee?"

Herbert took his pipe slowly from his mouth, looked first at Yvette, then again at John. He lowered his voice. "I hope you know what you're doing. Know what I mean?"

John look at him blankly for a moment and then laughed. "Oh God! I haven't started cradle-snatching yet. I met Yvette and her cousin in Chanteclair yesterday and had lunch with her parents today. The bread and the coffee's for them."

The corporal looked relieved. "You had me worried there for a moment." He pondered. "I don't see why I shouldn't be able to get that for you. When would you want it?"

"This evening, if possible. Say about eight-thirty."

"I'll see what I can do, son. Have a good time and I'll see you later."

John thanked him and went off with Yvette. She took him up the Boulevard, then turned off and they climbed a succession of steeply rising narrow streets until they arrived at the Sacré Coeur, which John thought the most inspiring church he had ever seen. The view from the dome, which they reached laughing and breathless after climbing the seemingly never-ending winding staircase, was magnificent. Yvette pointed out all the other places to which she would be taking him: the Eiffel Tower, the Arc de Triomphe, the Panthéon, the Louvre.

Later that afternoon they took the lift to the second stage of the Eiffel Tower and Yvette told him that Emile Zola claimed this was his favourite spot in all Paris, because it was the only place where he didn't have to look at that monstrosity of an Eiffel Tower. But John felt no empathy with that remark, excited as he was by the atmosphere and unable to imagine Paris without the Eiffel Tower.

Then they bought some fruit and took it to the Bois de Boulogne, where they sat in the shade of the trees beside the lake, relaxing from the sightseeing, eating cherries and apples, before hiring a rowboat. To their astonishment, when the boatman noted the time on a large card, it was already seven-thirty and they were able to spend no more than half an hour on the lake before leaving to rejoin Herbert.

The corporal was waiting for them at the same table, a large parcel in front of him which he pushed silently towards John.

"Thanks, Bert," said John. "How much do I owe you?"

"Nothing."

"Don't be silly. I must pay you for it."

"You have," Herbert said enigmatically. "But, if you like, I'll accept a beer."

So they all had a drink and Herbert insisted on hearing everything that John and Yvette had done that afternoon which, enthusiastically and excitedly, they were far from reluctant to describe.

They left after promising to have another drink with him later that week and made their way back to the house on the Quai de Valmy.

Claude was already there, engrossed in a game of chess with Yvette's father.

"Please don't stop playing," said John.

But Claude said, "There's no point in continuing." He pushed his king over. "He has me thoroughly beaten - as usual."

Although Claude had spoken in English, Monsieur Beaumont smiled and winked as if he had understood every word and fully concurred.

Then all three – Yvette's parents and Claude – insisted on being given a full account of their afternoon's adventures. And John, with continual interruptions by Yvette, repeated all he had told Herbert and, so great was his animation, he had to tell them in English, with Yvette and Claude translating.

Monsieur and Madame Beaumont kept smiling and nodding their heads in pleased approval, clearly contented by their daughter's healthily flushed cheeks and evident happiness.

When he had finished, John remembered the parcel on the floor beside him and solemnly handed it to Madame Beaumont. She opened it and her eyes grew wide as she saw the two rectangular loaves of white English bread and the large packet of ground coffee.

"*Ah non . . . c'est de trop . . . je ne peux pas . . .*"

John interrupted her protests. "It's nothing really. From the army. My pleasure."

But her protestations had been merely a formality and now she held up a loaf of bread for all to see. "*Mais ça, c'est du pain?*" she exclaimed. "What sort of bread is that?"

John laughed. "It's English bread. Very good."

"But it is not bread," she contradicted. "It's cake!" And she made Yvette cut five slices from the loaf so that they might all sample it.

It seemed strange to John to be eating a slice of English bread, albeit of typical pre-war quality, without butter or margarine. He feared the others would find it as stodgy as he did. But they all agreed with Madame Beaumont that it was indeed cake – a rather unusual cake perhaps – but cake nonetheless. And if they found it drier than they would have preferred, and even a mite stodgy, they were too polite to say so.

The Beaumonts thanked him again for his gift and then Yvette's father removed a large, old-fashioned timepiece from his waistcoat pocket and looked meaningfully at Yvette.

"Oh, Papa . . ." she complained.

"Come, Yvette," he insisted, "you've had an exciting day it is past eleven which, I am sure Monsieur Graham will agree, is late enough for a schoolgirl."

"Papa!" She blushed.

John Graham got to his feet. "I should be leaving anyway."

"Nonsense," Claude said. "Stay awhile and talk to us. It's only bedtime for little girls."

Yvette gave a small shriek, ran over to Claude and started pummeling his chest. He trapped her wrists in his hands and held her away from him, laughing.

"You beast, you beast," she cried.

"Now, now . . . little girls should be seen and not heard."

She struggled furiously to release her wrists from his grip, but realising that she had no possibility of escaping, suddenly subsided, panting.

"All right," she said. "I surrender."

Claude released her and, in a flash, she smacked his head and ran giggling to the other side of the room.

"Come now, Yvette," said her mother. "Say goodnight, and thank Monsieur Graham for being so kind."

"All right, *maman*. But John can come to lunch again tomorrow, can't he?"

"I don't think . . ." John began.

Madame Beaumont gave him no opportunity to object. "Of course he must."

Yvette kissed her parents and her cousin. Then, as she approached John, he held out his hand, but she ignored it and kissed him on both cheeks. "Thank you John, for a lovely day."

He felt his face redden and was annoyed with himself for being so easily embarrassed.

After Yvette had left the room, her mother excused herself and said the she also would go to bed and leave the men to their talk. Then Monsieur Beaumont got out a bottle of calvados and they settled back in their armchairs.

John could not understand the whole of the political discussion that followed, although the others spoke quite slowly so that he should not feel excluded. But, after asking him his views of the political situation in England under the new Labour Government (with which situation they actually appeared better acquainted than did John), and questioning him about his political affiliations (which he had to confess were rather negative), they proceeded heatedly to solve the internal problems of their own country. He gathered quickly that Claude was a member of the Communist Party and that the older man was some sort of old-fashioned radical.

Thereafter John found himself less and less able to follow the conversation, but reluctant to appear rude by suggesting that he leave. Two remarks, however, imprinted themselves on his memory. First Monsieur Beaumont said: "*Si les choses ne vont pas bien en France, c'est la faute du dirigisme du tripartisme déstructeur.*" He did not understand the meaning of the remark, although he gathered that it had something to do with the way the French Government was constituted being responsible for many of the problems. But the rhythm of the words appealed to him and on two subsequent occasions in his life the phrase was to return to him

Later, after a heated exchange, Claude said to his uncle: "*Le radical est comme le radis, rouge dehors, blanc dedans, et il se place dans l'assiette* à *beurre*." Then he burst into laughter. John took advantage of the interruption to ask Claude what this meant and Claude translated: "The radical is like the radish, red outside, white inside, and he puts himself in the butter dish – which probably doesn't mean the same thing in English, John, but I believe you have an expression about a gravy train? Is that it?"

After a while the effect of the calvados and the effort to keep up with he conversation induced a lethargy in John which Claude must have noticed, for he said, "If you feel like a breath of air I would be glad to walk with you as far as Barbès."

They took their leave of Monsieur Beaumont who, now that he no longer had the exhilaration of political argument, suddenly looked weary, and far older than his years. Then they walked slowly together through the dark Paris streets.

"I find it hard to understand," said Claude, "how so many English people seem to have so little political awareness."

"I haven't given the subject much thought," said John.

Claude grinned. "That is precisely what I mean."

"And yet you seem to have a new government every two weeks," retorted John, his national pride stung.

"Ah," said Claude, "that is because you have a two-party system. You have a stable government. But what do you achieve? We have a multi-party government in France and we achieve chaos. But out of that chaos will come order. One day we will have a one-party government here in France and then you will see how much progress we shall make."

They stood for a while beneath a street lamp at the corner of the Boulevard de Barbès. "I think I shall not see you again before your leave is ended," said Claude.

"Oh?" John queried.

"No. I depart tomorrow for a Party rally in Lyon and I shall be away for several days. But I hope that the next time you are in Paris you will get in touch with me."

"But naturally," said John.

"And one other thing, John." A hesitant note crept into his voice. "Please do not take this the wrong way, but be kind to Yvette, will you?"

"Of course I will. That's a strange thing to say."

Claude placed a hand on his arm. "You realise, don't you, that she has fallen in love with you?"

John laughed. "Please Claude. Let's not be absurd. She's only a schoolgirl and she's known me barely twenty four hours."

"That's true. But surely you understand that a schoolgirl's love is the easiest to conceive and the quickest to suffer? In its way it is no less deep than the love of an older woman, but it is without the older woman's experience to enable it to cope with real and imagined hurts." The shadows from the yellow street lamp gave his face a drawn and grave look. "And Yvette means a great deal to me," he added.

CHAPTER THREE

He had reported back to the guardhouse, as required, and now stared in dismay at the Nissen huts which made up the greater part of the camp. Fancy having to come back to this after the events of the past few days. Bloody roll on! Oh well, if he could wangle that "B-Release" for an early discharge, he wouldn't have much more than another nine months to do.

In the office he sat at his desk and glumly regarded the pile of papers before him. They certainly believed in thrusting a chap straight back into it. On the wall facing him a wooden hatch abruptly slid open with a harsh, grating sound, and Dusty Miller's red face appeared, framed in the opening.

"Welcome back, Graham." He grinned. "Had a good time?"

John chose deliberately to misunderstand him. "Well, no, actually. French railways are still bloody chaotic and the train crawled all night. Only got in this morning."

Miller screwed up his face. "I mean your leave, man, your leave."

"Oh that. Yes thanks, Sergeant."

"Reported to the M.O. yet?"

"No. Should I?"

"Too fucking true. Been to Paree, ainchya?"

"That's right."

"Well don't yer think you ought to see 'im? Might 'ave picked up a dose." Miller guffawed.

“I don’t think that’s likely, Sergeant Miller.” John felt his cheeks grow warm. Christ, why did they always have to bring things down to their own bloody level? Then, suddenly, he remembered what his original intentions in Paris had been.

“Aah, yer all the same, you young’uns. Always think you know best. Well let’s just ‘ope you remembered what your learnt at hygiene lectures.” He winked slyly. “What’s the crackling like there, these days, anyway?”

“Pretty fair,” he said. “Of course, we’re no longer the romantic conquering heroes you blokes were.”

The sergeant stared at him, clearly unsure whether or not this last remark was intended to be sarcastic. Then he said, “Well I guess there’d be sod-all use your seeing the M.O. anyway. You probably wouldn’t know what to do with it if it was offered you on a plate.” Having, to his mind, effectively countered the real or imagined sarcasm, the sergeant now smiled again. “As you can see, we can’t get on here without yer. We’ve had to save most of the fucking posting notices until you got back.”

“So I see.” John again looked at the papers on his desk. “Very kind of you.”

“Okay, Private Graham, get stuck in.” The hatch slid quickly and noisily back into place.

He got stuck in.

By lunchtime he had made a fair dent in the pile of forms, but he decided to give the cookhouse a miss. It was obvious that the sergeant had hit the exact tenor of the questions he might expect over the next few hours, and his questioners were not going to be satisfied with the terse response he had given the sergeant. Nor would they be likely to be satisfied with a recitation of his actual adventures, and would not doubt expect and demand a rather more graphic recitation. Consequently he asked someone to bring him a couple of sandwiches from the Naafi canteen and ate them in the office, exercising his imagination for a suitably impressive story to recount that evening.

“So I went back to the fellow and said: ‘What was that about pigs?’.” John surveyed his audience, noting with pleasure the looks of eager anticipation on their faces. Lofty’s mouth was actually hanging open.

“Yeah! And what did he say?” That was Scanes.

John grinned at him. “Well you must understand he had said it in French. *Films cochons*, or something like that. Of course, I had a rough idea what he was getting at. Anyway, he answered me in English. Did I want to see some special films? Not particularly, I told him. Then he started reciting a sort of list. He had something for every taste, he said. *J'en ai pour tous les gouts.* What was my fancy? Photos, a woman, two women, an exhibition – or would I prefer a man?" John paused dramatically. Really, he decided, it was quite easy once he had got started.

They were six, sitting around a Naafi table. Bernstein seemed a bit aloof, but the other four were hanging on every word.

"And . . . ? What happened then?" Pashley wanted to know.

John raised his glass and looked suitably surprised to find it empty.

"I'll see to that." Nobby Clarke grabbed the glass. "Don't go on until I get back."

In half of no time at all a full glass of beer was before him. "Cheers, Nobby," said John, raising the glass to his lips. "So, as I was saying, he ran through this list, and I said to him: 'What I want you haven't got.' He gave me a dirty look and said: 'We've got everything in Pigalle. You just name it.' I insisted that I was sure he hadn't got what I wanted and the poor chap got quite desperate trying to make me tell him what it was. You'd be surprised at some of the suggestions he made. I'd never even heard of half of them.

"Finally I took pity on him. 'Know what I want?' I said. 'I want a virgin. That's what I want, a virgin. And I bet you can't find me one.'"

They bellowed with laughter and John was gratified to note that even Bernstein joined in.

"Did he find you one?" asked Pashley.

"Of course not," John snorted. "The best he could suggest was one that was only slightly used. What he probably meant was that he hadn't been used much that evening. Anyway, I told him I wasn't interested, but that an exhibition might be amusing.

"Well, he took me round the corner and into a dingy little hotel. He made me give him a couple of hundred francs and another couple of hundred to an old crone there, and she took me up to a room where two babes were waiting." He winked conspiratorially. "One of them was black," he elaborated thoughtfully.

He was well into his stride now. All the details he had invented at lunchtime were coming out as smoothly as if he had actually experienced them. And his audience was really captivated. Even Bernstein now seemed interested, although John thought he could detect an occasional air of distaste in his expression at some of the more outrageous details. John paused at last and took a deep swig of his beer. This was thirsty work.

"And that was it," he concluded. "The climax of my leave . . . if you will pardon the pun." He grinned.

"Fuck me!" Lofty gulped. "Did they really do all those things?"

"I told you. You don't think I made it up, do you?"

"Christ, no . . . no." Lofty gulped again.

"And then I suppose you banged one of the tarts," said Nobby.

"Weeelll . . ."

"Which one?"

"Well I don't like to boast . . ."

"Fuck's sake," said Scanes plaintively. "I spent a seventy-two in Paris last month and I didn't come across anything like that."

"You just didn't know where to look," jeered Pashley. "Anyway, you probably didn't get your nose outside a pint all the time you were there."

"And if he had, he wouldn't have cottoned on to what the bloke was saying."

"Wouldn't have mattered," decided Pashley. "He don't know what it's for, anyway."

They dissolved into laughter, in which Scanes good-naturedly joined.

"Well I'll be there next leave," declared Pashley. "You can depend on't. Beats Blackpool into a cocked hat from all we've heard. Right! I'm for a game of darts. How about you, John?"

"Not for me, thanks," John said.

"What about you others?"

Four of them went off for their game, leaving Bernstein seated across the table from John.

Raymond Bernstein was two years older than John. Thick-set, with wiry black hair above thick black eyebrows, and a wide Edward G. Robinson mouth, he had had his call-up deferred two years while completing his degree at one of the red brick universities.

"How's it going, Bernie?"

Bernstein shrugged. "Still kicking my heels, as you can see. Don't know what's holding up my posting."

"Posting?"

"Didn't you know?"

"What am I supposed to know? You seem to forget, I've been away for most of the week."

"Sorry," Bernstein frowned. "I assumed you'd spotted it in the office."

"There's a five day backlog of posting notices," John grumbled. "If they'd at least taken the trouble to put them into alphabetical order, I might have dealt with yours by now. As it is, it's probably at the bottom of the deck. But does this mean you've got your transfer?"

"Yes. Obviously someone dropped a clanger at ABTU, though naturally they won't admit it. All they've said is, after reviewing the situation, I'm to be transferred to AEC and that my posting will come through normal channels." He snorted. "Normal channels!"

"But that's great! Army Education Corps! Carries automatic rank of sergeant, doesn't it?"

"Uh-huh. That's the lowest rank in the AEC. But in the meantime I'm bashing my fanny in this dump."

"Well I'll dig out your posting notice and rush it through."

"I'd appreciate that, John. Any idea where they might be sending me?"

"Probably Mönchen Gladbach. We've had quite a few education postings there lately. But wherever you go, we'll keep in touch, won't we?"

"Of course. And now I must buy you a drink. If I'd offered you one before you might have thought I was trying to bribe you."

John laughed as Bernstein retrieved their two glasses, to them to the counter, and then returned with two fresh beers.

"What do you intend doing, John?"

"I've no idea." John shrugged. "That's up to the powers-that-be, isn't it? I'm due for a stripe next month, but –"

Bernstein interrupted. "No, I mean when you get out of this mob."

"Oh . . . then. I'm not quite sure. I've been toying with the idea of a class B release and university. I took higher schools before I came in."

"Seems like a sound idea. Anything in particular?"

"Well, while I was in Paris I met someone . . ."

"So I gathered," Bernstein broke in dryly.

John hesitated. For a moment he was tempted to tell Bernstein the true story of what had happened in Paris. Raymond Bernstein was someone he admired and whose regard he esteemed. He wasn't like the others and would certainly place less store by the things most soldiers seem to value. But he thrust the temptation aside. He was committed to his story now and didn't want to risk Bernstein's respect any further by admitting to his childish trick of fictitious invention.

Now he covered his temporary confusion with a short laugh.

"No," he said. "I mean apart from that. There was this fellow, very intelligent, studying at the Sorbonne. We had quite a natter about politics and he made me realise how little I know in that area. I think maybe I might study political economy or something along those lines."

"To what end?"

"I don't really know. As I said, it's something I've only just started thinking about. I mean, what can one do with an economics degree?"

"Much the same as with any other sort of academic degree. I should know. I took classical languages." Bernstein smiled. "Know any old Greeks looking for a personal assistant? No, actually I don't think it matters much what you study, unless you want a professional, technical or scientific career. Any other sort of degree is just a key to a door. What you do once you're inside is up to you, but the degree will help to get you in."

"And how about you, Bernie? What will you do when you get out?"

"I'd like to have a shot at journalism."

"Funny," John mused. "This fellow in Paris said much the same sort of thing to me one evening."

"I'm glad to hear that the whole of your five days in Paris weren't spent jumping in and out of beds. Actually I suspect that that story you spun was a piece of fiction, but I must say some of the details sounded pretty convincing."

John felt unreasonably annoyed at Bernstein's implicit assumption that his story had been made up, and at the same time was angry with himself for being annoyed. And then, as if he had no control over his voice, he found himself saying, "But of course the story was true."

And immediately regretted his words. Now he had cut the ground from under himself and his last chance of confiding in Bernstein was gone.

"I'm sorry about that, John. You're too intelligent a fellow for that sort of nonsense."

"I suppose you would have spent all your time in the Louvre?" John said hotly.

"Yes, frankly, I would. I'm sorry if I've offended you. I know it's not my place to criticise, but when I think of all the things you could have done, all the places you could have seen, it seems a pity that so much opportunity has gone to waste."

"Well, there it is," John said. *Chacun a son gout*, or words to that effect.

But the only taste he had was a nasty one and, when he went to bed that night, he mentally replayed his time in Paris and cursed himself for a weak, stupid fool, realising how much he would have enjoyed describing his true adventures to Bernstein.

CHAPTER FOUR

Army life was becoming intolerable. In the three months since Bernstein had left, John Graham had gradually felt himself more and more tightly caught in the grip of a mentally corroding despair. He had found no-one else in camp to whom he could talk; nobody, that is, to whom he could try and express the subjective strain that was disturbing him, without having it treated with mocking laughter or ribald comment. When it was a question of discussing any subject other than work, drink or sex, a semantic barrier would appear or, even worse, the subject, through devious channels, would ultimately develop sexual connotations.

He had tried writing to Bernstein, now stationed in West Germany, and explaining what was troubling him. This had proved to be all but impossible. Somehow, in the writing, his thoughts got twisted, and the resultant plaint would appear childish and confused.

Bernstein, with typical understanding, had done his best to help. He had written to say that what John was experiencing was nothing more than plagued any other soldier possessed of intelligence and imagination living a stagnant and unproductive life.

But John felt that this was not the answer.

What made matters worse was that his application of a class B release had been rejected. The Army considered that he would have ample time to commence the next Michaelmas term at college on the expiration of his normal term of military service. Accordingly he was condemned to a full two years' engagement and, to his present way of thinking, this was tantamount to a prison sentence. Certainly a prison sentence could hardly be more oppressive.

Roll on death, demob's too slow. The old army catchphrase had real meaning for him. Even the corporal's stripes he had been able to acquire through an unexpected Establishment vacancy had done little to cheer him up. If anything, he found the company and conversation in the NCO's Naafi even less to his taste.

And yet could he be altogether sure that his mental torment was not of his own making? What was it Shakespeare had said about the fault lying not in our stars but in ourselves? He often thought about this and, in an effort to achieve better self-understanding, had taken to borrowing books from the education centre on psychology and philosophy. But the theories and phrases which seemed to register most significance were always those that merely thrust him into greater anguish: the death wish, the will to self-destruction. He recalled that statement of Monsieur Beaumont about the "destructive three-party system" and it appeared to have particular relevance to his condition, in a completely non-political sense, but he couldn't quite put his finger on it. The restrictive army routine and his own will seemed to form two sides of a triangle, but there was a third side which occasionally almost revealed itself to him and then vanished again behind an impenetrable veil. At these times it was as if something in his mind would say, "Here I am. Take me out and examine me. There is so much you can learn from me." And the moment he tried to grasp the proffered straw, it would be withdrawn.

He frequently compared his present mood of discontentment with the five amazingly carefree days he had spent in Paris. Had that really been a mere four months ago? What had happened in that short period of time to change his mental outlook so drastically? Or had it really changed so much? He had already started feeling dispirited and bored with life in Calais before he went to Paris; perhaps the five days he had passed there, plus the departure of Bernstein and the rejection of his early-release application, had merely hastened a previously-conceived process.

Yvette wrote to him regularly and frequently, her letters a mixture of schoolgirl gossip and cheerful family news. He always tried to reply promptly and to keep his letters suitably lighthearted, although it was sometimes a strain. But he could imagine that their correspondence was quite important to her, that it possibly added to her status at school to receive these letters from an English soldier.

At the moment when his nerves felt as if they were finally going to give out, a reprieve came in the form of seven days privilege leave. For a while he toyed with the idea of returning to Paris, and then he realised how unfair that would be on his mother who hadn't seen him in over six months.

London hadn't changed. That was his first, relieved thought as the number 19 bus made its slow, request-stop to fare-stage progress around Sloane Square, along Knightsbridge and down Piccadilly. Not that he had expected any changes, but it was always pleasant to have reality coincide with a mental image; something that all-too-rarely happened.

He wished he could say the same about mother. In six months she had aged six years. The unexpectedly grey hair had shocked him, and closer examination had revealed a gauntness to her cheeks and lines around her eyes which he could not recall having seen before. He hadn't said anything, though; merely hugged and kissed her, told her how glad he was to be home, and heaved an inward, grateful sigh at having decided to spend this leave with her.

He had been cross, too, that she had not asked for time off from her post-office job when she knew he was coming home. But she said that they were so short-staffed at the post-office, she hadn't liked doing that – and that was typical of her. She had added that, anyway, he didn't want to be saddled with an old woman on his leave, and although he had scorned her use of the adjective, it pained him to realise how much she had, in fact, aged in his absence.

John got off the bus in Piccadilly Circus and stared in surprise wonder at the statue of Eros at its centre. The last time he had been here it had been enclosed in ugly hoardings; now, in the mild October sunshine, the Circus seemed beautiful to him. Dressed once more in his favourite civilian outfit of Harris tweed sports coat and grey flannel trousers, feeling a part of the crowd of sightseers standing and staring at nothing in particular, he was suddenly happy. Calais and that dreary camp were in another world. He was home.

The Guinness clock showed twelve-fifteen. They would be open now, he thought. Funny how quickly one got back into the old ways: the ready acceptance of antiquated licensing laws. He crossed the Circus by the underground passage, through the circular booking hall, trying to decide which exit he should use to arrive at the pub he had spotted from street level. Suddenly he paused, seeing the sign *White Bear Inn*. He couldn't recall seeing this place before. Not that that was particularly surprising since the debut of his drinking habits coincided almost exactly with the start of his army life. He had probably walked past the place a dozen times last year without sparing it a second glance, or even registering the first. But it looked pleasant enough and, after all, a beer was a beer was a beer.

The Inn was quite crowded; mainly lunchtime office trade he imagined. He chose a table at which a solitary woman sat and, while waiting for the ancient waiter to reach him, lighted a cigarette and looked around.

His glance took in the woman sitting opposite him and, without deliberate intention, he found himself staring at her. God, she was beautiful! Honey blonde, shoulder-length waved hair, and a wonderful complexion. She seemed to be in her mid twenties. Well dressed, in a double-breasted black suit, with the currently fashionable broad lapels and heavily-padded shoulders, and a white silk blouse.

He reddened furiously as he realised that she had intercepted his stare and was looking back at him with an amused expression on her lips and a twinkle of merriment in her eyes. Discomfited and annoyed with himself, he turned away hastily, seeking the waiter, but the old boy was busy at another table. He cursed himself for a stupid fool. Why couldn't he conquer this habit of blushing at the least thing?

Then he became aware that she had spoken to him. He turned his still-flushed face back to her.

"I beg your pardon?"

She smiled. "I asked if you were on leave."

"On leave? No. That is, er, yes, yes I 'm on leave. How did you know?"

She pointed to the packet of cigarettes he had left on the table, the tell-tale, duty-free army issue.

"Oh, the cigarettes . . . of course." Now go on, you chump, here's your opportunity; think of something to say to her. "Err, would you like one?" He picked up the packet and clumsily started to open it.

She shook her head. "I don't, thanks." A smile still hovered at the corner of her delightful lips. "Where are you stationed?"

"France. Calais."

"Oh . . . do you like it?"

"Yes, it's all right." Now, why didn't he tell her the truth? And why couldn't he think of anything to say? What was the matter with him, anyway? He looked around again, trying to catch the waiter's eye.

"The service here is terrible at this time of day, isn't it? she said.

"Awful."

He noticed that she, too, had no drink in front of her and wondered if it were the done thing to offer her one. Their glances met and he quickly lowered his eyes, then raised them again as he realised he was staring at her bosom and the thrust of her breasts against her suit.

The waiter finally reached them and, after the woman had ordered a gin-and-tonic, John asked for the beer for which he now felt a desperate need. Until the drinks arrived he kept his gaze firmly riveted at a point somewhere over her left shoulder.

She raised her glass. "Cheers," she said.

"Cheers."

"You're really rather shy, aren't you? Not at all like most soldiers I know."

"You know a lot of soldiers then, do you?" *Had he really said that?*

She laughed, a pleasant, melodic laugh, and John felt that by chance he had hit exactly the right note for this sort of conversation.

"That's a leading question, isn't it?"

"Oh, I don't know," he said, "I reckon it's hard nowadays to go through life without coming into contact with the armed forces." It was much easier now he had started.

"So it's the whole armed forces now, is it?" she taunted him.

He didn't answer. Instinctively he felt that he should leave the next move to her; so he merely smiled in what he hoped was a knowing manner.

]"Well you're right, you know. I do know a lot of soldiers. But then, as I was in the ATS that's hardly surprising, is it?"

"No, I supposed not." He felt a twinge of jealousy, thinking of the men she must have known, must still know. "You're out now, are you?"

She nodded. "Thank the Lord. Three years were enough for me. What's your name?"

The question, coming without pause, momentarily startled him. "Err, Graham, John Graham," he said.

"Well, John Graham, it's been nice meeting you. And now I must rush or I'll be late back to work."

She opened her purse and sorted out change for her drink. John's heart started pounding and he became aware that he was holding his breath. He couldn't let her walk away and never see her again. But what should he say to her?

Leaving money on the table, she stood up.

"Goodbye, then" she said.

"I say –"

"Yes?" She paused by his chair and looked at him.

"Couldn't you . . . that is . . . couldn't we meet again?"

"Why?" That amused expression was back again, and so was his embarrassment.

"Well . . . I mean . . . this evening, say. Couldn't we have dinner together, or perhaps go to a cinema?"

She seemed to be appraising him, or perhaps she was just considering his question. "I don't see why not," she finally agreed.

"Wonderful! Where shall we meet?"

"Five past six, outside Swan and Edgar. All right?"

"Great! I'll be there. By the way, what is *your* name?"

"Betty. Betty Lane. 'bye now."

He turned in his chair to watch her walking away, admiring her slim, elegant figure, noticing with fascination the rippling calf muscles of her shapely silk-clad legs.

In a gesture of bravado which was entirely foreign to him he called out, "Waiter, another beer." Then he blushed again as people turned round to look at him.

In the distance Big Ben was chiming. He glanced at the Guinness clock, quite unnecessarily, for less than two minutes had passed since his last time check. Six-thirty. It was obvious she wasn't coming. What a fool he was to have waited. Well, he'd give her another five minutes. No, he'd wait until he finished smoking his cigarette. He looked at the butt and laughed sourly to himself; there were no more than two or three drags left in it. Perhaps she wouldn't come while he was smoking. It was curious, he had noticed, that people never seemed to turn up for dates while he had a cigarette in his hand. Perhaps if he threw it away . . .

A hand touched his sleeve.

"I didn't think you'd still be here."

He swallowed a sigh of relief and looked down at her. Her head reached to about the level of his eyes. Perfect.

"I was going to give you another five minutes," he said.

Suddenly he gave a gasp of pain and dropped the cigarette which had burned down to his fingers. Then he laughed.

"What's the joke?"

"Oh, nothing," he said. "Just a stray thought." In the neon-lighted dusk her face looked enchanting.

"I'm sorry to be late," she said, "but we had an unexpected stock check."

"Oh? Where do you work?"

She pointed to the store beside them. "Lingerie department, and before you . . ."

She was too late. "I wish I'd known," he risked saying, "I'd have visited you. I'd like to see you in lingerie."

She laughed politely. She had evidently heard it before. More than once!

"And now I'm famished," she said. "Does that dinner invitation still stand?"

"Of course. Where shall we go?"

"Do you like Chinese food?" she asked.

"I don't know. I mean, I've never tried it."

"Then you shall try it tonight." She smiled. "And if you don't like it, *I'll* pay for the dinner."

She tucked her arm in his with a feminine gesture that gave him a little thrill and he said, "I'm awfully glad you came, Betty."

"So am I," she said. "I thought I'd never get away, and I can eat a horse."

She led him to *Ley On's* in Shaftesbury Avenue and ordered for both of them. Sweet and sour pork, chicken and noodles, mixed vegetables and fried rice. Afterwards he lighted a cigarette and asked a waiter for the bill.

"You're paying, then?" she asked mischievously. "You must have like it."

He nodded. "Wonderful."

She wrinkled her nose slightly. "Not as nice as it was before the war. I suppose they still can't get all the proper ingredients."

"You knew this place before the war?" He couldn't keep the surprise out of his voice.

"Why yes." She laughed. "Do you think I'm too young to have known it?" And then as he fished for a reply she added: "How old do you think I am, then?"

He hesitated. One was supposed to be careful about guessing women's ages. He decided to be honest. "Twenty-five?"

"Oh you sweet thing. Add on five years or so and you'll be nearer the mark. And don't look so crestfallen. I'm not quite old enough to be your mother."

"Oh, I'm not . . ." he began a hasty denial.

"That's all right." She smiled at him. "I know I look younger than my years."

John took a sip of his Chinese tea, which he was not really enjoying but Betty had told him it was an acquired taste. He studied her over the top of his cup. She was a most enchanting person and she certainly didn't look anything like her age. He wondered if she had told the truth; he would more readily have believed her to be twenty rather than the thirty to which she admitted. Anyway, ten years was not a great deal of difference, and a woman was as old as she looked, he had heard.

"What shall we do now?" he asked abruptly. "Would you care for a cinema? Or we could go dancing."

She pondered his question. "It's such a pleasant evening. Why don't we just take a walk down by the river and then have a drink somewhere later."

He grinned at her. "If you're thinking of my pocket, you don't have to worry. One thing about the Army, they always make sure you have cash to take with you on privilege leave. But, of course, I don't have to tell you that."

"Silly," she said. "I wasn't thinking of saving you money. I could always pay my share anyway." She caught his sudden change of expression, the tightening of his lips. "Oh, oh . . . you're one of the old breed, are you?" She laughed. "No, look John, really . . . I don't feel like the cinema. And I've been on my feet all day, so dancing's out. But a gentle stroll and a drink or two will round off the evening nicely."

"Whatever you say." He paid the bill.

They paused for a while in Trafalgar Square. "You've probably never seen the fountains playing here, have you?" she asked.

"I'm not sure. I've a feeling I came here once with my parents before the war."

She sighed. "I wonder how long it will be before everything is normal again. It used to be so wonderful, with the water all lit up. Everything used to be so wonderful."

"It will all be wonderful again," he said.

"Will it?" Her face looked wistful, as if she were thinking of something else. Then she shivered slightly and gave a little laugh. "Come on. Somebody just walked over my grave."

They continued walking, down Northumberland Avenue and along the Victoria Embankment. On Westminster Bridge they stopped again and stared at the reflected street lighting in the black river. From far away a blue flash lit up the sky for an instant.

"Lightning," said John.

She shook her head. "Just a trolleybus."

Then the sky rumbled.

"What did I tell you?"

"Oh-oh." She clutched his arm. "It's started."

Sure enough, rain was spattering in large drops, disturbing the reflections in the water, causing the lights to dance.

John looked up and down the bridge. "We're going to get drenched here, and there's not a taxi to be seen. Trust us to get stuck right in the middle of the bridge."

She laughed. "Don't you like to get wet?"

"Looks like I've got no choice." For the rain was now falling steadily and heavily, and lightning flashed once more. "Come on. Let's run for it."

But she laughed again and raised her head to let the rain fall on her face. "This is just what I needed. Perfect. Lord, wash these sinners, purify us, make us clean again."

John was startled. Good God, was the woman mad? He looked around again for a taxi, then grabbed her arm. "Look, your clothes are getting soaked. Come on."

They ran to the northern end of the bridge and down the embankment steps into a subway. Out of the rain, John removed a handkerchief from his pocket and mopped his face and hair.

"Just look at us," he said irritably. "A pair of drowned rats."

But amusement and delight still showed on her face; her eyes were sparkling. Even with drenched hair and rain-bespattered face, John thought she looked beautiful.

"It's only water," she said. "It will dry." Then she abruptly became serious. "All right, John, there's a taxi rank near the other end of the subway. We'd better go somewhere and dry off."

They had the good fortune to find a solitary taxi waiting and John held the door open for Betty to climb in, then got in beside her.

The driver's glass panel slid open. "Where to, guv?" He sounded bored.

John looked enquiringly at Betty.

"Clifford Gardens, Kensington," she told the driver. The panel slid back.

"Where's that?" asked John.

"Where I live, of course. You don't think I'm going anywhere else looking like this, do you?"

They sat in silence, wetly uncomfortable. The warmth of the taxi and their own body heat caused their clothes to give off a dank, musty smell. Suddenly Betty tapped on the glass panel and called out: "This is it, driver." The taxi braked to a halt.

John leaned across her and opened the door.

"Shall I see you again?" he asked.

"Where are you going now?"

"Why, home of course."

She stared at him. "Aren't you coming up with me, to dry off?"

"May I?" He gawked.

She stepped out of the taxi and then put her head back in again. "You needn't worry. I don't bite. And I won't eat you."

John fumbled in his pocket for change.

"Three bob, sir," said the taxi driver.

John handed him a half-crown and a shilling piece, then joined Betty on the pavement. The rain had stopped.

He followed her up to the second floor of a large, old house, then waited while she found her key and opened the door. Inside she switched on the electric light and turned to him.

"Have you got a match?"

He reached into his jacket pocket and handed her a book of matches. "They're probably wet, too."

"They're okay," she said. She kneeled before a gas fire and lighted it. "Well I'm going to get changed. Make yourself at home." She disappeared into another room.

John examined his surroundings. It was a large room, comfortably rather than elaborately furnished. The parquet floor had a large sheepskin rug spread in front of the gas fire that was flanked by two deep, upholstered armchairs. In one corner was a divan, before which was a similar rug, and behind which a bookshelf ran along the wall. He went over and glanced at the books: some detective series Penguins, a copy of Forever Amber, a number of Foyles' Book Club selections. One could usually find out something about people by the books they read, but this collection gave nothing away.

He sneezed and felt for his handkerchief. It was a soggy ball in his pocket. Suddenly he felt a chill run through him and went back to the gas fire, bending down and rubbing his hands together. He hoped he wasn't catching cold. When Betty came back he would make his goodbyes and go home to bed. He looked at the door through which she had gone. Apart from the door through which they had entered, it was the only other door in the room. He wondered where it led. Possibly a bedroom – or did she sleep on the divan? It felt strange to be like this, in someone else's home; and she was a strange person. That peculiar business in the rain, for instance. For a moment there he had really thought he had a crazy woman on his hands, but perhaps it had been her way of joking. He sneezed again. This was no good; the fire wasn't drying his clothes, merely making them steam and smell. *Hurry up, Betty.*

Almost as if she had heard the thought, the door opened and she stood framed in the doorway, dressed in a red, silk dressing gown, looking at him in surprise.

"But you're still dressed!"

"Of course." Another sneeze shook his body.

"You fool! You'll catch your death like that. Why don't you take your things off and let them dry?"

"I can't do that here," was his shocked reply.

"You've got underwear on, haven't you?"

"Of . . . attishoo! . . . course."

"Then don't be so stupid. Take off your jacket and trousers while I make a hot toddy. And your shoes and socks while you're about it."

She opened a large, double-fronted cupboard door. Behind it was a small electric cooker and a sink. She filled a kettle and put it on the cooker. Then she crossed the room and, from a cabinet, assembled two beakers, a bottle of rum, and a bowl of sugar. She put rum and sugar into the beakers and took them over to the cooker.

She looked at him. "Shirt and tie, too," she ordered. He felt his face go red, as usual.

Betty went into the other room and returned with a large bath towel. "Here, give yourself a good rubdown."

The kettle emitted a piercing whistle and she rushed over to it, took it off the electric ring, and poured water into the beakers.

John was ashamed to look at her. He felt ridiculous dressed only in vest and shorts. Why had he obeyed her instructions in that way? Without demur. But he continued rubbing the towel over his arms and legs. Then he gave his hair a brisk rub and laid the towel over the back of an armchair.

"That's more like it," Betty said. "Now get some of this inside you."

He took a steaming beaker from her and sat in one of the armchairs. He held the beaker in both hands and slowly sipped the hot, strong brew. Elbows resting on lap, bent slightly forward, legs crossed, he studied the strands of the sheepskin rug at his feet.

Betty laughed. "God, you are shy, aren't you. You don't think you're the first man I've seen in his underwear, do you?"

He looked at her, his face aflame. She sat cross-legged on the rug, an elbow resting on the other armchair, sipping her drink. Her dressing gown, loosely belted at the waist, failed to disguise her abundant charms; her hair, piled high on her head, was held in place by a large comb. Over her steaming toddy her eyes mocked his embarrassment.

"How do you feel now?"

"Much better, thanks." He drank the last of the brew.

"See," she taunted him. "It always pays to do as the doctor orders."

She stood up and he caught a glimpse of white, smooth thigh before the folds of dressing gown overlapped again. She bent over him to take his empty beaker, and he was looking down the front of her gown at a white swell of breast. It lasted just a moment and then she had straightened up and was walking to the sink.

Despite the drink, his throat felt dry and his tongue was cleaving to the roof of his mouth. He felt his body stirring and, in consternation, folded his arms and laid them across his lap. He could hear Betty rinsing the beakers in the sink.

"I think I ought to go," he said.

"Your clothes are still wet." She dismissed his suggestion peremptorily.

He did not look up as her footsteps approached, but started examining the rug again, his thoughts in confusion, aware of an erection which he was sure his arms were not hiding. Then he was looking into her eyes as she sat on the rug at his feet. They seemed to be reading his thoughts and he was sure she was going to be angry with him. Instead, she smiled kindly and her parted lips seemed to hold an invitation, an appeal.

"Betty . . ." he said, his voice echoing foolishly in his ears.

Her face approached his and, impelled by the force of an emotion he was no longer able to resist, his hand stretched out to touch her.

Then their lips were together and he was overwhelmed by the passion of her response. This was nothing like the adolescent kisses he had exchanged during games of postman's knock and spin the bottle. Her tongue forced its way between his teeth and seemed to explore every part of his mouth. for a moment, a brief, shattering moment, he was shocked, and then his body was on fire and he surrendered himself entirely to her control, to her guidance.

He slipped out of the armchair and lay with her on the rug; she took his hand and directed it on to a smooth, firm breast beneath her robe. He could feel the nipple grow erect under his fingers. Betty's hands were moving against his chest, then down his back, over his head; her body was writhing and straining against him and he felt the startling response of his own body as her fingers explored him inside his shorts.

Suddenly she withdrew her lips from his and her hands from his body.

"Betty, oh Betty," he panted.

"You haven't done this before, have you?" she whispered.

"No . . . no." His voice was a groan against her shoulder; his limbs had turned to quaking, tremulous jelly; his breath was being expelled in short, harsh gasps.

She gently eased herself out of his arms, crossed the room and extinguished the light. Then she was back at his side.

"I'll help you," she said.

Her lips once more found his, her tongue flicking serpent-like in and out of his mouth, her hands doing things to his body, causing him to twist and squirm in an ecstasy of feeling that was almost painful. And then he lost awareness of his own actions, but felt himself alternately floating and soaring and then reaching, reaching, reaching, until all the sensations finally exploded in a vast, turbulent, detumescence.

How long he lay there, stretched out on his back in a torpor that was not quite sleep, he could not say. Ultimately, however, he raised himself on one elbow and gazed at Betty lying beside him. Her body was carved red mahogany in the flickering light of the gas fire, and her deep, even breathing suggested that she was asleep. He found himself studying the concavities and convexities of her body in fascinated wonder; it was the first time that he had seen a woman completely unclothed and he thought her indescribably lovely. He leaned over and pressed his lips to her breast. She gave a slight shudder and her arms came around his neck.

"I had such an awful dream," she said. Her eyes opened slowly and as she saw him she gave a startled gasp.

"What is it?" he asked. "Did I frighten you?"

The grip on his neck slackened and she sank back on the rug. "No," she whispered, her eyes closed again, "it was just that . . . for a moment . . . I . . . I. . ." and suddenly tears were running down her cheeks.

"Betty, Betty, what's wrong? What have I done?"

"Nothing, John, nothing." Her body shook with silent sobs.

John remained balanced on one elbow, afraid to move, afraid to speak. He couldn't imagine what might be causing her distress, but felt, instinctively, despite her denial, that he was somehow to blame. Perhaps he should try to comfort her, but that might make things worse; his inexperience in these matters filled him with apprehension.

Her sobbing stopped as abruptly as it had started and she gazed at him through wide, tear-filled eyes.

"I'm sorry, John."

He stroked her hair. "Are you all right now?"

"Yes, yes, I'm all right now." She forced a smile. "Put your arms around me, John."

He stretched out beside her once more and took her into his arms.

"Hold me tight, John. Tighter. That's better." Her voice was an anguished sigh in his ear. "Caress me, John. yes, there . . . and there . . . aah . . . that's it, John, that's it." She squirmed beneath his hand. "Now John! Do it now!" she urged, and then shuddered. "Clever, clever John. You do learn quickly, don't you?"

CHAPTER FIVE

Ironically, despite the new allure that London held for him, John was finding life at Calais far more tolerable.

True the town was still pretty ghastly, the camp quite grim, the work utterly boring; but he could endure these things now. He could even be tolerant of Sergeant Miller, a situation that he would not have believed possible one month earlier.

He actually took some pleasure now in listening to the others' accounts of their real or imaginary amorous adventures, where previously these variations on a single theme had begun to nauseate him. But then, he could afford to be indulgent now that he had adventures of his own to bolster his spirits whenever they seemed likely to flag. Not that his adventures were for camp consumption – oh no! They were too precious. His revered memories of tender and passionate hours with Betty were to be privately cherished; to be hoarded in his memory like a bottle of antique brandy which one saves for special occasions and then warms – oh so carefully – before luxuriating in that first heady aroma of its bouquet.

And that was very funny, really, for when he had returned from Paris, where nothing of importance (by camp standards) had happened to him, he had gone to elaborate lengths to invent that absurd story. This time he had carefully avoided even hinting at amatory success.

He still remembered the looks of incredulity and distrust on the faces of Pashley and Scanes when they had questioned him about his leave in London and he has said: "Really fellows, I spent all my time with my mother."

Immediately afterwards he had regretted his words, for he still felt guilty at the way he had neglected mother most of those seven days. He had spent one evening only at home, one evening when Betty had been unable to see him. Not that mother, bless her, had complained. On the contrary, she had expressed delight that he had found himself a "nice girl" (for he had told her about Betty, but had omitted any reference to her age) and had suggested that he bring his "young lady" home some time. But Betty wouldn't agree, despite all his entreaties.

Betty. Betty Lane. He found a magical ring to the sound of her name. Merely to repeat the name to himself seemed to bring her close and remind him of those wonderful evenings. He frequently fell into a reverie of recollection, reliving their walks and talks, their meals together, their visit to a theatre and a cinema, culminating always in that wondrous physical exploration and fulfillment. Was he in love with her? He supposed he must be. He had no yardstick against which to measure his feeling, but what he felt for Betty he had never felt before, and he could only conclude that it must be love.

And she loved him. He was sure of it. To hell with the difference in their ages. No woman could have behaved towards him – with him – as she had, unless it were for love. That first evening for instance, when she had suddenly cried, he was certain now that it had been because of her awareness of the age difference, and the fear that it would mar their relationship. This had to be the explanation, he had decided, and had never again referred to the incident.

He wrote to her every week and although he had only received one letter from her shortly after his return to camp, he was not disturbed. She had warned him that she was an atrocious correspondent and her one letter, with its simple expression of gratitude for their week together, was more meaningful to him than the sloppy, gushing stuff that many of the lads received daily.

In the office he reached for the calendar above his head and conscientiously cancelled the previous day with a thick pencilled cross. Then he turned the pages eagerly until he arrived at a date ringed in red, some six months ahead. He had followed this routine assiduously since his return from leave, noting the slowly decreasing distance to his "red letter" day, the estimated date of his next privilege leave. He felt alternately frustrated by the snail's pace at which time appeared to be passing, and buoyed up by anticipation of all the date was going to mean to him. On or near that date he would see Betty again.

He replaced the calendar and turned round as the office door burst open and Pashley came in.

"Hello, Pash."

"Hiya, John. You missed this this morning."

"This" was a letter which Pashley handed to him and then departed.

The envelope was addressed to John in Aunt Susan's handwriting. He studied it for a few moments, hesitating to slit the flap and remove the letter, intuitively anticipating the bad news which it might contain. Why should Susan write to him? What news could she possibly have that would not wait for one of his mother's regular letters? Apprehensively, he finally opened the envelope.

"Dear John,

"Bad news I'm afraid.

"Your mother had to go into hospital for an operation. It wasn't dangerous and she's home again, convalescing. But the doctor told me that the trouble was caused by something more serious and it may not be long before her pains come back again. Next time they don't think they'll be able to do anything for her. We haven't told her yet. Do you think . . ."

He finished the letter in a daze, his brain refusing to accept the implication of the news. For a space of time which lost all significance he sat hunched over his desk, submerged in thoughts which chased themselves around his head. Predominant was a nagging feeling of guilt. He should have known; he should have noticed. If he hadn't been so wrapped up in his own pleasures; if only he had given a little more thought to mother; if he had only paid more attention to the obvious signs of her failing health. If only . . . if only . . . if only. . .

Abruptly he left his desk, strode over and knocked on the wall hatch. It slid open and Dusty Miller's face appeared.

"What's up now, Graham?"

"I'd like an interview with the O.C." John said.

Miller snorted. "Well, corporal, you know the drill, donchya?"

"It's very urgent, Sergeant. I don't want to have to go through channels."

The sergeant laughed. "What's the matter, Graham, got a floozie in the family way? Nothing urgent about that."

"No, Sergeant." John forced calmness into his voice. "I want to apply for compassionate leave. It's my mother. She's very ill."

"I'm sorry to hear that." The mocking expression left Miller's face and he showed a sympathy which John would never have suspected. "But you know, Graham, you don't get compassionate leave that easy. Yer in the army, not the boy scouts. We don't go giving leave to every Tom, Dick or 'Arry just cos someone at home has a headache."

"But you don't understand. It's more serious than that. I think she's going to die." John was still holding the letter. Now he thrust it at the sergeant. "Here, read this."

The sergeant scanned it quickly.

"Well I can probably arrange for you to see Captain Harris," he said, "but I don't know as how that will do much good. It ain't as if she's dying at the moment, is it? I mean," he added hastily, aware that his words may have sounded callous, "the letter don't say she's *actually* dying. I don't see where they'd consider that grounds for compassionate leave."

"But there must be something I can do."

Sergeant Miller pondered the problem. "Look, I don't know if it'll do any good, but why not 'ave a word with he chaplain."

"The chaplain," John echoed.

"Yes. I mean to say, he can probably give you better advice than I can."

Captain R.E. Moss, army chaplain, stroked his thin moustache with a quick movement of his long fingers, a gesture at once nervous and impatient. The dark eyes, set deep into a narrow face, beneath bushy eyebrows, seemed to bore into John.

"I haven't seen you at voluntary services, have I?" he asked.

"No." John forced a brief smile. "No, I don't usually attend."

"I see." the moustache-stroking routine resumed. "You do not feel it to be necessary." A slight elevation of the last syllable converted the statement into a question.

"It's not that, sir . . ." John hesitated. "It's not something I've really thought about."

"But now you feel that I – that is, presumably, the Church – can help you." Once again it was statement and question combined. Captain Moss pointed to Aunt Susan's letter. "Isn't this really a matter for your Company O.C.? Captain Harris, isn't it?"

John nodded his head. "I suppose so. But frankly I haven't got sufficient grounds for compassionate leave in the normal way."

"Ah-hah!" The chaplain rubbed his hands together, gleefully almost it seemed to John. "Then why should you think I can help you?"

It was now obvious to John that the chaplain had no intention of helping him and he was beginning to regret having come to see the man. Well, he'd be damned if he'd butter the man up. He said, "Look, sir, I'm not coming to you with any sort of hypocritically religious plea. I don't profess to be a good Christian. I'm not even sure I know what a good Christian is, although I hardly think it can be measured by the number of times a chap attends church services. But I was baptised into the Church of England and I've got C.of E. marked in my paybook, and that's why I've come to see you." Spurred on by the pressure of concern for his mother, John was astonished to find himself adopting a tone and attitude quite alien to him. He was speaking, too, in an abnormally loud voice.

The chaplain raised his hands. "Calm down, my boy. You're not addressing a congregation. And will you please get to the point."

"The point, sir, is that I thought you would be someone who would appreciate a son's responsibility to his mother. My father is dead and I have no brothers or sisters. If my mother is dying I should be with her. Don't you think so?"

"Hmmmm." Captain Moss raised one eyebrow, thereby managing to convey the impression that the question was hardly deserving of reply.

But John did not notice this mannerism as he pressed on. "My entire concern is for my mother, not myself. But perhaps you view filial regard as less of a Christian precept than completing posting orders."

"Corporal Graham!" The chaplain's raised voice cut across John's remarks "That sort of comment is quite unnecessary. Or do you feel the need to preach *me* a sermon?"

"I'm sorry, sir." John's delayed reactions finally caught up with him in a burst of embarrassment, and his fingers played nervously with the badge on the forage cap he was holding in his lap."

"I realise you must be overwrought at the news you have received." The chaplain's face was hard and unyielding. "That's the only excuse I can find for your outrageous remark, and that's the only reason I'm not telling you to leave here this instant. Now, suppose you tell me exactly what you think I can – or should – do for you, and why."

"I don't know, sir." John felt no regret for his words, only for the impetuous way in which he had delivered them, and the fact that his thoughtless outburst had now forced him onto the defensive. "I just didn't know what to do. I thought perhaps you might have a word with Captain Harris, or even the C.O. It was silly of me . . . I'm sorry."

"No," said the chaplain. "No, it wasn't silly of you, corporal. You were right to want to see me. But you've come to see me for the wrong reasons. I can do no more for you with the Commanding Officer or your O.C. then you can yourself." Captain Moss rose abruptly and started pacing the room. "You know, you peacetime national servicemen are all alike. You seem to think that we're here solely to preside at church parades. It was different during the war. One really had the feeling he had a job – a worthwhile job – to do." He seemed to be talking as much to himself now as to John. "But then . . . I suppose it's much the same for you too now. Tell me, corporal," he turned suddenly and fixed his eyes on John, "what do you think my job is?"

"I . . . I don't really . . . that is, I suppose . . ."

"That's all right. You don't know." He shook a hand at John and his lip curled slightly. "Sometimes I find *myself* wondering. Oh, I could preach you a fine sermon about ministering to your spiritual needs, but

I'll save that for the pulpit." His eyes glinted mischievously. "Then you'll be spared the tedium of listening to it, won't you? But for heaven's sake, why don't you realise that you don't need an excuse to come and talk to me? Or rather, that the only excuse you need is that you want someone to talk to. Not just when you feel you might be helped to cut a few army corners, but just to be helped . . ." He paused. "You don't really know what I'm talking about, do you?"

John lowered his eyes and studied his cap-badge.

"Look, corporal, I can't promise anything," Captain Moss said. "I think you are right to believe that the army would not consider a request for compassionate leave on the grounds contained in your aunt's letter. But I'll look into it for you."

Like hell you will, John thought, but he said, "Thank you, sir." He got up. "And I'm sorry for my outburst earlier."

"Well, I did not disagree with the point you made, I just feel you might have chosen a more appropriate audience. In fact I may even refer to it myself, next Sunday." The chaplain smiled slyly. "Perhaps we'll see you at the service."

He was on his way home.

It was tremendous. Quite incredible, but true. In a few minutes the train would be arriving at Victoria Station. And he would be living at home, able to spend all his free time with mother, helping her, making it up to her for his past neglect.

That crafty old so-and-so Moss. When he had left him – was it really five weeks ago? – he had been sure the fellow was merely humouring him. But he had come up trumps. He had not got John the compassionate leave he had wanted, but almost certainly it was his intervention which had secured John the posting to a War Office department in Curzon Street. And Captain Harris had actually apologised for not being able to give him any compassionate leave. Compassionate leave! Christ! This was a thousand times better. But then, Captain Harris had been teasing him really. He had almost laughed. He was on the verge of laughter again when Captain Harris had referred to the chaplain, but then he had remembered that he was standing to attention. What was it Harris had said? Ah yes . . . "I don't know what sort of yarn you spun the chaplain, corporal, but you've had him pulling all sorts of strings at War Office."

And there he had been cursing himself, as the weeks had passed, for having blown his chances by approaching the old boy in quite the wrong way. A pity, really, that he hadn't had time to go and thank him.

But Moss would understand. The excitement of the moment; the rush to get away. It had all happened so quickly in the end that he had had little time for goodbyes. And Dusty Miller had astonished him again, congratulating him on his posting and hoping that he would find his mother much better than he feared.

Well he would soon know. The train was pulling into the station now and he would be with her very soon. God, he was looking forward to seeing her.

And Betty . . . he mustn't forget Betty.

He adjusted the knapsack webbing straps on his shoulders and hefted his kitbag off the luggage rack. Before the train came to a complete stop, he opened the door and jumped to the platform. Then he checked in with the station R.T.O. and took a taxi to the flat.

He sensed a strangeness, an aberrance, almost before his key had turned in the lock. As he wandered through the deserted rooms he *knew* something was wrong. According to Aunt Susan, mother should still be convalescing at home, but she certainly wasn't there; no-one was there. Fear brought perspiration to his brow and a chill to his chest. What could have happened? And then relief flooded through him. Of course, Susan had not meant she would be staying here, but at Ben and Susan's home, where they could look after her. Slipping the knapsack from his back, he left it in the hall beside his kitbag and rushed downstairs to his aunt's apartment.

In answer to his ring, the door was opened by his Uncle Ben. A smile of greeting appeared on his face. "Hello, John. We weren't expecting you quite so soon."

"Hello, Uncle. Is mother with you?"

Ben's mouth opened into an 'O'. "You don't know then? They took her away in an ambulance this morning. St. Mary Abbot's."

John turned sharply and rushed to the front door. Outside, in the dark December evening, a cold fog was beginning to swirl through the Kensington streets as he ran across the Cromwell Road towards the hospital. His heavy greatcoat seemed to be holding him back as he forced his legs to move faster.

At the hospital gates he muttered an apology to the departing visitor with whom he had collided and then spoke, with gasping breath, to the gatekeeper.

"Mrs Graham," he said." "Can you tell me where she is? She was brought in this morning."

The gatekeeper consulted a list. "Ask in Casualty," he said. "First right, first left, and it's on your right."

"Thanks."

In the casualty department he was directed to the ward where his mother had been taken and warned that visiting hours were almost over. Sitting on a bench outside the swing doors of the ward was Aunt Susan.

"John!" There was a note of relief in her voice. "Then you got the telegram."

"No," he answered tersely. "Where's mother? What's wrong with her?"

"Oh! Then how did you know? How are you here? We sent a telegram this morning, but you wouldn't have time. . ."

He grasped her arms, interrupting the flow of words. "Aunt Susan! Will you please quit your yammering and tell me what's the matter with mother."

"She had a relapse this morning. I've just left her. They gave her some drugs to relieve the pain and they're going to try another operation later. They said I had better let her rest. I don't know if they'll let you see her."

He stopped a passing nurse. "Excuse me, nurse. I've just got here. Is it all right to see my mother – Mrs Graham?"

"Just one moment," the nurse said. "I'll check with Sister." She went through the swing-doors and returned a moment later. "It's all right. You may go in. But please . . . just a few moments. She's been sedated. You'll find her on the left, behind the screens.

"Thank you, nurse." A wave of nausea swept over him and he became aware that perspiration was dripping down his cheeks. He removed his greatcoat and placed it on the bench beside his aunt, then he wiped his face with a handkerchief and walked into the ward, forcing himself to appear calm.

Behind the screen his mother seemed to be asleep. He felt the wet warmth of a tear trickle down his cheek as he studied the gauntness of her face, the pallor of her complexion. There was no movement beneath the sheets. Almost as if she is already dead, he thought, and the significance of the reflection brought the sick feeling back to the pit of his stomach. Then slowly his mother's eyes opened and she looked at him.

"John," she whispered. "You're here. I'm glad."

He took one of her hands in his. "How are you feeling, mum?"

"Better . . . much better now. But so sleepy . . ." Her eyes closed again.

A voice said in his ear, "I think you'd better leave her to sleep now."

He released his mother's hand, leaned forward and gently kissed her brow, then stepped past the nurse who had bent over the bed to tidy sheets which needed no tidying, and he went back to his aunt.

"I'm sorry, John," she said. "It must have been a shock to see her like that."

He couldn't speak. He pulled a pack of cigarettes from his pocket and then, not knowing if smoking were permitted, but suspecting that it was not, he replaced them.

"Was she awake?" asked his aunt. "Did she see you? Did she say anything?"

He stared at her uncomprehendingly. Then, dropping onto the bench, he rested his face in the palms of his hands. "God, oh God," he muttered. "Why does this have to be happening? Why can't they *do* something for her?"

His aunt put an arm about his shoulders. "You know we've been expecting it."

"Yes. But why now? Why now?" A sob caught in his voice. "Why now," he repeated to himself, "when I've got a posting to London and can spend some time with her?"

"I didn't know that," Susan said softly.

He raised his head. "Did you say they were going to operate again? I thought there was no chance."

"That's what they said last time. But now they think there's a slight possibility . . ." Her voice trailed off.

"When?" John asked. "When are they going to operate?"

"This evening. About nine o'clock. If you like we can go home now and come back later. We won't be allowed to see her again before the operation."

"No." The rebuttal came out more sharply than he had intended. "No," he repeated more gently, "I don't want to go home. I think I'll go for a walk." He put on his greatcoat and went to the head of the staircase, then turned back to his aunt. "I'll see you here later."

Outside the hospital he walked aimlessly, without paying attention to his surroundings, lost in miserable reflection. The now-thick fog seemed to press against him. Just like a shroud, he thought, and immediately cursed himself for the ghoulish association. He had to get his mind away from the hospital and the operation and the whole damned distressing business. There was nothing he could do, and he would certainly do himself no good worrying about it. But that was easy to say; not so easy to do. Then he thought of Betty and realised that he could surely not be too far from her apartment. He would visit her. Now. The decision acted as an instant remedial balm on his tortured mind and he felt comforted at the anticipation of talking about his worries with her.

He looked about him, trying to place his exact location, but it was impossible to discern any landmarks in the thick fog and in this district most of the streets looked alike. He walked to the end of the road and examined the plaque on the wall; Launceston Place. Well, if he turned right he should reach Cromwell Road somewhere in the vicinity of Gloucester Road; then it would be a matter of merely finding his way through the network of squares and gardens until he located Clifford Gardens.

The assessment was simpler than the act. Discovering that he had reached Onslow Gardens for the second time, he admitted to himself that he had no idea which way to go. A moment later he made out a dim figure approaching through the fog.

"Excuse me," he called out. "Could you . . .?" It was an American serviceman. "No, I suppose you couldn't."

The American laughed. "Well, buster, if you don't ask, you'll never know."

"I was looking for Clifford Gardens."

"And you've come to the right guy. Just turn round and take the first right and then first right again. Or go straight ahead and take the first left and then first left again. Depends what number you want."

"Er, number fifteen," John said.

"In that case . . ." The American interrupted himself. "Say, if that don't beat all. You wouldn't by any chance be wanting Betty Lane, would you buddy?"

"Why yes," John exclaimed in surprise.

"Well in that case, Mister, you'd better just postpone it, 'cos I'll be there before you. Happy hunting!" The American laughed again and strode away.

For an instant of time the American's words failed to impact John's brain and then he felt a sort of numbness creep down the side of his face as if he had been slapped hard on the cheek. It could not be right; it must be someone else; or he had misunderstood. He could hear the other man's footsteps gradually recede and then fade into silence, prematurely muffled by the fog. The words he had heard started to echo in his head and he knew that there was no mistake and no misunderstanding. The

Yank was visiting Betty and he had assumed that John would visit her later. And that could only mean one thing.

But that was impossible. Not Betty! Not *his* Betty!

It must be wrong. It must be some sort of crazy coincidence. There was probably another Betty in the house. But the Yank had said "Betty Lane", hadn't he? John tried to remember precisely what had been said, but couldn't be sure he hadn't imagined it. Well there was one sure way to find out. He hurried in the direction the American had taken. First right; first right again. As he turned the first corner he started to run. He was still running when a burst of light from an opened door penetrated the blackness ahead and, as a brief image projected on a screen, he saw Betty, *his* Betty, *Betty Lane*, greet the Yank and then the door closed behind them.

For several minutes he stood stock-still, as if his feet had grown roots into the pavement, his cheeks blazing with waves of shock and revulsion. A million crawling insects seemed to be performing a mad dance down his spine, and sweat mingled with the foggy dampness on his brow.

How could this be happening to him? It was not possible. There had to be a simple explanation. All he had to do was ring her doorbell; she would come to the door . . . and . . . He took two steps towards the house and then shivered. He couldn't do it; he couldn't call on her while that Yank was there. He moved into the areaway of an adjoining house and lit a cigarette with trembling hands.

He had just finished his third cigarette when the door to number fifteen opened again. This time there was no light from the hallway and the American, when he came out, was alone. John waited until he judged the man had reached the end of the road and then approached the house. By the light of a match he found Betty's bell and jabbed at it fiercely.

A moment later he could hear the sound of someone behind the door, then the door opened slightly.

"What do you want?" It was Betty's voice, speaking softly. "It's too late now. You should have telephoned."

"It's me. John."

"John!" The hall light suddenly clicked on and the door opened wide. "John," she repeated. "What are you doing here?"

"I want to talk to you." He pushed his way past her into the hallway.

"But we can't talk here. We'll disturb the people in the downstairs flats." He could see her face in the light. She looked as beautiful as ever, although he seemed to detect a hardness, a brassiness, in her face that he had never before noticed. It was just his imagination, he thought.

He said, "Then let's go up to your place."

"No!" she exclaimed, then lowered her voice again. "No, John, the place is a shambles. I was in bed, as you can see." She looked down at her dressing gown, the gown he remembered so well.

"I know you were in bed. I saw him arrive and I saw him leave." He glared at her. "Well? Are we going up, or are we going to stand here?"

She seemed about to protest, but then shrugged her shoulders and led the way up to her apartment.

In the room his eyes quickly took in the signs of disorder and then he turned to her. "Well?"

She went over to the sideboard on which a bottle of whiskey and two glasses stood, one of them partly filled. She raised it and gulped the amber liquid. then she faced him, her eyes blazing.

"Well – what?" she said. "You seem to know all about it, so what is there to say."

The anger and resolution which had built up in him downstairs now drained away, leaving him weak and exhausted. "But why, Betty? Why?"

"Why, Betty, why?" She mimicked his piteous tone. "I'll tell you why. Because I've stopped being a fool, that's why. Because I'm thirty years old and my body won't last forever, so why give it away when I can get paid for it? Does that satisfy you?

"You don't mean it. You can't mean it" His shoulders sagged and he could hear the whine in his voice.

She mocked him. "Grow up, little boy. This is the hard, cruel world, not a film on a cinema screen. Look at you," she jeered, "like a child who has just learned the facts of live and doesn't want to stop believing he was delivered by a stork. *You've* got nothing to get upset about. You had it free for a whole week, didn't you? Be grateful. It would cost you a fiver a time now."

His face screwed up in misery and distaste. "You filthy bitch," he said, shocking himself by the unaccustomed use of the words.

She gaped at him for a moment, then stepped over and slapped his cheek with an open palm. "How dare you presume to judge me," she said. "You'd better go. Go on, get out." She turned him round and propelled him towards the door.

Scarcely aware of his movements, he descended the stairs and left the house. In the street he rested his arms on the railings in front of the house, laid his head on them, and gave in to a fit of quiet sobbing.

"The bitch. The bitch. The bitch." He muttered the words between sobs. "How could she do this to me? Who is *she* to make me suffer this way?"

In his misery he could only see her behaviour as an act of treachery to him personally. There was no room in him for doubt or pity, or reflection of the events which may have led her to this impossible situation. His injured pride, his emotional immaturity, made him incapable of recognising that circumstances might exist other than a personal, callous affront to his pure – and, to him, unselfish – feelings for her.

How long he stood there, trembling and weeping against the cold, damp railings, he no longer knew. It was the rasping, inching movement of a motor-car, picking its way down the road through the fog that finally roused him. Then – only then – he remembered his mother and the operation.

With a final, desperate sob, he set off at a run in the direction of the hospital. Out of breath, his face streaked from fog-dirt and tears, he did not notice the pitying look the nurse gave him when he asked for his mother, but set off again to the building to which she directed him. Inside, in the bright light of the reception hall, he saw Aunt Susan and Uncle Ben and an icy band of pain clamped itself on his chest at their expressions: grief and reproof combined.

"John!" Aunt Susan grabbed his arm, her voice a painful accusation. "Why weren't you here?"

"Where's mother? What's happened?" But he already knew the answer and it was as if, for a moment, his life had come to an end.

"I'm sorry, John. They did their best."

Uncle Ben came over; his face, which he thrust forward until it was almost touching John's, a black mask of anger. "You selfish sod," he hissed. "Where were you?"

His aunt placed a restraining hand on her husband's arm. "She asked for you, John. Just before . . . just before . . ." Her voice choked on the words and a moan escaped her lips.

"Oh God!" He could not hold back the despairing cry. Shoulders slumped, he moved in a daze over to a chair and wilted into it. What have I done? What have I done? And suddenly the memory of the last few moments in Betty's apartment returned to him and his self-reproach turned outwards and fastened itself on her. It wasn't his fault; it was Betty's – that bitch Betty. She was responsible for all this. If it hadn't been for her . . . God, God, God . . . His mother . . . gone for ever . . . and that filthy bitch laughing and mocking him in her room.

His aunt was saying something to him, but he couldn't concentrate on her words. His agonised mind was screaming a torrent of abuse at the woman who had brought him to this. Well he would show her. And the others like her. This would never happen to *him* again. *His* feelings would never again be so deeply involved that they could be hostage to the behaviour of another person. If anyone was going to suffer in the future, it would not be John Graham.

PART TWO

Time was a soot-filled tunnel through which the slow train of life shuddered and groaned its dissolute passage. The motive power being hot air – what else? – it ran, as it must, on single track of narrow gauge.

My lips twitched in sardonic amusement. How symbolic the observation! And how apposite, too, the shuddering and groaning part. So appropriate – oh, yes, indeed! – so apt. And why not carry the analogy further? All I had to do was pull the communication cord and pay the fine. That was all you had to do in life, wasn't it? You broke a few of the rules and – if you were stupid enough to get caught – why, you just paid up with a good grace. The very least you could do was be gracious about it.

But how to apply that criterion of social law and justice to a moral code? And what of the *self-imposed* moral discipline? How was I to foot the bill when *that* was violated? And who was going to present the reckoning? I would simply have to be both debtor and creditor. And where did that leave me? I could pull the cord and jump off the train – and then what? I would probably end up in the foetid, airless tunnel, running like an idiot towards an exit that did not exist . . .

Her voice broke into my thoughts.

"Are you happy, darling? Was it all right?

I couldn't trust myself to speak. Bending over I kissed her cheek, then the side of her nose. She threw her arms around my neck and pulled me to her, burying her face in my shoulder, pressing her bare body against me, until the awareness of her small soft breasts and firm thighs produced the first stirrings of reawakening desire.

Turning slightly I reached over to the bedside table, picked up a packet of cigarettes and my lighter. If I could waste a little more time she would soon have to leave for her train to the suburbs.

"Should I light one for you, my dear?"

"No, thank you, darling. I'll share yours."

The flame springing from my lighter sent short, flickering shadows around the hotel room. The brass rail at the foot of the bed, thrown into relief by the light, served to depress me still further, made the whole episode somehow cheaper and more disgusting. This, of course, was the bill of account – or, at least, part of it – this torturing, nagging guilt; most of it self-induced, all of it self-inflicted. And how much more of it must I endure, I asked myself? My God, will it never end? Why did I put myself into this position?

But the answer to that, too, lay in the past: our infrequent – though continuing – correspondence and – following graduation – the casual mention that I was contemplating a continental holiday.

Her invitation had seemed to arrive almost before my letter had had time to bit the bottom of the postbox . . .

CHAPTER SIX

She startled him at the Gare du Nord by running along the platform, throwing her arms around him, and kissing his cheek. Not both cheeks. It was the way she used to greet him four years earlier. But that had been a skinny, saucy schoolgirl. This young woman was a slim, elegant, attractive stranger. Then he looked into her eyes and they were the same dancing eyes he remembered, and her smile was the same roguish smile, and Yvette – despite any biological developments – was still Yvette.

But he found it difficult to ignore those disturbing developments.

They took a taxi to the Quai de Valmy and she maintained a continuous excited chatter the whole way, asking him a million questions, giving him no chance to answer any of them. At the house she pressed the electric buzzer releasing the door-catch and, as he placed his suitcase on the ground to push the door open, she came up close to him and straightened his tie.

"*Ça y est,* now you look fine," she said. He had the impression that it was merely an excuse to touch him, to indulge in a small, intimate gesture.

She preceded him up the staircase and he was conscious of her shapely, slim, nylon-clad legs before him. He forced his eyes away from them.

The Beaumonts had already opened their apartment door – having presumably heard the approaching footsteps – and were waiting in the doorway to greet him. *Maman* Beaumont lifted herself on tip-toe to kiss him on both cheeks and *Papa* Beaumont took the hand which John extended in both of his own, pumping it warmly and excitedly.

They each said "John" in greeting. Nothing more. But the warmth and wealth of welcome they managed to convey in the one word filled him with such emotion that, for a moment, he had difficulty in swallowing.

"Isn't it wonderful?" Yvette said to her parents. "Don't you think he looks so much better out of uniform? Older and . . . and more a man, don't you think?" She squeezed his arm.

"*Dis-donc*, Yvette," her mother admonished. "A little calm, *n'est-ce pas*? You look fatigued," she said to John. "Yvette will show you to your room and you can unpack your bag, and wash and rest a little before dinner. You've had a long journey. Go on Yvette." She slapped her daughter's backside. "Take John's bag into his room."

"That's all right." John picked up the suitcase. "I can manage it. But I shall be glad to rest a little." And in truth he did feel weary and slightly ill-at-ease standing in the hall with the three Beaumonts; though he could not imagine why he should. "I'll see you later. I have so many questions to ask."

Yvette led the way into a small room containing a high, old-fashioned bed, a wardrobe, an armchair, a dressing table and a wash-basin in one corner. Yvette sat on the bed, swinging her legs.

"It really is wonderful that you are here, John. Why did you wait so long before you came back?"

He put the suitcase on the floor, lifted Yvette off the bed by her elbows and stood her by the door.

"Now then, young lady," he said, "all questions later. Remember what your mother said: *un peu du calme, n'est-ce pas*? Not for you, but for me. All right?"

"All right." She laughed. "I'll call you when dinner's ready." She opened the door and went out. A second later the door opened again and her head popped in. "By the way, this was Pierre's room."

He removed his jacket, tie and shoes and flopped out on the bed. His suitcase could wait until later, when he had recovered from the nine hours of almost continuous travel. It was probably nothing but the journey, he thought, that caused his uncomfortable feeling to persist. Hadn't he responded appropriately to their warm welcome? Hadn't he felt for a moment in the doorway as though he had come – yes, *home* almost – into a family circle in which he fitted intimately. But the nagging suspicion persisted that . . . that what? That he no longer had a right to be here? That he was not the person they had known before? He laughed sourly to himself. That was surely an exaggeration. And yet . . . and yet . . . it was almost as if he had a premonition of imminent disaster. He was crazy! Perhaps it was the room; Yvette's reference to her dead brother.

He sat up and looked around the room. Apart from some school photographs on the walls it had a completely impersonal air, as if it had never been lived in. But it had been lived in, and its impersonality only served to underline the grief the Beaumonts must have suffered at the loss of their only son. He wondered how many years Pierre's death had taken from his parent's lives. It did not help to consider how small a part this was of the suffering of Europe's people in the war years, nor to reflect on the greater tragedies which must still be taking their toll. He did not know those other people nor was he involved in their dramas; he only knew the affection and sense of consanguinity he had for the Beaumonts.

And he did not want to add to their grief.

Idiotic thought! How on earth could he do that?

No, it was not the room. The room added perhaps to his discomfort, but was not the cause of it. That lay deeper; that lay . . . His mind shied away from the consideration like a criminal slinking away from the scene of his crime. He pushed his thoughts back to the immediate approach of his uneasiness. It had started with Yvette's greeting at the station; it had deepened when they reached the house – when she had straightened his tie; when he had followed up her the staircase; when she had stood beside him in the hall. Then, when he had lifted her off the bed and, for an instant, her lips had been so close, her young woman's body touching his . . . Ugh! His thoughts sickened him. This was Yvette, little Yvette.

But he had to admit that the change in her was startling. All the way to Paris he had carried the mental image of a young schoolgirl – albeit grown slightly older – but still the baby sister he had never had. He had not imagined . . .

What had he imagined? That returning to Paris, to the scene of young, innocent pleasure, would automatically make him an innocent teenager again? Did he think he could wipe out three years of his life with a nine-hour train and boat journey? Oh he was a fine fellow all right. A clean-cut, fresh, upstanding English gentleman, coming to Paris for a quiet, homely holiday in the bosom of a family. What irony! From bosom to bosom! Not for him the illicit pleasures others might find in the French capital. Oh no, he could leave those behind in London. He could reverse the normal order of things. He could . . .

Stop it! Stop it, his brain shrieked at him. You're prefabricating a structure of disaster from a handful of worn-out straws. He was adult; he was intelligent. (*Well, wasn't he*?) So Yvette had grown up. So what? He might have realised it; should have expected it. It didn't change a thing. She was still little Yvette and the Beaumonts were still her parents, and Claude was still her cousin, and he could still behave in the manner they would all expect from him. (*Couldn't he*?) He would have to; *he would simply have to.*

A knock on the door and Yvette calling out that it was five minutes to dinner time roused him from his introspection. "Coming," he shouted back.

He swung off the bed, washed his face and hands in cold water, and dried himself on one of the two fresh towels which had been considerately laid out for him. Then he quickly put on a clean shirt and a different tie and joined the Beaumonts in the dining room.

Madame Beaumont immediately excused herself and went to the kitchen to finish preparing the soup. Yvette's father asked John if he would care for an *apéritif.*

"I shouldn't really ask for it before dinner," said John, "but do you still keep a bottle of *Calvados* in the house?"

Monsieur Beaumont's face beamed. "You remember then?" He removed a bottle and glasses from the cabinet. "And you, Yvette?"

"I'll have a *Byrrh*, Papa."

Monsieur Beaumont poured the drinks. "You know, John, where I come from in Normandy we do not drink this merely after the meal. We drink it before and during the meal as well. *Le trou normand* we call it. It helps us to eat more. The spirit burns a hole through the food and gives us more room in our stomach."

John laughed.

"It's quite true," Yvette said in English. "The Norman hole. And if we permitted it, *papa* would drink it at meals here too. But we insist he takes wine with the rest of us."

Since his arrival, John had been speaking only French. Now he said, in that language, "No English, please Yvette. I think I can cope in your tongue these days."

"*Tiens*!" said Monsieur Beaumont. "I had already remarked it. Your French is excellent now. But you haven't been back to France since you left the army, have you?"

"No," said John, "but I have studied French for three years at college."

Yvette pouted. "And when may I practise my English?" she complained.

"When we're alone," said John. "It's not polite when you parents do not understand what you say."

He was pleased with himself. Instinctively he had fallen into the pattern he used to adopt with her four years earlier. What had he been worried about? Of course he would cope. The spirit was warming him inside; the brief rest on the bed had restored his energy; he felt good. Of course he would manage.

Monsieur Beaumont evidently agreed. "That's it, John." He chuckled. "She needs a firm hand. Her parents are too old to discipline her these days."

John smiled at him as Yvette snorted disdainfully. It was not entirely true. The four years of returning normality had obviously treated the Beaumonts kindly and they seemed hardly to have aged. Madame Beaumont, as he noticed when she entered the room with a steaming soup tureen, had even put on a little weight and it would take a mighty gust of wind these days to blow her away.

But there had been no change in her culinary ability and now, with the food situation restored to normality, the successive courses she set before him, and her insistence upon heaping on his plate additional helpings of each course, was quite staggering. By the time the bowl of fresh fruit was placed on the table he felt like groaning under the weight of food he had eaten. But it was good. Damned good. Even the French loaf, which in 1946 had filled him with such dismay, now tasted fine.

Monsieur Beaumont winked at him. "You need *le trou normand*, I think."

John said, "I won't say 'no'. It was a fine meal, Madame. I even enjoyed the bread."

Yvette guffawed and then tried to compose her features.

"And what do you find so amusing, young lady?" he asked in a tone of mock severity.

"I must not say," she answered.

"But I insist."

She glanced at her mother. "Well, I suppose . . . after four years I may be permitted . . ." She started to giggle. "You remember the bread you once brought us?"

"Yvette!" This in a shocked voice from her mother.

"*Maman*, John will not mind." She looked at him. "Will you, John?"

"I don't see how I can, since I don't know what on earth you are talking about."

"Well . . ." She restrained the threatening eruption of laughter with an effort. "I suppose it was very nice, really. But you know, John, we really preferred to eat our horrible crusty French *baguette*."

Madame Beaumont's face was crimson. "You must excuse her, John. She should not say things like that. And anyway, the coffee was excellent." And her hand shot to her mouth as she recognised her own tacit implication that the bread was indeed not quite to their taste.

Both Yvette and John dissolved into laughter and even Monsieur Beaumont permitted himself a discreet chuckle at his wife's consternation.

"Well that will teach me to be more careful in a foreign country," said John. "You must blame that on my English missionary zeal."

Yvette kept her face absolutely straight and said: "Civilizing the savages, you mean?"

"Yvette!" Once more her mother was shocked.

John grinned. "She is only teasing, Madame."

He felt wonderful. The clock had indeed slipped back four years. He had had fifteen minutes of heart-searching and worry to no purpose at all. He had fallen back into the easy camaraderie – the acceptance and state of belonging – as though he had never been away. He might even permit himself a closer examination of Yvette without the embarrassment or misgiving that had caused him to avoid looking at her other than casually throughout the meal. He did so. He looked at the press of soft, young breast against her cotton frock; the indentation of her throat above the creamy skin, where the collar of her dress lay folded back; the stubborn little jut of chin; the lips, lightly rouged, partly open in a half-smile. She had very nice lips: full, but not excessively so. Kissable. That was the word. Totally kissable. The lips parted further, completing the smile, and he realised with a start that she was aware of him looking at her, examining her. He looked away in annoyance. What the hell! Why shouldn't he look at Yvette? And what had induced this feeling of shame simply because she had noticed him looking? Clearly it wasn't over yet. He wasn't yet in the clear.

"*A votre santé*." He raised his glass, breaking the silence which had actually lasted only a few seconds.

"S*anté*!" they echoed.

Yvette smiled again and to John – even though he knew it was imagination on his part – the smile suggested that they now had a secret to share.

The doorbell rang and Madame Beaumont hurried out.

"That will be Claude," said Monsieur Beaumont.

"Claude!" John exclaimed. "You didn't tell me he was coming."

"I wanted it to be a surprise," said Yvette.

"My word it is." He stood up from the table and moved forward to take Claude's outstretched hand. "Hello, Claude."

"John, my dear fellow. How good it is to see you again."

Yvette said, her voice an imitation of John's, "No English please, Claude. It is not polite. Milord Graham is now a Frenchman."

Claude laughed. "Ah-hah. You are teaching Yvette good manners, are you John? Excellent. She needs them."

"That's what I told him," said Monsieur Beaumont.

"Beast! Beast!" Yvette scowled. "You are all conspiring against me."

Yes, thought John. It will be all right now. This is what I needed: Claude's presence to restore my misplaced sense of values. He looked meaningfully at his watch.

"Isn't it time for little girls to go to bed?"

"Oh! I hate you!" But she joined in the general laughter.

Claude said, "Have you finished eating?"

"Yes," said Madame Beaumont. "You are just in time for coffee. Why don't you all go into the small salon and make yourselves comfortable and I'll bring the coffee in there."

"And so you went to university after all?" said Claude.

"Yes." John raised his cup and found it empty. Madame Beaumont brought over the coffee jug and filled his cup for the third time. "Thank you, Madame. Excellent coffee. Yes," he continued, "I was able to get a government grant – not very much – but with the little bit of insurance mother left, and working during vacations, I was just able to get by." He smiled ruefully. "Nothing over for holidays, of course."

(*Holidays indeed! This was the first break he had had in three years. And this was being achieved on borrowed time and borrowed money.*)

"But you left home, didn't you?" said Yvette. "The address you wrote from – in Hampstead – that was a flat you said."

"That's right. After mother died my aunt didn't really have room for me. It was all right while I was in the army: they gave me a lodging allowance. But afterwards, when I was demobilized, it was too difficult for my aunt. Then, when I went to college, I met this old friend – Norman Williams – and we decided to share a furnished flat.

(*Yes, he thought grimly, it really was difficult for Aunt Susan, wasn't it? Not to mention Uncle Ben. The incessant bickering, which he couldn't help overhearing and knowing he was the cause of it. And Ben's continual, infernal, unvoiced criticism and accusation. When Norman had suggested they find a place to share, he had jumped at the idea.*)

"What sort of a flat is it?" asked Yvette.

"Quite nice," said John. "Two rooms, kitchen and bathroom in a large block. Pretty expensive, of course. Four guineas a week. That's about eight thousand five hundred francs a month. But I pay only half of that, of course. And Norman's parents are quite well off, so he is able to get all the extras we need for the flat. Not to mention the enormous food parcels his mother sends him every couple of weeks."

(*Dear Norman. How would he have managed without the dear chap? How would he be managing now, for that matter, if Norman hadn't loaned him the money for this holiday? "Go on, John. It's only twenty quid.*

You'll be able to pay it back after two or three months work. And it isn't as if you'll have to pay rent at the flat for the week you're away." Nonsense, he had replied. Of course he would meet his share of the rent. But Norman had winked. "Don't be daft, chum. Why do you think I'm so anxious to get you away for a week? It'll be worth the extra two guineas.")

You mentioned working during vacation," said Claude. "What sort of work?"

"Oh, you know. The usual student things. Post office work during the Christmas break. Office work, factories, the railway. They used to pin a list of available jobs in the Registrar's office just before each holiday. The summer before last was slightly different. Norman and I went to work on a farm. Very good, in one way, because we lived there for the best part of two months and everything was included. You know: food, bed, etcetera. We also rented the flat to an American couple while we were away. Six pounds a week! But we didn't care to try it again last year. Up at six every morning. Sundays included. *Too* much like hard work."

(*Not to mention the entirely celibate existence for two months. It had just about driven them crazy. Where were all those hefty country wenches they had read about in Hardy and Fielding? The ones who couldn't wait to be led to the nearest haystack.*")

"And now it's my turn to ask a few questions," John said. "What about you, Claude? Yvette tells me you got married."

Claude grimaced. "It happens to the best of us eventually." He grinned at Yvette and John was surprised to see her glance at him and blush. "But I am one of the lucky ones. My Nicole is a remarkable young woman and our little Pierre makes me very proud."

"How old is he?"

"Six months. Last week was his *demi-anniversaire*. I am sorry that Nicole was unable to come here with me. She so much wanted to meet you. But you understand . . . with a small child. However, we have booked a baby-sitter for tomorrow evening and I hope we will – all four of us – be able to have an evening out."

"That will be wonderful. What about your work? Are you still with a newspaper?"

"Yes," said Claude, "I'm still a reporter with *l'Humanité*."

"Your political views remain unchanged then?"

"Foolish question." Claude smiled. "Have you acquired any political views yet?"

"Foolish question," mimicked John. "You should know better than to ask that of an Englishman. We do not hold political views; we hold political sway!"

"Mon Dieu!" Claude bellowed with laughter. "Right out of Kipling. But how the mighty have fallen, eh? The reign of the – what do you call them? – the *pukka sahib* is over now, alas. No longer shall your capitalists' boots be polished with the sweat of Indian labour. What are they going to do now, eh?"

John grinned and raised his hands in mock-alarm. "Steady-on, Claude. You'll not get me on to a political discussion tonight. There will be time enough for politics before I go back and – I promise you – you won't find me quite so naive as you did four years ago. I've learned a bit in the meantime."

"Ah yes. London School of Economics." He pronounced the name in a tone of contempt. "The bulwark of decadent British social democracy hiding under red camouflage."

"A cheap trick, Claude. I shan't be rising to *that* bait." John turned to Yvette. "And what are you doing these days, young lady."

She scowled at him. "Will you please stop calling me 'young lady'. Apart from being bad French, it is quite inappropriate."

"Now then, Yvette," her mother chided. "Remember your manners. John is our guest."

"No, she is quite right, Madame Beaumont." John rose and bowed deeply to Yvette. "My humble apologies, Yvette – dear little Yvette."

"And that is not much better," she complained, but smilingly. "But I will forgive you. And he is not our guest, *Maman*, he is one of the family, isn't he?"

Her mother smiled and said nothing. Both she and her husband had been viewing the verbal sparring of the three young people with obvious pleasure and an air of . . . fulfilment almost, John decided.

"And in answer to your question, John" said Yvette, "I am secretary to a director of an automobile company in the Champs Elysées."

"Bravo!" said John. "Shall I then call you Mademoiselle Secrétaire?"

"Do that," warned Yvette," and I shall come over there and box your ears."

The rest of the evening passed in pleasant, inconsequential chatter and, true to his words – and despite all Claude's efforts, aided occasionally with a mischievous smile by Monsieur Beaumont – John refused to be goaded into a discussion of anything more serious than a comparison of the standard of living in their two countries. He also learned that

Monsieur Beaumont was now retired from work and the Beaumonts were living on his retirement pension supplemented by Yvette's earnings.

Then, after making arrangements to meet Yvette and John the next evening, Claude took his leave of them, pleading – quite obviously in jest – that he wished to avoid incurring the wrath of a shrewish wife. After his departure it was clear that only politeness was keeping Yvette's parents, too, from their conjugal bed. John therefore used the excuse of his long day in suggesting that he would retire to his bedroom, although he was actually far from sleepy.

There was, however, a sense of pleasant physical relief in nestling down between the sheets of the old-fashioned but remarkably comfortable bed. Having switched on the bedside lamp, head resting on the round bolster, he prepared to finish the paperback detective story he had purchased at Victoria Station in London.

Suddenly a scuffling sound at the bedroom door caused him to sit up. It was Yvette. In long woolen dressing gown, hair pulled to the back of her head and tied with a ribbon, face scrubbed and shining, she slipped quietly into the room and approached the bed.

"I hope you do not mind my coming in here, John. But I saw the light under the door and knew you would not yet be asleep.

"What is it you want, Yvette?" His words were more brusque than he had intended. Momentarily a wave of fear threatened to overwhelm the defences he had built up during the evening.

She pouted. "You don't have to speak to me like that. I am no longer a child. I just wanted to speak to you alone. Do you realise that we haven't been alone since you arrived, except for ten minutes in the taxi."

"I'm sorry, Yvette. For a moment you startled me."

"You want me to go away?" He could sense tears close to the surface of her words.

"No, no. Of course not." (*What else could he say*?)

She smiled quickly and sat on the edge of his bed. "There were so many questions I wanted to ask you this evening, and it wasn't possible with the family there."

"That's all right." Close up, her scrubbed and shiny appearance somehow transformed her into the Yvette of four years ago – a somewhat overgrown schoolgirl – and conspired to still his fears. He reached for her hand and squeezed it. "Ask away."

All at once she looked shy and fell silent and, apart from a slight pressure of her fingers on his hand, motionless.

"Well . . .?" He smiled. "Have you forgotten all your questions?"

"No." Her mouth twitched slightly. "I just don't know how to ask them any more."

"Well I'm afraid I can't help you, since I have no idea what you want to know."

Suddenly, the words flooding rapidly out of her mouth, she said, "John have you got a girlfriend in London?" Then, in confusion, she looked down at his hand still holding her own.

"I see . . ." He smiled. "But of course I have." She glanced at him sharply as he paused. "I have dozens," he added.

She gave a sigh of relief. "That's all right, then."

"Funny statement," he commented.

"It's not at all funny." Her stubborn little chin jutted forward. "As long as you don't have one *special* girl friend, I do not mind."

He was tempted to treat her remark facetiously, to convert it into a joke, but one glance at her face convinced him that to do so would be not only a mistake, but in the worst possible taste. He contented himself with squeezing her hand.

"I'll go to bed now," she said.

Was there the merest hint of a question mark at the end of her words? Or was it just his imagination?

"Goodnight, Yvette, dear, dear Yvette."

She leaned over him and pressed moist soft lips to his. He sensed the faint aroma of talcum powder and taste of toothpaste and then, giving him no opportunity to respond to her kiss, she raised her head, withdrew her hand from his, and moved away from the bed.

"Goodnight, dear John. Sleep well."

Then she was gone.

As was any possibility of sleep.

Nor was he able to return to his book. Instead he made a deliberate effort to push aside the return of the turbulent emotions that had assailed him on and off all evening, and to examine his feelings calmly and dispassionately. Yvette's attitude to him, her regard for him, were clear and quite incapable of misinterpretation. But so, too, was his own response. After all, she was a woman, and it was as a woman that she affected his primary instincts. The complication arose from the fact that the woman had developed out of the girl – and the girl belonged to a life that no longer seemed any part of his. And he had changed. Dear God, how he had changed. The last three years had made him a different person.

His memory winged back, gliding through the years on a downdraft of unexpected recall; slipstreaming the lean period of frustration and sorrow and despair; soaring towards the ceiling of those last three years: the momentous years, the years of plenty; the ceiling of a new-found independence and freedom. A ceiling, moreover, that topped a singularly uninspiring facade; tucked away, out of sight, in a small street at the back of London's Aldwych. It was called the London School of Economics.

It opened up a completely new world to him. It was largely perhaps the reaction against having had to endure for too long the company of those with whom he had very little in common. But it was more than that. It marked a phase of greatly overdue development. He at last found himself evolving a personality and a character that had hitherto been stifled. A whole new range of interests and avenues of exploration were opening up, and each day was filled with wonderment and discovery. He was Keats's "Watcher of the Skies" and a host of new planets were swimming into his ken.

And that was only the beginning: the fringe of his recollection.

The purple, the black and the gold,
Are the colours of the schoo-oo-l
That we-ee-ee
Remember with a sigh . . .

So sang they in the college revue during his final year. And how true. How significant the words were proving. The cameos paraded through his reflections in cinematic review: "the old familiar faces". How much it had all meant to him: the companionship, the camaraderie, the easy-going acceptance of each other.

His memory suddenly fetched up short against a wall of self-annoyance. This futile resurrection was skipping the main issue, was seeking to shield him from the major assessment of his psychological development. He was avoiding the axis around which his life had revolved – and was, indeed, still spinning.

So back again, to probe, to assess, to judge.

Back to the beginning, to the first twist of the wheel, the setting in motion of his entire current way of life; that day in the Old Theatre, during his second week at LSE.

He had wandered in to attend a lecture, choosing to sit in the gallery where there was usually more room. The seats were formed from wide steps running elliptically around the hall. He placed his briefcase on the floor beside him and hunted through it for notebook and pencil. Suddenly a hand was clapped on his shoulder.

"*A oes lle yna*?"

Without reflection, engrossed in the search for his pencil, the strangeness of the request for room beside him being phrased in Welsh failed to impinge, and he replied in the same tongue.

"*Mae digon o' le yma*." There's plenty of room here. He moved his feet to let the enquirer pass and then, as the significance of the verbal exchange hit him, he glanced up. "Norman!" he exclaimed. "What the hell are you doing here?"

A grin spread over the other's face. "The same as you, I would guess, chum." He sat down beside John, placed his bag on the floor, and they clasped hands. "I guess it's pretty obvious that we're both here for the same reason."

"Yes, but . . . but . . ." Jon stammered excitedly. "I had no idea you were at LSE."

"Boy-bach, if you had taken to trouble to answer my letter, in the long-ago-and-far-away, we might both have known."

John looked shamefaced. "Sorry about that, Norm."

Norman Williams grinned gain. "That's okay, chum. I doubt if I'd have got around to writing a second letter myself. But Christ! How long has it been, anyway?"

John calculated rapidly. "Over three years."

"Jesus! That's right . . . Oh hell!" He had spotted a figure moving across the stage to the rostrum. "Sayer on banking. Look, chum, what're you doing for lunch?"

"Well I usually eat in the refectory."

"Refectory be buggered. Lunch is on me today, John-bach. We've got a lot of catching up to do."

Immediately after the lecture Norman took him to the Old Cheshire Cheese in Fleet Street and stood him the best meal he had had in weeks. Through the various courses they each pumped the other dry for details of their respective doings in the years between Llanelli Boys' Grammar School and the London School of Economics.

Finally Norman chuckled.

"Well, bach," he said, "here we are again. *Ymlaen Llanelli!*"

"*Sospan fatch*!" John grinned.

"*Cymru am byth.*"

"*Iechyd da bob cymro*."

"*Twll dyn bob saess*."

They both laughed happily at the old patter.

"Great days they were, John, eh?"

"You bet! Rugger at Stradey Park."

"Other games in Parc Howerd."

"Wouldn't know about those," said John.

"No. That's right. I forgot. Sanctimonious little prick you were in those days. Wouldn't even join me on the Sunday night monkey parade in Stepney Street, would you? Different story now, I'll wager."

John ignored the tacit request for information and said instead: "But I'm surprised to find you at LSE, Norm. I thought you were dead set on Aber' if you got Higher Schools."

Norman leered. "The crumpet, bach. Don't see any green in these eyes, do you? Aberystwyth could never compare with this."

"You're still into getting your share, then, Norman?"

"You know me, John-bach. Gets better all the time, isn't it? And if I only had a base of operations. By Christ, man," he gave his knee a mighty smite with an open palm, "that's it! That's it. Of course!"

"Of course – what? What's it?" asked John, puzzled.

"Look you, chum . . ." Norman placed his elbows on the table and leaned towards John. His brown eyes, set deeply into their sockets and partly concealed by an unruly lock of black, wavy hair, seemed to gleam fervently. He looked for all the world, John thought, like some early passionate evangelist. He had always been like that, John recalled. When he really got carried away with a subject he would appear to be simultaneously hypnotising you with his eyes and mesmerising you with his voice. It was, in large measure, the recipe for his success with the opposite sex. His implicit acceptance of – and belief in – his own infallibility and his assumption that others must necessarily agree with him, seemed to convince women that they stood to miss something really exceptional unless they fell in with his suggestions. Now the eyes shone and the voice declaimed convincingly. "It's like this, bach. I've the possibility of a flat in Hampstead. Terrific, it is! Two large rooms, kitchen, bathroom, hall, central heating, constant hot etceteras and all the doodallies. Ideal, it is. Fully furnished, part from bedding, kitchen equipment, and so on. Place called Gilling Court. But there's a snag, boy-back. A snageroo. Four guineas a week and three months in advance. I could borrow the money from the Da, but I couldn't afford to repay it and the rent too. Also I'd want to tap the folks for other bits and pieces, so the less I ask – to begin with – the more chance I'll have of getting the other things later. Now, d'you see what I've got in mind?"

"Not really."

"Okay, chum, I'll put it in words of one syllable. Look you, if we take the flat together, it'll mean half the rent each, half the deposit each, and – as they say – two can live as cheaply as one. So what do you think?"

John did not have to think. As soon as Norman had started explaining, he had felt his pulse race with excitement. It was a way out – a refuge – a flight from the strife and bickering and oppressive atmosphere at Aunt Susan's. Financially it would be difficult, but not – surely not! – impossible. It was, in short, a heaven-sent opportunity and one he was not going to miss.

"I'm game," he said.

"Good for you, bach!" Norman was gleeful.

It was a swinging success from the outset. A large part of John's meagre resources went into his share of the deposit, but an enormous parcel of linen from Norman's mother and a cheque from his father sufficient to equip their kitchen completely, relieved them both of a hefty item of expenditure which they had already budgeted. They decided to celebrate their good fortune and the eventual readiness of the flat by organising a house-warming party, that would also coincide with the end of term.

"A buffet is *de rigueur* boy-bach," said Norman. "But who is to organise it for us?"

"Julie," said John.

It was not a suggestion, but a statement which carried just a hint of astonishment that Norman had even asked. In the six weeks since he and Norman had met in the Old Theatre, Norman and Julie Grant – a fellow first-year student – had seemed to be inseparable companions.

Norman's lips turned down. "Hell, chum, once I let her loose in our kitchen, I'll never get rid of her."

John raised an eyebrow. "I wasn't aware you wanted to get rid of her."

"I've spent the last three weeks trying to ease myself out from under." Norman groaned. "Boy-bach, one thing I've learned: dating a dame at college is like giving a saucer of milk to the neighbour's cat. Once you've done it, you're stuck with it. You can't get away from them. Propinquity; that's the keynote of both mistakes. For three years you've got a woman hanging on your arm; like the bloody cat rubbing its furry body up against your trouser leg every time you pass your neighbour's door. Fine if you're a cat lover . . .

"And you're not?"

"Fickle, chum, that's me. A lover of cats rather than a cat lover."

"Yes, but look Norman, all joking apart. You can't mean that about Julie. Why, she's terrific! She's got everything: brains, looks, the lot!"

Norman put a hand on John's shoulder and fixed him with a pitying look. "John . . . Johnny-bach . . . sounds like you've got a crush on her yourself."

John laughed nervously and avoided Norman's eyes.

Norman abruptly flopped into an armchair, his long legs spread-eagling before him, and chortled for several seconds before saying, "It's true then. And I never suspected it."

"I don't see why you should find that so funny. She's only about the best-looking first-year female at LSE."

"Christ, chum, look at the quality of the competition!"

"Julie would be worth looking at in any company."

"All right, all right," Norman suppressed his laughter and held up a hand in surrender. "You don't have to persuade me. I've been knocking it off for six weeks and a doll has to have something special for me to bother more than three times. But I'm not prepared to end up with a ball and chain tied to my ankle, so the time has come to call a halt . . . unless . . ."

"Unless – what?"

"John-bach, how would you like to take her off my hands?"

John snorted. "A fat chance I've got of doing that."

"Oh, I don't know." Norman closed one eye slowly and gazed reflectively at John out of the other. "I'll make a deal with you. We'll get Julie along to cope with the eats on condition that you make a pitch for her. Okay?"

"Well . . . as you're no longer interested . . . I don't mind giving it a try. But I can't say I'm particularly hopeful."

Norman opened his eye and then closed it again in a wink. "Boy-bach, you may have a surprise in store for you."

The day of the party arrived and, in the afternoon, John answered the doorbell's ring and opened the door to Julie Grant.

"Hello Julie," he said cheerily. "Come in and let me get you a drink." He closed the door behind her. "Let me take your coat."

He had been anticipating her arrival for the past half-hour and had spent most of that time preparing himself for her visit, practising imaginary conversations.

She shrugged her coat off into his hands. "Where's Norman?" she asked tersely.

"Oh, he's out somewhere. Making last minute arrangements for the party I dare say." He waved a hand. "He's leaving it to me to give you a hand with the food. But how about a drink first."

He led the way down the hall into the living room. The door from the hall was located in the centre of one of the room's long walls. Left of the door as one entered had been furnished as a dining room; the right hand side as a living room. The dining section had a polished, uncovered parquet floor and a door leading directly to the kitchen. One side consisted entirely of French windows, in one corner of which was a built-in, upholstered seat. The remaining two walls were painted in soothing primrose and grey. By contrast the living area was brightly and sumptuously furnished. A deep pile rug covered the floor, at the centre of which were two large armchairs. Against one wall was a large settee, whilst against the gaily patterned wallpaper on the opposing wall stood a cocktail cabinet and radiogram.

Julie looked about her, evidently impressed. "Very nice," she said. Then she ran a finger across the top of the radiogram and lifted an ashtray overflowing with cigarette stubs. Her nose puckered. "But it's obviously being used by bachelors."

"That's right," said John. "You haven't been here before. Let me show you round."

He led her into the kitchen where she examined the electric cooker, opened the refrigerator and the built-in cupboards. Then they returned to the hell and entered the bedroom. He mouthed a silent prayer of thanks that both Norman and he had remembered to tidy their divan beds that morning. Finally she saw the bathroom with its shower stall.

Back once more in the living room he made her sit in one of the armchairs while he poured gins-and-tonic for them both. Then he sat in the opposite chair and studied her.

She had a forbidding expression on her face, almost as if there were a nasty smell in her nostrils, which was a pity, he felt, because it detracted from her otherwise attractive features: a pert nose, green eyes, full lips and gently waved ash-blond hair worn shoulder-length. He also found her body very exciting with its high, thrusting breasts, slim waist, and long shapely legs at present being effectively revealed by the depth at which the deep-cushioned armchair obliged her to sit.

He raised his glass. "Cheers."

"Cheers," she echoed and then, for the first time since entering the flat, she smiled. "I'm sorry if I've seemed a bit nasty, but I'm feeling angry."

"Oh? Why's that?"

"Norman," she stated flatly. "Although I should be used to him by now."

"What has he done?"

"Nothing much," she said. "Merely told me to meet him at Belsize Park Station. I've been waiting there for half an hour and finally decided I must have misunderstood our arrangement. But as he's not here either, I doubt very much if I did."

"I say, I am sorry."

"That's all right. It was silly of me to take it out on you. I should be used to him by now. Anyway, you're here, and I've come to do a job of work, so let's get on with it."

She hoisted herself out of the armchair and he stared, fascinated, at the brief revelation of white thigh above the stocking-tops as she stood up. Then, having replenished their glasses, he followed her into the kitchen.

By the time the bread had been sliced and the second glass of gin drained, he had his arm slipped around her waist. She made no effort to remove his arm, but continued to prepare sandwich fillings as though oblivious to the physical contact.

The completion of the canapés coincided with their finishing their third drink and, as she brushed past him in the kitchen, he gathered her into his arms and kissed her on the lips. There was an immediate response and then she withdrew from his embrace with a short laugh and the statement that they hadn't time for that sort of thing now. The "*now*" pleased him.

The arrival of the first guests found John and Julie on the settee, in an embrace as passionate as it was unexpected. He had, by now, lost count of the number of drinks they had consumed. She jumped off the settee with a groan of dismay and rushed into the bathroom to repair the ravages of her make-up, while he went to the door to let the guests enter.

Norman had still not returned, but somehow this no longer seemed important to Julie and they were both in exceptionally jocose mood as they bade the guests welcome together. In a very short time the party was going with a swing; the drinks were flowing liberally, and the buffet meal which Julie and he had prepared earlier lasted for precisely one hour and was then reduced to mere crumbs remaining on a few plates. Penurious students clearly appreciated good fare, particularly when it was free of charge.

Altogether there were eight couples in the room, apart from Julie and John, sitting around, talking and drinking, or dancing to swing records. Each of them had queried Norman's absence and both John and Julie had had to say that they simply had no idea what had delayed his return. Then, towards eleven o'clock, the apartment door burst open and Norman arrived, one arm around a buxom peroxide blonde.

"*Nos da*, boys and girls," he exclaimed cheerfully, apparently quite unfazed at his absence from his own party. "Excuse the delay, but I bumped into an old friend in town and completely lost track of the time. Still, the night's young, and we're all so beautiful, so let's eat, drink and be merry, for tomorrow we'll feel like hell."

He rushed around the room, shaking hands and kissing cheeks, and introducing his companion. "This is Cheryl . . . an old, old friend." With every introduction he resealed the friendship with a resounding kiss on Cheryl's lips. When he reached Julie and tried to embrace her, she hastily averted her face. "Now then, Julie ducks, whatsamarrer? I haven't got leprosy, have I Cheryl? Splendid job you're doing here, John-bach, isn't he Cheryl? Carry on the good work. C'mon Cheryl, let me show you the rest of the flat." He vanished with the blonde into the bedroom.

Gales of laughter greeted his drunken performance and his departure from the room. They all knew Norman and nothing he did could ever surprise them. Indeed they all seemed to expect such unconventional behaviour from him. All, that is, except Julie. John felt her arm linking in his and he looked at her. All evidence of her earlier drinking seemed to have vanished from her face, which looked a little white. John even imagined he could detect a slight tremble to her lips.

"Dance with me, John" she said.

Dancing was all but impossible in the crowded room and the blues record spinning on the turntable could barely be heard above the din. But he took her in his arms and joined the other couples indulging in a swaying embrace, which was all they could manage, to the hardly audible rhythm.

Suddenly Julie muttered into his shoulder. "Would you mind taking me home, John?"

"But Julie, how can I? The party . . . It's still early . . ."

"Damn the party," she exclaimed vehemently. "Norman's here now. Let him cope for a while. Of course, if you don't want to – I can go home myself."

"No, no, of course not. I'll take you. Let me get your coat!

They slipped quickly and quietly away from the flat. Julie did not want to make the round of goodbyes and John expected to be back long before the other guests started to leave.

But it was almost three hours later before he returned to an apartment which appeared deserted, except for Norman sprawled in an armchair, an almost empty whiskey bottle dangling from one hand. As John entered the room, Norman opened a red and bleary eye.

"What ho, chum. Everything go off okay?"

"You bastard!" John leaned over him. "What was the big idea of that performance?"

Norman grinned. "Simmer down, chum. Want to wake our guests?" John stared at him. "There're two couples sleeping it off – I presume they're sleeping it off – in the bedroom. Now why don't you just calm down, boy-bach, find yourself a drink – if there's any left – sit yourself down, and get that load off your chest. But calmly."

John dropped into the other armchair. "Christ, you're a sod, aren't you? You forget your own party; you break a date with Julie; you have the nerve to bring a cheap tart here; and now you just sit there grinning like a Cheshire cat."

"Finished, chum?" John sighed in reply and Norman said, "Then let me tell you a few facts of life. The party was a bloody great success, and you should know by now that I don't do things by accident. My boy, I've succeeded in killing about three birds with one stone this evening. As for you . . . don't tell me you didn't get what you were after. Don't tell me you didn't dip your wick, boy-bach."

John blushed. Norman guffawed.

"Okay, John," Norman continued, "let's get down to cases. It seems to me that your education has a few dull spots which need polishing. First of all, Julie. She'll get over it quickly enough." He chuckled. "If you did your stuff right, she's already well on the way to getting over it. What you do with her from now on is your business, but as far as I'm concerned, I'm off the hook. And, incidentally, Cheryl really was a tart! Cost me a fucking fiver. But a rather artistic touch, I felt. Appealed to my sense of the dramatic. Still, that's by the bye. The point is that we've got to establish a routine for the flat."

"What do you mean?"

Norman sighed. "Boy-bach, I'm beginning to despair at this evidence of how much you need to learn. Look, take women! You want to make out . . . right? So what do you do? You chase a woman who pleases you and – if you're lucky – you get there. How often do you get there? Perhaps one time in ten. So what do you do about it? I'll tell you what most guys do about it – they worry about their technique. They do their collective nuts. They rush around in ever-decreasing circles with the inevitable catastrophic rectal result. And – at the end of it all – if they're successful, why, they may end up doubling their average. Two out of ten!" He snorted. "Not me, boyo! One is ten is fine for me. My answer is to extend my field of operations, to regard every popsy I meet as potential bed-bait and go after it. D'you see? Where you would spend your time chasing ten dames and making out once or twice, I'll make a pass at a hundred. Just a pass, mark you, no time-wasting or brain-beating. But I'll wager that I'll make it with ten of them!"

John was flabbergasted. Norman's cool, calculating, clinical approach to the subject of sex was quite outside his experience. "You're not serious," he said.

"Serious? Too fucking true, I'm serious. Look you, bach, if we're sharing this flat, we've got to understand each other from the word go. I don't give a fuck if you want to play the game my way or not – just so long as we have a system. Believe me, boyo, a two-roomed flat can be a prison cell for two people unless they introduce a bit of organisation. Now you just think about it and let me know what you decide. Because, chum, I've got ideas and I've got plans, and I'm going to put them into practice. So it's up to you! You can come in with me, or I'll go it alone. It's no skin off my nose." Suddenly he grinned again. "Now, be a darling and find a bottle amongst that wreckage that's got something in it, and let's talk this thing out."

John found a half-full bottle of beer, took a deep swig and then handed it to Norman. He knew he was excited by the possibilities suggested by Norman's résumé; he knew he was nervous at the prospect of participating in it himself. Then he reminded himself of the decision he had consciously taken one year before – a hotheaded sudden decision to which he had not since given conscious thought or expression. He made another snap decision.

"Okay, Norm," he said, "I'm with you. But you'll have to be patient with me. I'll tell you frankly that I decided a long time ago that no woman was going to get her claws into me, but I'm afraid I haven't got your experience."

"Attaboy, John! You put yourself in Uncle Norman's hands and I can promise you, you won't go far wrong." He drained the remainder of the beer. "Now the first step in the plan of campaign is . . ." he paused and then added, significantly, "nurses' homes."

That was how it had all started. And now, lying in his bed in the

Beaumonts' home in Paris, John had to face another decision. After three years of subjection to the influence of Norman Williams, he found himself confused and bewildered by his response to what would have been, previously, a normal situation. But nowadays normality in his relations with the opposite sex betokened one thing only and, instinctively, intuitively, he knew it would be all wrong with Yvette.

He fell asleep, still pondering the problem.

CHAPTER SEVEN

John was stupefied.

There was no reason why he should have expected Claude's wife to be beautiful, or even attractive. It was probably a form of self-conceit that would not permit him to envisage the wife of a friend as being any less desirable than he would have chosen for himself.

And Nicole was far from attractive. She was – he had to admit frankly – downright plain! For a moment he felt a stab-wound of betrayal and then, as Claude presented her to him, he made a determined effort to keep the shock from showing, forced a smile to his lips, and assured Nicole how much he had been looking forward to meeting her.

He got his second surprise as she responded to his greeting. Her voice was throaty, huskily deep; a Marlene Dietrich voice, completely out-of-place coming from that unromantic exterior.

They met at the *Deux Magots*, and Claude and Nicole were already seated there when Yvette and John arrived.

As they sat around the terrace table, John studied Claude's wife. The long, lank black hair; the pale face, completely devoid of make-up; the heavy-rimmed, thick-lensed spectacles, seeming to magnify the pale, lack-lustre eyes behind them: all these added up to a creature he found completely insipid and lacking in allure. Her clothes too conveyed the impression of formlessness and gracelessness: a black cotton shirtwaist above a shapeless woolen skirt, black stockings and flat shoes.

Pointlessly he compared the fresh, young beauty of Yvette with the drabness of Nicole. Pointlessly, because the resolution he had made that morning, upon awakening – and had effectively maintained during his afternoon excursion with Yvette – should have absolved him from any feeling of contingent interest where she was concerned. But he could not suppress the childish feeling of satisfaction that of the two it was Yvette who was "his girl" and then, abruptly, he felt a sense of shame at his thoughts. Nicole was Claude's wife and Claude was his friend; and who was he to set himself up in judgement on the taste of others.

"Have you been here before?" Claude asked John.

"No, I haven't," John replied.

He looked around. The café was packed, both inside and out, with an animated, noisy, and generally young-looking throng. He was intrigued to see that many of the women were dressed similarly to Nicole: drably, that is, including the black stockings, and with similar long, lank hair. Politeness stopped him from commenting on the coincidence, but he made a mental note to question Yvette about it later.

In fact, Claude's next remark provided the key to the matter. Claude said, "This is quite a well-known café actually; this and the café opposite, the *Flore*. They each have phases of popularity with the existentialist set. At the moment this one is in favour with Sartre, so this is where they come – as you may have gathered from Nicole."

That was it, then. Nicole's dress was a sort of uniform, it would appear – although he could not imagine was the existentialist set might be. He said, "That would be Jean-Paul Sartre?"

"Yes," Nicole answered him. "Have you read his work?"

"Oh yes," said John eagerly. "We read some of it at college."

"What did you read?"

Only *La Nausée* and *Mains Sales*."

"Ah! Then you have not studied his philosophy?" Nicole's words conveyed the impression of smug satisfaction, as though his answer had confirmed an opinion. John found it somewhat baffling.

"I'm afraid my study of philosophy stopped short at Hegel," he said.

Nicole snorted scornfully. "Then you have not really studied philosophy at all. It *starts* with Hegel and continues with Marx." Her tone of voice carried an acrimonious challenge.

Claude laughed, a trifle embarrassedly it seemed to John. "I've brought my heavy armour with me tonight."

"So I see."

It seemed to John that Nicole's words were intended to draw him into some sort of argument, although he could not imagine why. It was a little unfair of Claude not to help him out. He could hardly be expected to cross swords with someone he had met a bare five minutes earlier – and a woman to boot.

"What's the matter, John?" Yvette asked. "Do you not have an answer?"

"I think there's a conspiracy afoot," John said feebly. "Don't tell me *you're* a communist, Yvette."

"Oh, no!" She giggled. "I take no real interest in politics. But I am always interested to listen when Nicole feels in the mood for an argument."

"So that's it," John said to Nicole. "You're an argument in search of a disputant – and I'm cast in the role of sacrificial lamb."

"Nonsense," she snapped. "That's a typical bourgeois jest to avoid facing a political reality. Why is it that reactionaries are always the same? Immediately they are asked to respond to a serious question, which it does not suit them to answer, they fall back on the childish device of making a joke, or avoiding the issue."

My God, thought John, and said to Claude: "How about coming to my rescue?"

"Oh no," said Claude. "I'm enjoying the position of onlooker too much. Why don't you just answer her? Don't worry about pulling your punches."

John felt his face redden with anger. "First of all I was not aware I had been asked a question. Secondly I do not see where she has the right to call me a reactionary – "

"It is quite . . . " Nicole began.

" – when you do not even know me." John over-rode her interruption. "I may not be well versed in Marxist philosophy, but I can recognise a typical, cheap dialectical tactic when I hear it."

"Bravo, John," said Yvette.

A waiter approached the table and took their order. When he left Claude said, "What *is* your political persuasion, John?"

"Persuasion!" John repeated the word disdainfully. "I'm not sure I have a political belief worthy of being so honoured. I suppose I'm somewhere between the Liberal and the Labour parties."

"Exactly," derided Nicole. "A reactionary!"

"Good God, woman! I know you communists. Anyone who doesn't toe the line is a reactionary, whether he's a dyed-in-the-wool, true-blue conservative, or a rabid anarchist with a bomb in each pocket. You seem to think you have a monopoly on freedom and progress and you have a larger vocabulary of abuse than every other political or socio-economic group put together. I know all right. At college I have been called capitalist, Trotskyist, Marxist-deviationist, petit-bourgeois-imperialist, chauvinist, and a dozen other names by so-called communists with whom I had the temerity to disagree."

Nicole wrinkled her nose in distaste. "If you received those names, they were probably deserved."

John turned to Claude in despair. "Claude, *mon vieux*, what does your *wife* want with me?"

"Don't ask me!" Claude held out his hands, palms upward, and gave a Gallic shrug. "To convert you, probably. I'm sitting happily on the sidelines for this discussion. I merely mentioned to Nicole last night your boast that you were no longer as politically naïf as when we first met."

"Naïf!" Nicole jeered. "Of course he is naïf. If he were not naïf he would realise that there is only one answer to the suffering and misery, the exploitation and starvation in the world today."

"Communism, I suppose?" said John. Nicole tossed her head; his question did not merit a response. "It doesn't occur to you, of course, that communism has added more than its fair share to the suffering and misery that exists in the world."

"That's a lie!" Nicole removed her spectacles, and the change in her appearance was extraordinary. She was still not beautiful, but the eyes which appeared as lifeless behind the glasses, now flashed with anger and brought an animated passion to her face. "Of course there is suffering under communism, but it is a fraction of the suffering that it has replaced and it is a suffering that is accepted willingly and even eagerly, because the People know that their destiny is in their own hands, and the future is being remade by them for themselves. It is the suffering of free people building that future, safeguarding it for their children; it is not the suffering of wage-slaves. When you own the means of production, you do not mind how much short-term deprivation you have to accept, for you know you will get the benefit of all the advancement you achieve in the future. You are not working to put profits into the pockets of your capitalist exploiters, but to put food into the mouths of your children."

"I was not aware that the French or English children are starving," said John mildly.

"Starvation is not a matter solely of an empty belly," snapped Nicole. "I was speaking metaphorically. We are starved of our heritage; of our birthright. We are starved of the right to achieve freedom of action and liberty of choice."

"And the Russian and Polish and Hungarian peoples are not, is that it? They have that freedom, do they?"

"Oh, a typical capitalist reply!" sneered Nicole. "The free peoples of the eastern European democracies are seeking to reach a standard of life in decades which it took us three centuries to attain in France and England. And they are doing it despite the loss of life and physical resources they sustained during the war. The peoples of the communist countries are voluntarily surrendering their immediate physical comforts in order to build a better life for the future. They are giving all in their power to give, so that want and deprivation may be ended for all time."

"Yes," said John, "I've heard that one before. From each according to his abilities to each according to his needs. Isn't that what you say? A very pretty phrase."

"It may be just a pretty phrase to you. To us it is a living reality; a dynamic expression of unselfish endeavour."

"And anyone who doesn't agree is purged, eh?"

"Oh, you make me sick!"

"Nicole!" Claude snapped at his wife. "You are going too far!"

"I'm sorry." She put a hand on John's arm. "Please forgive my bad manners. That sounded very rude, but I did not mean it personally, believe me. It is merely that this is a matter I find it impossible to remain calm about."

"That's all right," said John stiffly.

"No, it is not all right." Nicole turned to Yvette. "Tell him please Yvette that I always get carried away like this when I am arguing."

"It is quite true, John," said Yvette.

"And I only argue with friends, John," added Nicole. "So I hope you will accept what I have said as a friend and – as a friend – forgive my rudeness."

Suddenly – and he did not know why – John felt sorry for this plain young woman. He conceived the strange idea that she was not destined for happiness; it was a peculiar conception, empathetic rather than extrinsic. Her hand still rested on his arm and he patted it with his free hand.

"There's nothing to forgive." He smiled. "Any wife of Claude's is a friend of mine."

"And that is enough of politics - for the moment anyway," said Claude. "Let us drink up and then go somewhere to eat."

John enjoyed the fixed menu meal of chicken and red peppers which they ate at the *Restaurant Basque*. He enjoyed, too, the informal atmosphere of its small, crowded dining room and the Basque folk music with which three musicians entertained them. Under the mellowing influence of the *vin rosé* which accompanied their meal, all four of them were relaxed and comfortable, and the earlier spirited dispute was banished to a quondam limbo.

"How do you plan to spend your week in Paris?" Claude asked John.

"Relaxing mainly," said John. "Revisiting all the places I saw in 1946 and also spending at least three days at the Louvre. With Yvette at work during the day I shall have lots of time to myself." He smiled at her. "But she had better be prepared for some hectic evenings."

Yvette reached for his hand beneath the table and squeezed it.

"I don't think you will have much trouble persuading Yvette." Claude winked at her. "Eh, cousin? The only difficulty he will have is in getting away from you, *n'est-ce pas*?"

She snorted. "That's enough from you, Mister Clever. You can save your brilliant situation analyses for your newspaper."

"Oh-ho!" Claude raised a hand in mock-alarm. "I'm under attack now. *Au secours*, wife! Spring to the defence of your man."

"You defend yourself," said Nicole. "Yvette is quite right. You are an interfering old busybody."

She was clearly joking, but her expression remained serious. John realised that he had not seen her smile throughout the evening.

"All right, all right," Claude grumbled. "No further comments from me this evening. Remind me to make sure we have a bachelor night out next time, John." He grimaced. "Uh, I forgot, you would have to escape Yvette's clutches for that. Sorry, sorry," he exclaimed hastily as Yvette shook a fist at him. "I take it back; I give in. I shut up." He clamped his lips together.

"I sometimes find myself wondering about my husband," said Nicole. "I'm sure there is insanity somewhere in his family."

"Peace, peace." Claude raised a hand. "No more teasing; no more mocking; no more taunting. What did you two do this afternoon?"

"I took John to the *Bois de Vincennes*," said Yvette. "He was so anxious to meet you again, you see."

"To meet me . . .?"

"Yes." Yvette nodded her head gravely. "I thought he ought to meet your simian relations at the *jardins zoologiques*."

"John!" Claude yelped. "Are you a party to this scandalous aspersion?"

John grinned. "Well, we *did* go to the zoo this afternoon – and we did visit the apes. But if there was any resemblance to be seen, it wasn't obvious to me."

"Thank you . . . my friend!"

"Yes," John continued. "They seemed far too handsome a collection of apes."

Nicole's sole concession to the dismay on Claude's face may have been a slight softening of her expression – and then again it may have been John's imagination. Not so Yvette, however; she started giggling in most unladylike fashion.

"That does it!" said Claude. "I'm through with you, you . . . you. . . reactionary!"

"Oh, oh, oh," gasped Yvette. "Why did you wait four years to come back to Paris, John? This is the first time I've seen Claude so completely deflated since Pierre was alive." Instantly her hand flew to her mouth and she looked quickly at Nicole. "I'm sorry . . . I . . . I . . ."

Claude interrupted her stammered apology. "What do you intend doing tomorrow, John?"

He had obviously interposed the question to cover up an embarrassment for which John could imagine no reason. He said, "Yvette plans to take me to Versailles, that is, on having me take her . . ." He interrupted himself, caught up in the precipitate play of emotions on the faces of Yvette and Nicole. "I say, there's nothing wrong, is there?"

"Of course not." Claude smiled, but John could see that the smile was forced. "But I think perhaps we should get home before our baby-sitter loses patience with us."

"No," said Yvette. "You stay and have a few drinks with John. I'll go back with Nicole, and John can pick me up later."

"Are you sure?" asked John. "We can all go back, if you like."

"No." Nicole struggled to bring her emotions under control. "Our apartment is too small to entertain. I think Yvette's idea is best. You two stay out awhile and Yvette can come back and keep me company." She got up and Yvette, glancing unhappily at Claude, followed suit. "We'll see you later."

After the women left, Claude called the waiter and, rejecting John's attempt to pick up the bill, settled up and suggested they find somewhere quieter to have a drink.

They walked slowly and silently in the direction of Montparnasse. Claude was deep in thought and John – although puzzled by the abrupt turn in the evening's mood – discreetly held his tongue. Eventually they entered a small bar and seated themselves at a corner table, away from the few other patrons.

"What will you drink, John?"

"A beer please."

"Good! That will suit me too." Claude ordered and they remained in silence until the drinks arrived.

"Santé," said John.

"Cheers."

The emotional turmoil of a little earlier – that inexplicable, precipitate disturbance of their evening – still hung between them: a Gordian knot of uneasiness.

John forced a chuckle.

"What is it?" asked Claude. "I should be pleased to hear something amusing."

"I was remembering that discussion you had with Monsieur Beaumont one evening in 1946, and what he said about the *dirigisme du tripartisme déstructeur*. I think if I get a good degree result in my French exam it will be partly due to that phrase."

"Oh?"

"Yes. In answering one question I quoted the phrase." John laughed. "*Selon Monsieur Léon Blum* . . .etcetera."

Claude grunted. "Happily then, John, it was a French examination and not a test of political knowledge. If you attributed the phrase to Blum it would be obvious to the examiner that you had no real comprehension of Blum's politics."

John saw that he had failed to penetrate the veil of gloom with which Claude had surrounded himself. He made another effort. "Hmm. In that case I'd better confess to another area of ignorance. Would you mind explaining to me what an existentialist is?"

"Ooof," wailed Claude. "You do not ask much, do you? Unfortunately there is no short answer to that question as existentialism covers a large number of doctrines and a large number of philosophers."

"Not just Sartre, then?"

"Eh? No, not at all. Hediger and Kierkegaard, Bosanquet and Green, to name just a few. The basic concept behind existentialism is nothing new. But I know what you mean: here in Paris the existentialists are in fact followers – disciples you might say – of Sartre. Their main belief is that Man has freedom of choice and must therefore create his own values; the way to create those values is by action and devoting ones self to the business of life: the act of living. Do you follow me?"

"Not completely," John confessed.

"Well, let me put it this way. Basically existentialism postulates that existence precedes essence. As an example of what I mean: suppose you wanted to build a house; who would you approach?

John thought for a moment, taking a sip of his drink. "An architect?"

"Just so." Claude nodded. "It would be set out on a blueprint and that would provide the basic concept of your house: the *essence*. Later the house would be built; would come into *existence*; but the essence of that house would have preceded it. Now existentialism believes that no similar essence preceded the existence of Man. Man exists without a blueprint and is therefore free to choose for himself what he is to become".

Signaling for the waiter to bring another drink, he continued, "If he just sits back and accepts all that is provided for him by the environment – and by that I mean his political, social, economic and moral environment – he will have an essence stamped on him from outside; he will be formed by conditions over which he has effected no control. But man has the ability to control his conditions – and not just the ability - a duty to do so. He must consciously and deliberately set out to develop his own essence by living his life to the full and, by his actions, creating his own set of values."

Claude paused. "Is that any clearer?" he asked.

"Um, I think so. That means that existentialists are inevitably atheists."

"No, not necessarily. It means that they cannot accept Man as being conceived in the image of God, with a pre-selected objective set of values; of universal values, that is. But there is nothing to stop them believing in a Creator; just as there is nothing to stop you building your house without employing the services of an architect."

"And what sort of a house would that be?" scoffed John.

"Probably most insecure, lacking form and stability, perhaps even quite dangerous. But – think a moment! – what sort of a world have we, anyway?"

"Yes." John grinned. "I take your point. But how then do you equate that concept of freedom of choice with the repression of free choice under Communism?"

A flicker of a smile from Claude as he replied, "That's a cunning way to beg a question, John. You surely do not expect me to agree that free choice is repressed under communism, do you?" He narrowed his eyes. "But, leaving that on one side, let me say first that I am an existentialist with a small 'ee'; Nicole is an Existentialist with a capital ‘ee’. Therefore I believe that Man is born a blank mould, with the ability to impress on himself his own set of values, his own essence. I do not however agree with all the theories of Sartre. But Nicole would tell you that communism is a form of group existentialism: that we communists – by the exercise of our free will – are prepared to subdue our personal desires and actions to group action, to achieve a higher good for all people, so that all people may live their lives to the full.”

_“In that case,” said John, “you may call me a communist with a small ‘cee’. Anyone with a grain of compassion or humanity must prefer to see a world without misery or suffering; with affluence in place of poverty; with abundance in place of want. But Communists – members of the Communist Party –” he sniffed contemptuously, “Communists are people, human beings with human failings. In a perfect world – the sort of world we would all like to see, with perfect people: unselfish, considerate, loving their fellow beings – we could have a society where everyone is free to follow the dictates of their private conscience, to chase their own set of values, and we would be safe. We would *know* that it would be impossible for one person, or one group, to cause the suffering of any other person or group of people.” He paused.

“I am prepared to grant you,” John continued, “that of the millions of communists in this world, ninety-nine percent may be sincere and full of love for their fellows. Unfortunately the leaders of any Communist group in power – as with any other totalitarian power group – inevitably belong in the remaining one percent. It follows that – surrounded by opposition and animosity – they have to be the strongest members of their group, unencumbered by the weaknesses of sentiment and tenderness, in order to ensure the preservation and strength of their regime. Communist countries simply cannot afford to have the thinkers, the intellectuals, the idealists at the head of State – in fact they find these people an embarrassment once the revolution has been achieved. Leon Trotsky is a perfect example; for an intellectual – a thinker – cannot stop thinking, enquiring or criticising simply because a higher stage has been reached. There is no boundary line to the exercise of the intellect. And the Man-in-Power cannot afford to tolerate criticism. Hence the Communist purges.

“No thank you,” John concluded, “I’ll bear with the decadence of British democracy and the knowledge that I can criticise my Government – *and* do everything in my power to change it if I feel so inclined – without fear that my head may be placed on a chopping block.”

“I’ll grant about one-tenth of what you have just said, but as for the rest . . ." Claude snorted. "You have really provided an answer to your own argument. Communists *are* just people: human beings with human failings. However it is not the communists but the capitalists, the bourgeois exploiters, the imperialists, who are the greatest totalitarians. They are the ones who achieve the maximum degree of immutable oppression by the simplest of all devices: economic necessity and control of the means of production. Of course they permit criticism! The vocal escape valve – which you British are so proud of – is the most effective single method of ensuring the avoidance of practical rebellion. Oh, yes! I have heard of your fabulous Speakers Corner. The poor idiots who stand there and spout – and the even more pathetic fools who heckle them – are not aware that in verbally excoriating the existing structure of their society they are providing the strongest possible bulwark for its retention."

Claude rubbed his eyes wearily. "But you know, John, I think we've done enough arguing tonight."

"I'm sorry," said John. "I've suspected that something was wrong. Is there anything I can do?"

Claude looked at him through eyes that were red-rimmed and watery from the rubbing they had received. "There is nothing you can do . . ." He hesitated, then added, "but you are entitled to an explanation, I suppose."

"That's all right, Claude. If you had rather not tell me . . ."

"No! You should know, if only for Yvette's sake." He paused as the waiter placed two fresh beers on their table and removed the empty glasses. He drank deeply from his glass before continuing. "It is really quite a long story, which goes back to the wartime. You may know that Pierre – Yvette's brother – and I were in the FFI – the *Maquis*."

"Yes," John murmured.

"You will not know, I think, that Nicole was also one of us. We were – all three of us – operating together with the same partisan group in the *Vosges* region. I will not bore you with the whole story, but on one raid Nicole got caught by the Germans. We did not know whether she was alive or dead, but three days later we heard that she was being held for questioning by the Gestapo near Epinal. Nicole was Pierre's girlfriend – fiancée really. They had been together from their schooldays and it was always assumed that they would eventually marry. Throughout the three days Pierre was, as you can imagine, frantic with worry and grief. But when he heard that Nicole was in the hands of the Gestapo, he was like a madman.

"You see it was a normal thing with us to assume we were living on borrowed time. Every week reports came of comrades from neighbouring groups being captured or killed, and even our own group had suffered its losses. We knew too that capture almost inevitably meant death by firing squad. The thing we never thought about – something which did not bear thinking about – was being put into the hands of the Gestapo for questioning." He laughed sourly. "The Gestapo had rather primitive methods of questioning – particularly when they were dealing with women. But towards the end of 1944, when this occurred, our partisan activity had increased so considerably in support of the battles being fought by the Allied Armies in the north of France, that the Gestapo were taking a more and more active part in dealing with FFI captives in an effort to locate our supply bases and headquarters.

"Partly because of Pierre, but mainly because of the considerable risk involved should information fall into German hands at that particular point in our activities, we decided to organise a rescue operation. Once again I will not trouble you with the details, but in the operation – which was otherwise successful – Pierre was killed.

"That is all really, except that after Nicole rejoined us it was as thought part of her also had been killed in the raid, and for weeks afterwards she was tortured with guilt, blaming herself for Pierre's death. It was not until our marriage that she would accept the friendship of Yvette and the fact that Yvette did not judge her guilty of her brother's death. And to this day she has not been back to the Beaumonts' apartment, despite their frequent invitations, because she cannot bear to face them.

"We named our son Pierre. We both wanted it, but if she had objected I would not have insisted. Yet even now – six years later – Nicole gets intolerably upset whenever Pierre Beaumont's name is mentioned in outside company. You saw how she reacted to that thoughtless – though quite natural – remark that Yvette made. She still has this . . . I suppose a psychologist would call it a guilt complex. She feels responsible for Pierre's death and while – when she is alone with me or Yvette – she can discuss her feelings nowadays fairly rationally and calmly, the moment an outsider is present she develops this emotional reaction." His brow creased with the pain of his thoughts. "I do not want to sound dramatic, but I get the impression that she feels herself marked with a stigmata which immediately becomes apparent when Pierre's name is mentioned.

"Well, now you know." Claude smiled sadly. "I did not want to burden you with our family problems, but it seems to me that you are so much almost one of the family that you would be better hearing it from me, rather than questioning Yvette."

John felt as though he had been thrust into an emotional grinder. Claude's story had a fantastic, unreal quality and had revealed a depth of tribulation that he would never have suspected. He had so many questions to ask, so much to understand; yet he could not bring himself to speak.

Claude, with typical understanding, said, "You do not have to say anything, John. It is just one of those things and, eventually, all will be normal. But – alas – these things take time. Already, since the birth of little Pierre, Nicole is a much changed person." He sighed. "Now! I feel much better for having got that out of my head, so let us change the subject." He gripped John's arm. "Tell me, my friend, what do you think of Yvette after all this time?"

"She's a very lovely person," said John. "I had the surprise of my life when I saw her again. And I also think – " he paused and grinned, " – I think you were right when you told me something about her, all those years ago."

Claude returned his grin. "That she was in love with you?"

"You have not forgotten then?"

"Forgotten?" Claude chuckled. "She has given me no opportunity to forget."

John said seriously, "You told me something else at that time. Do you remember that also?"

Claude shook his head.

"You told me to be good to her."

"I did?" Claude raised an eyebrow. "Well, that was a piece of superfluous advice, wasn't it?"

"In those days it was. Nowadays . . ." Uncertainty etched a furrow between his eyes. "I'm not sure."

"What do you mean, John?"

What did he mean? There was no longer a problem, was there? He had decided to treat Yvette as a dear, close friend; he had determined to exercise sufficient restraint to avoid involving himself – and Yvette – in too great a degree of intimacy; he had concluded that, at nineteen years of age, her feelings for him could hardly be so deep as to endure for long if unreciprocated. Why then burden Claude with his foolish doubts?

He passed off Claude's question with a flippant laugh. "Nothing at all, Claude. I'm just being a tease. Come on, let's push off and I'll take Yvette home. And *I'm* paying for the drinks here; I consider I got off lightly."

Yvette came to the door of Claude's apartment as soon as the two men arrived. Nicole had already gone to bed with a migraine, she said, and she was ready to leave immediately with John. It was a short distance to the house in the Quai de Valmy and they decided to walk.

In the street Yvette held John's arm and said, "I'm sorry about this evening."

"That's all right, Yvette. You do not have to explain. Claude has already told me."

"Everything?"

"Yes. All about Nicole and Pierre and his death in the war . . . I'm sorry," he interrupted himself, "is it all right to talk about it?"

"Of course. I did not know the whole story myself when we first met, but I long ago learned to accept the reality of my brother's death. He was really a hero, wasn't he?" she asked proudly.

"Yes," agreed John. "He was a hero."

"But then, so was Nicole," she said with angry bitterness. "Did Claude tell you what the Gestapo did to her?"

"No." John shivered although the night air was still warm. "And I would rather not know, I think."

"Oh, that's all right. It's not my place to tell you, anyway. But she put up with their torture for two days, without disclosing anything. And nobody forced Pierre to do what he did. I wish the foolish girl would realise that – far from blaming her – everyone who knows the story is really very proud of the way she conducted herself. But the affair still keeps eating at her – even after all these years."

Were the subject of their conversation not so grave, John would have been amused at the way this young person had referred to Nicole as a 'foolish girl'. He said, "How old is Nicole?"

"Twenty-nine."

"She is older than Claude?"

"Yes. About three years older. She and Pierre were the same age."

They had arrived at the Beaumonts' apartment. As Yvette unlocked the door she said, "Would you like something to drink, John?"

"No thank you, my dear. But can we sit and talk a while? There are still some questions I would like to ask you."

"Of course. But quietly please. My parents will be asleep now."

She led the way into the *salon* and sat on the settee. John sat beside her and she moved close to him, resting her head against his shoulder. He leaned over and kissed her forehead, then gently eased his body away from hers, arose, and sat in an armchair.

"I'll not be able to think of a single question with you so close," he explained.

She pouted. "Would that matter very much?"

"I'm afraid it would. Now, get rid of that little-girl expression and give me your attention."

"Yes, sir!" She jumped to her feet, saluted him, and then gave him that *gamin* grin that he recalled so well. She was amazingly volatile, he thought, and abruptly felt such a wave of affection for her that it required a deliberate effort to retrieve his thoughts and questions.

"I don't know if I have the right to ask you this," he said, "but why did Claude marry Nicole?"

"Why?" she repeated perplexedly. "Because he loved her, I suppose."

Ask a silly question, thought John. "And she loved him?"

Yvette frowned. "I'm not sure. I know she always had a genuine affection for him and I know, too, that he nagged her constantly for almost two years before she agreed to marry him. But it has been good for her. You cannot imagine what she was like before their marriage. I think it has been good for Claude also," she added thoughtfully.

"Hmmm." He pondered her reply. "Then you would say they have a happy marriage?"

Yvette grimaced. "I find it hard to apply the word 'happy' to Nicole. I think she has lost the capacity for real happiness – really profound happiness, that is. Satisfaction . . . yes, that she is capable of; and fulfilment too, as one can see when she is nursing little Pierre. But I think that they have a good marriage. Nicole is a tremendous source of help and energy to Claude in his political work." She paused reflectively. "You know, John, Nicole was not terribly interested in politics before the war – or so I have gathered. Pierre, of course, was a very staunch communist. do you think that her political activity now is a form of rationalised compensation for her feelings of guilt? That she may feel it her duty to carry on where Pierre left off?" She inclined her head and gazed at John with an expression of grave contemplation.

John smiled. "I think you are a very astute young lady."

Slowly and deliberately Yvette left the settee and approached John. She stood over him a moment, her head on one side, her eyes narrowed in purposive appraisal. Suddenly she threw herself into his lap and started pummeling his chest.

"I warned you not to call me that."

"Hey! Steady on!" He caught her wrists in his hands. "I forgot. It was a mental aberration." He laughed, struggling to hold her wrists.

"Then you had better prove it."

She ceased her efforts to escape his grasp and lowered her face until their eyes were on the same level. Gazing steadily into his eyes, she pressed her lips firmly against his. John released her wrists and pulled her gently towards him, his hands in the small of her back. He responded to her kiss as warmly as possible, while retaining control of his feelings – forcing himself to remain dispassionately objective despite the almost overwhelming inclination to fervent response.

Suddenly she drew he head away and gasped, "John, you're hurting me."

He became aware that his fingers were bunched into fists, pressing into the small of her back in a subconscious effort to stop them from exploring her body. He quickly unclenched them.

"I'm sorry, darling."

Damn it! He was angry with himself for the instinctive use of the endearment. The last thing he wanted to do was to treat Yvette with the glib technique that he used with his casual dates in London. But Yvette sighed contentedly. "I don't mind, John – dear, dear John. 'Darling' is an improvement on 'young lady'. But you know what your trouble is?" she said solemnly, holding his face between her hands, "You cannot relax. You cannot adjust to the fact that I am no longer a little girl."

Hell, he thought, *you don't know how right you are*. Or perhaps the reverse would be even more to the point: that he had adjusted only too well to the fact of her maturity.

He said: "You know what the trouble is? I am tired. We've had a long day and a late night. Tomorrow we are making an early start. My trouble is that I am thinking of bed."

"So . . . ?" She smiled mischievously.

"God, what an imp you are." He laughed. "We have an expression for girls like you in England."

"What is that?" she asked seriously.

"Never you mind!" He pulled her to him again, kissed her quickly and coolly, then forced her from his lap. "Now! Bed for you, young . . ."

"John!" She scowled

"Sorry." He grinned and stood up. "Bed for you, Yvette."

"Oh . . ." Her lips puckered in disappointment.

He resigned himself to the inevitable. For the third time he said, "Bed for you . . ." and then added deliberately, ". . . darling."

A beatific smile burst upon her face. She raised herself on tip-toe, her arms encircled his neck, and she kissed him with partly-opened lips. "Goodnight, my dearest. It is wonderful to have you here."

It was wonderful to be there, he agreed mentally when he got into bed. The Beaumonts were the family that he lacked in England, and he felt grateful and humble for the way he had been allowed into the drama of their unhappy past. He felt, too, an intense relief at having successfully controlled his reaction to Yvette. His habitual hedonistic behaviour would not only have been out of place, but a certain source of subsequent embarrassment. A mere twenty-four hours had sufficed to restore the set of values he had spent three years discarding. The normality of the lives of these Parisian friends, erected on a foundation of pain and grief besides which is own sufferings paled to insignificance, was enough to ridicule the infantile pleasure-seeking that had formed his personal antidote to adversity.

He felt on the verge of a great discovery; the revelation of a sublime truth. For a bare moment his mind groped, grasped, and then let slip. And it was gone. His efforts to retrieve the substance of his vanished thoughts served only to drive them further from the surface of his mind and he surrendered the attempt with a feeling of hapless frustration.

Instead his mind returned to Norman Williams: dear, foolish Norman, with his unsophisticated, uncomplex anodyne – a simple answer to all problems. In John he had found a willing – nay, zealous! – participant in his adventures. And adventures they had been! But adventures cast in the same mould, with the same basic approach and the same monotonous conclusion. No! Not monotonous! He had to be honest. Monotony implied boredom and that was one state they had never achieved. In fact it was probably true to assume that he way of life had been necessary to its context – had fulfilled a vital function. But that need was now past. He would discuss the whole subject with Norman on his return and would make the fellow see it his way. If only he had managed to retain control of the vagrant thought of a few minutes earlier; he was sure it would have provided the key to his newly-felt aspiration.

Yet, as he fell asleep, a part of his mind – that small, untarnished, still-honest part – caused him to wonder momentarily if he would not, on return to London, once again fall under the spell and influence of Norman.

On the basis of a casual meeting with a student nurse at a bottle party, Norman had viewed an entire new field of profitable sexual enterprise.

"Boy-bach," he said to John, "I want you to consider this. Don't give me an immediate answer, but think about it, reflect on it, roll it around your tongue – I mean your head – and then give me your considered opinion. Right?" He paused, accepted John's puzzled expression as an indication of assent, and added, "Where do we find the biggest conglomeration of available females in London?"

Unhesitatingly John answered, "Holloway Prison."

Briefly John enjoyed the unique experience of a mutely awestruck Norman Williams. It lasted a bare moment and then, his poise restored, Norman said, "Brilliant, brilliant. You may give the pencils out tomorrow. If you want the privilege of cleaning the blackboard too, you may now tell me how we are to get them out of the jug."

"Ah, but we don't," John replied. "We put on wigs and dresses and commit a felony. If we're lucky we get to join them inside."

"Oh brother!" Norman groaned. "Have pity. It's four o'clock in the morning. Try and give the matter some serious thought."

"Okay, Norman." John poked his tongue out of the corner of his mouth in what he hoped was an air of deep reflection. Then he said, "Nurses' homes."

"What!" The unbelievable had happened. John had once more succeeded in dumbfounding his flatmate. "How did you work that out?"

"Easy," said John. "You told me yourself. Barely two hours ago."

"I did?" Norman glared at him in suspicious accusation. Then his face lit up with a smile of incredulous wonder. "That's right. So I did!"

It was immediately after their housewarming party. They had finally managed to eject the last of their guests and were now facing each other across the four-foot space between their divan beds.

"Of course," John comforted his friend, "I wouldn't say you were on top form at the moment. How the hell much did you drink last night, anyway?"

"Don't ask, boyo." His face assumed a pained expression, his eyes closed, his head shook from side to side in metronomic rhythm. Suddenly he flopped out on his back.

"Hadn't we better postpone this inspiring discussion until you're in better shape?" suggested John.

"No-o-o-o." The abruptly uttered negative transformed itself into a moan of anguish. "Oh, my poor aching head" All right, Johnny-bach," Norman conceded, "we'll leave it till the morrow." He rolled over onto his stomach.

"And one other thing." John decided to profit from Norman's weakened condition to air an irritation. "Do you think you could desist from those ridiculous forms of bastardised Welsh appelations?"

"Yrrriii," Norman groaned into his pillow.

"What did you say?"

Raising his head slightly in somnambulistic gesture, Norman repeated, "You're right." His head dropped. "G'night, boy-bach."

The scheme he outlined to John over a pint of beer in their 'local' the following lunchtime was wondrous in its simplicity. They would not go out hunting for women; the women would come to them. A series of bottle-parties was the answer; the bottles to be provided by the male guests. From this provision, of course, the hosts themselves were precluded. And there would be no repetition of the costly and unnecessary supply of food, such as had marked their housewarming party. Thus their actual expenditure would not only be held to a minimum – a supply of soda water, tonic water, ginger ales and soft drinks – but, with skillful husbandry, they could manage to hoard sufficient alcoholic beverage for their own day-to-day needs.

They would insist on a minimum amount of drink from each male guest, the lure being the availability of unattached females. These they would obtain through Norman's nursing contact, with an open invitation to the parties for any of her colleagues as might be free to come.

"It can't miss, John," he enthused. "She told me that they can't resist the lure of parties. Most of them are from abroad – mainly Irish lasses – and have no family and few friends in London. Their usual Saturday night out is the Hammersmith Palais or the Lyceum, but they are underpaid and overworked and the bait of a party which isn't going to cost them a penny will be irresistible. Plus the opportunity to meet men of marriageable status in relaxed conditions.

"Hmmm," John murmured, only partly convinced.

"Look you, chum. They come to our parties. We sort the sheep from the goats and butter-up those that are truly bed-worthy, and date them separately and at our leisure. D'you see? And then there's another possibility. The hospitals often organise dances for the nurses and invite nurses from other hospitals. Now strange as it may seem – but my informant assures me this is the absolute truth – the main need at these dances is a supply of men. Fine! We wangle invitations to the dances, thereby extending our contacts to other nurses homes." He gurgled merrily. "It's a self-expanding, self-perpetuating, and far-from-vicious circle. You'll see."

And John had seen.

Looking back at intervals, in amazed recollection, increasing numbers of women of greatly varied physical attributes and often dubious virtues, paraded themselves before his inner eye. Norman's standard of bed-worthiness was open to extremely liberal interpretation and they both applied the standard with far-from-conservative restraint. And their ratio of amatory conquest greatly exceeded Norman's conservative estimate of success.

And not merely nurses. They eventually, through contacts made in public houses and coffee bars, discovered another rich vein of amative supply: women's hostels; Hampstead boarding houses devoted exclusively to women, hostels provided by the larger London stores for their female sales assistants, and by the major hotels for their staff.

They organised a working system which would give maximum scope to their sexual adventures, while allowing enough time for their studies. During the week they would each spend at least three evenings studying in the college library, and by coordinating those study evenings they could each have the apartment available in total privacy at least twice a week. At weekends they would arrange their exploits synchronously. It worked perfectly.

For John, the most pleasing aspect was his success in divorcing the sexual act from any emotional entanglement. He modelled himself completely on the style of his colleague and mentor. He developed a clinical approach to his liaisons.

Except in the case of Julie Grant.

Despite the constant scorn and derision with which Norman treated his continuing relationship with Julie, John found himself unable to shake off a sense of emotional obligation. He told himself that there was no reason why he should want to rid himself of this involvement, for Julie was singularly undemanding. Ever since he had taken her home from the housewarming party, she had refused to set foot in their apartment, except on his absolute assurance that Norman would not be there.

With Norman she maintained a cold, neutral relationship. Since it was impossible to avoid him altogether at college, she accepted the inevitability of their occasional contact. When he spoke to her, she answered him. But she made no effort to seek him out, nor to encourage any display of familiarity. Sometimes she would express the view to John that his continuing friendship with Norman was undesirable; was, in fact, unhealthy; that Norman was holding John back from the higher things of which he was capable. But she never pressed the point. And she seemed to recognise that, while he continued to share the flat with Norman, her claim on his free time would inevitably be limited.

She apparently accepted the situation, for she made no effort to end her association with John. Also, as far as he could gather, she had formed no alliance elsewhere, although she must have had ample opportunity and abundant offers. All her spare time, except that spent in John's company, was devoted to study.

Therefore, he told himself, there was no worldly reason why he should disturb the situation. So why did he suspect his motives?

CHAPTER EIGHT

Back again in London.

Regret surged through him; regret and unhappiness. Regret at having to leave the refuge of communal warmth. Unhappiness at having to vacate the asylum of familial intimacy.

Regret. Regret and unhappiness, with more than a slight admixture of fear. In fact, if he were to be completely truthful, fear was the dominant emotion from which the other two stemmed. But fear of what?

Fear of facing up to the new responsibilities which now confronted him? Apprehension of the shortly-to-be-announced examination results? Doubt of his ability to cope with the currents of life into which he would now be plunged?

The feeling had been building up in him throughout the long journey back to London. At first a vaguely uncomfortable unease, followed successively by the regret, the unhappiness – and now the fear. Earlier he had tried to dismiss the sensation as a reaction to the journey. He had even tried to laugh if off as homesickness; to find amusement in the concept that he should now regard Paris as home. And it was partly true. When his mother had died he could still be secure in the associative homogeneity of the army, feeling himself one of many, even though he had little in common with his associates. Then he had gone to college and the feeling of kinship – of belonging – had increased, for now there was a community of interest where, before, there had been merely a propinquity. Finally to Paris and, to the other affinities, had been added that of intimate acceptance.

What could he look forward to now? The struggle for survival? The search for a job? The battle for economic advancement? Christ! He sounded worse than Claude and Nicole. Perhaps some of their communist influence had rubbed off on him.

And so melodramatic! God, he felt miserable.

Well, at least he had friends . . .

Back now in Hampstead.

The lift to street level at Belsize Park. Out in the mellow warmth of the June evening air. Haverstock Hill bathed in the red glow of shepherd-delighting sunset. The pub-crawlers, the Sunday-evening strollers, the be-sweatered men and be-slacked women (Hampstead uniform: you must conform to prove your nonconformity). This too, of course, was home of a sort.

Belsize Grove. The apartment block. The lift to the third floor. His key in the lock. (*Please god, let Norman be home*.)

He left his suitcase in the hall and walked into the living room. Nothing. Ashtrays spilling over. Remains of dinnertime crockery and cutlery cluttering the dining room table. Greasy plates and coffee-stained cups. Magazines and newspapers littering armchairs and settee. Dust on radiogram top. Jumble of bottles in the corner.

In the kitchen the sink piled high with unwashed dishes.

He suppressed the desire to burst into tears and opened the refrigerator. One bottle of beer. Well that was better than a kick in the arse. He removed the crown cork and returned to the living room, dumping journals from one armchair into the other, and sat down with bottle raised to lips. Across the bottle's length he saw Norman.

Naked. He padded on soundless soles from the carpeted hall into the carpeted room.

"Thought it was you, boyo. Welcome back."

John had an insane desire to giggle and cry simultaneously. The sight of a mother-naked Norman with hand outstretched in greeting was too incredible to be true. Or would be incredible for anyone but Norman. He swallowed hard and forced his voice into a calmness which he did not feel.

"Christ, Norman! Were you still in bed? Or should I say '*already*'?" He shook his friend's hand.

"Neither, chum, neither. The word is '*again*'." He leered. "And not alone."

"*Plus ça change . . .*" John murmured.

"Eh? What's that?"

"Nothing, Norm. Nothing at all." He pushed a playful fist into Norman's stomach. "Jesus, it's good to see you, you great tub of lard."

"Tub of lard!" Norman screeched. "There's no fat there, chum." He examined himself anxiously. "Well, maybe just a slight swell to establish the fact of easy-living. And speaking of swell, you've got to meet Megan. Swells all over the place, she does. Oh, honey," he called towards the hall, "come on out here, my beauty. Can you hear me, sweetie? Just a minute, John, I'll roust her out." He padded back towards the bedroom.

"Norman," John said. His friend stopped in the doorway and looked back. "Would you mind saying 'boy-bach' just one?"

"What? What d'you mean?"

"Oh, nothing. Go and fetch your Megan." John smiled contentedly, lay back in the armchair and began drinking his beer.

"And go easy on that beer, chum. That's the last bottle in the flat." Norman slipped out of the room. Noises off. Bedroom door opening. Norman's voice: "Honey, aren't you out . . .?" His voice was cut off by the closing of the bedroom door.

Scarcely a pause. The sound of the bedroom door reopening. Norman's voice again: "Now come on, my beauty. There's no need for that; it's only John. Here, put this on." The rich thwack of palm of hand connecting with flesh of rump. A squawk of pleasureful anger. Norman returning.

A respectable Norman. Norman conforming to the dictates of propriety, dressed in jockey shorts. Behind him, a tangle of corn-coloured curls and with flushed cheeks (all four, presumably, but only two visible), tripped Megan. Megan Morris, personifying the beauty of Wales; the richness and fullness of Wales barely hidden by Norman's silk dressing gown descending to ankles, revealing where it should conceal. The abundance of Welsh mountains and valleys.

She tendered her hand. A smile parted her rosebud lips revealing an even line of whitely gleaming teeth. "I have been looking forward to meeting you." A hint, a mere whisper of the sing-song Welsh accent. Honeyed musical tones.

John was impressed. More than impressed, he was smitten at a glance.

"I wish I could say the same, but I'm afraid Norman has never mentioned you." John looked at her admiringly. "I can see why he wouldn't."

"Woof! Down boy!" Norman chuckled. "And you can let go of her hand. She's old enough to stand up without assistance. Now, where's that beer?"

John leaned over the armchair, retrieved the empty bottle.

Norman's face dropped.

"There's a bottle of Merrydown in the cabinet," chanted Megan, her voice sending a tremor along John's spine.

"Merrydown! Grrr." Norman shuddered. "See if there's any whiskey left, sweetie. You can use the glass on the table." He pushed newspapers off the settee with an impatient gesture and dropped into its cushioned depth with a contented sigh.

Megan dug up a whiskey bottle from the jumble of bottles and poured a liberal measure. Soda water was added with a steady hand, and the whole presented to Norman with arrogant disdain.

"Will that be all, O master?"

"For the nonce, wench."

"Then shift your big arse." Thump of fist on thigh and a muttered oath from Norman as his legs slid off the settee.

Megan planted herself beside him, head against his arm, legs spread along length of settee. The dressing gown gaped wide from swell of thigh to wiggling, red-painted toenails. John gaped too, and then quickly closed his mouth.

"Are you a nurse?" asked John.

Both Norman and Megan laughed. He a raucous, choking cackle; she a rolling, tumbling cascade of golden sound, conjuring up the image of a meandering Welsh mountain stream.

"I take it I have said something funny," said John, genuinely puzzled.

"You can't imagine *how* funny. Norman has told me all about your infantile escapades. Childishly dissolute and completely moronic. You'll be pleased to hear that they are a thing of the past. I have plans for Norman and I am led to believe that you may be included."

Behind her back Norman gave a surreptitious but pronounced wink. "I'll tell you all about it later, boy-bach."

"Norman." Her voice was quietly menacing. She swivelled in the settee. Vertiginous revelation.

"Ahem!" John cleared his throat.

The significance of the sound was not lost on Megan. She gathered the folds of robe together.

"Excuse me, John. The morally-debilitating influence of a week spent in the company of this animal." She turned her attention back to Norman and punched his chest.

"Hey!" he squealed. "What was that for?"

"For forgetting."

"Forgetting – what?"

"You know." Meaningful emphasis.

"Oh yes." He grimaced at John. "I am being pressured into discarding my – quote – terminology and mannerisms deriving from the anthracite pits of South Wales – end quote. Copyright reserved. All requests for reproduction to be addressed to author, Miss M. Morris. And careful how you interpret that reference to reproduction. Ow!" The exclamation resulted from a further hefty wallop administered to the lumbar region.

John said, "Well, for that at least you have earned my undying gratitude, Megan. And now tell me, since you are obviously not a nurse, what are you?"

Dirty laugh from Norman. Megan raised a fist threateningly.

"Don't you dare! You strike me once more, woman, and that bottom gets spanked. Here. In front of John."

"Oh! You wouldn't dare."

"Wouldn't I just." He made a grab for her.

With a scream of simulated fright, Megan darted from the settee and, before he had a chance to guess her intention, deposited herself in John's lap, hugging his neck.

"Protect me, John."

"Put that woman down," Norman growled. "You don't know where she's been."

"Don't listen to him John. You hang on to me. Thank heavens you're back. You can't imagine what it has been like staying here with that beast. Do you want to see the marks?" She reached for the cord at her waist.

"No! No!" John protested hastily. "I'll take your word for it." He felt a warmth creeping up the back of his neck. Hang on to her, indeed! Her arms had tightened around his neck; even if he wanted to, he could not escape. Her small, compact body pressed into his groin. Bulge of breast flattened against his chest. Cheek to cheek. He was throbbingly conscious of each point of contact; uncomfortably aware too of a growing erection and of seven days without physical release.

Suddenly she jumped from his lap. "John!" Horrified exclamation. "You're worse than Norman!"

Bellows of laughter from Norman suggested he had made an immediate and exact interpretation of her remark. "You see what a week in Paris does for him? Stop showing off, John. And as for you, wench, you'd better come back here where you're well off."

The glow from the back of his neck had spread to John's cheek. It was less embarrassment than anger at his own lack of control. Megan looked at him with tender understanding. She took his face between her hands and planted a gentle kiss on his lips.

"I'm sorry, John. It was my fault. I'm afraid I'm just a terrible tease."

"That's all right, Megan." He smiled at her. "I'm a big boy now. I should be able to behave like one."

"Oh my God," muttered Norman disgustedly. "Why don't you two go into the bedroom and make a production of it?"

She turned on him crossly. "Why don't you go into the bathroom and wash your mouth out with soap?"

"Pardon me for breathing." Norman looked from John's face, flushed with unease, to Megan's flushed with anger. "Oh, hell! I'm getting dressed and going out for some beer."

"No you're not," corrected Megan. "*We're* getting dressed and you can walk me to the tube. What you do after that is your affair."

Her attempt to walk haughtily from the room, encumbered as it was by the long dressing gown, brought a grin to John's face. Norman patted John's shoulder and shrugged an apology. Then he too grinned and padded after Megan.

John sat for a moment in warm discomfort. A bath was the answer, he decided abruptly. The depths of his memory yielded the recollection of the cats screeching in the Nuneaton alley, and the vociferous female exhortation from a neighbour to "chuck down a bucket of water". He sniggered inwardly as he went to the bathroom. That's what he was: a tomcat in heat.

In the bathroom he removed his clothing and stepped into the shower stall. A pounding on the bathroom door. Norman's voice.

"What are you doing in there, John?"

"Taking a shower," he called back.

"A cold one, I hope." Norman guffawed. Norman was his own most receptive audience.

But right on the nail, damn him. "What do you want?"

"What do you think I want? To come in, of course." He added, "To wash – that's all."

"Go and wash in the kitchen. And, while you're about it, wash up the dirty dishes."

He turned on the tap full blast and yelped as the icy jet hit his shoulder blades. He adjusted the shower-head to a fine spray and immediately felt better. The bathroom door withstood another battering. He turned the tap off.

"What is it now?"

"Damn you! Open the fucking door, there's a good chap."

"Oh hell, all right. Don't blow a gasket."

He parted the plastic curtains, stepped gingerly from the stall and slid the door-bolt back. He hardly had time to retreat a step before the door burst open.

"What's the matter, chum? Turned shy?"

"Oh, go boil your head." John returned to the shower, adjusted the temperature to 'warm' and luxuriated in the relaxing spray. Outside he could hear the muffled noise of Norman's ablutions. Then Norman's voice.

"Okay, ducky, I'm through. You can come in now."

"Hey! Just a minute!" John turned the water off. "Pass me a bathtowel first."

"Get it yourself." Norman chuckled. The bathroom door opened and closed.

"Is that you, Megan?"

"Why yes, John. Are you still showering?"

"I've just finished. Be a love and pass me a bathtowel. There should be one hanging on the door."

Inserted in the curtain gap, a creamily-pale arm, slender wristed, fine fair down and fingers clutching bathtowel.

"Thanks." He rubbed briskly, then draped the towel around himself, toga-fashion, and stepped out.

Megan bending over sink. Panty-girdle and bra. Figure trim and rounded. Thrust of bosom intolerant of unnatural restraint. He gathered her into his arms and pressed his lips to hers. Momentary struggle and then response, and her tongue half-way down his throat. He maintained the embrace a moment more, then, as he felt the towel begin to slip from his shoulders, he released her and stepped aside.

"Now we're quits," he said.

Megan, breathless and panting. Bosom rising and falling, threatening to escape its snare. Lips parted, teeth gleaming.

"You dog," she said.

"You'd better tell Norman."

She laughed her golden laugh. "You can tell him if you like."

He laughed back clutching the towel to his body. "He would never believe me."

He went into the bedroom and slipped quickly into fresh pants, sports shirt and slacks, and slippers from his suitcase. The bedroom was untidy, but not noticeably so, apart from the two divans which had been pushed together with bedclothes in lively disarray. Of course, aesthetic sensitivity would demand a certain amount of order in a room in which they spent most of their time. He smiled at the thought and went to the living room.

Norman, deeply ensconced in an armchair, grinned at him.

"Well, you young bugger, what have you been doing with yourself?"

"Do you mean before, or since I made time with Megan in the bathroom?"

A sudden flash of astonished annoyance. Then the grin again. "She's really something, eh?"

"She's really something," John agreed. "Where did you meet her?"

"Full details later. You're staying home this evening of course."

"Why of course? Actually I was thinking of phoning Julie."

"Ugh!" Distaste scored Norman's face. "You're not going to carry on with that, are you? *Now*?"

"I'm sorry," John said. "The significance of the '*now*' escapes me. Has something changed since I've been away?"

"Johnny, boy-bach – " He flicked an impatient hand. "Uh, I forgot! Haven't you noticed the change? I repeat: full details later. You'll wait for me to get back? I'll only be gone ten minutes."

"I can't promise. Perhaps."

"Well, suit yourself. If you're here, you're here. I'll be bringing some beer back anyway."

"Well that's the first thing you've said that makes sense. Now *that* might be worth waiting for."

"Johnny-boy," Norman extricated himself from the depths of the armchair and grasped John's arms, "it's good to have you back. We're going to have some great times again. And not like before. But . . ."

"I know," John interposed. "Full details later."

"Full details of what?" This from Megan in the doorway.

Megan, coolly poised. Lilac linen outfit displaying to advantage the trim and curvy figure. High-heeled open sandals and flesh-coloured nylons, showing to perfection the slim flexure of calf. Megan, with overnight bag in hand and quizzical expression on face.

"Seven days in Paris." Norman leered at her. "Are you ready?"

"No. I'm carrying this bag for decoration."

She approached John and held out her hand. John gripped it and an unspoken message passed between their eyes and the pressure of the hand-clasp. A promise. A warning that their friendly duel had not been played to the end; that there might be scenes to come before the final curtain descended.

"Goodbye, John. We'll be seeing each other soon." A statement admitting of no doubt.

"Goodnight, Megan. I'll be here when you get back, Norman."

After they had gone John paced the room nervously, trying to feel anger with himself at the speed with which his thoughts had reverted to their habitual pattern. But he could feel only an indefinable sense of excitement intermingled with frustration. That Megan! She was womanhood incarnate. She oozed sex from every pore, with every movement of her body, with every syllable she uttered. His immediate response to her presence, the way she had set his pulse and imagination racing, the affect and response that he had not experienced since . . . Well, there was no percentage in pursuing that line of thought.

In a burst of decision he left the apartment and descended to the telephone cabin on the first floor. He inserted his coppers and dialed Julie's boarding house number.

He did not recognise the female voice which answered the phone.

"May I speak to Miss Grant, please."

"Just a moment. I'll see if she's in." He waited impatiently, transferred the phone to his other hand, then, "I'm sorry. She seems to be out. Is there a message?"

"No. No message."

He replaced the receiver and returned to the apartment, feeling unreasonable resentment that she should not be available when he wanted her.

He raised the bottle to his lips and drank deeply of the gassy beer. Too deeply. He gagged and made a choking sound.

"Steady on, chum. Where's the fire?"

"A fine ten minutes that was." He wiped his mouth with a handkerchief. "You were gone half an hour."

"For fuck's sake! It's a gorgeous evening. We walked down to Chalk Farm and I took the tube back. What's the matter with you, John?" A worried frown appeared on Norman's face. "For a few minutes after you got back you were fine. Ever since, you've been snapping my head off. Didn't you get your share in Paris?"

"That's all you can think of, isn't it?" John replied hotly. He knew he was being absurd, but the imp of obstinacy forced him to continue. "Why don't you buy a new record?"

"Hell, man, I wash my hands of you. When you recover your reason you can talk to me again." He turned his face away from John and began guzzling his beer. Hostility thickened the air between them.

Five minutes later John said abashedly, "Sorry, Norm."

"Figured you might be." Norman faced him with a grin. "Want to tell me about it?"

"There's nothing to tell, really. You holed out in one. A week – an entire week – without a sniff."

"Never!" Voice vibrant with disbelief. "In Paris? You?"

"No opportunity. Spent the whole week with the family."

Disgusted by the apologetic tone he heard in his voice, John added, "Don't misunderstand. I had a great time – really great. Didn't want to come back. But then I started to feel the effect."

"You poor sod." His face lit up with sudden perception. "Aaaahh! Now I understand. You mean seeing me here with Megan. Can't say I blame you either. She'd give a Trappist monk the horn." His voice softened in sympathy; this was in his field of comprehension. "Want me to get on the blower? Fix you up with someone?"

"No," John smiled. "I'm all right now. But you can start filling in those details if you like."

"Later, chum, later. First you complete your catharsis by giving me a rundown on the past seven days."

"I'll do better than that. I'll illustrate it for you. Joe Tourist, that was me. Complete with camera. I had the snaps developed just before I left Paris. Just a moment while I fetch them."

"Fetch me some beer while you're about it."

"Good idea," agreed John. He collected the snapshots from the bedroom, picked up two bottles of beer from the kitchen, and sat on the arm of Norman's chair. Norman took the snaps from him.

"Didn't realise you were so photogenic."

"Idiot!" John mussed his friend's hair. "That was the day we visited the zoo. Yvette said we had to snap the chimp and show Claude the resemblance – not to me, but to him."

"Yvette?"

"You know. I told you. The Beaumonts' daughter."

"Oh yes, the schoolgirl."

"Um." John refrained from comment.

Norman turned the snaps. "And where was this?"

"Versailles, last Sunday. Wonderful place. Spacious grounds, beautiful gardens, lakes and fountains . . ."

"Charming," Norman broke in.

"It was." Defensively.

"Each to his taste. And these, I suppose, are the Beaumonts."

"Yes." John pointed. "That's the *Quai de Valmy*. It was taken in front of their apartment house. You can see the canal behind them."

"Uh-huh." Norman looked at the next snap and wolf-whistled. "And who's *this*?"

"Oh, that's Yvette."

Norman held the print up to his eyes, studying it. "*This* is the schoolgirl?"

"Well . . . you know . . . Time passes. She's grown a bit since 1946."

"And how!" He flipped rapidly through the remaining pictures and then returned to the one of Yvette. "Man, she's terrific!"

"Mmm, yes, she's not bad," John conceded, deliberately refraining from showing the enthusiasm he felt.

"Not bad, indeed! How old is she?"

"Nineteen, going on twenty."

Norman snorted. "And you wanted me to believe you spent a week without a woman. You lying hound! What about her? Don't tell me you treated her like a sister."

"Well, yes. I mean we kissed a couple of times. You know."

"I don't know. Tell me."

"There's nothing to tell." John shrugged. "That was all."

"You mean she wouldn't let you," Norman sneered.

"Oh, she'd have let me all right. I mean I didn't try."

"What!" Norman's voice rang with incredulity and he reached up to lay a hand on John's brow. "What's the matter with you, man? Got a fever?"

John gathered the snaps together with a sigh and returned to the other armchair. "I didn't expect you to understand."

"Too fucking right! I *don't* understand."

John ran a hand nervously through his hair. "Well, I'm glad the subject's come up. I was going to raise it anyway. Look, Norman, I want you to concentrate. Try and let what I say sink into your – what were Megan's words? – dissolute and moronic brain."

"I say," Norman broke in. "Take it easy, John. Megan can get away with things like that; she has a way of earning the right which, in your case, simply wouldn't interest me, if you know what I mean."

"You don't have to draw a picture."

"And her remarks applied just as much to you."

"I know. That's what I'm getting at." John breathed deeply. "Okay, Norman, let's start again. In Paris I discovered a fundamental truth about our way-of-life. At least, I thought I did, but after I got back here I decided it might have been a load of shit. However . . ." he paused for emphasis ". . . in the half-hour you were gone I thought it all out again, and I've come to the conclusion that while the life we've been living has been great fun, I can't accept that it's the *right* way. I just can't see it. I can't adopt one set of standards in my day-to-day life and then – suddenly – switch to another set. I don't know if you can follow this. It's like trying to plug a DC radio into an AC socket and you discover that you need an adaptor. Or at least I did when I got to Paris. And Norman – seriously – if I had treated Yvette the way you treat Megan, it would have been the biggest mistake of my life. I would never have forgiven myself afterwards. And make no bones about it, the temptation was there. Christ! You've seen what she looks like. Well, I've got to do something about it. The trouble is that what seemed so clear cut while I was in Paris, has now got all snarled up again and I don't know what the answer is. Can you understand all that?"

"Of course I can, man. Jesus you must take me for a fucking idiot. Almighty Christ, chum, how the hell do you think I treat Megan? Haven't you noticed that this one is different? This is it, boy; the big one, the jackpot. Have you ever know me spend a week – an entire bloody week, mark you – with one woman?" He winked. "Not that I'd be against getting a nit of nooky on the side, if it's possible.

"Hell, man, I've done some thinking too, while you've been away. It's one of the things I need to talk to you about. Meeting Megan has been about the greatest thing to happen to me. And man, she *is* the greatest. And that's from an expert. But what makes you think your Yvette is something different? She's a woman, isn't she? If she wanted it, you should have given it to her. And if you didn't – whatever excuses you made to yourself at the time, or afterwards – all I can say is you were either a selfish sod or a stupid one."

"I guess you just don't understand, Norman," John said wearily. "What you do with Megan is one thing. As you said yourself, she is different, and Yvette is not different. I know, I know . . ." He held up a hand to cut off Norman's attempted interruption. ". . . that isn't the way you meant it. But it's true nonetheless. Megan knows what she is doing. I'm not sure Yvette would have known. But I damn-well do know what I would have been letting myself in for. I can't hope to explain my feelings to you, living with her family, being treated as if I were one of them. I just know that I could have been intimate with Yvette only if I had been prepared to carry it to a normal, conventional conclusion. And by that I mean marriage. And you know as well as I that even if I wanted to get married – which I do not! – I'm in no position to think about it yet."

Norman snorted. "Are you quite through playing God? What in hell gives you the right to assume the responsibility of what is, or is not, the proper thing to do, when a woman obviously wants you? Jesus, we've been together three years and I'd have expected a little more sense and understanding to have rubbed off on you by now. But evidently not. You've still got that prudish core of misplaced Victorian respectability. You still have the feeling, deep down, that women are different from men; that they're the weaker sex or something; that they've got to be handled with kid gloves. One week away from me and you go to pieces.

"Aaaarrh," Norman groaned, "believe me, man, women have the same feelings and desires that we have. You've had enough proof of that, haven't you? And I'll tell you something else, boyo, they're far from weak." He laughed ironically. "They're a damn sight stronger than us in many ways. I don't think you did your Yvette a damn bit of good by adopting that self-righteous attitude. And you can put that in your pipe and smoke it!"

It was not true, John thought. It all sounded logical enough the way Norman put it, but he couldn't *know*, he hadn't been there; the sole basis of his conclusion was a snapshot and a few words from John. And it would have been a mistake, John was certain, if he had allowed his desire to get the upper hand. He had handled Yvette perfectly. Exactly the right amount of response with the right degree of restraint. It had taken an effort, but he had won out. He felt proud of himself, but Norman could never be made to see it. There was nothing to be gained by pursuing the argument.

He said, "Okay, Norm. I'll assume you're right. But that's water under the bridge. The question is: what do we do now? I'm not going to be so hypocritical as to say I've changed, that I've taken the pledge. You wouldn't believe me anyway. But frankly the thought of returning to that crazy whirl of bottle parties and your so-called African gang-bangs, and what have you . . . Well I'm just not up to facing it!"

"And you won't have to, chum." Norman slapped his thigh with a gleeful yell. "You haven't heard my news yet. As I said, I've been doing some thinking too. The time has come – with apologies to the walrus – to think of other things. We're poised on the threshold of the great, wide world. Our oyster! There's nothing we can't do. Think, chum, we've got the whole world before us." His voice filled with awe. "Jesus, there's exciting it is! And we need a new system befitting our new status."

"Back to systems again, are we?"

"Don't interrupt! We've had a good run for our money, but time it is to think of higher things. Not just scatterbrained, dumb, tit-and-arse spread upon a mattress, but women. Real women. Women with something between their ears as well as something between their thighs. Women to take out as well as get into. Women suited to our new station in life."

"Which is?"

"Money-earners. Career men. Up-and-coming young executives."

John laughed hysterically.

"What's the matter, chum? What did I say that's so funny?

"No-o-o-o-o-o-thing."

"Then try and control yourself, you nut. What's the big joke?"

"Us. You. Me. Career men. Executives. Ha-ha-ha-ha. Ho-ho-ho-ho." John quelled his laughter with difficulty. "Christ, Norm, we haven't even had our exam results. We haven't even started looking for a job."

"So what? There's no doubt in your mind that we destined for success, is there? There's certainly none in mine; it's just a matter of time, that's all."

"Christ, I wish I had your confidence."

"It's not a matter of confidence, man. It doesn't matter a brass farthing whether we've got our degrees or not. The important thing is that we've spent three years at LSE. We've had a university education. We know how to mix with people; how to talk to them; how to show ourselves to maximum advantage. Not that I'm really in doubt about the exam results, but do you know what some Indian students do when they plough their exams? They sign themselves as Mohammed Bannerjee – or whatever their bleeding names might be – failed BSc Cantab – or whatever, wherever they've failed. Now there's confidence for you. Fucking insolent confidence. In my case it's not confidence but belief. Belief as opposed to doubt."

Norman's single-mindedness of purpose – regardless of the purpose itself – was so deeply ingrained in him, John realised, that he could neither see, nor appreciate, his own super-abundant self-confidence.

"Sounds as though Megan has had you on a diet of Dale Carnegie for the past week," John said. "For my money, belief and confidence seem the same thing. But tell me anyway what this new system is."

"You've got the crux of the matter yourself when you mention Megan. She's the golden key to our future, boyo. She's going to open the door for us." He gurgled delightedly.

"I don't follow. Who is Megan exactly? Where did you meet her?"

"As to where I met her, that was at LSE, one evening in the Students' Common Room."

"Then how is it I've never seen her before? How long ago did you meet her?"

An unprecedented look of guilt appeared on Norman's face. "It was about a month ago," he began apologetically. "Don't take this the wrong way, chum. I didn't keep her from meeting you with any ulterior motive. It's just that it took me a while to make any headway and I didn't want to spoil things by treating her like all the others."

John felt a surge of joy. "So," he accused, "you're the man who doesn't waste his time or beat his brains out over a woman, eh? You're just a fraud, lad. And, good god, I do believe I'm seeing you blush for the first time."

"Nonsense," he denied irritably.

It *was* nonsense, but John laughed at his friend's discomposure.

"Look you, chum, I've been aware for some time that change was the order of the day, but I wanted to get it all worked out before mentioning it to you. As for Megan, I judged that it had to be handled with finesse and that I would do right to build up to the climax of a week at the flat. Now you see why I was so happy to get rid of you for a week."

"You bastard! And I thought it was just because you believed I needed a holiday. I imagined you were glad to think I'd be spending some time elsewhere than in Llanelli with you. Well, well, well, aren't the home truths coming out tonight. And what was Megan doing at LSE?"

"She'd come to visit Pat Simpson. As soon as I saw them together I thought: 'This is it!" and invited them both out for a drink. Then I got in touch with her again through Pat. She's a bright girl, you know. Megan I mean."

"So I noticed."

"No, really. Got a Second at King's last year."

"Uh-huh. How old is she?"

"Oh, twenty-one or –two. I'm not quite sure."

"All right, you bastard. I forgive your deceit. Now what's this fabulous door she's going to open for us?"

"The ADVERTISING WORLD." Norman pronounced the words in capitals. "Her father is Managing Director of Sanderson-Morris, one of the second rank advertising agencies – but very up and coming. Megan works for him. Account-executive or some such. She's going to get me in there. And – and this is the point, man – she can get you in too. They're always on the lookout for bright graduates." He saw John's sudden frown. "What's the matter, chum? Don't you want in?"

"It's not that, Norm. And I appreciate your thinking of me. But I'm not sure I want to get into advertising."

"Don't be crazy, man. Advertising is it! It's the most. The prospects are limitless. And you've heard the talk about a commercial television channel, haven't you?"

"No."

"Well, you'll have to take my word for it, but it's coming. It's got to come. And there'll be fortunes to be made, believe you me. Now's the time to get in – on the ground floor."

"I don't know, Norman. I know it was proved to us at college that advertising expenditure doesn't necessarily add to the selling price of a product – that it may even reduce the price through increased sales. But it has always struck me as a rather specious argument, and I can't lose the feeling that advertising men are somewhat spivvish, making a living out of the efforts of others."

"But of course they are! A bloody great expense-account life! Why should that stop us? Why shouldn't we carve ourselves a slice of the cake? What would you rather do, start a crusade against the immorality of advertising? That won't stop it."

"I didn't say advertising was immoral; I said that advertising men struck me as being spivs."

"So, what the hell? Someone's going to do the work, so why shouldn't it be us? Incidentally," he grinned smugly as he revealed his newly-acquired knowledge, "they are known as admen in the trade. Seriously though, chum, what do you plan to do? You've got to find a job – and quickly. Well, here's a heaven-sent opportunity. For both of us."

It was tempting. John recognised instantly that it would remove one large source of anxiety. But there were snags, the greatest of which was that he would be thrust into Norman's company twenty-four hours a day. He couldn't lose the thought that it was time to break away from that proximity, not increase it; time to stand on his own two feet. Also the fact was that he really could not see himself in advertising – an adman as Norman termed them.

"I still don't know, Norman. As to what I plan to do . . . I really haven't a clue. But I do know that I would prefer to get into commerce rather than advertising."

"Commerce!" scoffed Norman. "That's a little word that covers a bloody large field. What exactly do you have in mind?"

"Well, I was discussing this question of work with Claude in Paris. His uncle has a timber business in French West Africa – *Dumard Frères* – and they do a lot of business with a London timber broker named Reid. Claude got me a letter of introduction to Reid from his uncle, and I was planning on phoning tomorrow for an appointment."

"Yuk!" said Norman. "Sounds bloody horrible, man."

"Well, as you yourself said, each to his taste. I think I'd like to give it a try."

"Suit yourself, chum. One thing for sure: if you can't find anything else, I know we'll always be able to get you into Sanderson-Morris."

Incredible! The man's conceited self-assurance was almost terrifying, thought John. He hadn't even been interviewed for a job yet, and already he was talking as if he were personnel manager of the company. As always, John could not help being impressed by his friend's confident assumption that the world had been created for him, personally, as one enormous playground.

"Okay, Norman, let's leave it like that."

"Fair enough. And now let me tell you all about Megan. But first, have you got a fag?"

John got up and handed a cigarette to Norman, then gave him a light.

"Thanks, chum. And before you sit down again, would you mind passing via the kitchen and fetching another couple of beers."

"God you lazy bugger. I've never known anyone like you for getting others to do their fetching and carrying. I'll get your beer, but promise me that if ever you marry Megan and need any help, you'll give me first refusal."

CHAPTER NINE

The City of London; the heart of the British financial world.

In a Lyons's teashop, John Graham looked around him, endeavouring to typecast the other patrons. There was a uniformity to most of the men, in their clerical-grey, single-breasted suits, which rendered this task well-nigh impossible. They could be bankers, brokers, underwriters, accountants, solicitors – or simply junior clerical assistants in the latest shade and cut from Montague Burton. The women were far more suitably dressed for the summer in brightly coloured, brightly patterned cotton frocks. There was a sprinkling too of men in overalls: typewriter mechanics? telephone engineers? window cleaners? Joe Lyons, the great City leveller. The company director sitting cheek-by-jowl with the man who cleaned his office windows. Saville Row rubbing shoulders with the Thirty Shilling Tailors. John found something vaguely reassuring in the thought.

He glanced at his wristwatch and discovered he had five minutes to his appointment. He drank the last of his coffee and left the tearoom.

Moorgate smouldered in the late-June mid-afternoon heat, the pavements refracting the sunlight in a mirage-like shimmer. He crossed into London Wall and entered the building which housed Alfred Reid Limited. Inside, the sudden cool contrast with the external heat brought a shiver to his back and the awareness of a light film of perspiration on his upper lip. He mopped the dampness with a pocket handkerchief, while studying the rows of nameplates in the dim entrance hall, then walked past the lift and on up the stairs to the first floor.

Left and right on the landing were swing-doors, each bearing nameplates. The left-hand side stated: REID-PARRY ENTERPRISES LIMITED; the right-hand side, ALFRED REID (TIMBER) LIMITED and, in smaller print, *Alfred Reid (Produce) Limited.* He turned right and pushed through the swing doors. Halfway down a long corridor a sign, RECEPTION, above a deep mahogany counter. On the other side of the counter a solitary female switchboard operator. She turned to face him, revealing her teeth in a professional expression of greeting.

"Good afternoon," he said. "I have an appointment with Mr Reid."

"Oh." The teeth vanished. From the manual of receptionists' technique appeared expression number two: regret with a dash of sympathy. "I'm afraid Mr Reid is out at present. You say you have an appointment?"

"Yes. Graham. John Graham."

"Oh yes, Mr Graham." Return of teeth. Greeting, by some indefinable magic, transmuted to welcome. "You are expected. Mr Parry will be seeing you. Would you care to sit in the waiting room? I'll let him know you are here." She pointed to an open doorway on her own side of the counter.

"Thank you."

He pushed through the counter's gate and walked into the room, seating himself, with reflex action, in a chair facing the door, where he could examine the receptionist's legs. Instant regret. They ballooned from a point immediately above thick ankles to a fleshy calf wherein no sign of muscle was visible. She had plugged-in to the switchboard and was speaking in sweet tones to – he imagined – the mysterious Mr Parry. After a moment she removed her earphones and the switchboard plug.

"Mr Graham," she called out.

"Yes." He left the room.

"Mr Parry will see you immediately." Her tone left no room for doubt that he was being singularly honoured. "You'll find him down the corridor. Second door on the left." She smiled once more.

"Thank you again," he said, returning her smile as he once more pushed the counter-gate open. She had a pleasant face, even if the range of expressions seemed unnaturally cultivated. Pity about the legs.

The second door on the left bore the legend: *Matthew Parry, Company Secretary*. He knocked and, in response to a barely audible shout, entered the room.

Across the maroon-carpeted floor, behind an enormous glass-topped desk, Matthew Parry stood up and was instantly dwarfed by the desk. As if aware of the fact, he shook hands with almost impolite haste, motioned John to a chair, and promptly sat down again. Seated he barely managed to hold his own in stature with the desk.

"Mr Reid asked me to apologise on his behalf. He was called away at short notice." Parry inclined his head as though beseeching forgiveness. "But for all practical purposes I am able to deputise adequately for him. That is, unless you have reason to discuss your business with Mr Reid personally."

"Oh no, no," John protested. "It was just that Monsieur Dumard's letter was addressed to Mr Reid."

"Ah yes. The letter from Dumard. You have it with you, of course?"

"I have it here." John removed the letter from his inside breast pocket. It was sealed, and he had no precise knowledge of its contents. He handed it to Parry. "I have also prepared a CV which is not very useful perhaps because I have not yet had a full-time job, but I have given details of my vacation work." He passed the single sheet to Parry.

Parry slit the envelope carefully with an ivory-handled paper-knife. He smoothed out the letter slowly and deliberately, then removed glasses from a spectacle-case and balanced them on his nose, accompanying his actions with an occasional encouraging smile. Finally he settled down to the business of reading the single sheet.

John spent the time studying the short, dapper company secretary, finding himself strangely drawn to the plump, rosy-cheeked, white-haired little man of benign expression. He appeared to be in his fifties. Of course, John told himself, Parry's name, combined with the slight trace of an accent in his voice, had immediately given him a head-start in John's popularity stakes. Funny how his life had always been subject to Welsh influences. He wondered if he would have found Welsh people quite to sympathetic and friendly had he not lived in Wales during that formative period of his life.

Finally, having disposed of the letter, Parry turned his attention back to John. Worrying an ear lobe between thumb and forefinger, he said, "Well, Mr Graham, you come to us highly recommended. Yes indeed; very highly recommended."

"Oh yes," said John, as Parry paused. Evidently some sort of comment was called for, but in his ignorance of what Dumard had written, John hardly knew what to say. "Very kind of Monsieur Dumard," he muttered.

"Oh I've no doubt his comments are fully deserved," said Parry generously. "Tell me, Mr Graham, were you on the sales or administrative side of the business?"

"Well neither, actually," John confessed awkwardly. "I have not worked for Dumard Frères."

"Oh? But you are well acquainted with Mr Dumard?"

"Er no. That is, not in a commercial sense," he hastily covered his error. "I am very friendly with his nephew. We have known each other for several years."

"Hmm . . ." A frown produced a slight furrow above Parry's nose as he turned his attention back to the letter. "Yes. I see he says you have been known personally to him for some years. I had assumed he meant in a business capacity. What has been your experience, then?"

"None, actually," said John with a nervous little laugh. He began to describe his academic career and Parry placed his elbows on the desk, put his palms together in a position of prayer, and tapped forefingers gently against his lower lip as he listened to John's recital. Finally John finished.

Parry smiled briefly. John felt that, had it not been for the letter of introduction from Dumard he would, at this point, be shown politely to the door.

"Well, Mr Graham, it is hard to know exactly what we can do for you. You are somewhat older than is normal for an apprentice timber salesman and, in any case, our quota of apprentices is filled at present. Suppose you tell me what you had in mind."

This posed a problem, since John had nothing in mind. He ad-libbed "I thought that perhaps my economics studies and my French might be of some help. If there is any statistical work or French correspondence that I could do, while learning the trade . . ." His voice tailed off lamely.

Parry's sigh was apologetic. "Unfortunately all our correspondence is conducted in English, and as for statistics . . . Do you know the sort of work we do here?"

"I know you sell timber for Dumard from their French Cameroons concessions," John ventured.

He was tempted to make his excuses and beat a retreat from this office. He was experiencing, too, the first insistent craving for the relaxing effect of a cigarette, but, although Parry's desk boasted a large ashtray, the virginal spotlessness of its Venetian-glass surface was sufficient to inhibit the desire.

"We do a little more than that," explained Parry, smilingly patient. "We import and sell hardwoods from West Africa and the East Indies, softwoods from Canada and Scandinavia, essential oils and nut kernels from South America. I'm afraid it's all extremely specialised. Of course, you could learn, but – as I said before – at your age and level of academic achievement you would undoubtedly be better advised to seek another field. Although . . ." he paused reflectively. "No! I was thinking of our accounts and shipping departments, but there is no vacancy in those at present."

Suddenly Parry's hand smote the desk. "But, of course! I should have thought of it earlier." He looked at John for a moment as though weighing up a possibility. "I think this may be the solution."

Parry depressed a switch on his inter-office phone, picked up the receiver and, after a moment, spoke into it.

"Mattson? Would you come over here, please."

He smiled at John. "Mr Mattson is the manager of our associate company, Reid-Parry Enterprises." He paused, glanced at John's CV on his desk, and then added, "Tell me, Mr Graham, did you enjoy living in Wales?"

"Oh yes," said John enthusiastically, "I count my years there among the most memorable of my life."

Parry nodded with an air of satisfaction. "You speak Welsh?"

"*Dim llawer*," John grinned.

A knock on the door was followed without pause by the door opening. The man who entered was tall and thin, his height somewhat disguised by a barely-perceptible stoop to his shoulders. A lock of fair, lank hair fell across his forehead, above frameless spectacles. A cigarette, half smoked, hung from his lips. He removed it when he saw John.

Parry introduced them: "John Graham, Mr Mattson."

They shook hands and Parry signalled Mattson to sit down.

"Mr Graham has been sent to us by Dumard," explained Parry. "He is looking for a job, but there's nothing we can really offer him on the timber side."

"I see." Mattson's expression belied his words.

"About the assistant you need, Mattson. It's possible Graham could be the answer."

Mattson turned to John. "You've experience of exporting, have you?"

"No, sir. That is, as I explained to Mr Parry, apart from odd office jobs during college vacations, I've no real commercial experience."

A momentary flicker of disgust behind the spectacles, which John decided he must have imagined, and then Mattson looked back at Parry, his thin face quite expressionless. "I thought we had agreed . . ."

"Parry waved an impatient hand. "You're going to need someone in six weeks time."

"Yes, but . . ."

Parry seemed determined to give him no opportunity to finish a sentence. To John, observing the interplay between the two men, it was almost as though they were fighting a psychological duel. "Mr Graham is a very intelligent young man. He comes highly recommended by Henri Dumard. He speaks several foreign languages . . ."

"Only one," John murmured. Parry ignored the interjection.

". . . and he is, moreover, very keen to embark on a commercial career. I consider these to be eminently desirable qualifications."

For a moment John thought Mattson would lose his temper. He stubbed his cigarette viciously in the ashtray, ravaging its chaste purity, ignoring the expression of distaste which this act induced in Parry. But when he spoke it was calmly, with an air of resignation. "I need someone to relieve me of the routine work: shipping documents, accounts, export credits, invoicing . . ."

"I'm sure Mr Graham would be prepared to learn these things."

"Oh yes," agreed John eagerly.

"You see, Mr Graham," Parry explained, "Mr Mattson is leaving in six weeks time for a tour of our West African customers. We've been thinking in terms of an assistant who is already experienced in export procedures to deputise for him while he is away. That is why I did not consider the position for you immediately. But I now see that there is absolutely no reason why we should not use the intervening time to give you a basic grounding in the work." Parry smiled. "Do you think you would be interested in the opportunity?"

"I think so," said John.

Parry turned to Mattson. "After all, I shall be here to help keep things under control."

Mattson stared expressionlessly at Parry and John decided abruptly that he didn't like this man. He seemed to lack elementary good manners and breeding. He seemed furthermore to have decided – instantly and without apparent reason – that John would be unsuited for the job. What gave him the right to deny John this opportunity to demonstrate his ability? Not that the job, as such, made much difference to him, but he would welcome the chance to show this sourpuss Mattson how quickly he could absorb knowledge and apply it. Fortunately it seemed that Parry had the same idea.

"What do you say, Mattson?"

Mattson shrugged his shoulders. "The decision is yours."

"Oh come now . . ." Parry spread his hands, smiling. "That hardly seems a very gracious way of offering our young friend a job. I'm afraid Mr Graham will end up with a very strange impression of us. We don't want that, do we?"

"No, sir," said Mattson wearily. "I would naturally do everything possible to help Graham before leaving for West Africa."

"And no one could ask more." Parry beamed at John. "Could they, Mr Graham?"

John smiled back at him, thinking how charming and friendly Parry was. He was astonished by a muttered oath from Mattson beside him, so *sotto voce* that he was unsure whether or not he had imagined it.

"What do you say, Mr Graham," pursued Parry, "does the idea of working with Mr Mattson appeal to you?"

An unfortunate way of phrasing it, thought John, and said, "I would certainly like to try it, Mr Parry. I'm sure I'll give Mr Mattson no reason to doubt my willingness to learn the job."

"I'm sure you won't. Now are there any questions you would like to ask us?"

"I dare say I'll have nothing but questions once I start work, but for the moment the only matters of urgency are: when would you require me to start, what are the hours of work, and of course," he paused uncomfortably, "er, the matter of salary."

"Well, our hours are nine to five-thirty with occasional Saturday mornings and you may start when you wish – obviously the sooner the better under the circumstances – tomorrow if you like. As for salary . . . he glanced at Mattson and then quickly back at John, ". . . I think we could start you at five hundred. Would that be satisfactory?"

This time there was no mistaking Mattson's muttered curse, but John was too excited to be bothered by it. He had been thinking in terms of three-fifty or four hundred. He gulped. "Oh yes." He forced the eagerness from his voice. "That will be quite satisfactory. And I am certainly free to start tomorrow."

"Well, well, that's settled then." Parry reached across the desk and held out his hand. "Welcome to Reid-Parry Enterprises."

John shook Parry's hand and then turned to Mattson. That surly individual, however, had no intention of indulging in so welcoming a gesture as a handshake. His hands planted firmly in his lap, he spoke to Parry. "I suppose we had better introduce Graham to Mr Reid."

"Unfortunately Mr Reid's not in this afternoon. Tomorrow will be time enough for that. I suggest however that you take Mr Graham over to your offices now and introduce him to the staff."

Mattson rose abruptly and walked swiftly from the room. John, with a quick smile at Parry, followed him. As he passed the counter in the corridor, chasing Mattson's long, impatient strides, he glanced at the receptionist and was greeted with a pleasant nod of her head. John felt a wave of empathy. He wanted to vault the counter and shake her hand, to tell her they were now colleagues. But he hastened after Mattson, through the swing doors, across the landing, through the further set of swing doors, into a small, dimly-lit, square hall, boasting just four doors. Two doors were located in the opposing wall and one door in each side wall. Three doors were marked PRIVATE. The remaining door yielded the information, REID-PARRY ENTERPRISES LIMITED: *Regd. Office.* It was through this door that John passed, on the heels of Mattson.

Inside, a large room, dully painted cream and brown; a brown worn carpet; un-curtained windows giving on to a quadrangle surrounded by office windows; two desks, flanking a small telephone switchboard. There was a large filing cabinet in one corner of the room, and two large cupboards on the opposite wall; the large intermediate floor area was starkly, grimly empty. Between the cupboards was a door.

At the desks two young women ceased their typewriting and turned in their chairs as John entered the room. They looked at him incuriously a moment, then exchanged glances, and were about to return to their work when Mattson spoke to them.

"This is John Graham," said Mattson. "He is coming to work here."

A second exchange of glances, rather more significant than the first, it seemed to John, and then they looked at him again with more interest.

Mattson presented them. "Miss Anderson, our shorthand-typist. Miss Rogers, invoice-typist and shipping clerk."

John shook hands with them. Miss Anderson, the older-looking of the two – in the early thirties he judged – accompanied a cool, limp hand by a cool, slightly disapproving glance. The invoice-typist, in contrast, smiled winsomely and exerted slightly more pressure perhaps, with the tips of her fingers, than the situation called for.

With a terse "Come on, Graham", Mattson opened the door between the cupboards and John joined him in a smaller room, less starkly furnished than the outer office, dominated by a large double-sided desk at its centre, with a smaller desk in one corner. The single window, also without curtains, overlooked the same quadrangle. The wall facing the window contained a door which, John surmised, led to the hall and was one of those marked PRIVATE.

"Will I be working in here?" asked John.

"Mattson's lips curled away from nicotine-stained teeth, more a sneer than a smile. "Not unless you're planning to take over my job."

"Gosh. I didn't mean . . . that is . . ."John swallowed. "It's just that I didn't see a spare desk in the other room."

"We'll move that one outside tomorrow." Mattson indicated the small desk in the corner. He seated himself behind the large desk, his back to the window, and motioned John to sit down in the facing leather-covered swivel chair. When he was seated Mattson said, "So you think you are able to do this job?"

John forced a smile, determined to appear friendly to the man. "Well, I don't really know what I have to do yet, do I? As I told Mr Parry, I intend to do my best."

"You'll do that all right," Mattson snorted. "I only hope your best is good enough. This business is too small to carry passengers. Parry has offered you five hundred a year, and I expect you to do five hundred a year's worth of work. And that doesn't mean nine to five-thirty, five days a week. We've got no time for trade-unionists here. You've got a lot to learn and I expect you to learn it on your own time, and that means staying here until the work's done. So if you have any objections you'd better air them now."

"I didn't expect to be paid for nothing," John retorted angrily.

"That's all right then. You won't be disappointed." Mattson lit a cigarette and let it dangle from his lips while he spoke. "I'm not going to ask you to do anything I'm not prepared to do myself. Nor anything I haven't done myself. This company was started by me from scratch, and I've built it up to the position it's in today. And that wasn't done by working City hours. Well, now I've been given an assistant and, by Christ, he's going to assist. Which means he has to learn everything and be able to do everything when I'm not here. And that means that unproductive work, like book-keeping, is done after office hours, after five-thirty, or on Saturday mornings.

"Don't misunderstand me. If it turns out that you really can learn to do the work and provide me with the much-needed assistance I've been after for so long, nobody will be more delighted than I. It will make a nice change if I'm able to get home to my wife one or two evenings a week. Frankly I doubt it. I'll be quite honest with you, Graham. I've got nothing against you personally, but what this office needs is someone with at least two years experience of office procedures. That's what I've always told Reid and Parry, and I see no reason to change my mind now. However I've been given as assistant and there's little likelihood that I'll be able to change him before I leave for Africa in August, so I'm going to do my damndest to turn him into someone who can do *my* job *my* way when I'm gone.

"I hope the point I'm making has got home to you. It means you can count on my absolute co-operation as far as learning the work is concerned, but I give you fair warning, Graham, I shall be on the lookout for mistakes and slackness. So don't try to pull the wool over my eyes. I'm too old a campaigner to be hoodwinked by old-soldier tricks."

"That's honest enough," said John. He was seething inwardly and only angry pride held him back from calling the whole thing off there and then. "I hope to make you eat those words, Mr Mattson."

A surprising grin from Mattson. "Nothing will give me greater pleasure, Graham. I only wish I could believe it. Anyway, you know what to expect now, don't you? Is there anything you want to ask me?"

He knew what to expect all right. My god, he would show this man Mattson a thing or two. A typical small-minded bastard with a limited knowledge of a specialised area of work – which couldn't be that difficult if *he* was able to do it – and his pigeon-brain could not conceive of someone else possessing the logic or intelligence to reach the same level of competence. If it was the last thing John did, he decided, he would rid the sad, skinny sod of that smug and detestable conceit.

John said, "Do we only have these two rooms?"

"Yes. We're the poor relations in the Alfred Reid family."

"What about the other offices on this side?"

"They belong to Timber. They're the accounts and shipping departments."

John nodded. "Who will show me what I'm to do?"

Mattson stubbed his cigarette and brushed ash from his coat. "I'll show you what to do. And that's something else we'll be doing in the evenings, because I'll be too busy during the day."

"But what about Mr Parry?"

Mattson pointed a nicotine-stained finger angrily at John. "That's another thing. You can forget about Parry. In this office I'm the boss. Any problems you have, any questions that need answering, you bring tome. Understand?"

John understood all right. It was clear the man was jealous of Parry. John made an instant mental resolution that, whenever the opportunity presented itself, he would speak to Parry rather than this boorish individual.

"Is there anything else, Graham?"

"No. I think that's all for the moment."

"Fine. Then I suggest you push off now and I'll see you in the morning. Go through that door and you can avoid the general office."

John paused with his hand on the doorknob. "Good afternoon, Mr Mattson."

"Goodbye, Graham. Oh, just one more thing. You'd better get in about quarter to nine in the morning and we'll move the desk outside."

By the time he reached Gilling Court, John's anger had dissipated itself and the memory of Mattson had been supplanted by more pleasant thoughts. He whistled softly, cheerfully, while waiting for the lift to descend. He had a job. He had a *job*. HE had a JOB. And five hundred pounds a year. That was almost ten pounds a week. Between seven and eight pounds after tax and insurance had been deducted. Over five pounds left after paying his share of the rent. He could repay Norman his loan in about three months and would then be able to buy some much-needed clothing.

He was still whistling as he entered the flat and the tune jarred cacophonously with Norman's fortissimo baritone rendering of All Through the Night, issuing from the kitchen. Grinning broadly he modified his whistle to an accompaniment of Norman's tune and marched into the kitchen. Norman was pouring coffee into a cup.

"Hell, man, I think you can smell the bloody stuff in the Underground. Want me to pour you a cup?"

"That's what a call a right friendly offer, boy-bach," said John.

Norman interrupted his activity with a scowl of simulated disapproval. "Hey That's my copyright."

"Not any more, boy-bach. Have you forgotten?"

"Right." The coffee pot hit the table with a thump. "One more boy-bach out of you and you pour your own bloody coffee."

"Hmm. That's too big a price to pay for the dubious pleasure. Go ahead, chum, pour it out."

"Oh brother." Norman groaned. "What's bitten you? Come on, come on, 'fess all to Uncle Norman."

"Nothing much to tell." John put on a smug air. "You are now looking at one of your up-and-coming young executives."

For an instant Norman's face dropped, then he composed his features. "You mean you've got a job?"

"Uh-huh."

"Office boy? Tea maker? Stamp licker?"

"Guess again. No, don't bother. You'd need the proverbial month of Sundays. Before you stands one John Graham, BSc. Econ, or perhaps Failed BSc. Econ, Assistant General Manager, Reid-Parry Enterprises Limited."

"Never!" Norman scoffed. "What do you know about managing anything? Or even assisting anyone? Let alone managing to assist generals."

"Norman, I do believe you're sorry I got a job."

Norman grinned sheepishly. "I must confess I still harboured the hope we would be working together." And then with typical *bonhomie* he slapped John's back. "But congratulations, man. That *deserves* a cup of coffee. And while I'm pouring it, you can congratulate me."

"You mean . . . you too . . ." John roared with laughter.

"Trainee-executive, that's all. Nothing so grandiose as your title."

"Norman, that's great! Terrific! This calls for a celebration."

With a self-satisfied smirk, Norman opened the kitchen cupboard and revealed the heaped packages of newly-acquired foodstuffs. "Same in the fridge," he proclaimed proudly, "including a bottle of top quality, vintage, no-expense-spared, white Italian bubbly, indistinguishable from the real stuff. I felt we ought to celebrate whether or not you got your job today. I took the liberty of ascertaining that there would be a job for you at Sanderson-Morris if you wanted it."

"Norman! You didn't! Not while you were being interviewed?"

"But of course."

"Jesus. How far can friendship stretch?"

"And that's not all, boyo. We're taking it easy tonight. Megan's doing the cooking . . ." Then, seeing John's grimace, "What's the matter?"

"Uh, I can't tonight, Norm. I've arranged to take Julie out to dinner."

"Oh hell, man. Postpone it. This doesn't happen every day."

"I can't Norm, even if I wanted to. She's going home for a fortnight tomorrow. anyway, ours is in the nature of a similar celebration. She got a post in market research last week. She'll be starting sometime next month."

"Christ, man, that's awful. I more or less promised Megan you'd be here. And look at all the stuff I bought." His features twisted into a worried frown. Look you, Johnny-boy, this thing between Julie and me has gone on long enough, don't you think? We're big boys and girls now; we ought to behave accordingly. Can't you talk her into celebrating with us here tonight?"

John groaned in dismay. "Norm, you don't know what you're asking."

"Then I'll have a word with her."

"No!" John exclaimed. "No, that would really put the kibosh on it. You know what she thinks about your smart-aleck dialectics. Look, I'll ask her. But I can't promise anything."

"Good lad. And do it now, will you. Megan will be along in an hour's time and Julie could help her with the cooking."

"My God, you've got an angle on everything."

In the telephone cabin John drummed his fingers nervously, waiting for his call to be answered, and was relieved to hear Julie's voice.

"Hello, Julie?"

"John? Yes, it's me. Is something wrong?"

"No, nothing's wrong. How are you?"

"John Graham, you didn't ring me up to ask how I am when we've got a date to meet later. Did you now? Come on. Out with it. What's up? Can't you make it?"

"Eh? Oh, yes. Yes, I can make it. Only I wonder if we can change the arrangements slightly."

"Oh?"

"Can you come to the flat instead?"

"Of course." Her voice sounded relieved, even pleased. "You mean we'll be alone there this evening?"

"Uh no, not exactly. You see there's a sort of celebration . . ."

"Nothing doing." Testily. "You should know my feelings by now."

"Julie, Julie, this is different . . . and Norman said . . ."

"I'm not interested in anything Norman may have to say."

"For heaven's sake, let me finish a sentence. He said it was time to bury the hatchet . . ."

"He has a point there," Julie interrupted again. "I'd like to bury it right in *your* head. Now tell me, John Graham, for the last time: are you taking me out tonight or not?"

"If you'll only give me a chance," he pleaded desperately. His collar was sticking to the back of his neck and he loosened his tie. "Look, I got a job today . . ."

"John! You didn't! That's marvellous news."

"And Norman got a job too. Now he has organised this dinner at home and his girl-friend's coming to cook the meal. Well, they would like us to be there. Is that so ridiculous? And I said I would only accept if you were there too. Otherwise I would be taking you out to dinner."

"Did you John? Did you really say that?" Her voice was softly feminine.

"Of course I did!"

"And did you mean it?"

"You know I did. Hell, Julie, I haven't seen you in ages. And you're going away tomorrow. If it's a choice between celebrating at home with Norman or celebrating elsewhere with you . . . well as the Americans would say, that's strictly no-contest."

"John, why didn't you say that in the first place. You can tell your Norman to start sharpening his hatchet."

Hell! Female logic! How could a simple-minded chap hope to cope with the intricacies of their mental processes? He heaved a grateful sigh. "And Julie . . . can you come over in about an hour's time? We'll be having cocktails first." He decided that diplomacy called for no mention of Norman's suggestion.

They said goodbye and he rejoined Norman and gave him the good news.

"That's great, man. Now tell me all about this job you've got."

"Later, Norman. First I've got to get out of these clothes and into something comfortable."

He took a brief shower and changed into sports shirt, slacks and sandals, then returned to the living room and stretched out on the settee, smoking a cigarette.

"Okay, Norman, what would you like to know?"

"Everything, boyo, everything. What sort of work is it? Apart from assisting the General."

John shrugged. "I don't really know yet. It's a subsidiary of the timber firm. An exporting company. The manager has to go to West Africa in August and I have to take over while he's away. I gather the work is pretty diversified: documentation, shipping, insurance, and so on."

Norman pulled a face. "Rather you than me. Think you're going to like it?"

"Too soon to say. I think it might be interesting mainly because it's a small company and I'll get greater all-round experience more quickly, particularly as the training will have to be very intensive with the manager going away."

"What's this bloke Reid like?"

"I didn't see him. I saw his co-director, Parry, one of your countrymen. Charming fellow. Friendly, helpful, considerate. Seemed almost paternal. I'm sure I'm going to like him. The manager's another kettle of fish." John grimaced." "The nicest thing I can say about him is that he's a rotten sod. I gathered he doesn't hit it off too well with Parry and he made it clear he resented my being brought in over his head."

"That doesn't sound too good, chum. Hardly the most pleasant environment in which to start your career."

"Oh, I don't know. Mattson – the manager, that is – may be a bastard, but I think the interest of the company comes first with him. I don't think he'll sabotage me – not until after his African trip anyway. In a strange, nervous sort of way I'm looking forward to the challenge. But that isn't the best part of the job . . ."

"I know," Norman broke in with a suggestive wink, "it's the crumpet."

"I might have expected that from you. Actually there are two birds there, neither of them bad looking. And there are probably a lot more in the timber company, but I only saw the receptionist. But that's not what I was thinking of. I meant the money."

"Which is?"

John permitted himself the luxury of a complacent smile. "Five hundred a year."

"Christ! And I thought I was doing well."

"What are you getting?"

"Four-two-five."

"Well, never mind, lad," with mock-sympathy. "There'll be fortunes to be made, you said. Give it time. Next year you'll probably own the business."

"All right, you sarcastic bastard, you'd better do your laughing now. You won't see me for smoke when I get going. And that remark about owning Sandersons may not be so far off the mark."

"What do you mean?"

"I mean, Johnny-boy, that I've decided to marry Megan."

John gasped. "What? When did you pop the question?"

Norman chuckled delightedly at his friend's astonishment. "I haven't asked her yet. I don't intend to marry for at least a couple of years. I've taken the decision, that's all. Jesus man, if she knew. . . I'd never get her off my back – and I've got a bit of living to do first."

As always, John was filled with awestruck fascination at this further example of his friend's conceit and confidence. And yet it wasn't vanity, which would imply an awareness of himself as someone special, set apart from his more ordinary fellows. Norman lacked this awareness of his apparently overweening self-esteem. With Norman it was simply an implicit assumption that we would achieve whatever he set out to get, undemanding, unquestioning and unaccompanied by any self-examination. So that when he said he intended marrying Megan, the statement permitted of no doubt that he would succeed in winner her acceptance, whether it be in two or twenty-two years time.

"Well it would seem that congratulations may be in order. At least I can congratulate you on your good taste."

"That's it, boyo. She's got it all. Looks, brains, body and technique. And her old man's got the money. What more could I ask?"

"What about her father? What sort of a man is he?"

Norman shrugged. "Haven't a clue. Never met him."

"Didn't you see him this morning?"

"Uh-uh. I was interviewed by the personnel manager. Megan's folks left on holiday yesterday." He gave a lecherous laugh. "I'm spending the night at her home."

"So I'll have the flat to myself tonight?"

"It's all yours, chum."

John sighed with relief. "Well that's one problem solved."

Relief was also a predominant feeling later. Relief that Julie and Megan, after quickly summing each other up with that special look women seem to reserve for other women, had apparently hit it off. Relief that Julie had offered to help Megan in the kitchen and Megan had accepted the offer. Relief that Norman, either out of consideration for John's feelings, or under Megan's influence, had been politely charming to Julie in a subdued manner quite unlike his usual taunting exuberance.

When they had finished eating, Julie offered to help Megan wash the dishes.

John said, "I'll give you a hand with the dishes, Julie."

"Thank God," sighed Norman. "For a minute there I thought you were going to suggest that I help you."

Megan glared at him. "He shouldn't have to suggest it. You should have offered."

"Oh Lord," Norman groaned. "Heaven protect me from nagging women."

"Leave him alone, Megan," pleaded John. "He's had an exhausting day. He made the coffee this afternoon."

He and Julie removed the dishes to the kitchen to the accompaniment of Megan's vocal excoriation of Norman.

In the kitchen.

"You wash, I'll dry," said John.

Okay." She looked up at him. Smiling green eyes. Up-tilted pert nose. Lips slightly parted.

"Julie," he said.

She came into his arms with a little sigh and he held her tightly, feeling the silk of her hair against the angle of his chin.

"Julie," he said again.

She tilted her head back and he lowered his until their faces were together and he could taste the sweet flavour of her lips, the sweet caress of her breath, the spine-tingling play of her tongue. His arms tightened further round her and then relaxed as he felt his senses beginning to swim towards the depths of abandon.

She rubbed her cheek against his jaw. "Welcome back, darling. I've missed you."

"And I you." And at the moment of saying it, it was true. "But we'll get no dishes washed this way." Reluctantly he released her.

"And I am glad I came here this evening," she confessed. "Megan's very nice, isn't she? And Norman seems to have changed somewhat, seems more restrained."

John picked up a dishcloth. "A regular little ball of sex is Megan." He laughed. "And restraint is still not a word I'd apply to Norman."

Julie gave him a look of mock-severity. "John Graham, you know darned well I didn't mean it that way. And you'll keep your eyes and thoughts off that little ball of sex this evening, if you know what's good for you."

"Julie, my love . . ." He responded with simulated shock. "Jealousy is a new emotion for you, isn't it?"

"Listen, you." She jabbed a finger into his chest. "What you do when I'm not around is your own business. But when you're with me I expect to have first claim on your thoughts, and all your attention."

"Ah, Julie, this is so seldom."

"I'm serious, damn you." She whipped round from the sink, clasped his cheeks between two dripping hands, and pulled his head down until their eyes were level."

"Julie," he complained. "You're soaking me."

"Then soak, damn you." She pressed her lips to his, harshly, possessively. "There. Now you're branded for the evening."

He laughed. "The whole night, if you like. Norman's spending the night at Megan's" He put his mouth to her ear and whispered.

"John!" She drew her head away sharply, a red spot flaming in the centre of each cheek. "You're incorrigible."

"You're only saying that because it's true."

She chuckled. "Come on, these dishes won't finish themselves."

When they returned to the living room Norman and Megan drew apart hastily on the settee.

"Don't let us interrupt you," said John.

"That's all right, chum, nothing to interrupt."

"In that case you'd better wipe that lipstick off."

"Uh-uh." Norman licked his lips. "Flavour of the month. Welsh rabbit. Come to that, your own lips could use some treatment."

John pulled a handkerchief from his pocket, scrubbed his lips briskly, and then examined it. "You lying hound. There's nothing there."

Norman grinned. "You weren't sure though, were you?"

"Belt him one for me, will you Megan." John crossed to the radiogram, switched it on, and lifted the lid. He removed several records from the storage slot and examined them. "I say, what's all this?"

"I brought them over last week," said Megan.

"Very nice," complimented John. "Shorty Rogers, Barney Kessel, Bill McGuffie, Ella sings Cole Porter. That I must hear. He placed the record on the turntable and said to Julie sitting in an armchair, "Up, woman."

Obediently she stood up and he planted himself in the armchair.

"Oh, I thought you wanted to dance."

"No, ma'am. I want you here." He pulled her down into his lap. She kicked her shoes off and snuggled into him, her head resting on his shoulder.

"I gather you're off to Cheltenham tomorrow, Julie," said Norman.

"That's right. A fortnight with the family." She raised her head and looked at John. "I was going to suggest you come down for a week, but now that you're starting work tomorrow, that's out of the question."

Norman snorted. "I should think John's had enough of family life for a bit."

"What do you mean, Norman?" Julie raised her eyebrows in enquiry.

"He's just had seven days of family life in Paris." He groaned despairingly. "In *Paris*, mark you."

Megan punched his arm. "That's the one you asked me to give him, John." She punched him again, harder, and Norman yelped. "And that's one from me. I can imagine how you would have spent seven days in Paris, you single-minded bugger." She clambered swiftly away from his groping hands, a flurry of plump thigh beneath cotton skirt, and glimpse of cleavage behind low-cut blouse.

John felt his arms tighten involuntarily around Julie, reflecting the crazy desire which Megan's unconsciously lascivious movements induced in him. He found himself studying the Welsh girl, his imagination playing tricks with his libido, thankful that the pressure of his arms seemed to be accepted by Julie as the result of her own closeness. He found himself, too, comparing the two women in a sudden rush of wonder at the effect Megan had on him. From an aesthetic viewpoint there was no comparison: Julie's long legged body, which moved with such athletic grace, her thrust of bosom, so uncompelling that one became aware of its abundant appeal with a sense of shock almost, the delicate bone structure of her face with its slightly luminous skin, the texture and colouring of ivory, the ash-blond hair, so fine that the merest hint of breeze sent wisps of it curling away from her head. In contrast, Megan was coarse and dumpy, her body too short for the inordinate swell of breast, her face too fleshily sensual, her walk too obviously derived from wanton awareness of her lascivious appeal; a walk of conscious sexuality contrasting with Julie's unconscious grace. No, the appeal Megan made was a direct appeal to his animal instincts: an obvious, conscious, deliberate flaunting of her libidinous charms. Why, even her red hair. Red hair! Now he knew what had been vaguely nibbling at his mind all evening.

"I see you've dyed your hair, Megan."

"Do you mind!" Righteous indignation. "I have merely restored its natural shade."

"I can swear to that, chum." Norman chuckled.

"Norman!" Megan raised a small, plump fist menacingly.

"Don't you dare, woman!"

"Ugh, you're disgusting," she said.

She jumped out of the settee to the refrain of Norman's lewd laughter as Ella Fitzgerald began singing *Love for Sale*.

"My favourite track," Megan said. "Julie, do you mind if I borrow John?"

"Not at all, Megan." Julie had been following the conversation with a look of sardonically tolerant amusement. She drew John's arm away and stood up.

"Come over here, Julie," Norman said, "and tell me all about your exams."

As Julie joined Norman on the settee, John took Megan in his arms and marvelled at the incredibly perfect fit of her against him, so natural as to feel habitual. She arched her body backwards with inveterate sexuality, forcing his own body to bend forward. He could feel the whole disturbing line of her pressing against him, from rounded stomach, through softly bulging breast, to plumpness of cheek against shoulder, with her hair in the depression of his jaw. Behind him, as if in another existence, he was aware of Julie talking to Norman.

John lowered his head and pressed his lips to Megan's ear. "You're an unholy terror," he whispered.

"I know," she whispered back. "Isn't it nice?"

He didn't answer. He didn't have to answer. Through the mists of semi-conscious awareness and the slow rhythmic movement of their bodies in sensual harmony he could hear the strangely appropriate words of the song:

Appetising young love for sale;
Love that's new and quite unspoiled,
Love that's only partly soiled;
Love for sale.

"What is Paris like?" she asked.

"Wonderful. Have you never been there?"

"No." Wistfully. "I want to go sometime. But not on my own."

"Is that an invitation?"

"Who knows?" Soft chuckle. "The statement alone is mine. The interpretation I leave to you. And you've got no way of finding out, really, have you?"

If you want the thrill of love,
I've been through the mill of love,
Old love, new love,
Every love but true love.

"Norman's quite a guy, isn't he". It was a safer topic, John thought.

"Uh huh. I shall probably marry him."

It took more restraint than he suspected he possessed to suppress his laughter.

"You've told him, of course."

"Of course not!" Sharp snort. "I'm not ready for marriage yet."

This time he couldn't hold his laughter back.

"What's the joke?" called Norman.

"Private," replied John. "When will you be ready?" he whispered to Megan.

"Oh . . . when I've done a bit more living, perhaps." Her nails made little indentations in his flesh through the thin sports shirt.

If you want to buy my wares
Follow me and climb the stairs,
Love for sale.

"That was a fine exhibition, I must say." From the other end of the settee Julie glared at him.

"What do you mean? What exhibition?"

"That dance. Dance!" She corrected herself scornfully. "More like vertically mutual masturbation."

"Hey, steady on!"

He had been aware of a slowly smouldering anger in Julie from the time the dance had ended to the moment Norman had left with Megan. Now he looked at her tenderly, a smile hovering on his lips.

"You *are* jealous, aren't you?"

"Oh!" Disgust. He felt it was directed more at herself than at him. "Little ball of sex, indeed. Flaunting, shameless hussy is more like it."

He raised his eyebrows. "Really. How very Victorian. Stop being so foolish, Julie. Megan doesn't mean anything to me – she's Norman's girl. Anyway, I thought you liked her."

"I did. While she acted like Norman's girl. But I know that type. She's every man's girl. A regular sexual Bedouin."

"I say! That's rather good! I particularly like the bed bit."

Julie chewed on her lower lip, fighting back laughter. John slid along the settee, put an arm round her shoulders, and planted a gentle kiss on her cheek.

"Julie, this isn't really you. You're not really upset, are you? Anyway, I'll let you into a secret. Norman and Megan are getting married."

"Are they?" She turned round with a suddenness that brought her head into sharp contact with his chin. "Oh, John." Dismayed anxiety. "Did I hurt you?"

He moved his jaw from side to side. "I think it's still in one piece."

Her hand stroked his chin for a moment, and then they were holding each other, and all the pent-up emotions of the past week, climaxed by the suppressed desires of the last two days, escaped through his lips and his tongue and his fumbling anxious hands.

For a while she responded to his kiss and accepted his caresses, and then she calmly forced him away from her.

"Don't get too excited, John. I haven't finished talking to you yet."

He endured a momentary, panting, unreasoning resentment at the broken contact and flopped back in the settee, hands clasped behind his head, arms pressing tightly against his ears and temples.

"What is it now, Julie?"

"And don't get irritable, either. There's something we have to have out."

"Oh hell. Don't tell me. Let me guess. Here's where we get all Victorian again and have the what-are-your-intentions bit."

"No we don't." she said angrily. "At least, only so far as I want to make something clear. We're no longer students. You start work tomorrow and I start in a few weeks. For the best part of three years I've made no unreasonable claims on your time or your emotions. But the time has come for a certain understanding . . ."

He interrupted her. "Look here, Julie, let me tell you something before you go any further. I have no intention of getting married. Certainly not yet at any rate. If you're thinking of what I said about Norman and Megan, well they're not likely to marry for at least two years, and anyway . . ."

She did not let him continue. He caught her wrist a moment before her palm connected with his cheek. "Damn you! Damn you, John Graham!" Her eyes misted with barely-restrained tears, and her face flushed with outraged pride. "I had no intention of mentioning marriage. And I don't give a damn what your precious Norman and his precious Megan are going to do."

"Julie, I'm sorry." He pulled at her shoulders until her face came away from the back of the settee and pressed into his chest. He held her there with one hand in the small of her back, the other stroking her soft, fine hair. "Forgive me, darling. It was the strain of being away from you and the reaction to my interview today, perhaps. I had no right to say that." But he knew it was more than that, even as he said it.

Her body was heaving against his with small sobs. He smoothed her hair away from her temple and kissed the side of her eye, feeling the salty wetness on his lips.

"Oh John," she murmured, "it's my fault too. I did feel jealous before and I am behaving with Victorian prudery." She raised her head, a smile trembling on her lips.

"I suppose you have the right, really." The glib smugness of his words almost sickened him and he instantly regretted having uttered them.

"Do I, John?"

He was committed now. There was no turning back. Damn it! "Well, nobody else has."

At the base of her throat a slight pulsation. He bent over and pressed his lips to it. Her words crept softly into his ear.

"I'm not going to ask you if you love me, John. That's a word you'll use when you feel ready to use it and not because you think I want to hear it. And I mean in circumstances other than those in which you've already used it. So I don't want you to feel under any sort of obligation. Do you understand?"

"Yes, darling." His hand started to stroke her breast, feeling the nipple become erect.

"And I want our relationship to continue, John. But only if you want it to continue. And not the way it has been, on the occasions when you've had nothing better to do. If you want it to carry on – *really* want it – then I must come first with you, as you have always come first with me. Is that what you want, John?"

"Yes, sweetheart. That's what I want" And at that moment he really did. The nipple was now fully erect under his fingers and he slid his hand down, smoothed it over the slight swell of stomach, fingers pressing into the concavity of her groin, caressing the long expanse of thigh.

"Oh, John." She sighed. "Dearest. I'm not even going to ask you to be faithful to me. Only that you never let me find out. It's just that I want to feel a part of your life now, and to know that you are a part of mine. Is that very, very foolish?"

"No darling. It's not at all foolish. It's sweet and touching and very, very flattering." His hand reached with long, gentle, practised strokes, under her skirt, feeling the warmth and softness of her skin above the tightly-suspendered nylons, and the moistness of her panties.

She stopped the progress of his hand. "Not like this, John."

"Can you stay here tonight?"

"Yes," she whispered. "Oh, yes please, dearest."

CHAPTER TEN

He would never get along with Mattson.

Heaven knew he had tried hard enough these past four weeks, but it was as though the man were determined to give him no opportunity to penetrate the stark, impersonal barrier he always maintained between them. Admittedly he never obstructed John in his work, was always prepared to answer reasonable questions, to respond to reasonably solicited advice; but there it ended. It was as if he were saying "Okay! You wanted this job and you've got it. I don't think you're the man we need, but if you can prove me wrong, go ahead. Only don't expect me to prop you up in the process." Not that he had ever said anything like that, but John had the continual feeling that Mattson had him poised on the edge of a precipice and was just waiting for him to topple over.

He finished balancing the July cash account. Ledger column, plus contra column, equals bank column . . . and carry the balance forward to August. He was sitting at the small desk in the corner of Mattson's office which had replaced the larger desk he habitually occupied in the outside office. They had decided it was more useful for him to share Mattson's office in the early mornings, when they examined the daily mail together, and in the evenings when he did the bookkeeping.

Now he turned to Mattson. "The books are finished."

Mattson grunted. His head was bowed over figures of his own. He was working out his monthly expense claim. A cigarette hung from his mouth, burned down almost to his lips, a half-inch of ash on the verge of dropping off.

John looked at his watch.

"It's almost nine o'clock," he said.

Mattson raised his head. Cigarette ash dropped on his desk. He cursed and brushed it away with the side of his hand. "Have you got a date this evening? Somewhere you've got to be?"

"I'd like to get home sometime."

"Well, just wait a few minutes. I've got to get this done and then I want to speak to you." He returned to his figures.

Annoyed, John pushed his chair back, making as much noise as possible. He stretched his legs and lit a cigarette. This was typical, he thought. He was lucky if he got away from the office before nine twice a week. And he knew Mattson was just waiting for him to complain. Well, he'd be damned before he gave Mattson the satisfaction of spinning *that* rigmarole again.

Christ, he could recite it by heart. The this, the that, the other they would never achieve by working City hours; the hours that he, Mattson, had put in getting the company on its feet; the disgust that Mattson felt for the 'old soldiers' and 'trade unionists' who hadn't the foggiest idea what an honest day's work was. Above all – and it always came down to this – the fact that if he, Graham, found the strain and effort of the work too taxing, he damned-well knew what he could do about it.

Five weeks. He had been there only five weeks. It felt like a lifetime. Initially he had forced himself to remain because he was not going to be beaten by Mattson. Now he stayed despite Mattson, because he actually found the work interesting.

The excitement of receiving new orders, orders to be confirmed and placed with manufacturers; delivery dates to be negotiated with suppliers; shipping space to be booked and shipments arranged; deliveries to be invoiced and suppliers paid. Then the host of other duties: marine insurance, credit insurance, documentation, correspondence. And every day brought problems of a financial or technical nature that had to be sorted out with the banks, the customers, the suppliers, the shipping lines, or one of the relevant Government departments. And over and beyond all this he was expected to maintain the company's books of account.

John was pleased with himself. He felt he had grasped the essentials of the job quickly and assimilated his duties adequately. He didn't expect praise – although it would have been nice – but was constantly irked by Mattson's failure to express even a mild satisfaction with the way he was handling the work. In the mornings, going through the mail, Mattson would explain in meticulous detail how each letter or order had to be handled, frequently scribbling terse notes in the margins of the letters. On one occasion John had pointed out that most of these instructions were unnecessary: he knew what had to be done. Mattson had glared at him.

"While I'm in the office, we'll do things my way," Mattson had barked. "There'll be time enough for you to make mistakes when I'm in West Africa. And I've no doubt you'll make plenty."

It was the first and last time John had complained.

He looked at his wristwatch again. Nine-ten. Mattson was still hunched over his expense sheets and petty cash box on the other side of the large desk. Would the man never be through? John stretched out further in his chair and closed his eyes, recalling his first day at the office.

Mattson had started him off reading the correspondence files for the previous six months, and studying the invoice files, and he had been amazed at the volume and variety of business transacted by this small firm. The exported everything from safety pins to ten-ton cranes. The bulk of the exports went to West Africa and were mainly connected with the timber industry: trucks, trailers, tractors, sawmill machinery. But they also had customers in South America, the Dutch East Indies and the British West Indies.

That afternoon he had met Alfred Reid . . .

Mattson burst into the outer office. "Come on, Graham." John looked up from the file he was studying. "Reid wants to meet you." Mattson tore out of the room.

John closed the file quickly and stood up. Across the room the Anderson girl was busily typing, but young Pat Rogers swivelled in her chair and flashed him a conspiratorial wink. He smiled at her and hurried after Mattson, catching him up halfway along the timber company's corridor.

Mattson knocked on a door and entered the room, holding the door open for John to enter after him. John walked in.

Across the room, the largest man John had ever seen. He filled the wide boardroom chair as though he had been poured into it and the pourer, with heavy-handed generosity, had added the one-for-the-pot which now overflowed the chair's sides. The chair was some small distance away from the desk to allow breathing space for the man's pendulous paunch. The man's head, in fatly huge proportion to his body, was completely bald, the face fleshly florid, the button-eyes almost hidden in layers of fat. He might be an old fifty-five or a young seventy. John was reminded of the film actor Sydney Greenstreet in a Humphrey Bogart movie of a few years earlier. This, he assumed, was Alfred Reid.

On the other side of the desk, Parry was not merely dwarfed but Lilliputian in comparison with his obese co-director. John's memory made an instant recall of the same movie, but he decided that Parry looked nothing at all like Peter Lorre, apart from the obvious difference in size with Reid.

There was something intimidating about Reid. And not just his size, but rather the way his mere presence seemed to pervade the room's atmosphere. Never in his life – even during his two years of military service – had John met anyone with such an aura of authority. As a consequence he did not know exactly what was expected of him: whether to advance and shake the man's hand, or wait for Reid to make the first move. For a moment he had the idiotic feeling that an obeisance might be in order; a bending of the knee and a swearing of fealty to his vassal liege-lord; a ceremonious kissing of his master's shoes.

In the event he nodded a greeting at Parry and stood by the door.

"Come in. Come in, boy." Reid's voice boomed and reverberated through the room; the RSM Brittain of the boardroom. "Sit down."

John sat.

"So you're Graham, are you?"

"Yes, sir."

"We're expecting great things of you, boy."

"I'll do my . . ."

"*Great* things. Reid-Parry Enterprises is going places. You settle down, learn the job, listen to Mr Parry and Mr Mattson, learn from them . . . you'll go places too."

"I hope that . . ."

"How's Henri, boy?"

"Henri . . .?"

Reid shook his head impatiently. The flesh shuddered. "Dumard, boy. In Paris."

"Oh, yes sir. Well, I believe."

"Good. Good. Tell me about yourself."

"What would you like to know, sir? Background? Education . . .?"

"Just talk, boy, that's all."

"Well, sir, I was born in Nuneaton and educated in Wales to Schools' Certificate. Higher Schools at the Quintin School in Regent Street, then two years in the Ordnance Corps, and finally three years at the London School of Economics. I don't know yet if . . ."

"Not one of those, are you boy?"

"One of *those*, sir?"

"Not one of those, is he, Mattson?"

Mattson, leaning against the wall beside the door said, "I don't think so, Mr Reid."

"Because I'll tell you flat, Graham, we've got no time for bolshies here. Got no use for the Webbs' young men, understand. We're here to work. Do your work, you'll get ahead. Try the other and that's the end. Glad to have you with us, boy. Give my regards to Henri when you see him."

Reid turned to his desk and examined some papers. The interview was evidently at an end. John was reminded of an occasion in the army, when he was marched into and out of the CO's office, for a minor misdemeanour. He would not have been altogether surprised to have heard Mattson's voice from the door: "Abaht turn. Forward march. Hep, ri, hep, ri . . ."

"Thank you sir," he said to Reid's shiny pate. He smiled at Parry, turned away from he desk, and went out through the door that Mattson was holding open for him.

In the corridor Mattson revealed his uneven, tartar-stained teeth in a derisory grin. "Well, what do you think of our Mr Reid, Graham?"

"Rather a formidable character, isn't he?"

"If you had half his brains and one-tenth his money," Mattson jeered, "you'd be pretty well off." He entered his private office and John followed him.

"It doesn't take brains to make money," said John.

"Oh?" Mattson's lips turned down in a sneer. "You're an expert on money-making, are you? In addition to your other accomplishments."

John ignored the irony. "From what I've read and heard, intelligence is less necessary to success in business than a fair share of luck and a certain single-mindedness of purpose: the conviction that you're going to make it no matter who you have to tread on in the process."

"Is that so? Well, well. I'm naturally glad to have the benefit of your research. Believe me, I feel the honour deeply. Intelligence is not necessary, you say? Imagine that. Aren't you wasting your time here, in that case?"

John, on the point of retorting angrily, suddenly sensed the futility of involving himself in the sort of argument Mattson seemed to want to provoke. Calmly he said, "Mr Mattson, I don't know what you're trying to achieve by these cheap debating tactics. You know very well that that is not what I said. If you're trying to goad me into losing my temper, you can save your breath because I have no intention of doing so. If, however, you've decided after my four or five hours in the office that I'm totally unsuited to the work, then I suggest we both go back to Mr Reid right now and you can put your case to him. Otherwise I'd better get on with my work."

It was worth every bit of restraint he had exercised just to see the look of dumbstruck amazement on Mattson's face. He stood there a moment, giving Mattson a chance to reply, and then returned to the outer office.

Mattson had not tried to needle him in the same way since. But now, five weeks later, John still experienced the same sense of futility in his frequent verbal exchanges with the man. And he could not avoid these exchanges, for Mattson checked his work with a fine tooth-comb and missed no opportunity to point out errors of the most insignificant kind: a misplaced comma that he had failed to notice before signing a letter; an error of addition on an invoice, rendered insignificant by the fact that the whole point of checking invoices was to discover such errors; an incorrect entry in the books of account which would automatically come to light in the end-of-month reconciliation.

These were mistakes anyone might make, let alone someone who was trying to cram into less than six weeks a proficiency which might normally expect to take one year. And someone, moreover, tired from the effort to concentrate on accounts work at the end of a very long, hard day. Well, at least he had avoided the big one, the one significant mistake that would have justified Mattson's early opinion of him; that would have allowed Mattson to use John as a lever in his authoritarian battle with Parry.

And now it was done. Now the weeks of effort and application and waiting were at an end. This was the last Friday evening before Mattson left for the Gold Coast. Thank God, from Monday morning he would not have to put up with Mattson's penny-pinching control of his every action.

As though he had read John's mind, Mattson locked his cash box, put it in a desk drawer that he also locked, and gave both keys to John.

"Give these to Parry in the morning, will you."

"Won't you be in tomorrow?"

"No, Graham." He laughed mirthlessly. "It's all yours, and by . . ." Mattson paused irresolutely, as though unwilling to express the criticism that John had come to expect. He continued calmly, "Can you join me for a drink?"

The contrast in tempo, the unusualness of the request, momentarily confused John. "Why, yes . . . yes, I'll be glad to. Mind if I make a phone call first?"

"Go ahead." Mattson lit a cigarette and slumped in his chair.

John went into the outer office and dialed a number.

"Miss Grant, please," he said to the voice which answered. Then, after a moment, "Julie? John."

"Hello, darling. Where are you?"

"In the office."

"Oh, John . . ." Dismay thinly veiled the annoyance in her voice.

"I'm sorry, Julie. Something has cropped up."

"Does that mean I won't be seeing you tonight?"

"I don't think so. I don't see how I can make it."

"John. This is ridiculous. It's not reasonable to expect you to work all the hours in creation. It isn't even as if you get paid overtime."

He laughed. "We're not a union shop, I'm afraid."

"It's not a joking matter. It's quite absurd. And quite wrong. You're worn out whenever we meet. I could understand if it was once or twice a week, but it isn't, it's practically every evening."

"Julie, please . . ." He felt the lassitude creep over his body and the weariness filtered into his words. "I've had just five weeks to learn the job and this is Mattson's last evening before he leaves. There are things he has to talk over with me. And I knew damn well what I was letting myself in for when I took the job. Now you can either be understanding and reasonable, and help me cope with the strain, or difficult and demanding, which will just make my task harder."

"I'm sorry, John. I suppose I am being selfish. But I am worried about you."

"I know that, darling."

"We'll meet tomorrow, won't we?"

"Of course. We'll make it a celebration. Dinner and a show in town. How's that?"

"Wonderful. But if you're too tired, I shall be happy simply spending the time quietly with you. Goodnight, darling."

"Goodnight, Julie." He replaced the phone and palmed his eyes, elbows resting on desktop.

"You look as though you could use a drink." Mattson from the doorway.

"You're right. let's go."

They locked the office door and went to a nearby pub. Over a pint of bitter ale Mattson stared at John, then he put his glass down and held out a packet of cigarettes.

"Go on. Take one."

"Thank you."

Mattson lit both their cigarettes, then, "Tell me, Graham. Do you think you're going to be able to cope?"

"I think so." He could have kicked himself for adding, "Aren't you satisfied with my progress?" It was an open invitation to another of Mattson's sardonic comments.

But all Mattson said was, "Frankly, yes. You've done better than I expected."

John took a quick sip of his beer, trying to hide his pleasure at the unparalleled compliment.

"Mind you," Mattson went on, "you've still a hell of a lot to learn, and I'm not yet convinced that you're prepared to learn it."

"What do you mean?"

"I mean that if you continue to apply yourself to the job, if you realise that nothing in this work is routine and everything has to be checked and double-checked, if, above all, you try to do things my way, you should have a good future with us. But if you don't – if you continue to think that you can learn more from Parry than from me – I give you fair warning, you won't last long after I get back from West Africa. Because there is one thing you can depend on absolutely: if you try to do things any other way, you'll slip up. I don't know how, or when, but one day you'll slip up. And I'm only waiting for one slip."

"You've confused me now," John said, forcing himself to remain calm. "I really don't know what you mean."

"Don't you?" Mattson peered at him from behind his spectacles. "Don't you think I know how often you've gone running to Parry for help? The only reason I've said nothing until now is because I've made damn sure that the only advice of Parry's you've followed has been advice of an accounting nature and not one of policy."

"I still don't understand." John was honestly puzzled. "After all, Mr Parry is a director of the company."

"That's right." A half-smile touched the corner of Mattson's lips. "He's also a very nice man, isn't he?"

"Yes. Yes, he is."

"And I'm not very nice, am I?"

"Well I wouldn't . . ."

This time Mattson actually smiled. "Go on, say it. I know what you think. I'm a rotten bastard." He paused, as if waiting for John to agree. "Okay, Graham, I won't take unfair advantage of you. It's perfectly clear what you think of me. But just remember one thing. Mr Parry may be a director of our company, but I'm the general manager and if ever it should become a question of you or me having to quit, I can tell you which one it will be. Your friend Dumard notwithstanding."

"No, just a minute Mr Mattson . . ."

"No. I know what you're going to say. But I'm laying my cards on the table. Reid-Parry Enterprises is my life. I've put my blood into that company. And it's a company which has earned a reputation for prompt and efficient service. A lot of people, both in England and overseas, have a lot a confidence in us, and I intend to see that that confidence is not misplaced. Reid and Parry may have put their money into the business, but a lot of other people have put their trust into it and, when I get back from Africa, perhaps I'll have persuaded some of them to invest money too. At my suggestion and on my assurances. So I'm thinking of a lot more than the money of Reid and Parry. I'm thinking of my personal reputation, the company's reputation, and all the people who trust me."

"I understand all that, Mr Mattson. I just don't see what you have against Reid and Parry."

Mattson grunted. "What makes you think I've got anything against them? My personal feelings for Reid and Parry have nothing to do with the right or wrong way to run our business."

"But you seem to have this . . . this thing about Mr Parry."

The only subject I have a thing about, as you put it, is the efficiency of Reid-Parry Enterprises. When I'm in Africa you will be the custodian of that efficiency. All I want to know is: can I rely on you?"

"I'm sure you can."

"All right, then we'll say no more about it. You'll be getting daily reports from me and occasional cables. There will be matters for you to handle promptly, according to instructions I'll send you. I'll expect you to see to them exactly as I tell you to. Is that clear?"

"Yes."

"Fine. Then I'll say goodnight."

"Won't you let me buy you a beer? It's my shout."

Mattson grinned unexpectedly. "No, thanks. I'd like to get home too." He got off his bar stool and turned to leave. Then he turned back to John. "On second thoughts I will have that drink. It occurs to me that I ought to tell you a little more about Reid-Parry Enterprises than you already know. It may help give you a slant on the type of work you're doing, and a better understanding of my anxiety of what may happen in my absence."

John ordered the beers.

It started immediately after the end of the war, Mattson explained. With post-war reconstruction, the timber business boomed, while the governmental control system ensured that losses on timber imports were virtually impossible for companies who were allotted import quotas. Alfred Reid Timber Limited was one of the companies who were very favourably placed to benefit from the generous government arrangement.

They were fortunate, too, in having a number of excellent timber shippers, particularly in West Africa. Good quality timber – and even timber of a quality which, in more normal times, would have been rejected out-of-hand – was often sold even before it had been imported and inspected. Profits were soaring, salaries and wages rising, trading conditions excellent. They were making up for the excessively lean years of the twenties and the early thirties, and showing a profit on the exchange.

But there was a snag.

Delivery promises were rarely maintained and, when frantic cables were sent asking why there was a delay, the answer would inevitably be that obsolescent equipment had broken down and the shortage of replacement parts and new equipment was causing complications in production.

In an effort to ensure the continuity of their timber supplies, Alfred Reid would endeavour to find the needed spares, or locate alternative equipment, for their overseas shippers. The task of find this equipment and shipping it overseas was entrusted to Mattson, who had working for them as an accounts clerk ever since his discharge from the Army.

At first it was a mere trickle of equipment that Mattson obtained and shipped abroad, but the native bush telegraph system must have gone to work for, after a while, requests for different types of machine, or vehicles, or spare parts, were being received at an ever-accelerating rate.

Ultimately Mattson found he had a full-time job on his hands, simply buying and shipping these supplies, and he was staying at the office later and later in the evenings in order to cope with the backlog of his accounts work.

About this time, too, considerable numbers of ex-Army vehicles were being put out to public tender, and surplus supply companies were mushrooming. In a fit of enthusiasm for his job, Mattson took to sending lists of available secondhand equipment to the timber shippers overseas, and was suddenly overwhelmed by a flood of requests to have items of equipment surveyed and, if found suitable, purchased and shipped abroad.

It is unlikely that the extra work devolving on Mattson had any effect on the subsequent decision of his employers. What is more likely is that they suddenly discovered that the five percent purchasing commission they charged was unreasonably swelling their already excessive timber profits.

Whatever the reason, they decided they would be better off having their export business handled by a subsidiary company and Alfred Reid, as Managing Director, and David Parry, as Company Secretary, formed Reid-Parry Enterprises to handle exclusively these overseas demands. Mattson was taken off accounts work and given the job of managing the company, aided by an invoice typist from the timber company's typing pool.

Mattson was still not content. Over the years the available supply of surplus vehicles and equipment had gradually dwindled, while production of new equipment had slowly increased as factories, reverting to peacetime operation, got into their stride. The Government, too, was encouraging exports and a large part of all factory production was automatically allocated to export sales. Mattson recognised that the goodwill he had built up with these factories could be turned to profit if he could persuade some of his overseas customers to act as agents for the manufacturers, and purchase goods not solely for their own use, but for resale. He had had preliminary discussions with a number of manufacturers and was now about to visit his West African connections and persuade them to take on the agencies.

"And that's it, Graham." Mattson removed his spectacles and rubbed his weak-looking, red-rimmed eyes. He peered at John myopically. "The first full month I spent in Reid-Parry Enterprises we achieved the phenomenal turnover of slightly in excess of £8,500. You've just finished balancing the July accounts. What was the approximate turnover figure?"

"I can tell you exactly," said John. "£33,920. 8. 8."

"And July is not usually one of our better months. Furthermore, if I succeed in this trip, we can expect another four-fold increase within one year!"

"That's quite a success story," John said, admiration evident in his voice despite the animus he still felt towards Mattson."

"Yes. And if I've had any luck, I've made it myself. And I haven't consciously trod on anyone in the process."

You've done your best to tread on me, John thought, while admiring the man's memory. He said, "You haven't become particularly wealthy in the process, though, have you?"

Again the unexpected grin as Mattson replaced his spectacles. "No," ruefully, "I grant you that one. Now I'm off."

"Good luck, Mr Mattson. I'll do my best."

"I hope so. Goodnight Graham." He got off the bar stool and turned towards the door, then abruptly faced John again. "Incidentally, and merely apropos your earlier comments, you might be surprised to learn that Parry is my youngest son's godfather."

And he left the pub.

John ordered another beer and sat thinking about the conversation they had had. Mattson had revealed a new side to his character. He had been almost friendly. But why had he treated John almost as a leper for five weeks? And what was the point of that last remark about Parry? Mattson had ability, that was clear. And energy. If John had found the going tough, the hours long, the work exhausting – what then of Mattson? He had worked equally long hours and just as hard; and he had, moreover, the additional strain of training John and thoroughly checking all his work. But that did not excuse his foul temper and bad manners. There was no law that made ability antithetic to good conduct.

And then the answer hit him and he was lost in wonder at the man's low cunning. Naturally, going away for several weeks, Mattson would make an eleventh hour attempt to woo John away from his obvious preference for Parry. And, thinking about it, the attempt now seemed to have been singularly crude. The suddenness of Mattson's change of approach had obviously been due to his abrupt realisation that this was his last opportunity to win a measure of loyalty from John.

The sentimental allusion to Parry's family relationship was clearly a further attempt to suggest a solidarity of understanding with the little director, which patently did not exist. John wondered if Mattson's last remark was actually true. There was no way he could find out.

Damn Mattson! He must think John an absolute simpleton. The background to the growth of Reid-Parry Enterprises was fascinating, but John saw no reason to change his opinion of Mattson himself, nor to deviate one inch from his own determination to place his trust in Parry rather than the contemptible general manager.

CHAPTER ELEVEN

It was working out exactly as he had hoped.

He was coping with the work. More than coping; he was smugly satisfied that even Mattson would not have done the job better. Nothing had gone wrong. Correspondence, invoicing, shipping and accounts were all up-to-date; cabled requests from Mattson had been handled promptly and correctly; he had even succeeded in changing Mattson's system in a few small ways which had resulted in a speeding-up of output, so that he rarely had to remain in the office beyond seven o'clock.

Each morning he would open the mail, date-stamp it, and then take it across to Parry to discuss the non-routine matters it might contain. Sometimes Reid would be present at these early-morning discussions, but more often not. And this pleased him. He had got over his initial awkwardness in Reid's presence, but the Managing Director clearly had little understanding of the export business, and his occasional suggestions (given in he form of commands rather than recommendations) were usually embarrassingly ill-advised.

But Parry was beginning to bewilder him. It was nothing he could put his finger on, but every time he asked Parry's advice he was left with the feeling that he had himself supplied the answer; that Parry had in some subtle way steered the conversation so that John was making suggestions and proposals rather than obtaining the benefit of Parry's experience. Yet it was always done so charmingly as to leave him wondering if it were imagination on his part. He would ask Parry's advice and Parry would smile encouragingly and say, "Well, Mr Graham, what do you think?" The question would always be accented in such a way as to flatter John that his opinion was very important to Parry. Then Parry would consider John's response gravely and make pertinent comment. Always, however, in a form to induce further input from John. Finally John would return to his office, the problem resolved, with the feeling that had he not bothered to approach Parry, he would nevertheless be doing exactly the same.

His main source of irritation was the Anderson woman. He always thought of her as the Anderson woman and addressed her as Miss Anderson. Pat Rogers had quickly become just Pat, but Patricia Anderson, sharing the same given name as her colleague, had so discouraged any attempt at even polite familiarity that their relationship had remained stuffily, formally businesslike.

At Parry's suggestion he had moved into Mattson's room and was working at Mattson's desk. Whenever he sent for Miss Anderson to take dictation, she responded promptly enough, but always with an air of grudging reluctance. She did her work quickly and professionally, but never demonstrated the same willingness and quietly helpful zeal that marked her activity for Mattson. John was often tempted to tax her about her attitude, but there was nothing tangible he could point to. In the army it would have been called dumb insolence.

By contrast Pat Rogers took every opportunity to enter his office with questions and problems that he would have expected her experienced enough to handle. She was always winsomely feminine. When she sat down in his office, she always revealed a little too much thigh. When she stood over him, while he explained something, it was always a little too close. Whenever he entered the outer office she would turn in her chair and smile at him.

On one occasion he imagined he heard the two girls arguing about him, but he could not be sure.

Of one thing he was sure. Pat Rogers would not be averse to a bit of extra-curricular activity. For that matter he would not be averse to it himself. But instinct warned him that such a relationship might well have an adverse effect on discipline in the office, not simply with Pat, but also with the Anderson woman. Anyway, she always left the office long before he did, and his weekends were devoted exclusively to Julie.

Mattson was apparently finding his tour both more demanding and more rewarding than he had anticipated. He had already spent six weeks in West Africa and was not expected back for another two weeks. It felt strange to John to reflect that he had now spent longer at Reid-Parry Enterprises without Mattson than with him. The past six weeks had seemed to pass with twice the speed of the preceding six weeks, and the feeling could not be accounted for entirely by the shorter hours he was now working.

The external phone rang. He picked it up.

"There's a Mr Pearce on the line," Pat Rogers informed him.

"What does he want?"

"It's something to do with tractor spares."

"All right. Put him through . . . Mr Pearce?"

"That's right." The voice was quietly authoritative. "Who am I speaking to?"

"My name is Graham."

"Well, Mr Graham, I believe you can supply me with Grasshopper spares for West Africa."

"Yes. I think so. What do you require exactly"?

"These will be genuine Grasshopper spares, I take it?"

"Of course. What do you have in mind?"

"Do you have a pencil and paper handy? I'm afraid it's rather a lengthy list."

"In that case, Mr Pearce, don't you think it would be better if you sent it through the post?"

"No." John thought he detected a slight chuckle at the other end. "It's pretty urgent. I'd sooner have you ring me back, if that's possible."

"Well, you realise I won't be able to give you a delivery date before checking with the factory?"

"That's all right." Once again the suspicion of a laugh. "As long as you can quote me prices and delivery conditions. You can do that, can you?"

"Oh sure. I can do that." John sighed. "Okay, Mr Pearce, I'm ready."

Pearce began dictating part numbers and quantities. It was almost fifteen minutes later before he finished. Then he gave John a Mansion House telephone number to call back as soon as possible; that same afternoon if he could.

John said he would do his best, and hung up. He picked up the internal phone and Pat Rogers answered.

"Oh, Pat, would you please bring in the price list from Tees-Tyne Tractor and Equipment, and also their invoices for the past six months."

"Yes, Mr Graham."

She came in a few minutes later, walked around to his side of the desk and leaned across him to lay the documents before him. It would have been much simpler for her to have passed them across the desk from the other side.

"Is there anything else I can do for you, Mr Graham?" Determined to show him she had Macleaned her teeth that morning.

"No, thank you, Pat." He returned her smile. "That will be all."

Immediately she had left the room he started calculating prices. One hour later he phoned Parry.

"Graham here, Mr Parry. May I come over and see you?"

"I'll come over there, Graham."

Parry bustled into the office and beamed a greeting.

"Well, Graham, what's the problem?"

"It's not really a problem, Mr Parry. I've just had a telephone enquiry from a man named Pearce for Grasshopper spares and I've worked out the prices. He wants me to phone him back."

"And . . ."

"And the total value is in excess of fifteen thousand pounds."

Parry pursed his lips in a soundless whistle. "This Mr Pearce . . . where's he from?"

"I don't know. He didn't give the name of his company."

"I see." Parry smiled. John knew what was coming next. "Well, Graham, what do you think?"

"It's hard to say. I can't see any harm in giving him the prices."

"No-o-o-o. We can get the parts all right, can we?"

"Oh, there's no difficulty there. We get them from the Grasshopper agents in the north-east of England. Mr Mattson has a special arrangement with them."

"Hmmmm. Terms of payment?"

"Depends on the company, I suppose. Normally cash on readiness at factory, if it's being paid for in England. Sight draft if it's being paid for abroad, subject to ECGD approval, of course. Otherwise Letter of Credit."

"Y-e-e-es. Well, there's no harm in quoting, is there?" Parry grinned. "It would be rather nice to have an order like that under our belts when Mr Mattson returns, wouldn't it?"

"John nodded. "It would. I'll ring him back then, shall I?"

"I think so. Ask him for the name of his company so that you can confirm the quotation. I'll stay here will you speak to him."

John asked Pat Rogers to connect him with Mr Pearce at the Mansion House number. When his phone rang he picked up the receiver."

"Mr Pearce?"

"Yes."

"Graham here. Reid-Parry Enterprises. I have those prices for you."

"Oh, yes. Thank you. I'll take them down if you will kindly give them to me."

John dictated the prices slowly. When he had finished he said, "Is that in order?"

"Perfectly," replied Pearce. "Now what are your terms of delivery.?"

"Well, those prices are net f.a.s. Newcastle or Leith. There would be a supplementary charge for delivery Liverpool or London."

"Sounds fair enough. Thank you very much, Mr Graham. I'll be letting you know."

"Just a moment, Mr Pearce. Could you let me have your full name and address. We would like to confirm the quotation in writing."

This time there was no mistaking the mirth at the other end. Pearce said, "We're the Amalgamated Africa Corporation. You'll find the address in the phone book. My initials are B.G. And the name is spelled with an E.A., not an I.E. Have you got all that?"

"Yes, thank you Mr Pearce. We'll get the quote off tomorrow."

"No hurry, Mr Graham. I have the important details. Goodbye."

John recounted Pearce's side of the conversation to Parry. When he got to the name of Pearce's company, Parry's eyebrows shot skywards.

"Getting that order would really be a feather in our caps," the director said.

"Oh? Why is that?"

"Amalgamated Africa is one of the largest companies in Africa, with world wide connections. Get that quotation off as quickly as possible, Graham."

It was a bronzed Mattson who returned from Africa, his hair perceptibly lightened by the sun.

John, who had moved back to the outer office on the eve of Mattson's return, saw little of him the first day. Having greeted John rather less warmly than the two office girls, and reassured himself that there were no problems of a pressing nature, Mattson instructed him to carry on with his work as if he – Mattson – were still away. Mattson then spent the entire morning making phone calls and dictating letters, and the afternoon closeted with Reid and Parry. At five-thirty he rang John on the intercom and suggested that he pack up for the day and get in a bit earlier than usual in the morning.

The next morning John arrived at eight-thirty and found Mattson already in his office, his desk piled high with correspondence and invoice files.

"How did it go, Graham?"

"Pretty well, I think, Mr Mattson."

"No snags? No insuperable problems?"

"Nothing we couldn't handle."

"Not much new business, I see."

"No." John frowned. "That was something I couldn't quite understand. Orders from West Africa dropped off sharply after you left."

Mattson grinned, but there was little humour in the grin. "You didn't get your order from AAC, then?"

"AAC? Oh, Amalgamated Africa. How did you . . .? I suppose Mr Parry told you."

"No Graham," grimly, "Parry did not tell me."

"Then you must have seen my quotation in the files."

"Yes." His lips lifted away from his teeth. "Yes, I did see it in the files. But I heard about it before I left Africa."

"I'm sorry," said John, genuinely puzzled, "I don't follow you."

"That is quite apparent. You know who AAC are, I suppose?"

"Well I've been told they're a pretty big outfit."

"You don't know that they are official Grasshopper agents in West Africa?"

"No, I didn't know that." He was suddenly struck by the significance of Mattson's announcement. "In that case, why did they ask me for a quotation?"

"Exactly, Graham. Why indeed? I'll tell you, should I? AAC are not interested in purchasing Grasshopper spares from us. Why should they pay our prices when they can get them at full trade discount themselves? But they are interested in finding out how bootleg spares are getting into West Africa when they are supposed to be the exclusive suppliers in the region. Well, now they know. As a result of your hot-headed anxiety to bring off a big deal in my absence, you may have been instrumental in costing Tees-Tyne their north-east franchise for Grasshopper. Plus the fact that we are no longer in a position to supply those parts to our West African customers.

John felt his little world of proud achievement crash in pieces around him. For a moment he was tongue-tied as the significance of Mattson's remarks penetrated his understanding. Then he said, "My God, how could I imagine there would be repercussions like that? What can we do about it? And how did Amalgamated Africa find out where our spares come from?"

Mattson gave a disgusted sigh and pulled an open file towards him. "Here," he said, pointing to John's quotation. "You told them yourself. Price delivered free alongside steamer Leith or Newcastle. You might just as well have said price ex Tees-Tyne factory. And as for what we can do about it . . . I'll tell you in one word: nothing! Nothing except to write a letter of apology to Tees-Tyne for our failure to let them know we were shipping the spares to West Africa – a letter that they can show to the Grasshopper Corporation. And you had better start praying that the Grasshopper people accept that explanation from Tees-Tyne."

John felt like a schoolboy hauled before the headmaster for a misdemeanour he was unable satisfactorily to explain. A sour taste replaced the sweet flavour of pleased complacency with which he had awaited Mattson's return. "I don't know what to say. I had no idea anything like this could happen."

Mattson's eyebrows drew together in a puzzled frown. "You admit you are responsible, then?"

"Why yes. Of course. There's no question, is there?"

Mattson drew a deep breath. "I may have misjudged you, Graham."

"I don't follow."

"Didn't you discuss the AAC enquiry with Parry?"

"But of course. He was in this office when I phoned them back with the prices."

"Isn't the mistake Parry's responsibility then? Shouldn't he have told you not to quote them?"

John hesitated. It seemed that Mattson was giving him a chance to get off the hook. It was an answer that had not occurred to him. But why not? Parry was, after all, a director of the company. And Parry had assured Mattson that he would keep things under control in Mattson's absence. Furthermore John had actually expressed doubt to Parry about the authenticity of the enquiry. Why then this reluctance to lay the blame squarely on Parry's shoulders. He found himself recalling the many other meetings and discussions he had had with Parry; Parry's failure on every occasion to give him a clear-cut line of action, except in matters of banking, accounts, or insurance. And suddenly he knew why he had not passed the buck; why he had avoided the easy way out.

He said, "The responsibility is entirely mine, Mr Mattson. I discussed the enquiry with Mr Parry as a matter of principle – as I have discussed all enquiries with him in your absence. But I learned very quickly after you left that Mr Parry has less understanding of this business than I had imagined. He doesn't have the *feel* for the business that you can only get by working here, in this office, all the time. I probably should have used my own judgement with the spares enquiry and not asked Mr Parry at all. But, honestly, I would still have made the same mistake."

"No. You were right to ask Parry." Mattson's lips tightened into a thin line. "But I'm beginning to think the mistake was almost worth making if it has taught you something I couldn't drum into your thick skull through six weeks of trying."

"You mean that Mr Parry . . ."

Mattson interrupted him. "I want you to understand this, Graham. Mr Parry is a director of this company. He is my superior as well as yours. And make no bones about it, he's a damned smart little man. He can spot things instantly in a contract, or a letter of credit, or an insurance claim, that you or I would never notice even after an hour or two of study. He has learned the practical aspects of accounting and financial procedure in the best school of all – the tough school of experience.

"But Parry is essentially, basically, an accountant: a book-keeper with a book-keeper's mentality. And it's a funny thing about accountants; they always seem to think that their knowledge of the backside of commerce turns them into commercial wizards. You once asked me what I'd got against Parry. Remember?"

John nodded.

"Well, I've got nothing against him when he sticks to the things he knows. But that is something he seems to be incapable of doing. It was his decision, remember, not mine to bring you in here as my assistant. I didn't think it would work. I'll be frank with you and say it has worked far better than I dreamed possible. However, had I got the sort of assistant I wanted, one who already had export experience, I could have spent the training period on the more intangible aspects of this business, instead of wasting so much time on basic procedure. And then the Grasshopper fiasco might have been avoided."

"John gulped. "Does this mean you're going to ask me to leave?"

"No, Graham. I'll tell you bluntly that last week you wouldn't have had to ask that question. You'd have been out on your arse in no time flat if you'd been around when the AAC manager in Lagos spoke to me.

I won't tell you what he said, but he couldn't have chosen a worse moment. I was in the Lido, a local night spot, with some pretty important people, and I can tell you it made me look damn foolish." Mattson grinned wryly as the memory returned to him.

"And now . . ."

"Now I've had time to think about it, and I've spoken to Parry."

"I thought you said Parry didn't tell you anything."

"Exactly. Don't look so puzzled. I know Parry well enough now to be able to read his silences even better than his speeches. When I mentioned the trouble with AAC he said absolutely nothing. That's when I decided to give you another chance. You'll never know how close a thing it was. If you had tried to crawl out from under by laying the blame on Parry, that would have been it."

"I don't understand."

"I don't expect you to understand. Call it my warped sense of integrity, if you like."

"What can we do about it now?"

"Not a great deal." Mattson scowled. "I've already told you. We've got to try and get Tees-Tyne off the hook, but apart from that there's nothing we can do."

John rubbed his brow. "Mind if I sit down?"

Mattson pointed to a chair. John sat.

"There's still something I can't quite grasp," John said. "We've been shipping those spares for years, presumably. Why did AAC wait so long before doing anything about it?"

"Mattson laughed sardonically. "Because up to the present we've been doing them a favour. Their agency arrangement is with the American factory and their contract specified that only American spares were to be sold. Because of import restrictions they have never been able to get enough spares to service their customers' tractors. We've been shipping spares of British origin and, by helping to keep Grasshopper tractors in operation, we've inadvertently kept their customers happy. Recently the Americans agreed to allow them to purchase spares from England, so they decided the time had come to get moral and display some righteous indignation."

"Then surely the Grasshopper Corporation should be equally glad that spares from their north-east agents have been used to supplement the American spares in West Africa?"

Mattson sighed. "Tees-Tyne's contract is with the English factory – an autonomous concern. They are not very happy when their English customers - who are also incidentally experiencing a spares shortage – are denied parts rightly theirs. The only way I was able to get the parts from Tees-Tyne was because their manager is a friend of mine."

"I see now."

"I hoped you might. Now let me tell you something else, Graham. So far you've learned the ABC of exporting. And learned it quickly and thoroughly. But if you intend to stay with us, you've still got the other twenty-three letters to master, and it's not going to be easy. So make up your mind right now. If you thought your first five weeks were tough, just wait and see what I've got lined up for you in the future. I should imagine that the experience you gained here would enable you to find another job fairly easily. One where you can work regular City hours and be a regular City gent in bowler hat and rolled umbrella. But if you stay here you will continue to do things my way; you'll work my hours and at my speed, and there's no prospect of promotion or rapid advancement while I'm here. So think about it carefully and let me know."

"I don't have to think about it. I'll stay."

"Then let me make another point. I gather that while I've been away you've taken it upon yourself to make various procedural changes."

John blinked. "How do you know that?"

Mattson shrugged.

"Oh, I suppose the Anderson woman told you yesterday," said John.

"The Anderson woman, as you so rudely call her, has been with me four years. She was given to me as an invoice-typist with a slight knowledge of shorthand. She is now as efficient a secretary as I could wish for – only for Christ's sake don't let her know I called her a secretary, I don't want any class distinctions outside. Anyway, it doesn't matter who told me what. The point is that I've only one comment to make on your changes: if they work, that's fine. But if they don't work, if they are responsible for any sort of error in this office . . . Well, let me put it this way: I'm still waiting for you to make that one unjustifiable slip."

"That's fair enough, Mr Mattson. I'll stand by anything I do and I'll accept any blame that is rightly mine."

A grin spread slowly over Mattson's face. "Okay, Graham." His hand shot out. "Welcome to Reid-Parry Enterprises."

Christmas eve in the City of London.

By tradition the day of the great unbending. The chain of command, the usually-inflexible desert of disparity, the normally-rigid chasm of class-consciousness, the impassable, impossible expanse between company director and office boy magically yielding, fracturing, finally breaking.

The magic? Nothing but old demon drink himself.

From eleven-thirty in the morning the City offices disgorge their hordes of workers and the public houses open their doors wide in an exuberance of Christmas spirit: an exuberant anticipation of spirituous profits. God rest ye, City publicans, let nothing you dismay; for wine shall flow like water on this *your* Christmas day. And so tradition bridges the gap and, beneath the carefully hung mistletoe, slightly glassy-eyed office girls turn their heads aside with a giggle, and always fractionally too slowly, while the company director and his office boy become as one in their simultaneous advance to the ritual touching of lips.

But before all this, another tradition to be honoured. The exchange of goodwill in the form of the bonus cheque.

John Graham, standing to attention in Reid's office for this sophisticated version of the army pay parade, gratefully accepted the sealed envelope, gravely shook the hands of Reid and Parry, cordially reciprocated their Christmas greetings, and took his leave. He went directly to the washroom and locked himself in a closet, fervid fingers ripping at the envelope in anxious enquiry. Would it be the equivalent of one or – dare he hope? – two weeks salary?

He removed the cheque and pay slip and read them. His hands trembled, his brain went numb. The cheque was for a sum slightly more than one hundred and twelve pounds. The pay slip showed a bonus figure of one hundred and fifty pounds and a deduction for tax. There must be some mistake. They must have confused his envelope with another. He studied all three pieces of paper carefully. The envelope, the pay slip, the cheque: all three of them bore his name in Parry's meticulous hand. He gulped. He took advantage of the toilet bowl's proximity. He returned to his office.

"Oh Miss Anderson, would you please go over to Mr Reid's office."

He sank weakly into his chair, scarcely aware of Miss Anderson's stiff progress from her desk to the door, hardly aware of Pat Rogers's uneasy question.

"Mr Graham." He raised his eyes. "I asked if you were feeling all right."

"Yes, thank you, Pat. I'm fine." He grinned. "Happy Christmas."

Relief showed on her face. "For a moment I thought you might have been given the sack."

"On Christmas eve? In a Christian community? You've been reading too much Dickens, Miss Rogers," he accused.

She laughed. "Are you coming to the Stirling Castle later?"

"I'll be there, Pat. Never fear. And watch out for the mistletoe."

"Not me, Mr Graham." She opened a desk drawer and removed a sprig of green with white berries. "I carry my own supply. You're the one who will have to watch out."

"How about a quick practice session?" He pretended to get out of his chair.

She giggled. "Not while Mr Mattson is here."

"Mattson? When did he get back?"

"While you were with Mr Reid."

He walked over to the inner office door and raised his hand to knock on it.

"Watch yourself in there," cautioned Pat Rogers. "He's been out drinking with someone. He was walking a chalk line all the way through the office, trying to appear normal."

"Where did he get the drink at this time of the morning?"

"I imagine he has his sources. Actually, though, I think he had it in someone's office."

John tapped on the door and walked in. Mattson was sprawled in his chair, a vacuous smile on his face, a corona-corona in his mouth, feet crossed on desktop.

"Come in, Graham." He reached into his top pocket and threw something at John. "Have a cigar."

John caught the cigar and stuffed it into his own pocket.

"Feeling pretty good, Graham."

"I can see that, Mr Mattson."

"Not me, Graham. You. Full of Christmas cheer. On top of the world. You, Graham. Me too, of course. But you particularly. Know why? I'll tell you why . . ."

A knock on the door and regal entry of Patricia Anderson. A glance at John. Nose-twitching disdain. A radiant beam at Mattson. Eye-sparkling admiration. Mattson's legs slid off the desk.

"I'd like to thank you, Mr Mattson. And to wish you a happy Christmas."

"Well, thank *you*, Patricia. It was no more than you deserve." There was a quiet deliberation to his speech; a conscious effort to keep the sibilants from slurring. "But aren't you coming out to celebrate?"

"I don't know, Mr Mattson." A glance at John. "I hadn't thought . . ."

"Nonsense, Patricia. We must shel-celebrate as always. All of us. You and Miss Rogers go on down to the Stirling Castle. Most of the timber people are already there. Mr Graham and I will join you shortly."

"All right, Mr Mattson." She left the office.

"Splendid woman that, Graham. Fine shec-secretary. But never tell her I think of her as a secretary. No clash dish – class distinctions in *my* office, eh? Come over here, Graham." He pointed to a chair by the side of his desk. "Then I shan't have to shout."

John sat down by Mattson's side and Mattson leaned towards him collusively. John reeled slightly under the dual impact of cigar smoke and whiskey fumes.

"I know why you're happy, Graham. Thanks to me, that's why. I talked the Board into giving you a pretty nice bonus, eh?"

"*You* did that, Mr Mattson?"

"Call me Matt, Graham. Christmastide and all that." He leaned further forward and tapped John's chest with a brown forefinger. "Yes. Didn't expect that of the old bastard, did you? Well, I hope you're going to be worth it, Graham. Because you're going to have to earn it. And your salary increase."

"Salary increase?"

"Didn't Reid tell you?"

"No, Mr Mattson."

"Matt, Graham . . . Matt."

"Er no, Matt."

Mattson chuckled. "Salary increase to match your promotion, Graham."

"Promotion . . . er . . . Matt?"

"Office Manager, Graham, from first Jan. Hundred a year rise to mark the position."

"Office Manager?"

"Graham, you're beginning to sound like an interrogation mark. I expect Parry or Reid will give you the glad tidings after Christmas. I'm jumping the gun, so mum'sh the word, eh?"

"Yes, Matt. But I don't understand how I can become Office Manager. You're not leaving, are you?"

"Leaving?" He guffawed and the discharge of stale breath overwhelmed John. "What gave you that crazy idea? We've both been promoted, Graham. I've been promoted to the Board."

"You're a director?"

"Graham, that's another thing I like about you. You catch on so quickly. So I'll let you into another little sh-secret. We're going places, you and I. You know, Graham, when you first came here I didn't like you. I thought you were one of those intellectual pipsqueaks whose head was bigger than his arse. A know-it-all, just because you had learned a bit about demand and supply curves and opportunity cost. That surprises you, eh? Didn't think the old bastard would know anything about economics, eh? Not quite the bloody ignoramus you took me for." He leaned further forward, trying to put an arm around John's shoulders, and almost over-balanced. John pushed him gently back into his chair. "Well, I've changed my mind about you, Graham. There's a bit of good in you somewhere and, by Christ, we're going to bring it out. It's already started coming out slowly and, as soon as you've forgotten all the rubbish you learned at 'varsity, we'll have you really learning something. Then you'll be able to train your assistant."

"Assistant?"

"Oh, God." Mattson removed his spectacles and covered his eyes with the palm of his hand. "Stop repeating everything I say with a bloody question mark at the end. An assistant, I said. You know what that is, I suppose? Someone who assists. There's going to be a lot more work from the first of next year, and we're going to need someone to relieve you of the donkey work, so that you can relieve me of some of my work, so that I can do more work. Understand?"

"I think so."

"Remember those orders I brought back from West Africa?"

"Very well. About fifty thousand pounds worth. That's why so few came in while you were away."

Mattson tapped the side of his nose and winked. "That was a little lever I used to prize old man Reid away from his money box. But it was chicken feed, Graham. What we've got to do now is to invest some of our own money in West Africa; to take on a few agencies ourselves, in our own name . . .

"Jesus! I've got an attack of verbal diarrhoea. Christmas Eve's no time to talk shop. C'mon Graham, let's go down and celebrate."

The basement of the Stirling Castle was thronged, airless, and hazy with tobacco smoke, as they pushed their way through to the Alfred Reid crowd.

"Will Reid and Parry be coming down here?" asked John.

"Doubt it," muttered Mattson, elbowing an entwined couple out of his way. "Parry may turn up for a sherry, but Reid would never manage to squeeze in here."

John laughed and forced his own way through.

"Come on, boy." An arm embraced John's shoulders. It belonged to one of the timber company's salesmen. "You're way behind. What'll you have?"

"Pint of bitter," John shouted above the din.

"Coming right up, boy."

His shoulder was released at the same moment that his arm was gripped. Pat Rogers. "You'd better have something to eat first," she counseled. "We've got some sandwiches on the table."

"Fine. Lead the way." She released his arm and he instantly grabbed her hand. "But first, what about that kiss?"

"Don't be silly." She laughed nervously and pulled her hand away.

"Miss Rogers, you are clearly all bark and no bite."

"Try me when we're alone some time."

"Miss Rogers! This is so sudden."

She giggled. "Here you are. Beef, ham, egg, or cheese. What will you have?"

"One of each."

"Pig!" She piled the sandwiches on a plate and handed it to him. Across the table Miss Anderson was struggling, in very ladylike fashion, to escape the clutches of another timber salesman rather the worse for drink. She was trying to catch the eye of Mattson, but that somewhat tipsy gentleman was himself engaged in gymnastics with the timber company's receptionist who, in even more ladylike manner, was not struggling at all.

John leaned over the table and offered his hand to the salesman. "Merry Christmas, George."

"And all the best to you, John."

An arm was withdrawn from Miss Anderson's back and a hand outstretched. With a quick look of gratitude at John she slid along the bench and stood up.

"I say," George called out in dismay. "Where are you off to?"

"Don't worry, George," said John, "there's lots more where that came from."

"George's left eye closed in a wink. "Very true, John," he said sagely.

A beer was thrust into John's hand.

"Cheers, mate."

John struggled to balance beer and half a ham sandwich in one hand,

and the plate in the other. "Cheers," he said, somehow managing to raise the glass to his lips.

"Here. Let me take that." Pat Rogers took the plate of sandwiches from his hand and put it on the table. "But keep an eye on it, or it'll vanish."

"Thanks, Pat."

Miss Anderson approached, sipping daintily at a gin-and-tonic. "Thank you for your help, Mr Graham."

"Call me John, Patricia," he said, taking a leaf out of Mattson's book. "Christmastide and all that."

She stared at him as if trying to decide that he might not be wholly obnoxious. Evidently undecided, she said nothing, but took another sip of her drink.

The afternoon swept on in a whirl of exchanged greetings, a fluster of vanished rounds, a flurry of changing faces. People left and others arrived. Parry dropped in for a quick sherry and left immediately afterwards. There was a crazy kaleidoscopic effect to the proceedings.

Mattson's face appeared before him. Their noses were almost touching. "Know something, John? When you first came to us I didn't like you."

"I know, Matt. I didn't like you either."

"Buddies now, eh?"

"Buddies, old buddy. Matt."

Mattson's arm was flung around his neck. "What'll you have, old buddy?

"Another bitter, Matt."

Mattson weaved away from him, then weaved back. "Know something else, old buddy? Patricia didn't like you either."

"Oh, didn't she?" said John. "We'll see about that."

He stumbled his way through a group of people by the table, to where Patricia Anderson was sitting and talking to the receptionist.

"Now then," he said, " no shop-talk at Christmas. Come here, Miss Anderson, I've something to tell you." He took her hand and pulled her to her feet.

"What is it?"

"Not here. It's too crowded." He lead her under a lamp from which hung a sprig of mistletoe. "Merry Christmas, Miss Anderson." He kissed her. She kissed him. The room began to move under his feet, like an underground train. He broke away. "Miss Anderson, you've been drinking," he accused.

"Call me Patricia," she said. "It's Christmas time."

"What about me now?" It was Pat Rogers, smiling demurely at him.

"You, Miss Rogers, are about two hours too late, or two hours too early." He frowned and swayed. She leaned against him, counter-balancing his movement. "I'm saving a special one for you, young Pat."

"Drink for you, old buddy." Mattson again, somehow succeeding in holding a brimming glass without spilling a drop. John grabbed it. "And a Christmas greeting for you, Pat." Mattson bent his long frame and planted a wet kiss on her lips. "And I'm off home now. . . if I can make it."

"I'll come along with you if I may," said Miss Anderson. "That way we may both stand a chance of making it."

"A very good idea, Miss Anderson."

"Call me Patricia."

"Christmas and all that," said John. "Bye-bye you two. Happy Christmas."

Patricia Anderson leaned forward and kissed him. "Happy Christmas, John."

They left.

"What about you, Pat?" John said. "Ready to make a move?"

"Mm-hmm."

"Well I'll see you to the station. Liverpool Street, isn't it?"

"That's right."

"Merry Christmas everybody," John called out, and they left to the chorus of reciprocated greetings.

The City was cold and damp. The clock about the London Wall Restaurant showed almost four-thirty. They hurried through the streets. Everywhere, from almost every building, came the sounds of merrymaking. Shop windows glowed with their Christmas decorations and displays. On impulse John excused himself and entered a confectioner's. He bought a large box of chocolates and handed them to Pat.

"Sorry I didn't think of anything earlier, Pat. That's for you."

"Oh, you shouldn't have. I didn't expect a Christmas present, and I haven't got one for you."

"It's not a Christmas present, Pat, it's a thank-you for the past six months."

"Thank you, John."

He was sobering up rapidly in the winter evening air. He didn't want to. He wanted the pleasant, mellow glow to continue; the feeling that he was suspended about six inches above his shoes. At Liverpool Street he said, "What time's your train?"

She glanced at the departure board. "There's one in about fifteen minutes."

"Then we've time for a quickie." He led her into the crowded station buffet and, by discarding any pretence at good manners and ignoring hurt feelings and loud complaints, forced his way to the bar and ordered a beer and a gin-and-tonic.

They drank in silence and left the buffet. The drink had restored his earlier mood.

"Where to you have to go?" he asked.

"Seven Sisters," she said. "Why don't you come along?" She lowered her eyes. "There's no one at home."

He didn't hesitate. "Delighted."

He purchased a ticket and they found the train waiting at the platform. It was a local train, without corridors, fairly empty, and they had no trouble getting a compartment to themselves. He took a corner seat, opposite Pat, and she immediately go up and sat beside him as he knew she would. He wanted it that way. As far as he was able to think logically – and that was not very far – he knew that whatever he did this evening, a day of reckoning would arrive. Therefore he wanted to appear blameless, at least in Pat's eyes. Let *her* continue to make the suggestions. Let *her* make all the advances. Let *her* take the initiative. That way he would have nothing with which to rebuke himself afterwards and – even more important – Pat would not feel she had any real claim on him. He would be able to state afterwards – quite credibly, should she become in any way difficult – that he had not known what he was doing, that he had been well and truly under the influence, and that he was not even aware he had done anything.

The train juddered off. Pat's head slipped onto his shoulder. He put an arm around her. Now it begins, he thought. This was the way to handle it. Gently and easily . . . easily and gently . . . it was clear what she wanted . . . what she wanted was . . . what she wanted . . .

"John! John, you're falling asleep."

"Wha. . . what?" He forced his eyes open, found the strain too great and closed them again. "No, I'm not," he said, "I've just got my eyes closed."

The train shuddered to a halt. Somewhere in his head a whistle blew and the jogging motion began again.

"Aren't you going to kiss me now?" she whispered.

"Mmmm."

He turned slightly in the seat, trying to open his eyes, finding the effort impossible. It felt as though she were all over him, her lips plastered firmly to his. Instinctively his mouth moved, opening, and she responded with bewildering swiftness. He turned round further in the seat, pushing his hand out in an attempt to brace himself against the swaying, dizzying motion of his body. His hand encountered bare flesh. It felt nice. Dimly, half-consciously, he was aware of the train stopping and starting again, while their kiss continued. His fingers explored the flesh beneath them, gingerly, almost disinterestedly. It was her thigh, he decided. Plump and warm. Megan's thigh must be something like this. Not Julie's. Julie's thighs were smoother, longer, firmer. Julie was altogether a different . . . a different . . . a . . . Julie! They were supposed to be travelling together to Cheltenham this evening. He had arranged to meet her at Paddington Station at eight-thirty. He gasped and sat up, forcing their bodies apart.

"John! What's the matter?"

"Nothing, Pat." He forced his brain to function. "But we shouldn't be doing this. It's not right."

"Don't be silly." She smiled and leaned towards him. Her teeth had lipstick on them. "If you're thinking I might have had too much to drink . . . don't worry. I know exactly what I'm doing."

"No, Pat." He held her insinuating body away from him. "You'll only regret it tomorrow."

"Nonsense." She continued smiling, trying to make the smile seductive.

The train drew into another station. He glanced out of the window. Rectory Road. He leaped from the seat and lowered the window all in one motion. His fingers groped for the handle.

"It's not nonsense. You'll thank me for this in the morning."

He jumped onto the platform and slammed the door shut as the train moved slowly off. Through the window he caught a glimpse of her face, moving with surprise and disappointment and pain. And then she was gone.

CHAPTER TWELVE

"Well, chum, it's almost the end of another year."

Norman shook the cocktail shaker with an up-and-down motion of his wrists, listening appreciatively to the chinking of the ice.

"What exactly as you supposed to be making, Norm? That is, if I may be so bold as to ask."

"To tell you the truth, chum, I don't really know. Megan decided she would like some cocktails served at this party of hers tonight and she promptly elected me head mixer and shaker. I thought I ought to get some practice in first."

"Oh no, you don't," John protested. "Not on me you don't."

"Now then, man, where's your sense of adventure? Where's the spirit that made Britain great? It's all in the cause of science, you know."

"So is vivisection, but I don't propose to make myself a guinea pig. Anyway, what have you put in there?"

Norman scratched his head. "To be perfectly honest, I can't remember. Be a sport now, Johnny-boy, and try a glass. I promise you, if it has any adverse effect, I'll put you promptly and painlessly out of your misery."

John groaned. "Oh, you steaming nit. If you don't know what's in it, how are you going to repeat it this evening?"

"Ah yes," Norman conceded, "you have a point there. But look you, John, if you don't try it and give me your opinion, I'll be afraid to repeat it this evening."

"Aaahhh . . . all right. But only if you join me in a glass."

"Delighted, dear chap, delighted."

Norman swiftly uncapped the shaker and filled two shallow cocktail glasses. The liquid came out colourless and cold, frosting the glasses.

Norman raised his glass, a faint smile playing around his lips.

"Iechyd da!"

"Iechyd da.!"

John took a careful sip and rolled the liquid around his tongue. He looked at Norman in surprise, then produced a careful frown. "Not bad," he said. "Not bad at all. If I might hazard a guess I would say roughly equal amounts of *aqua tapata*, *chateau-la-pompe*, *eau du robinet* and . . ." he took another sip, ". . . undoubtedly tap water. Now do you mind telling me what you're doing with a cocktail shaker full of iced water."

"Not at all, dear fathead. Megan has the recipe and the ingredients for the cocktail. I'm merely trying to perfect my shaking technique."

"Saints preserve us," John moaned. "And the idiotic expression goes with the shaking, does it?"

"Now you've hurt my feelings."

"Impossible. Who's going to be at this party tonight?"

"Well, there'll be you and me. Megan, naturally. Julie. You are taking Julie, aren't you?"

"Of course." John looked at his watch. "I'll have to leave in a few minutes to pick her up."

"So . . . that makes four of us already. I don't know who else will be there. Friends of Megan I suppose. And friends of Megan's friends. And friends of theirs. You know how these parties are."

"Yes. What about her parents?"

"Oh, they'll be seeing the New Year in at the Savoy as usual. The pater naturally expected me to take his daughter there as well, but I said to him, 'Sir,' I said, 'on the meagre pittance you casually dispense for my unworthy efforts on your behalf, I can't even afford to take your scrumptiously corrupt and dissolute daughter to Joe's Eats Stand at the eastern end of the Old Kent Road. And that, as you are undoubtedly aware, is the poorer end.'"

"Really?" John grinned. "And what did he say to that?"

"He didn't like the aspersion very much, of course. 'My dear Williams' he retorted. 'Sir?' I said. 'Williams,' said he, 'if you don't appreciate our undeniable generosity, you should join Reid-Parry Enterprises Limited, where salaries are doubled every six months, where promotions are sprinkled like confetti, and where gents who assist generals to manage, or who manage to assist generals, eventually end up managing to direct assistants, or conversely and otherwisely, directly assisting managers. In general, that is. Witness your friend Graham.'

"Naturally I could not allow such scurrilous and scandalous ignorance to pass without comment. 'Sir,' I said, 'my friend Graham suffers the single unfortunate disadvantage of being unable to knock it off with his boss's daughter. In that respect, Sir, and begging y'r honour's pardon, you are of far more liberal disposition than Mr Reid, or Mr Parry, or, for that matter, any of their assistants, managers, generals, or non-coms. And for that, Sir, from the bottom of me 'eart, Sir, I thank you.'

"And speaking of parents, how did you make out with Julie's over Christmas?"

"Fine," said John. "A very sweet couple. She also has a delightful young brother, who nearly decapitated me with a boomerang he was given for Christmas, and two charming twin sisters whom I promised to seduce for their twentieth birthday in approximately nine years time. Why the sudden interest in Julie's family?"

"Oh . . . nothing really. It's just nice to know you hit it off with your prospective in-laws."

"Nuts!" John hurled a newspaper at his friend. "The day I marry Julie I'll personally treat you and Megan to an evening at the Savoy."

"Then why, me old darling, are you stringing the girl along?" Norman looked serious. Serious, that is, for Norman.

John flushed. "Because it suits me. All right?"

"All right with me, chum. You know me."

"Okay." John got up. "If you've got no more asinine questions I'll push off. See you at Megan's."

"Right." Norman resumed his shaking.

It was a large house adjoining Primrose Hill.

In answer to their ring the door was opened by Megan herself

"Julia. John." She kissed them both quickly on the cheek. "I'd just about given you up. What kept you?"

Julie looked at John and, with a touch of embarrassment, said, "It was my fault I suppose. Everything went wrong. I bust a suspender and . . ."

"Never mind, my dears," Megan interposed. "You're here now. Let me take your coats. You'll forgive me if I don't take you round and introduce you to everyone, but there are so many people here now and I don't seem to know half of them. Just wander around and make yourself at home. The party's spread out on this floor and the next. You can go where you like. The bar's the second room on the left and dancing is upstairs – you can hear the music. Just one thing: at five to twelve me must all get together in the ground floor front room. Go on now, enjoy yourselves."

She went upstairs with their coats and Julie and John wandered towards the bar room.

"It was all your fault," Julie hissed. "I told you we'd be late."

"It's not important." He grinned. "I liked that ad lib about the suspender belt breaking though."

"Oh!"

The bar was located in the corner of the room. Behind it was Norman, dispensing drinks, jokes and crackpot philosophy.

"My friend," he said as they approached. "And you, too, John. Name your poison."

"Hello, Norman," said Julie.

"Where's the cocktail shaker?" asked John.

Norman pulled a face. "It was not an outstanding success," he admitted. Incidentally, where were you two? Uh, never mind, you don't have to answer that."

"I'll have a scotch and soda," said John.

"Make mine a gin and Dubonnet," said Julia.

Norman mixed the drinks. "By the way, John, someone's been looking for you. One of the friends of friends."

"Oh? Any idea who it was?"

Norman looked around the room. "He's not here now. Perhaps he's upstairs dancing. Or in the television room, seeing how they bring in the New Year in Tsien-Tsin." He frowned. "Or is that the other side of the International Date Line?"

"Wherever it is, it won't be the same time as here, will it?" said Julie.

"Did you catch his name?" asked John.

"Burman, or Barman. No, that's me, isn't it. Or Bechstein. Something grand like that." He laughed at his own joke. "Short dark fellow, with glasses."

John considered the description. It didn't mean much to him. He suddenly felt excited. "Couldn't have been Bernstein, by any chance?"

"That's the fellow. Give the man another banana."

"Good God," said John.

"What is it?" asked Julia.

"And old army friend," John explained. "Haven't seen or heard of him since 1946 in Calais. The glasses fooled me for a moment. He didn't wear them when I knew him. Come on, love, let's see if we can find him."

They looked in the front room. The television set was playing to a non-existent audience. They climbed the stairs, heading towards the strains of a record player and shuffling feet. The room allotted to the dancing was enormous. It had been formed by knocking down the intervening wall between two rooms, each of which had been large by ordinary standards. Despite its size the room was jam-packed.

"You'll have trouble seeing him here, Julie said.

"No I won't," John contradicted. "There he is!"

"Which one?"

"There. A bit left of centre. Dancing with the short, plump brunette."

"Oh yes, I see. With hair down to waist level."

"No. He's got a crew cut."

"Idiot. Shall we wait for the dance to finish?"

"Might never find him again. Come on, let's dance over to them, if we can force a passage." He put their glasses down and took her in his arms.

It was less a dance than an excited, hopping incursion into every gap they could spot or make, but eventually they ended up behind Bernstein. John tapped him on the shoulder. "Hello, Bernie."

Raymond Bernstein turned his head. His wide mouth spread wider in a delighted grin. "John! It is you, then. I couldn't believe it. I was sure it would be a different John Graham."

They clasped hands.

"The very same John Graham," John said. "And this is Julie Grant. Raymond Bernstein."

Raymond pushed his partner forward. "And I'd like you to meet Ruth. Mrs Bernstein, that is."

They were being jogged to-and-fro by the shuffling, rhythmically pressing throng.

"Can't we get out of here?" Raymond said.

"Good idea. The television room's deserted."

Raymond looked at his watch. "And it won't start filling up for at least an hour. Come on."

They pulled three armchairs into an arc and sat facing each other, with Ruth Bernstein on a pouffe at her husband's feet. For a few minutes the men were silent, grinning at each other in an incredulous and slightly imbecile fashion.

"Are you a Canadian, Mr Bernstein?" Julie asked.

"Ray, please."

"Ray," she agreed.

"No, why?"

"Well, John said you two were in the army together and . . ."

"That's right," John broke in. "You've got a trace of American accent now, Bernie. Been seeing too many Westerns?"

Bernstein chuckled and rumpled his wife's hair. "Her influence," he said. "She's a colonial."

"Colonial, indeed." His wife snorted.

"You're the Canadian then, are you, Mrs Bernstein?" Julie asked.

"American," she corrected. "From New York. And the name's Ruth."

John said, "You've been in the States then, Bernie."

"I'm living there, John. Been there . . . how long is it exactly, honey?"

"Two years and eleven months," his wife said.

"Well, what are you doing there? And what are you doing here? And how did you know I would be here?"

"Hey! Hold it! One question at a time. Let's see now . . . Question one: I'm working for a news syndicate. Question two: we're in London on vacation. Question three: I didn't know you would be here. At least, I didn't know it would be *you* who would be here, if you follow me. Ruth and Megan were at King's College together. That's when I met Ruth. And, when we got to London, and they were talking to each other, Megan mentioned her boy friend and the guy he was living with. From what she said, it seemed to figure that you'd be the same John Graham I knew, but I couldn't be sure."

"Hell, Bernie, it's a small world, if I may coin a phrase."

Julie reached across and took John's glass. "Ruth, Ray, you're not drinking. Can I get you something?"

"I'll come with you," Ruth said, "and we'll have a drink alone first. I can sense a bubble of man-talk just itching to burst." She pushed herself upright, a small, plump bundle of barely concealed energy.

"Bring me a scotch on the rocks," Raymond said.

"And I'll have the same again, Julie."

Raymond stretched across and slapped John's thigh. "Hell, boy, I still can't believe it's you. What have you been doing with yourself? I gather from Megan that you got to LSE after all."

"That's right. That's where I met up with Norman."

"So I heard. Got your degree okay, huh?"

John screwed his face up. "Just a pass, Bernie. Spent too much time of extra-mural activities, I guess."

Raymond guffawed. "Same old John. Actually I heard about those activities from our hostess. You and her boy friend – Norman – together, huh?"

John snorted. "That woman talks too much. And as for her precious Norman, he was ten times worse than me and ended up with an upper second."

"There are some people like that, John. Drop them in a sewer and they'll come up smelling of violets."

"That's Norman described all right."

"So . . . the more it changes, eh? I still recall your trip to Paris in forty-six."

This would be a good time to clear up that little misunderstanding,

John thought. But, hell, four years had passed and there was no point in raking over cold ashes.

"I'm a bit more conventional in my approach these days," John said.

Raymond nodded towards the door. "That seems a pretty swell girl you've got there. Is it serious?"

"Uh-uh."

"Okay, boy, you know me. No questions, no pack drill."

"The same old understanding Bernie. I'm sorry we lost touch like that."

Raymond shrugged. "You were going through a pretty tough time as I recall. When your letters stopped I figured you had a reason and would write again when you were good and ready. Later I got caught up in things myself and, when Ruth went back to the States I followed her and we got married. I did twelve months tutorials at Columbia U and then got this job with WSNS – that's Western Syndicated News Service."

"I don't quite follow. I thought you said Megan and Ruth were at college together."

"Yeah. But Ruth's final year was Megan's first year."

"Oh."

"And what are you doing now, John?"

John drew a card out of his wallet and handed it to Bernstein. "I'm office manager for these people. We're export merchants."

Raymond studied the card. "Like it?"

"It's all right. Keeps me on my toes, and the pay's good. I don't know how long I'll remain there, but I want to stay in commerce and I like the export business. Keep the card. You've got my phone number there."

Ruth and Julie returned with the drinks.

"We'd better move these chairs out of the way," Ruth said. "There's sure going to be an influx into this room in a minute."

And true enough, people were already coming in on the heels of the two women. Outside the door John could hear Megan's musical tones urging her guests into the room. Then she came in herself.

"Who turned the television off?" she shrieked. She rushed over and turned it on again. "It'll be midnight soon."

The room was rapidly filling up. John and Julie, Raymond and Ruth, were pushed into a corner and squeezed together by the press of guests. Many more of them were in the entrance hall, unable to gain access to the front room. The television came on and someone switched the overhead light out. The room was lit by one table lamp, the television screen, and the hall light flooding through the open doorway. From the television came the sound of community singing. John could not see the screen, but imagined it would be showing the crowds in Piccadilly Circus or Trafalgar Square. There was an unceasing hubbub of talk all around him and it was becoming increasingly difficult to draw a normal breath.

Suddenly the singing stopped and the first chimes of Big Ben announced the arrival of midnight. Simultaneously the sounds in the room died out and it was as if their collective breath was being held in anticipation of the first stroke of twelve.

Bong!

"Happy New Year. Happy New Year." The shouts echoed around the room. In millions of homes, in hundreds of thousands of restaurants and hotels and night clubs, in streets, in church halls, on boats, all over the country, the ritual greeting was now being exchanged. John felt his fingers and toes tingling. It never failed to move him.

He lowered his head to Julie's. "Happy New Year, darling."

"Happy New Year, dearest."

The kissed; a sweet, warm, lingering kiss, devoid of passion, filled with tenderness and closeness and sentimental response to the occasion. For an instant John had the absurd wish that this moment might last forever; that life might consist of nothing more than this wonderfully intimate, yet curiously asexual feeling of togetherness. It was as if they were sharing a conjoint happiness which, once broken, might never be recaptured, might indeed end in disaster. Then they drew apart.

"Happy New Year, Bernie."

"Happy New Year, John."

They clasped hands. A pulsation of friendship, a reaffirmation of brotherhood passed between them. What a wonderful moment for a reunion of this sort, John thought.

"Happy New Year, John."

"Happy New Year, Ruth."

They kissed. A friendly, moist touching of lips. John's heart went out in empathetic love of his old friend's wife.

Then all four of them were parted as the crowd swirled around them, drawing them away from the wall, mixing them up in an ever-changing pattern of handshakes and kissed cheeks and New Year's greetings.

John found himself out in the hall and, still greeting the strangers about him, gradually wormed his way to the fringes of the crowd. he drew a deep breath.

A hand clasped his arm, worked its way down to his hand. "Happy

New Year, boyo."

"Happy New Year, Norman."

They stood there grinning at each other like a pair of mischievous schoolboys.

"This is going to be a great year, Johnny-boy."

"They're all going to be great years, Norm. The world is our oyster, as you once said."

"That's it, boyo. There's nothing we can't do."

"*Iechyd da bob Cymro*."

"*Twll dyn bob Saess*."

"Made your new year's resolutions yet, Norm?"

"Yup. Gonna set a new record this year, chum."

"Well you can add another resolution for me."

"Oh?"

"You can ration yourself to two chums, two boyos, and two Johnny-boys a day. And in return I'll allow you two boy-bachs when Megan isn't around."

"Grrr. Be seeing you, boy-bach." Norman elbowed his way into the crowd.

John raised himself on tiptoe, trying to spot Julie or Raymond in the throng, but they were not to be seen. He felt in his pocket for a pack of cigarettes, pulled it out and opened it. Empty. There was another packet in his coat pocket. Where had Megan put his coat?

He climbed the stairs. On the first floor, the large room in which they had been dancing and a study-cum-library also constructed out of two rooms. No coats.

He continued to the second floor. Four doors, one of them open, revealing a lighted double bedroom. Black and white decor and regency curtains. Twin beds piled high with clothing. God, he would never find his coat in that jumble. He'd better lift some cigarettes from the bar and fill his empty packet. He started to turn –

"Guess who?" Two hands came over his shoulders from behind and covered his eyes.

"A certain little Welsh tease," he replied. He turned round and faced her.

"You haven't wished me a happy new year yet, John." She pouted.

"I always save the best things for last." He placed his hands on her shoulders.

"Not here, John." She took one of his hands. "Let's do this New Year's greeting in style."

She led him into the facing room and shut the door. He had a quick glimpse of pink coverlet on a bed before the door closed. Then darkness.

Absolute quiet except for the whisper of their breathing. He put out his hands and pulled her to him. She came into his arms with a little sigh, straining against him, her mouth open before their lips touched. Her kiss seemed destined to last forever, and his senses reeled as their bodies swayed together. He felt the edge of the bed pressing into the back of his knees and fell backwards, sitting on the bed, breaking their embrace.

"Heady stuff, that," he quipped. "You should bottle it and sell it in the off-licences. You'd make a fortune."

She did not reply. He heard a metallic sound in the dark; a grating, sliding noise, then a rustling.

"What are you doing?" he whispered.

She gave a little laugh and sat next to him on the bed, pushing his body prone, pressing herself against him. His hands reached out and touched the bare flesh of her back, the single strap of her bra.

"Megan, we can't do this."

"What's to stop us?"

Christ, she was teasing him again. But it was different now; he could not – dare not – respond. She was Norman's girl. They were going to get married. Norman was his best friend.

"Your guests will be looking for you."

"Let them look."

A whisper of soft, deep-throated chuckle and their lips were together again. He could feel himself sinking, giving in to that languour from which there was no return. Her hand removed his from her back and there was a crisp snap. Then she was wriggling her body to the accompaniment of further rustling sounds. All the time her lips and tongue played with his.

She reached for his hand again; placed it between her thighs.

He gasped. "Megan, you don't really want to do this. We must stop."

He said it and didn't mean it, and he knew that she knew he didn't mean it. But it was wrong. It was nasty. It was an act of treachery. To Norman and to Julie.

"I told you once that I still have some living to do." That golden laughter, fresh as a mountain stream, tumbled from her throat. "Well, let's live a little." Her hands reached down to his belt, unfastened it, unzipped his trousers, reached inside . . .

"Aaahhh . . . Megan . . ."

"Happy New Year, John." She bent down and he felt her lips enfolding him.

He ceased his mental resistance and succumbed. And he did it with a curious feeling of relief, as though it had been inevitable from the very start, that beginning so long ago, so far away. It was fated to happen; if not in this way, then in some similar way; if not with her, then with someone else. And it was necessary. He had to plumb the depths, to sink so low that no further downward movement was possible. He had to bury himself in the mire of self-disgust, the grime of self-debasement, until he was finally, thoroughly sickened. Only then would he be able to rise again to the surface.

At the very last, as his orgasm exploded, it was as if something had abruptly come to an end, or perhaps something had just begun. And he knew it was more than merely and old and a new year.

PART THREE

A kaleidoscope of faces and places; an ever-changing pattern of thoughts and actions and events; a tourbillon, rushing and gyrating and encircling, taunting and teasing and withdrawing; an intermingling and a juxtaposing of memories and voices; a ghastly retributional rhythm.

I discovered I was mouthing soundlessly:

O Lord I pray Thee
Grant this day
I count my dead
Another way.

My dead. If only they were. If only they would stay buried. If only the torment, the torture, the ceaselessly racking reminiscence would grind to a halt. I didn't want it this way. I had changed. I had left that other self in the bottomless chasm of nemesis. Why wouldn't it remain there?

That tract I had once been handed at a revivalist meeting in Wales. How had it started? To will is present with me, but how to perform that which is good I find not. Oh they were great for revivalism in Wales. But religion wasn't the answer. Morality had to come from within, not be imposed from outside. Law was not morality, even though it might be moral. And religious laws were no different from any other. They operated by fear. Fear of the consequences of disobedience. Civil disobedience, or moral disobedience, what was the difference? To do the right thing was important – of course it was important! – but how much more important to do the right thing because you knew it to be right, because you wanted to do it, and not just because you were told you ought to do it.

And I wanted to. Dear God, didn't I want to? What was stopping me? What was getting in the way?

Shouts from the street interrupted my thoughts. I glanced at the open windows across which the wooden louvered shutters had been drawn. Outside it was still raining, but the rain had done nothing to relieve the August heat. Damn the rain, I thought. And damn the heat. But most of all, damn me, myself, for trying to attribute my annoyance to anything but my own selfish weakness.

Beside me she had drifted into a shallow, contented slumber. Damn, damn, damn, I couldn't go on this way. The calming effect of a night's sleep would bring no solution, would change nothing. There was no solution. I knew that now. For the facts were ineradicable, incontrovertible, and neither a night, nor a week, nor a year would change them. I had spent my life digging one pit after another to fall into. But this last pit . . . when had I dug that? I had been so careful, so very careful. I had tried so hard to avoid this involvement. It had been so important to have just one thing, one person, one relationship, to which I could point and say: *This at least I have not sullied. This at least is good and clean and right.* And now. . .? The irony of it caught in my throat. Dame Fate, determined to have the last laugh. She must have started chuckling that day when the phone rang in the office . . .

CHAPTER THIRTEEN

"Call for you, Mr Graham."

"Who is it, Sally?"

"I'm not sure. I think it may be Dumard. It's from Paris."

"Well put it through right away."

There was a click on the line.

"John?" A woman's voice.

"Yes. Who is that?"

"Yvette."

"Yvette! How wonderful. What are you doing in Paris? How are you?"

"John . . . I'm coming to London. I'm at Orly Airport. My plane leaves in thirty minutes. Can you meet me at London Airport?"

"Of course. But . . . I don't understand. Are you alone?"

"Yes."

"Have you booked a hotel room?"

"No . . . I. . . I. . ."

"Yvette, you sound funny. Is something wrong?"

"You . . . it . . . it's. . ." He could hear the tears in her voice. "I'll tell you all about it when I get there. You will meet me, won't you?"

"Don't worry, Yvette, I'll be there. And I'll see to a hotel for you. How long will you be staying?"

"I don't know . . . I . . . goodbye, John."

The line went dead. He replaced the receiver with a puzzled frown. Across the room Mattson was slumped in his chair, his eyes half-closed, a look of bored disinterest on his face; it was his habitual attitude these days. He had spent the whole lunch period drinking, John imagined. That too had become normal. How was it possible for a man to have changed so much in four years? Whenever John questioned him, he had one answer, always the same cryptic answer, always uttered in the same listless tone: "The buggers are beating me, John . . . they're beating me."

He got Sally Carter back on the phone.

"Sally, would you please ring round the hotels. The ones on our second list. Try and book a single room with bath, for a Miss Yvette Beaumont from France. I don't know how long she'll be staying, but I imagine it will be at least two nights from tonight. And do it immediately Sally, please."

He turned to Mattson.

"I'd like to leave a bit earlier, Matt. Is that okay?"

A flicker of interest in the bloodshot eyes behind the frameless spectacles and then that withdrawal again, a return to defeated lethargy.

"Do what you like."

"Mitchell has everything in hand. Patricia has a few letters of mine which she can sign for me if you don't feel like signing them yourself. But there are some bills of lading which need . . ."

Mattson cut him off. "Don't go on, John. I'm quite sure you have it all under control."

John felt like making an angry retort, but forced himself to remain silent. What was the use anyway? One might as well try to pick a quarrel with a corpse.

"Okay, Matt. I'll push off then."

No reply; no comment; no reaction.

John tidied his desk and went into the outer office. George Mitchell was speaking on the telephone. He inclined his head and looked at John expectantly. John, with a slight flutter of his hand, let him know he was not needed. He walked over to the two women.

"I'm leaving now. Sign my letters for me Patricia."

She looked towards the inner door, her eyebrows raised in silent enquiry. He shook his head and a momentary expression of anguish appeared on her face. The change in Mattson had hit her hardest of all.

"Mitchell can check anything you're not sure of, Sally," he said to the other girl. "Have you been able to fix that hotel room?"

"Yes, Mr Graham. I've booked her into the Cumberland."

"Fine. Thank you, Sally." He looked across at Mitchell still on the phone, showing no sign of terminating what sounded like a particularly trivial conversation. "Tell Mitchell I've left and shan't be back. He can take the bills of lading to Mr Mattson for signature, or hold them for me to sign tomorrow."

She gave him a quick smile. A big-boned, clumsy girl, with owlish bespectacled eyes, acned complexion, and a fixed, shallow smile, she nonetheless did her work efficiently enough, and with Sally Carter at least there was no risk of a repetition of the embarrassment that had developed with Pat Rogers. For the best part of four months following Pat's frustrated Christmas-time attempt at seduction (*her attempt, or his*?) the atmosphere in the office had been unbearably tense. She must have felt debased, he had decided, degraded by his seeming rejection, and there was nothing he could say which would not have made her feel worse. So she left. And Sally Carter came. And Patricia Anderson remained. And George Mitchell arrived and survived, occupying Johns previous place in the outer office, while John now shared Mattson's office, the corner desk having been replaced. And for three years the company had performed with professional efficiency. Except, of course, for Mattson.

He slipped into his raincoat and went out into the April drizzle, bending his head forward against the windswept rain as he walked to the bombed side where he had parked his Ford Anglia that morning. He unlocked the car door, swiftly removed the raincoat and threw it on the back seat, then threw himself into the driving seat and slammed the door shut. He brushed at a few drops of rain on his trousers and inserted the key into the ignition lock. Let it start please, he prayed silently. He had no wish to fiddle with a cranking handle in this weather, but the battery had been playing up lately. He pulled at the starter and the engine managed a slight, stuttering cough. He gave it some more choke and tried again, holding his breath anxiously. This time the engine fired, caught, and chugged away merrily. He released his breath with a grin and drove off.

Life had been good to him. Who would have dreamt, four years ago when he left college, that he would have gone so far, so quickly? And this was the most recent symbol of his success. Not that it was especially grand: a seven-year old model with tell-tale rust under the doors and around the windows, chrome-work requiring considerable effort with wax and rag to reflect even a modest, pitted shine. But it was all his, purchased outright with his last Christmas bonus – and a few pounds over for gifts.

And his salary; ninc hundrcd pounds now. Sufficicnt for him to rctain the flat at Gilling Court despite Norman's departure and the recent pound-a-week rise in rent.

Yes, life was good. Good enough for him to be able to count his blessings for a change without being overpowered by the ever-recurrent unease of self-doubt.

He drove through Islington, Holloway, Highgate and Hampstead Garden Suburb to the North Circular Road, avoiding the Central London traffic. The car chuffed happily onward at its maximum fifty-five miles an hour along the derestricted ring road. Wouldn't Yvette be surprised at being met in this affluent style! He hadn't yet got around to writing and telling her about it. He owed her a letter, too. How long had it been now? Months! He had sent a Christmas card to Menton and another to

Claude in Paris, and had received New Years' cards from each of them. And he had not written since. He felt a twinge of shame. He hadn't been that busy either, apart from the driving lessons in February.

And now Yvette was on her way to London. She'd probably be crossing the Channel at this moment. He stopped at the Chiswick roundabout and waited for a break in the traffic, then cut in and turned into the Great West Road. Why was she coming to London so suddenly, so unexpectedly? He should feel guilty about her, he supposed. He had promised to go back to see her before too long, and that had been four years ago, and he hadn't seen her since. He worked on the feeling, worrying at it, nagging it, but the guilt would not come. All said and done, when the Beaumonts had bought that hotel in Menton, she must have known it would be difficult for him to raise the fare.

His first summer with Reid-Parry he hadn't had a holiday at all, had he? Not a *real* holiday. He had been too busy. There had been too much work to be done. He had merely taken a number of long week-ends with the continual threat of immediate recall to the office, having to telephone Mattson every day to provide answers to any of Matt's questions after he had opened the daily mail. In his second year there had been that enjoyable foursome in Cornwall with Megan and Norman and Julie, driving there in the Standard Eight which had been Megan's twenty-fourth birthday present from proud papa, adman-de-luxe. Nothing de-luxe about the car, of course. But it had got them to St. Ives and back without incident, which was more than he would be prepared to guarantee for his own dear jalopy. That had been shortly before Norman's marriage and the Beaumonts' removal to Menton, and about six months before Yvette had sent him the news of Monsieur Beaumont's death.

Last year he had not been able to afford a holiday, what with having to meet the doubled rent at the flat after Norman had left. It had been a great temptation to give up the flat and find somewhere more moderately priced, but he had struggled on and now he was glad, for the end of the year had seen his biggest salary increase to date: one hundred and fifty. Julie had spent a fortnight in Sweden with a girl friend, and he had been alone in London because they had originally planned to take their holidays together. He had spent most afternoons bathing in the Serpentine or the Finchley lido, and his evenings, when he was lucky, with the dates he had made in the afternoons or, when luck had not visited him, with Norman and Megan. Not terribly exciting and certainly no effort made to prolong any of the casual relationships he had formed by the side of the swimming pool. That would have been too risky now that Julie had her own key to the flat.

He reached London Airport, parked the car and entered the arrivals building. The timetable showed only one plane which coincided with Yvette's departure time, the AF814, due at six. He had fifteen minutes to wait. He bought a coffee and sat in an armchair.

Yes, there were few ripples to disturb the tranquil placidity of his life at present. Norman, Julie and Mattson were the only minor irritants.

It was several weeks since he had last seen Norman. And that hadn't been a very happy meeting. Nor the two meetings before that. There was no tangible reason for the changed – estranged one might say – relations between them. No reason, that it, which had been aired. It was simply that Norman had turned cold towards him, had stopped joking, had stopped suggesting going for a pub drink, had stopped telephoning him. And John had eventually thought: *to hell with him.* Norman could make the next approach. But Norman had made no approach.

John had the feeling that the marriage was falling apart. This would account for a degree of abstraction on Norman's part, but not for the cold, deliberate way he had turned his back on their friendship.

Megan was altogether a different kettle of fish; no lack of warmth there. On the contrary, he reflected wryly, she had never stopped trying, contriving situations which would bring them together – alone. Not quite so bad since her marriage, but there had been that one awkward time when he had visited them, and Norman had been away. It had taken even more argument than usual to persuade her that he really was not interested. And then she had not believed him. Hardly surprising, of course, since it was not true. Not true, but essential to maintain the pretence. He had fallen once, once only, and that was another weakness to be chalked up to experience – like the very first mistake, so long ago, in that earlier other-life – never to be repeated.

And Julie. With marriage more and more in her thoughts if not in her speech. How much longer could he go on accepting the solace, the comfort of companionship and more, that she provided, without giving more back; specifically the security of position that she naturally desired? And that was something he was determined to avoid. He could live with Julie quite happily; he knew that. He had even suggested that she move in with him, but she had refused. She had agreed to take Norman's key when he left, but that was the limit of her acquiescence. With Julie it was marriage or nothing. But marriage was out of the question. Even to think about it filled him with neurotically unreasoned dread. The trouble was finding a way to break things off. So long as she refused to bring her thoughts about marriage into the open, he had no way of using them as an excuse to sever their relations. Even if he was really convinced he wanted to do so.

Finally there was Mattson, and the totally inexplicable change in him, marked by a lack of interest, a loss of energy, a disintegration of spirit – alcoholically induced. When had it started? It was hard to pinpoint the first signs precisely, but certainly he had been all right up until his second trip to West Africa. It must have begun sometime after that, but whether it was caused by business or personal considerations John could not say, for the change had also been marked by a reluctance to indulge in confidential disclosure which had not been previously evident.

It was, he decided, more likely something in Mattson's private life, since the company's business had been continually expanding. The agency agreements which Mattson had negotiated following his first African trip, and extended during his second, had worked out well and were extremely profitable. He had secured some very good agencies: Mammoth tractors, Lodemore trailers, a heavy and a light truck agency, a popular and a luxury car agency, and several agencies for woodworking machinery and cranes. The profits on purchasing and shipping alone were enough to justify the expense of Mattson's two tours, let alone the return on capital investment which Reid must be earning. The amount of capital investment was unknown to John, was handled by the timber company's accounts department, but had to be considerable for two of the more important West African timber shippers had established large separate sales and service organisations just to handle this side of the business.

How then could Mattson be suffering from business worries? It did not seem possible. Yet the fact remained that he was always in his most depressed states after his frequent meetings with Reid and Parry. Perhaps he was one of those people who are only happy when they are fighting an uphill battle; for whom success tastes bitter unless they have another out-of-reach goal.

It was ten past six, and arriving passengers were starting to exit from Channel Eight. He walked slowly over and arrived there just as Yvette came through the door. He waved. She smiled briefly and walked towards him.

"Yvette,"

"John."

She placed her suitcase on the floor and raised her face, turning her head so that me might kiss her on both cheeks. He marvelled at her cool poise, her self-possessed maturity. The Yvette of 1954 seemed as subtly different from the Yvette of 1950 as she had, in turn, differed from the self of 1946. Funny how their meetings seemed to follow four-year cycles.

Suddenly her face pressed into his chest and her shoulders heaved with silent sobs.

"What is it, Yvette?"

Her body gave a last tremble and was still. She looked at him, dry-eyed, but with eyes slightly red-rimmed as though she had been crying earlier.

"I'm sorry, John. The reaction, I suppose. Seeing you again."

"Are you sure everything is all right?" He surveyed her anxiously. "On the phone earlier . . ."

She smiled, a pained, tremulous parting of her lips that was not reflected in her eyes. "I'll tell you about it later. I do not want to talk about it here."

"All right, Yvette." He picked up her case and took her arm. "Let's go to the car."

"You have a car?"

He wrinkled his nose. "Only an old banger." She frowned. "*Une vieille bagnole*," he translated.

Getting into the car she said to him, "Life must be going well for you, John."

"I can't grumble," he agreed.

He started the engine, engaged first gear, and set off. Yvette was making no attempt to explain her unexpected visit to London. She would doubtless tell him in her own good time. He fished a packet of cigarettes out of his pocket.

"May I have one please, John."

"Eh? You smoke now?"

"Not often, but I would like a cigarette at the moment I think."

He handed her the packet and a cigarette lighter. "Light one for me too then, please."

The cigarette she placed between his lips carried the faint and pleasant flavour of her lipstick. She slipped cigarette pack and lighter into his jacket pocket and her hand stroked his arm gently before she straightened in her seat.

"Where are we going now, John?"

"To your hotel. I've booked you into the Cumberland, near Marble

Arch.”

“I don’t want to go there.”

Stopping at a set of traffic lights he looked at her in surprise. She was inhaling and puffing out cigarette smoke in short, nervous bursts. “Where do you want to go?”

“To your apartment.”

The lights changed to green and they moved slowly away. “We can go there later. First you’d better check into the hotel.”

“You do not understand. I do not want to go to the hotel at all. I want to stay with you.”

“But Yvette, you can’t. That’s not . . . it’s not . . .”

“You’re not married, John?”

“Of course not.” He laughed.

“You are not affianced?”

“No. But . . .”

“You are not sharing your apartment with someone?”

“Certainly not. But . . .”

“Then I want to stay with you.” It was less an expression of desire than a determined statement of fact.

He made a final attempt to dissuade her. “But Yvette, it’s really not possible. I have only one bedroom.”

“You used to share it with a friend, did you not?”

“Well yes . . .”

“Then there must be enough room.” Flatly. Resolutely.

He didn’t answer her. At the North Circular Road he turned left towards Hampstead, although his intuition was urging him strongly to continue towards Central London and the Cumberland Hotel. For several minutes they did not speak.

Then she said solemnly, “I do not wish to be alone tonight.”

He held his tongue. Let her tell him now, he pleaded silently. Let her please clear up this mystery.

“I am very unhappy, John.”

He removed a hand from the steering wheel and laid it on her thigh. “Do you want to tell me about it>”

“I’ve got to tell you, John, but I do not know how to tell you.” And then the tears started.

He sought a suitable place to park and pulled into the side of the road, then turned to her, leaning forward so that her head might rest on his shoulder, ignoring the discomfort of the gear lever pressing against the inside of his thigh. She was crying quietly, in a piteous, broken way.

"What is it, Yvette, *chérie*? Have you done something wrong? Are you in some sort of trouble?"

"No John. It's n-not me. It's Claude and N-Nicole and . . . and . . ." He waited for her to continued. Suddenly she blurted out, "They are dead! Claude and Nicole."

"God, no! How? What?"

Her sobbing changed to short, wracking gasps. "Claude was killed in *Dien-Bien-Phu*. He . . . he . . . was flown in by . . . by helicopter . ." She took a deep, tremulous breath. "He wanted . . . wanted to find out for himself . . . the truth . . . for an article. The authorities did not want . . . want him in *Indochine* . . . but he managed to persuade an army pilot to take him to *Dien-Bien-Phu*. He . . . he . . . got killed . . . two . . . two days later." She gave way to another fit of sobbing.

He waited until she had calmed down again, trying to visualise Claude as he had last seen him, trying to make some sense out of the story Yvette had told him, trying to accept the fact of his death, the fact that they would never meet again. But he could only feel a sense of numbing disbelief.

"My God, that's awful," he said. "I can't . . ."

"And Nicole," she broke in, "Nicole . . . she . . . she . . . Oh *mon Dieu*!" Yvette shuddered. "Nicole killed herself."

"What!"

"I had . . . I had . . . I hadn't . . ." She choked on her words.

He could feel the dampness on his shoulder where her tears had penetrated his clothing. "Don't tell me any more now, Yvette. Wait until we get home."

"You . . . you see why I do not want to be alone."

"Yes, darling. You won't be alone." He pushed her gently back into her seat and drove off again towards Hampstead.

"So that's why I was in Paris."

He nodded. "Finish your drink. You will feel better for it."

"I'm feeling a bit better already." She drank the last of her brandy.

He took the empty glass. "Do you want another?"

"No thank you, John."

He put the glass on the table and sat down beside her on the settee. "So Pierre is with Nicole's parents?"

"Yes. She took him there the afternoon she heard of Claude's death. Then she went home. When her mother tried to phone later, and there was no reply, her parents got worried and went round to her home. They could smell the gas on the landing. We still cannot understand how the neighbours failed to notice anything. When they broke in it was too late."

"But why? Why? I know it must have been a shock, but . . . with Pierre to live for . . ."

"She left a letter. She said that she could only bring disaster to anyone who loved her. First Pierre, then Claude . . . she . . . she didn't want little Pierre to suffer also."

"But that's crazy."

"Crazy. Yes. We thought she had recovered – that she was normal again. I suppose it was there under the surface all the time."

"God, what a mess."

Yvette gave a laugh with more than a trace of hysteria in it. "A mess. An ironic mess. Claude was killed by the very people whose cause he was trying to help. Ugh! Politics and war and death. What sort of a world are we living in, John?"

"I don't know, Yvette."

"I'm sorry to involve you in our problems, John. But after the funeral I felt I had to get away and . . . and I wanted to be with you. I had to tell you, and I wanted to be with you when I did so. Do you understand?"

"Yes, darling, I understand. Let's stop talking about it now. You've got to have something to eat."

"I am not hungry, John."

"I'm hungry, Yvette. And I refuse to eat alone." He put out his hand and helped her to her feet, then put an arm around her shoulders and led her into the kitchen. "I'm afraid I've only got eggs in the refrigerator," he apologised. "I wasn't expecting a guest this evening."

"That's all right. I'm really not hungry. But let me make you an omelette; I will feel much better doing something. Show me where everything is."

"As you wish. But I insist you also have something to eat."

She gave a faint smile. "We will see."

They ate the simple meal in the kitchen. The activity of preparing the food, the ordinary act of eating, seemed to calm Yvette. It was as if the injection of everyday behaviour into her actions had restored a sense of normality.

After eating they returned to the living room

"It is not really difficult for you to have me stay here, is it, John?"

"No, of course not," he assured her. "I'm pleased though that the

Cumberland accepted my telephoned cancellation of your room."

Thank goodness, he thought, that Julie is going out with a girl friend tonight. Her arrival upon the scene would really set the cat among the pigeons. But she would have to know sometime that Yvette was staying with him. The best thing he could do would be to make up a bed for himself on the settee and telephone Julie in the morning to explain the situation. He would invite her round to meet Yvette. When she heard all the circumstances of the unexpected visit, she would be sure to understand.

"How is the hotel business, Yvette?"

She shrugged. "It is quiet at the moment. The season will not begin for another month."

"But you can manage all right? You and *maman* alone?"

"Oh, we are not alone. A cousin of *maman* and his son are with us. And it is only a small hotel with fourteen guest rooms."

John's mouth twitched ruefully. "I'm sorry I have never accepted your invitation to visit you."

Yvette got out of her chair and sat on the floor at John's feet, her elbows resting on his knees. "Why didn't you, John? When you left Paris all those years ago you promised you would soon be back to see us. I was afraid I had done something to upset you."

"Of course not, silly." His fingers played with her silky, dark hair. "I had too little time while you were still in Paris, and too little money after you moved to Menton."

And now it was too late, he reminded himself bitterly. For the first time since Yvette's arrival he began to feel the true effect of her news about Nicole and Claude. He supposed he had always retained a deep-seated satisfaction in the knowledge that there was a family in France which looked upon him as one of its own. First Monsieur Beaumont and now Claude. Madame Beaumont would not be there forever and eventually Yvette would be as alone in France as he was in England. He began to feel with Yvette the deep shock that Claude's death must have been, and then with the added horror of Nicole's suicide . . . it was understandable that she should want to be here in London with him. He was a tenuous link with happier times.

He bent down and pressed his face to her hair. "Claude was more a brother than a cousin, wasn't he?" Her head nodded beneath his face. "I realise that I can never take Claude's place but – this is going to sound terribly trite – but I would like you to think of me as your brother now, Yvette darling."

She raised her head and looked at him, her breath catching in her throat. "I do not want to think of you as a brother. That is not why I came to London."

"I don't understand."

"I want . . . " She hesitated and blushed. "I want us to be lovers."

It was plain to see how much courage it had taken to utter the words. He stared, not knowing what to say. Under his gaze the redness in her cheeks increased and she turned her head away from him abruptly, with an embarrassed moan.

"For heaven's sake," she said angrily, "don't look so shocked. You make me feel ashamed of myself."

"Forgive me, Yvette. I'm not shocked, just surprised. You must admit it's not often a man gets such a tempting offer." He tried to make a joke of his words.

"Oh I know what you are thinking, John. You think this is just the reaction to the past days. You think I am miserable and lonely, and want your love and comfort." She looked at him again, the redness in her cheeks concentrated into two spots in their centre. "That may be true, but it is not the whole answer. It is something I wanted to happen four years ago, and it has taken Claude's death to give me the courage to speak to you."

"But Yvette . . . darling, darling Yvette . . . you can't just say to me, 'I want us to be lovers,' and expect . . ."

"But John, you love me. I know you do."

"Yes, Yvette, I love you. I think I love you more than anyone in the world. But it's not the same thing. Not in that way."

She tossed her head angrily, pulling away from his hand. "What's the matter, John? Don't you find me attractive? Am I not desirable?"

"You know I do. Dear, sweet Yvette, I find you almost too desirable."

"Then what is it, John. Have you never slept with a woman?"

He laughed bitterly. "Oh yes, I have slept with a woman. With a great many women. That is why it is different with you. Those women, mainly, did not mean anything to me. I have never been involved with them to the extent of wanting to marry them."

She burst in furiously. "I have not mentioned marriage, have I?"

"I know you haven't, but . . ." He broke off as he became aware of her eyes brimming with tears. Instantly he was filled with compassion, tinged with worry as he perceived that the matter was getting quite out-of-hand. "Darling, please understand . . ."

"Oh! *Idiot. Imbecile.*" She pronounced the words the French way.

"Don't spoil things. I know what I am doing. I am not asking for anything but you . . . your love."

"Come here Yvette," he said gently, patting his thigh."

She got up obediently and sat in his lap, burying her face in his chest.

"Yvette, I want to tell you something. And I want you to listen carefully. All right?" Her head moved against his chest. "You already have my love. *I love you.* I loved you already in 1946. I loved your high-spirited schoolgirl vivacity, your sincerity, your affectionate befriending of a foreign soldier far from his own family. I loved you in a quite different way in 1950. I loved the beautiful woman that had grown from the cheeky schoolgirl; I loved her intelligence and charm, and I loved knowing that I still had her affection and trust. And I love you still, Yvette. I love you too much to risk losing that affection and trust."

She raised her head and ran a hand tenderly down the side of his jaw. "John, *mon chéri*, you are using a lot of words to say nothing. If you really love me, as you say you do – as I love you! – then you will want to prove it to me. Or is there someone else?"

He snorted. "There are too many others, Yvette. I know that's not what you mean and, yes, there is one special girl friend. But that's just the point. If I were the sort of man you think I am, she would mean far more to me than she does. I've known her for six years, and instead of thinking of marriage, all I can think of is how I can end it. Is that the sort of person you want for a lover, Yvette?"

"Oh, John." She smiled at him, laid her arms over his shoulders and entwined her fingers behind his head. "You are talking of marriage again. Marriage does not enter into it. I am not trying to tie you down to anything. Tell me, do you lovc this girl fricnd?"

"Love?" He frowned. "I don't see how I can. Perhaps, once, I may have thought I did. I am very fond of her; very grateful to her. I would not deliberately hurt her. Yes, I suppose I do love her, in a way. But I am not *in love* with her, if you can tell the difference."

"And you are not in love with me either." She laid her cheek against his. "But you are in no doubt that you love me, are you?"

"You know I'm not."

"Well then." She rubbed her cheek lightly against his, then brushed the back of his ear with her lips. "Do I mean less to you than she does?"

"Yvette, you are twisting my words. I didn't mean love in that way."

"Dearest, darling John," she murmured into his ear. "How many different ways of loving someone are there? You know, I should be offended: the rejected woman. How do you say it in English? Ah yes, the woman spurned. But I know you are not really spurning me; it is just your quaint English idea of being a gentleman."

"A gentleman!" He scoffed. "I am far from being a gentleman, particularly where women are concerned. Do you know that of all my relations with women, there is only one of which I am proud? And that is my relationship with you, Yvette." He became aware that his hand was spontaneously stroking her back, and he stopped the movement. "Do you want me to spoil that too?"

She drew her head away and looked into his eyes "That did not stop you from kissing me and demonstrating your feelings for me in Paris."

"That was different. That was simple affection."

She chuckled softly. "Ah, John, you are so funny when you are pompous. I really think you are afraid of me."

"I am not afraid of you, Yvette; I am afraid of myself."

"Then are you too afraid to demonstrate some of that simple affection now?"

He kissed her quickly. "There."

"Oh, John, you can do better than that."

"Yvette, you're determined to compromise me, aren't you?" The words came out more sharply than he had intended.

"If I am compromising anyone, John, it is myself." She spoke huffily, clearly hurt by his words. "I did not think I would be reduced to begging you. Now you *are* making me feel cheap."

With a sudden, startling movement she left his lap and threw herself on the settee, burying her face in her arms. After a moment her shoulders started to tremble.

He went over and sat beside her, stroking her hair. "Yvette, there is no question of your begging me. Perhaps you still do not understand what I have been trying to say. You do not have to use your powers of persuasion on me; I am trying very hard to persuade myself not to give in. Oh, hell! I'm not making much sense, am I? Look, my dear, in Paris it took every particle of my self-control not to carry our love-play too far. And I wanted to; I really wanted to. But I felt it would be wrong and, afterwards, I was glad. Now I know it would be wrong."

She turned a tear-streaked face to him. "How can it be wrong? If we love each other it cannot be wrong."

He had no answer for her. In other circumstances he could well imagine using the same argument himself. He could not even account for his own reluctance in a satisfactory manner, for it was a mental reluctance based on intellectual reasoning, quite at odds with the physical desire which had been bubbling close to the surface of his body from the time they had begun talking. He supposed it was a selfish reluctance really; a need to prove that he could still resist the challenge he had imposed on himself four years ago. But was he being fair to her? Was he even being fair to himself? The mere act of questioning his motives was serving to weaken his resolve and now, with her eyes still regarding him in mute appeal, the front of her white silk blouse rising and falling sharply with each breath, he could feel the last shreds of his control vanishing.

He lay beside her and put his arms around her shoulders, drawing her to him. "I'm being rather horrid, aren't I, darling?"

He suddenly recalled Norman's words, bitter and mocking, so long ago, asking him where he got the right to play God in a situation similar to this one. And that too, he realised with a shock, had centred round the smug satisfaction of his self-denial with Yvette. Norman had been right; he had been – he was being – selfish. What was he trying to prove, anyway, by this single, isolated, stoical stand? He remembered a few lines of poetry he had once read:

. . . we ourselves thwart.
Thwart with this struggle
Inherently vile:
Life's lasting tourney
'Gainst love's chilling smile.

He up-tilted Yvette's face. "I think I need you too, Yvette."

And then he kissed her. And her lips moved against his, expressing the hunger, the loneliness, the fear, the misery, the myriad other emotions she was feeling. Their bodies swayed and shifted together, their fast heartbeats and breathing mingled, their hands roved and groped. Their lips drew apart and he kissed her cheeks, her ears, her nose, her eyes. Her eyes were wet.

"Darling, you're crying again."

"Tears of happiness, dearest. I was right, wasn't I? We do love each other, and it can't be wrong."

"Yes, sweetheart, you were right." He kissed the point of her chin. "Funny little stubborn chin. I should have know better than to argue with you."

"John," she spoke his name with shy enquiry, "will you take me to bed?"

Once again her directness shocked him.

"Are you quite sure . . .?"

"Oh, yes, yes, yes, yes."

He stood up and took her hand, helping her to her feet. He switched off the lamp and led her into the bedroom. They stood for a moment in the dark, holding each other tightly.

She said, "John, would you mind very much leaving the light off? I'm not used to this . . . and . . ."

"Of course. I'll get undressed in the bathroom. Knock on the wall when you're ready."

When he returned to the bedroom she was lying in the divan-bed with the covers drawn up to her chin. The bedside light was switched on.

"If I'd known you were going to put the light on, I'd have worn pyjamas," he said laughing.

"No. I . . . I like your body, John." Her voice quavered nervously and her face was flushed. "But I'll put the light out now."

She did so as he got into bed beside her. He was immediately glad he was not wearing pyjamas, which might have further embarrassed her, for she was quite naked beneath the sheet.

As their bodies touched she said, "Do you think I am terribly brazen, John?"

"Brazen? No, of course not. Why do you ask?"

"Do you not remember teaching me that word?"

"No. Did I?"

"Mmmm. In front of *La Source*, one morning in 1946."

"Do you remember everything I taught you?"

"Everything," she confirmed vehemently. She turned on her side and snuggled up to him. "That is because I have always loved you."

As her body pressed against his, he could feel desire mounting in him. He put his hand on her waist and marvelled at the incredibly smooth texture of her skin. Her arm came up and tightened around his neck, and her body strained to meet his, while a sound like a sob came from her throat. Her breath was sweetly moist against his face and he lowered his head and pressed his lips into the soft warm hollow at the base of her throat. Then they were straining together in an intense primal rhythm, holding each other and kissing, caressing, enfolding. His erect penis was throbbing with urgent command and his hand moved over her body, stroking, exploring, probing . . .

She gasped and shuddered in his embrace.

"Be gentle, please, darling," she whispered.

He felt his body tighten with a deep sense of shock. "Yvette! Why didn't you tell me?"

"There was nothing to tell."

"But you . . . I . . . I didn't realise . . ."

She came to his rescue with the same directness that had astonished him earlier. "You did not believe I was still *jeune fille*?"

"If I had know . . ."

"If you had known," she murmured gently, tenderly, "I should have had even more difficulty with you. But it makes no difference. I *wanted* you to be the first. I have never been able to imagine myself with another man. You see now why it was so important to me. Darling, darling John, I have waited four years to you to come back to me, and I could not wait any longer. Now more than ever I *need* you. You will not deny that need, will you?"

"No, sweetheart." He pressed his lips softly, briefly to her breast. "But under the circumstances I think I had better . . ."

She interrupted him. "I may be inexperienced, darling, but I am not completely ignorant. It is quite safe."

She reached for him and, with primeval female instinct, stilled his remaining fears. And they consummated their love with pain, and tears, and a deep, overwhelming, ecstatic sense of fulfillment.

Somewhere, in the graveyard of his memory, he could hear Claude's voice, wistful and grave, *Be good to her, John.* Forgive me Claude, his mind cried out. Forgive me, dear kind friend, whom I will never again see. I tried. You know I tried. I promise I shall never hurt her.

CHAPTER FOURTEEN

Morning coffee in bed was a new and pleasant experience for him, particularly since it was accompanied by a tenderly warm awakening kiss. Clearly they had the right idea about female upbringing in France.

She hovered over him anxiously. Was the coffee all right? Was there enough milk and sugar in it? Did he want anything else?

She was beautiful in a pale lilac, brushed wool robe, her hair in a pony tail held in place by a matching lilac ribbon, her cheeks glowing with health, her eyes alive and gay. Despair and grief were banished; they no longer belonged to the previous evening, but to a previous life, another world.

He placed the empty cup on the bedside table and reached for her wrist, pulling her onto the bed beside him. She came into his arms with a sigh, and they kissed, a slow, sensitive, affectionate kiss of friendship and reassurance; a reaffirmation that the passionate night had not disturbed the tranquility of their relationship, that the depth of their intimacy did not detract from what they had shared, but had added to it a new dimension, a fresh understanding, a deeper acceptance.

"Darling," she murmured, "I was afraid I might have spoiled things, that you might think . . ."

"Hush," he said. "I love you, you little French minx."

"What is minx, John?"

He laughed. "I don't know the word in French, but it's what you are. I had no idea you were so tempestuous."

"Was I too brazen, John?" Her eyelashes fluttered in simulated modesty, but behind them her eyes were sparkling.

"I'm beginning to think that's your favourite word, and it fits you perfectly."

"You are joking?"

"Yes, I'm joking."

She kicked her slippers off her feet and nestled up to him under the sheet. "Do you mind, darling? I mean, having to have *all* my love now that I have so few people to share it with."

He squeezed her. "I love you, Yvette, and I *want* all your love."

She drew a deep, contented breath. "I meant what I said last night. I am not going to tie you down. When I came to London yesterday I was broken into little pieces and you have made me a complete person again." She hugged him. "This was all I wanted."

"Aah, sweetheart." His body moved against her. "Sweet, wonderful, generous Yvette. I think you are the one who has done the rebuilding job. On me." He could feel desire stirring in him.

She felt it too. She pushed him away gently. "John, what time do you go to work?"

"Christ!" He twisted in the bed to examine the clock. "Ten past eight. I'll have to get ready. Thank heavens you woke me up. I forgot to set the alarm last night."

She slipped out of bed and groped for her slippers. "Can I make you some breakfast."

"No time," he said. "But I could use another cup of coffee. What will you do while I'm at work? And I still don't know how long you're staying in London."

"I think I can stay until after *Pâques*."

"Easter? Of course. Day after tomorrow is Good Friday. I'd forgotten. Well, that's fine; perhaps we can go away somewhere for the weekend. But today and tomorrow will be difficult. I really can't afford to take any time off work."

"That's all right, darling. You go off to work and I will make believe I am the little housewife. Actually there's some washing to be done." She reddened. "It's a good thing you had a blanket under the sheet."

He laughed. "The result of experience." He caught the look of hurt shock in her face and leaped from the bed, oblivious to his nakedness. He took her in his arms. "I'm sorry, sweetheart, that was a joke in bad taste."

"I'm a silly little – minx – am I not, John?" She ran her hand down his body. "Go on, darling. Put a dressing gown on quickly or I will not let you go to work."

He slipped into his gown. "Look, sweetheart," he said thoughtfully, tying the cord, "I think I can probably take tomorrow off if I work late this evening. Do you have any money?"

"Only francs."

He got his wallet from his jacket pocket and counted out some banknotes. "I'm afraid I haven't very much at home, but I can leave you five pounds. If you want to change any French money, let me have it and I'll send someone from the office to the bank. Why don't you spend today in Hampstead? If it's fine you can go for a walk on the heath. It's a large open park, a bit like the Bois de Boulogne, and it's only five minutes away from here. There are also some nice little shops and restaurants just up the hill from here. Otherwise you can stay in the flat and relax – play some records – anything you like. I'll leave the key with you. And, if you can buy some food while you are out, perhaps you could prepare some dinner for us this evening. I'll bring some wine back with me. I would take you out to dine, but if I'm working late, I shall probably be tired. What do you think?"

She nodded and smiled. "I would like that."

"Good. Now I'm going to the bathroom and you can get busy on that second cup of coffee."

Later, weaving his way through the City-bound traffic, he thought about their night together, the passion and storm with which she had responded to his invasion of her body. There had been an urgency in her at first, as if she were using the pain of rapture to cast out the devils of heartache and suffering. Then later she had become calm and tender, and shyly exploratory.

He was astonished at his own reaction to their lovemaking; it had contained an element with which he was unfamiliar. For him this coupling of the bodies had always been a complete act in itself; the sensations, the sensual summit, the detumescent ecstasy representing the ultimate object of his endeavours. With Yvette, however, he was conscious of an extra feeling which was foreign to him: a slight emptiness, as though the sexual act was less important an end in itself than a symbol of something else, a more profound union.

He worked on the feeling, trying to isolate it, trying to give it form and substance, but it would not come. It was almost as though there was a gap in his experience where the answer would normally reside; an incomplete jigsaw puzzle. And suddenly it was terribly important to find the missing piece, to gain the measure of self-understanding which was lacking. He was still pondering the problem when he walked into his office.

Although it was nine-thirty, Mattson was not yet there. He was less surprised than he would have been six months earlier. Now that the office was running smoothly there was, of course, no reason why Mattson should not relax a bit after his years of overwork. But John knew this was not the reason.

He had opened the first letter in the pile of morning mail on his desk when Mitchell entered from the outer office.

"Good morning, Mr Graham."

"Good morning, Mitchell." It *was* a good morning and John gave Mitchell a warm smile which seemed to startle that individual.

"Mr Mattson's been on the phone for you. About five to nine it was."

"Did he say what he wanted?"

"Asked for you to ring him back, he did. As soon as you came in. Said for me to tell you he wasn't at home." Mitchell laid a slip of paper on John's desk. "That's the number."

Mitchell went out. John waited a moment, then dialed the number Mitchell had given him.

A gruff voice said, "Anchor Hotel."

"May I speak to Mr Mattson, please."

"Mackson?"
"Mattson. M-a-double t-s-o-n."
"Oh yeah. 'alf a mo'."
There was a noise on the line like radio atmospherics, and then Mattson's voice. "Yes?"
"John here, Matt."
"Christ, about time. How much money have you got?"
"Money? About ten bob, I think."
"That's no fucking use. What's in your cashbox?"
"I'm not sure. Ten or eleven quid."
"Right. I want you to get it out and bring it to the Anchor Hotel in Victoria. I'm not sure of the street, so take a taxi, the driver will know where it is. Got that?"
"Yes."
"And do it right away."
"I can't, Matt. I haven't gone through the mail yet."
"Jesus bloody wept! Give the mail to Mitchell. Ring Parry and make some fucking excuse. But get here. Pronto!"
"Okay, Matt. I'll do my best." He hung up, thought a moment, then rang Parry on the intercom. "Graham here, Mr Parry."
"Good morning, Graham. Anything good in today?"
"I haven't gone through the mail yet, sir. I've had Mr Mattson on the phone. He's at a meeting with Leylands in Hanover Square . . . Oh, didn't he? He must have forgotten. Anyway, I've got to take a file over there urgently . . . No, sir, Mitchell can't do it. There's something Mr Mattson wishes to examine with me . . . Yes, sir. I'll tell Mitchell to bring the mail over to you."

The Anchor Hotel, when the taxi driver finally found it, was exactly as John had imagined from the coarse, offhanded voice of its receptionist: a dingy, stale-smelling dump, undeserving of the title of hotel. For that matter, and judging by the unwashed, unkempt shirt-sleeve-and-braces appearance of the receptionist himself, it had probably ceased being a legitimate hotel some time ago. John was shocked. This was a new low-tide mark for Mattson.
Following the man's surly instructions, John climbed to the second floor and knocked on a door. There was a barely audible grunt from inside the room. John turned the handle and went in.
His eyes slowly swept the room, absorbing the sordid details, like a

television camera panning an area which contains too many significant details to be disclosed by a single long shot. He felt sickened by the sight of the grease-stained carpet, its faint pattern barely discernable after long years of wear, the brass-railed bed with covers in disarray, revealing ugly stains, the single bed-lamp with its broken, cheap plastic shade, the empty bottles and glasses on the floor beside the bed, the brown-stained, chipped porcelain sink with its dingy mirror cracked in several places. And Mattson. Mattson in crumpled trousers and singlet, slumped in a canvas-backed chair, drinking directly from a whiskey bottle.

"Pretty, isn't it?" Mattson put the bottle down and sneered.

"Don't you think you've had enough?" John could not keep the disgust from his voice.

"Oh, I've had enough, all right. That one was strictly medicinal." His laugh was devoid of humour. His face, always thin, was now almost cadaverous, more suited to an inmate of Auschwitz with black pouches under the eyes, whites flecked with red.

"You've really tied one on this time, Matt."

"Ugh." Mattson gagged dryly and took another swig of whiskey. He grimaced. "Nothing more to come back. Got the money?"

John pulled out his wallet and extracted eleven pound notes and a ten shilling note. He couldn't bring himself to enter further into the room, but stood by the door with the money in his hand.

"Thanks, John. Would you pay the man downstairs and then wait for me. I'll be down in a couple of minutes. He'll want to take for two bottles of whiskey and four bottles of beer. Plus one night's lodging . . ." He paused, then added with unconcealed self-loathing, "for two people. Give him eight quid. If he doesn't like it, tell him I'll see him when I come down."

The man downstairs accepted the eight banknotes with stubby fingers and grimy nails. He made no comment. When Mattson came down and he and John left, the receptionist didn't even glance at them.

"Did he say anything?"

"No."

Mattson grunted. "He's probably already had his rake-off. I dare say he expected a complaint instead of eight quid."

"How do you mean?"

"Let's get some coffee and I'll tell you."

In Victoria Station's buffet they drank tasteless coffee from thick cups.

"What did you tell Parry?"

"That you had a meeting with Leyland and needed my assistance."

"Hmm . . . You've done a fair bit of covering up for me lately, haven't you?" John didn't answer. Mattson went on, "Well, it's all over now; I won't be bothering you any more."

"You've finally seen the light, have you?"

"I'm through. Last night was the last straw."

"So we can expect things to return to normal in the office?"

"I can see we're talking at cross-purposes." Mattson put his cup down. His hand was shaking and the cup clattered against the saucer. "I'm leaving the company. I've had it up to here."

"But why? Business has never been so good."

"We're not in business, John. We're nothing but a fucking post office. I thought I could take it, but I can't. Let me tell you about last night."

"That's not necessary," John said stuffily.

"Ah, but it is. I've got to tell someone or I'll go daft." Mattson's lips twitched. "When I left the office yesterday I had a few drinks in the Stirling Castle. I wanted you to come with me, but you left early."

"Sorry about that. It was unavoidable."

Mattson waved a hand. "I'm not blaming you, I've brought this on myself. Not entirely by myself. I've had a little help from a slimy , psalm-singing, sanctimonious little bastard who – but that's beside the point. I don't remember where I went after I left the Stirling Castle . . . it's all a bit hazy. I've a feeling I got kicked out of another pub, but I might be confusing it with another time. I do recall, vaguely, sobering up very slightly in a drinking club, with a fat, ugly-looking bitch with peroxided hair, telling her I'd been waiting all my life to meet her. Then things go dim again. But I'm pretty sure we left the club together and went to that hotel. Hotel!" He snorted. "I woke up this morning alone, lying in my own vomit."

He shivered with the recollection. "God! I feel sick and filthy and . . . Anyway, I was alone this morning and all my money had gone. I may have spent it all before we got to the hotel, but I doubt it. I left the office with about twenty quid. Jesus, man, I hope nothing like this ever happens to you. I looked at myself in a cracked mirror over a filthy wash basin. It was like looking at a stranger; someone I wouldn't toss a tanner to if I met him in the street. For about five minutes I thought seriously of killing myself. Then I found there was some whiskey left and drowned the thought. Thank God they had hot water and towels in the room. I scrubbed myself until . . . well, it's past now. There was a phone on the landing and I rang the office and spoke to Mitchell. You know the rest."

John shook his head slowly. "You don't do things by half, do you? But there must be a reason why you're doing this to yourself. It's been going on for ages. What has this got to do with the office?"

Mattson sighed. "Parry. Reid and Parry, but particularly Parry. He's beaten me, John. The little bugger's beaten me. I wasn't going to let it happen. I've been fighting him for six years. When you joined the company he had an ally." He help up a hand, cutting off John's anticipated interruption. "I know. I know it wasn't deliberate. You didn't know what was going on. But there was a time I could cheerfully have murdered you, when you were playing right into his hands. That was when I went to West Africa the first time. Luckily for you one or two things went wrong, and Parry had a finger in the pie each time. You straightened out. Too well!" He smiled, but with irony, not humour. "If you hadn't learned to run the office so well, I doubt if I'd have got into this mess. I'd have either resigned myself to the inevitable limits of the company's progress, or I'd have left. But the office was running well. Damned well. We made a bloody good team. And there was no reason why we shouldn't have expanded and built up a business to be proud of."

"Excuse me for butting in, Matt, but why this use of the past tense? Haven't we done all that? Isn't Reid Parry a business to be proud of? You're a director of the company; we've got some first-class agencies in West Africa, which are expanding all the time. I know there's a hell of a lot still to be done, but what's to stop us from doing it."

"You're not listening, John. I've told you. Reid and Parry. They're too smart for me. And the smartest thing they ever did was to put me on the Board. It was the most effective way of tying my hands."

"But they sent you to West Africa again two years later."

"Yes, they threw a crumb my way. They decided I needed to work off some of my restless energy. Either that or they wanted a few weeks peace. And they made damn sure that I would spend most of my time on their fucking timber business."

"But what about their investment in the agencies?"

"What investment? They haven't put a brass farthing into anything. That's the whole point. They never had the least intention of doing so. We haven't got a single controlling interest in any of the agencies, nor have we even got a say in what's being done with them. Everything has been organised and paid for by the West Africans themselves, and we're just acting as their messenger boys. A fucking post office! The orders come in and are routed through our office. The goods go out and are shipped by us. For the magnificent remuneration of five percent buying commission and the freight rebates."

"That's ridiculous," John exclaimed. "I thought you said after your first trip that we were going into the business for ourselves. Why the hell didn't we?"

"Aahhh . . ." Mattson lit a cigarette from the stub of his last one. "Why the hell didn't we? Why don't you ask me a simple question, like where I can lay my hands on a million pounds. If I knew the answer I could possibly do something about it. But the answer is that there is no simple answer. Perhaps the key factor is fear. Parry is afraid and Reid is afraid, and they have two different kinds of fear. Parry's fear is of Reid and his own job. He was taken on by the timber company as a bookkeeper during the late twenties when the timber industry, most industry, was in a big slump. He'd been out of work for some time. Since then he has built himself a nice safe little niche, with a nice salary, a nice home in Hertfordshire, and a nice little world of minor authority. He's done it by knowing when to say yes and when to say no, but mainly when to say yes. If he doesn't clean Reid's shoes, it's only because Reid has never thought to ask him. And he lives on a permanent brink of fear – dead scared that someday he may wake up and find himself on the dole again. So most of the time he's nice and friendly – a real father-figure to his staff. Proud as hell when one of them asks him to be a godfather. A pillar of the church; Sunday school teacher; bible thumper. A real Christian, with all the virtues. And totally lacking in honesty; the honesty of self-examination. Two completely different sets of ethics: preaching charity on Sunday, and then wrapping it up and locking it in his desk drawer for the remaining six days of the week. He's like an old maid with shares in a brothel: wanting his money, but not wanting to know where it comes from.

"As for Reid, he's another kettle of fish entirely. He's scared too, but his fear is less tangible, less capable of analysis. It's mainly a fear, I think, of loss of authority. The biggest thing in his life is his personal achievement and the power that it's given him; the power to have lots of little Parrys running around to his word of command. I doubt he was always like this. I think he always liked to feel the big man, the puppet master, but I've noticed a change in him these last few years. You know what they say about power corrupting? I think the change is simply due to the addition of the fear element; the realisation that he's getting old and that his minor empire will someday fall into other hands. So he's not anxious to have it develop in directions that are foreign to him.

"You see, John, if Reid had invested in vehicle agencies in Africa, he would have had to leave it to me to handle them. It would have meant a loss of power, or at least a delegation of power, because he would have to rely on me. But there's more to it than that. Do you remember Graumann coming over to see us about six months ago?"

"The director of United Swiss Timbers?"

"Yes. We had a night out together. I got to know him quite well in Dunkwa. At the moment they are Reid's biggest shippers of *obechi* and *sapele*, two hardwoods. Graumann told me in confidence that they are selling their timber concession and concentrating on the vehicle agencies we got them. You know what will happen then?"

"What?"

"Reid will lose the timber account. The new boys will have their own brokers in London. After that it's just a question of time before we lose Graumann's agency business. He's not going to pay us five percent when he can get the work done by someone else for half that. I told Reid months ago we were gouging. Oh, it was okay when we were in a sellers' market. When you joined us, our customers were so desperate they would have paid anything for the equipment we shipped to them. But the situation has changed, and we've got to change with it. You know what Reid believes? That we should think of ways of charging more commission, not less. He has absolutely no understanding of our business. Parry knows better, and could back me up at board meetings. But Parry just smiles his hypocritical smile and says 'Quite right, sir.' So there it is. Four years ago I could have argued the toss with them – and frequently did. But I'm a director now, which means I have to accept board decisions and the responsibility that goes with them. When Graumann asks me, over a friendly drink, if I don't think we're being unreasonable, I have to remember that I'm a party to the decision and argue the case from Reid's viewpoint. And the business is going to the dogs, John. We're tied totally to the timber accounts. United Swiss are only the first. Reid will lose others. I doubt if Dumard will stick with him forever.

"We've put all our eggs in one basket. At present the basket is overflowing, but the bottom will fall out of it one day, and we'll find ourselves holding a handle-full of air. So I'm getting out before I drink myself to death, or my wife leaves me."

"Surely your wife doesn't know what you've been getting up to?"

"She'd have to be blind or stupid not to have noticed. And she's neither."

"But Matt, I don't understand why we don't find new accounts elsewhere, while we still have the West African business to bolster us up."

Mattson gave him a pitying look. "Don't you think I've thought of that? When I made my last trip to Africa it was after I'd pestered Reid for months to let me plan a trip to the West Indies, for just that reason. As I said before, they simply fobbed me off with a second trip to West Africa. So that I could bolster up their timber business. I tell you, they're scared little men, hanging on to what they've got, and afraid to give anyone else a chance.

"They're worse than that; they criminally fucking blind. They think the whole world is still just waiting to knock on our door, so we continue to sit on our arses and wait for the orders to come in. Any day now those orders will stop coming in. A business has to be dynamic, it can't remain stationary; if it doesn't move forward it will inevitably go back; it's like a living plant which has to be nurtured and fed and developed, or it will fade and die. But try telling that to Reid. Well I'm through, finished, washed up."

"So what are you going to do?"

"First I'm going to phone my wife and tell her I've come to my senses. Then I'm going to a Turkish bath and try to get my body clean. I'm afraid my mind and memory will take a bit longer to recover. And, by the way, I'd better take the rest of that money, so I can buy a shirt and some underwear. Then I'm coming to the office and having a showdown with my charming co-directors."

"I didn't mean that, Matt. I meant after you leave Reid-Parry."

"I'm not quite sure. I've got a few ideas, but I want to chew them over. When I've done that it may be that I'll want to speak to you again. But we'll see."

"Okay, Matt. I'd better get back to the office now. Any message for Parry?"

Mattson laughed. "I doubt that you'd deliver the message I have for him. Just tell him I'll be in after lunch. And don't worry, I'll let him think I was with Leylands this morning."

At Bank station John looked at his watch and found it was almost eleven-thirty. He cashed a cheque at his bank in Lombard Street, changed Yvette's francs at the foreign exchange counter, then hurried back to the office.

He entered through the general office and stopped for a moment in the doorway. With sudden percipience he realised that, unless Parry brought in someone over his head, he would shortly be in sole charge of the office. The thought gave him a pleasant tingle of pride. The two women and Mitchell had turned around in their desks and were looking at him.

He nodded at them and addressed Mitchell. "Anything I should know about?"

He could sense a new feeling of authority and hoped it did not show in his voice. He recalled Mattson talking about power corrupting . . .

"Put the mail on your desk again, I did," said Mitchell. "Except for invoices and acknowledgements of order, and one new order that Parry kept."

"What was that?"

"Pretty large order, it was. From Dumard. Two Mammoth tractors."

John whistled. That would be worth in excess of twelve thousand pounds. Why, the freight rebate alone would be more than six hundred pounds.

"What did Parry say?"

"Wants you to go over and see him, he says."

"Who? Dumard?

"No. Parry."

"Oh." John sometimes felt his patience stretching thin at Mitchell's inanity and peculiarity of speech. This was one of those times. "Sally, please ring Mr Parry and tell him I'm on my way over."

He walked across the landing to the timber company's offices, feeling pleased with himself. These would be the first Mammoths Dumard had ordered. At present they were using nothing but Cats. It wasn't certain that the order was the result of the French correspondence that he had sometime ago persuaded Parry and Mattson to let him try, but it must have helped. People must prefer to get letters in their own language.

Parry was seated at his desk, writing, when John entered the room. He continued writing, gave no sign of noticing John's presence. John did not interrupt him. He had learned long ago that Parry got pleasure out of keeping visitors waiting. With Mattson's words still fresh in his mind he imagined this was a power-thing with Parry, a form of compensation for thirty years of subservience to Alfred Reid. So John waited in silence until Parry put his pen down, placed both elbows in desktop, making a steeple of his hands, and started tapping his fingertips together. He let Parry speak first.

"Did you meet up with Mattson?"

"Yes, sir."

"Where?"

The question came so sharply, with such obvious innuendo, that John was sure it was a snare of some kind.

"I don't follow you, sir," he said, playing for time.

"No-o-o. I suppose you don't, Graham." Parry was visibly angry now. "It wasn't at Leylands, was it?"

"No, sir, it wasn't."

"Well, where was it then? You must have met him some place. It wasn't on the astral plane, was it? And I hope you had some good reason for lying to me this morning. Well, man, can't you speak?"

"I'm sorry, sir. I don't feel at liberty to disclose that. Mr Mattson will have to tell you himself when he comes in after lunch." He shifted his feet, nervously, and repeated, "I'm sorry."

"That's not good enough, Graham. We tried to reach you at Leyland's offices to discuss an order which has come in and you were not there. Neither of you. But of course you know that. I'll give you another chance to tell me where you were this morning."

"I'm sorry," John said once more, feeling the back of his neck getting warm, "I can't add anything to what I've said." He now knew exactly what was meant by the hope that the ground would open up and swallow him.

"Well, I'm not satisfied Graham, and the matter will not be allowed to rest there. You can expect to see Mr Reid this afternoon."

Parry returned to his writing and John, with a sense of relief, left the office. He walked back to his own office in a far less happy frame of mind than earlier. Events were moving altogether too swiftly. He had returned from Victoria with the hope of a general manager's job, if not a directorship, in the palm of his hand, and now it seemed he would soon be looking for a new job.

Far from hungry, but even less inclined to stay in the office, he went to the Stirling Castle and compromised on a cheese sandwich and a glass of beer. When he returned to the office Mattson was already seated at his desk, hunting through drawers. A different Mattson from the morning, looking better than John had seen him look for months. He commented on it.

"I *feel* better," Mattson said. "Amazing what an hour in a Turkish bath will do for you. They were able to valet my suit while I was there, so I feel up to bearding the lion in his plush-carpeted den."

"I hope you still feel up to it when you hear what I've got to say."

Mattson raised his eyebrows.

"Reid and Parry know you weren't at Leyland's this morning," John said grimly. "They tried to reach us there."

"Christ, that's buggered it for you, John. I'm sorry. What did you tell them?"

"Nothing." He smiled bitterly. "The prisoner reserved his defence. I told Parry he should hear it from you. He wasn't very happy about that. I haven't seen Reid yet."

"Jesus, John, I didn't intend for you to land in a mess."

"I told Parry to expect you after lunch."

"Right. I'll push off for a quick bite and see them when I get back."

It was almost three o'clock before Mattson returned to his desk. He looked tired and grim.

"They're waiting for you in Reid's office."

"What did you tell them, Matt?"

Mattson sat down wearily, removed his spectacles, rubbed his eyes. "I think I've got you off the hook. I told them I phoned you this morning and asked you to come to Hanover Square with Leyland's file, that I led you to believe I was visiting Leyland. I said I was waiting for you outside their offices."

"Didn't they want to know why you wanted to see me?"

"I covered that too. I said I had stayed in town overnight and needed some cash. I also told them I was resigning and that you know of my intention, and that's why you felt you couldn't say anything until they had heard from me."

John expelled his breath audibly with relief. "Well you've certainly made me sound a paragon of virtue. I only hope they believed you. Didn't they want to know why you needed the case?"

"They asked me, but I told them it was none of their business. I said I had told you the same thing."

"Sounds as if you had a pleasant meeting."

Mattson groaned. "You've no idea. You have absolutely no idea. They want me off the premises immediately."

"Can they do that? After all, you are a director."

"I don't know and I don't care. t suits me to be away from here as soon as possible. I didn't expect anything else.

The intercom rang and Mattson picked up the phone.

"Yes, Mr Reid. I've just told him and he's on his way over. He had to finish a phone call first."

John waved a pair of crossed fingers at Mattson and hurried out.

When he entered Reid's office the director's normally florid face was purple with anger. Across the desk from him sat Parry, hands in lap, looking uncomfortable and wary. Mattson seems to have done a good job on them, John thought.

"Come over here, Graham," Reid boomed.

John walked over to the desk and stood before it, hands clenched behind his back.

"You know Mattson's leaving." He paused, waiting for an answer, even though it had not been a question.

"Yes, sir."

"You knew it this morning."

"Yes, sir."

"Didn't tell Mr Parry, though. Didn't see fit to inform us. Lied about it in fact. Eh, boy?"

"It was not quite. . ."

"Can't have that, Graham. Can't have liars working for us. Start lying about small things, who knows where it'll end."

John shot a glance at Parry, a silent appeal for help, for intercession to explain the circumstances of their afternoon conversation. Parry studiously avoided his eyes.

"Well, by, got nothing to say for yourself?"

"I did what I thought was right, sir. I felt it was Mr Mattson's duty to inform you first. In fact I felt that he should not even have told me before you knew." He managed to get a degree of righteous indignation in his voice. He could almost convince himself it was the truth.

"That's all very well, boy. But who pays your wages? A director about to resign or us?"

"It's not . . ."

"You mentioned duty, Graham. There's also such a thing as loyalty. Your loyalty is to us. You understand that, don't you?"

"Yes, sir."

"You see now that you behaved wrongly, Graham."

"Yes, sir."

"We'll say no more about it this time, then. Call it a misplaced sense of honour, eh? But don't let it happen again if you want to stay with us. You do want to stay with us, eh, Graham?"

"Yes, sir."

"All right. Parry, tell him about the Dumard order."

Parry plucked a sheet of paper from the desk. "We had to get this translated outside, Graham, when you weren't here."

Reid broke in. "That's another thing, boy. Understand you've been writing in French. That's to stop. English has always been good enough for us here in Timber. Those Frenchies write it pretty well. Can't encourage them to write in a foreign language. Next thing they'll be doing it with the timber contracts."

John was torn between the desire to make an angry retort, and the urge to laugh at Reid's unbelievable stupidity. He did neither. He remained silent.

Parry went on. "It's an order for two Mammoth tractors. Now that Mattson's leaving, you'll have to handle it. Do you think you can manage that?"

"Yes, sir."

"You can well imagine, Graham, that this has been a great shock to us. We've treated Mattson more than generously. It was like being rejected by one of our own family." Parry's eyes seemed to mist with pain. He actually believes that rubbish, John thought. "As you can appreciate, Mr Reid and I have a great deal to discuss. The office will have to be thoroughly reorganised. We may have to bring in someone to replace Mattson. We just don't know. In a way it is up to you. We are looking to you to prove that you can do the work adequately by yourself. For the time being, therefore, you can look upon yourself as acting General Manager, responsible directly to me. If you think that is too much for you, you'd better tell me now."

"No, sir, I . . ."

Reid interrupted. "Tell him about his salary, Parry."

"Hrrm, yes." Parry smiled, producing a series of little lines beside his eyes. John was reminded of Mattson's father-figure description. "You're getting nine hundred a year at present, I believe." John nodded. "And you got a two hundred and fifty pound bonus at Christmas. That's eleven-fifty altogether. Well, in view of the extra responsibility you will be undertaking, we propose to augment your salary to that as a basic figure. Eleven hundred and fifty pounds a year. Plus expenses and bonus, of course."

"Well, boy, what do you say?"

"Thank you, sir. I'm sure I'll be able to cope."

"Right, Graham. We'll want to discuss it further with you tomorrow."

His words reminded John that he had promised Yvette he would take tomorrow off. Dare he mention it? Dare he? What the hell, he might as well start off on the right foot – and that meant boldly. It was obvious they couldn't do without him.

"Actually I had planned to take tomorrow off."

Parry's eyebrows seemed to be trying to join forces with his hairline; Reid's face grew apoplectic. Before they could speak, John added, "Dumard's niece is in town and I promised him I would show her around." He silently thanked Dumard for the timeliness of his order. "Dumard's nephew – my friend – died recently in Dien-Bien-Phu, and she came over to give me the news personally."

Reid's face bore the signs of a struggle: unease at the significance of John's relationship with Dumard's family battling with anger at the thought of loss of authority. Parry stared at his co-director, his face expressionless, waiting to get his lead from Reid.

Anger lost. "Hmmm . . . yes . . . well, I suppose . . . in that case. What do you think, Parry? Can we leave it until Friday?"

"Excuse me, sir. Friday is Good Friday."

Parry said, "I think a good solution might be for you to bring the young lady to the office tomorrow morning, since you will probably be coming to town anyway. We would like to meet her, wouldn't we, Mr Reid?"

"That's it," said Reid, seeing an opportunity to grant John's request with no loss of authority. "A good idea, Mr Parry. I'd like to hear how Henri's getting on. That all right with you, Graham?"

"Yes, sir. I'm sure Miss Beaumont will be delighted to meet you."

"Beaumont? Beaumont, you say?"

"Yes. Her mother was a Dumard."

"Right, boy. We'll expect you here at ten. Mattson's leaving tonight, so you'd better get back to your office and get things tidied up with him."

John trod air all the way back to his own office. Mattson was flopped out in John's chair, his feet on John's desk.

"Wipe that silly grin off your face, and sit at your new desk."

"Well, Matt, how did you know?"

"It was obvious. I can probably tell you word-for-word what they said. First Reid bawled you out for not telling Parry about my resignation. Right?"

"Right."

"Then he very generously decided to let bygones be bygones. Right?"

John nodded.

"Then they offered to make you general manager in my place. Correct?"

"No. Acting general manager until they decided what they're going to do."

"Pikers! They decided that within ten seconds of my leaving them. You're the general manager, lad, but without the title. How big a raise did they give you?"

"Two fifty. Upped me to eleven fifty."

"You accepted?"

"Of course."

Mattson chortled. "Oh the cunning bastards. You should be on twelve fifty at least, and probably fifteen hundred. They have no intention of bringing anyone else in. They'll have you doing your work *and* mine. And they'll be saving two thousand a year. I'm afraid you've let them pull a fast one, John."

John felt himself getting irritable. "I'm quite happy with the arrangement, Matt. I don't think it's a bad salary at my age. And as long as they let me do my job I shall be perfectly satisfied."

"Okay, keep your illusions while you can. I suppose they also told you to get everything straightened out with me?"

"They did."

"Well most of it will be verbal. I don't have to remind you that I haven't been doing much paperwork lately. So we can discuss it over a coffee after you close the office. But I warn you, I won't be making a late night of it. I want to get home to my wife."

"Don't worry, Matt. I've got plans of my own for this evening." His words came out more stuffily than he intended.

"Pardon *me*. I didn't realise we were so touchy." Mattson smiled. "We're going to part as friends, aren't we?"

"Of course. I didn't intend to sound so stuffy. I hope we'll remain friends, Matt."

"Good. For two reasons. First because I may want to cash in on that friendship in the new future. Secondly because I'm afraid I'm responsible for you losing your secretary."

"Patricia?"

"Yes. I told her I was leaving. She said she also wanted to leave. She didn't want to stay if I wasn't here."

"But that's ridiculous. Why should she say that?"

"She has her reasons I suppose."

John stared at him, and Mattson looked uncomfortable. "Matt! You haven't? You and Patricia . . .?"

Mattson nodded his head and refused to look John in the eye. "Don't, for Christ's sake, let her know I told you. It started one day when I'd had a drop too much . . ."

"Don't tell me," John broke in. "Let me guess. Christmas 1950, right?"

"Right,"

"Matt, aren't you ashamed of yourself?" He was teasing; after all he was not one to cast stones. But Mattson took him seriously.

"Why should I be? I've made no claim on her. She's made no claims on me. She knows I love my family and I've no intention of leaving my wife. She also knows there's little likelihood of getting married herself. Don't ask me to explain that statement, just take my word for it. So why shouldn't she get a little happiness out of our relationship? And I've needed her as much as she needed me. I'd have gone overboard years ago if I hadn't had someone to talk to, someone who knows the office."

"You could have talked to me."

"You're not my type." He grinned. "No, you're right. I could have talked to you. And if I hadn't had Patricia, I probably would have talked to you. But talking wasn't enough. She has been able to comfort me too. For heaven's sake, I don't have to explain, do I?"

"Hell, no, Matt. I'm teasing you. Anyway I'm hardly in a position to make moral judgements."

"Well, you see how it is. You can understand why she wants to leave. Perhaps if we'd been able to see more of each other, I wouldn't have ended up as I did last night. But we were only able to meet once or twice a month."

"Well I suppose I shall just have to contact some of the agencies."

The phone rang on John's desk and Mattson picked it up. "Yes, all right, Sally, I'll tell him." He turned to John. "There's a call for you, and Sally says to remind you that it's after five-thirty and the letters still need to be signed, and they want to know if they may leave."

John took the phone from him and grinned. "How would you like to do your last job of work for Reid-Parry Enterprises, Matt? Sign the letters for me, huh? And tell them they can go. I'll speak to them in the morning. Oh, and tell Mitchell I'll be in late tomorrow. He's to open the mail and hold it for my arrival."

"Yes, sir. Will that be all, sir?"

"That's all. Dismiss." He spoke into the phone. "Hello, Graham here."

"John? Is that you?" It was Yvette.

"Yes, Yvette. How are you, darling?"

"Oh, John, I think I have made trouble for you." She sounded tearful.

"What is it, sweetheart? What has happened?"

"A woman came to the apartment a few minutes ago. She came in by herself. I was in a . . . a . . . you know, a *fauteuil*."

"An armchair."

"Yes, an armchair. She looked at me for a moment and then left again. She did not say anything. Could it be the girl friend you mentioned?"

"Yes. Undoubtedly." His face twisted. Christ, with all that had happened today he had forgotten to telephone Julie.

"What are you going to do, John?"

"Don't worry about it, darling. I'm sure no harm's been done. I think I had better visit her on my way home. Do you mind?"

"No, of course not."

"I shall be home about . . ." he looked at his wristwatch ". . .about eight o'clock. All right?"

"Yes. Are you sure it is in order?"

"Of course. Just put it out of your mind. I'll see you later."

He made his voice sound confident but, as he replaced the receiver, he wondered how the hell he was going to explain the situation to Julie.

He hesitated with his finger six inches from Julie's doorbell.

It still wasn't too late to turn around and go home. He could telephone her later. He could avoid what threatened to be a difficult confrontation. It would be easier on the phone. How could he explain it to her now? He could not longer invite her round to meet Yvette; their relationship was no longer an innocent one. Yvette would be embarrassed.

Oh, he'd think of something to say once they began talking.

He pressed the bell.

Moments later he heard her footsteps, then the door opened. She was dressed in a flowered housecoat. He face seemed pale. Her eyes opened wide when she saw him.

He leaned forward to kiss her, but she turned her head aside and his lips brushed her cheek.

"What do you want, John?"

"I want to talk to you."

"Oh. I suppose your – your *inamorata* told you I'd been round. Or are you going to tell me she's a relation?"

"No, I'm not going to say anything of the kind. The woman you saw at the flat is Yvette. I've told you who she is. I just want to explain . . ."

"All right, John," she cut him off wearily, "you'd better come in."

She led the way into her bed-sitting room and sat in a chair. John remained standing, his hands thrust deep into his trousers pockets.

"Well, John?" I thought you had something to explain."

"Yes. You're obviously jumping to conclusions, and . . ." He paused, uncertain how to continue.

"What's the matter, John? Can't you remember the story? Suppose I tell you something, before you think up a convincing lie. Peggy cancelled her date with me last night. I came round to the flat . . ."

"You came round to the flat?" he repeated stupidly. "I didn't hear . . ."

"No, you didn't hear the door open, did you? You were in no state to hear anything, I imagine. But I could hear plenty. I went round again this evening to pick up my things. She's still there, isn't she?"

"Yes, she's still there," he agreed miserably. "But I didn't invite her. And I couldn't help what happened. You've got to understand . . ."

"Don't worry, I understand only too well. I'm through making excuses for you."

"What do you mean? What excuses have you had to make for me?"

She glared at him. "You don't think this is the first of your indiscretions I've found out about, do you?"

"What indiscretions? What are you talking about?"

She sighed and shook her head slowly from side to side. "Give me a cigarette. You're clearly determined to have it spelled out for you, letter by letter."

He handed her a cigarette, took one himself, and lit them.

"What about Megan, John?

"Megan? What about her?"

"Haven't you wondered why you never see Norman these days? Don't you know their marriage is on the rocks and she wants a divorce? You don't think the little bitch would keep her affair with you a secret, do you? It's given her the utmost satisfaction, I'm sure, to let both Norman and me know what's gone on between you."

"My God! You surely don't believe that!"

"Isn't it true, John?"

"Once! Just once!" he exclaimed with indignation. "And that was her doing."

"You are incredible. Always the injured party! My heart really bleeds for you. Megan and now this. . . this other woman, and heaven knows how many others . . . and none of it has been your doing, has it? What insufferable conceit. Well it's over, John. You're going to have to learn you can't continue charming your way through life, taking all the time, and not giving anything back. I'm through being a convenience to be used when the need arises – like a credit card. And to think I once wanted to marry you."

"So that's it! That's what brought this on! The fact that I've never asked you to marry me. Well, that's one thing I've always been honest about. I've never made any promises, have I?"

"My God, you haven't understood a word I've said. How can anyone be so vain. You think you're a strong-minded individual, but you're not. You're weak. Your only strength is that incredible vanity, and you're too stupid to see that it's your greatest weakness. When I think that one day you may really fall in love, I can feel almost pity for you, as I feel pity for any woman who falls in love with you. Because really you're afraid. You're unsure of yourself. You're lacking something, and you don't know what it is. One day you will have to look inside yourself if you want to find the answer, and you won't like what you find."

"Well thank you for the parlour psychiatry. Have you quite done?"

"Yes." Bitterly. "Yes, John, quite, quite done. I don't suppose it'll worry you too much. Your supply list must be pretty long, even when my name's been crossed off."

"Okay," he said, hurt and angry, mainly because he could recognise the truth in much of what she had said. "Suppose you let me have the key back."

"I left it on the hallstand in your flat."

"Thank you. I'll get your things back to you somehow."

"Don't take the trouble. The only thing I want back, you can't give me: the last six years of my life."

As he left the room he thought he heard the sound of her crying behind him.

CHAPTER FIFTEEN

Twilight was enfolding the valley and a cool breeze caressed the leaves of the trees. Far below the river wound its way carelessly through the fading evening light while, in the distance, the sinking April sun had become a ball of fiery glory, gilding the hills with its last rays, dissolving softly into patient night.

The stood silently, hand in hand, scarcely daring to breathe lest they break the spell of the evening's magic, until finally the last ray of the declining sun disappeared, leaving them in darkness. Then they turned to each other and embraced. This was a moment to be cherished, he felt: this experience they had shared, filling them with the imagery of poetry, making their two souls one.

"Darling," he whispered.

"Sshh." She laid a finger against his lips. "Not now."

She was right. Words were not necessary. They turned and walked slowly back to the village inn.

The bar was filled with locals, most of whom stared with friendly curiosity at the visitors. Occasionally one would nod or wink in warm acceptance. It was pretty certain, he reflected amusedly, that the whole village was aware of the Grahams occupying the solitary guest bedroom of this Herefordshire inn.

They finished their drinks and climbed the narrow staircase at the rear, hearing the sudden outbreak of voices behind them as they left the bar. In the bedroom John threw open the small latticed window and gazed out at the night sky. After a moment Yvette came and stood beside him.

"The stars always seem so much closer in the country, don't they?" he said.

She did not answer. He did not expect an answer. He held her in his arms and said, fervently, "If only this could go on for ever and ever."

He face looked wistful in the starlight. Far off an owl hooted, and from below came the sounds of people leaving the inn, making their farewells.

Taking his arm, leading him away from the window, she said, "I do not think I would want this to last forever. It would cease to be so precious. It would become familiar and tarnished and spoiled. We would start to take it for granted. Perhaps we would take each other for granted also. This way we will always remember it exactly as it is. Am I not right, John?"

"Yes. I suppose so. And yet I don't think I have ever felt so much at peace with myself. Is it so strange for me to want t to last?"

"I know," she murmured. "I know."

Later, in the old-fashioned down bed, he looked at her. Her head was resting in the crook of his elbow, her eyes closed, although her breathing suggested she was not yet asleep. Her hair, long and black and silkily thick, fanned out over the pillow.

He felt again the slight ache of emptiness that he had tried unsuccessfully to identify after their first night together. He was happy – he was sure he was happy – and he couldn't understand why he should feel that something was missing. It was . . . yes, it was the knowledge that this happiness was transitory, that it would not endure the dawn and the successive dawns. And he wanted it to last. He wanted the permanence of belonging. It was what he had always wanted; what he had always striven for. Was marriage the answer? With a shock of confusing discovery he found he could think about marriage for the first time without the instinctive revulsion that always turned his thoughts away from the subject. Marriage . . . marriage to Yvette . . . would that give him what he needed? In the stillness of the room he could hear the thudding of his heart. Perhaps that was the missing substance of his blind desires and irrational fears. But he mustn't rush things. He must consider it calmly and unemotionally, not just in the pulsating response of night, but in the impassive light of day.

Her eyes opened, stared at him, her lips smiling. "What is it, John? Aren't you sleepy?"

"No, sweetheart, I'm afraid to waste a moment of this precious night."

"Darling." She nestled to him. "Have I made you happy?"

"You know you have." He pressed his lips to her forehead.

"Have I made you forget that other girl?" she asked slyly.

He winced with the memory of his last meeting with Julie. "There was nothing to forget."

"That was funny, in your office the other day, John. I felt very important. What would those two men have said, had they known I am not really related to Monsieur Dumard?"

He laughed. "The point is they didn't know. I didn't know myself. I thought he was your mother's brother."

"No. His brother married my aunt, my mother's sister."

"It doesn't matter, darling. The fact is you were very good with Reid and Parry."

She giggled. "It was like playing in a *pièce de théatre*. I did not like them, you know."

"Who? Reid and Parry?"

"Mmm." She wrinkled her nose. "The big man was horrible. Like a great big frog. And there was something about the little man . . . I cannot explain. He was very friendly, but I did not trust him. He smiled too much."

"Woman's intuition. What about my own staff?"

"Oh . . . the man was . . . um . . . nothing, you know? He made no impression. The big girl seemed nice, very genuine. The other woman looked unhappy."

"Well, well, perhaps there is something in woman's intuition after all. But I told you once before that you were very astute, do you remember?" He hugged her.

"John, darling . . ." She spoke softly, hesitantly. "I do not want to make you feel . . . *unquiet*?"

"Uncomfortable?" he suggested.

"Yes, uncomfortable. I am not trying to . . . to imprison you." She clicked her tongue impatiently. "Oh I cannot find the right words."

"Just speak your mind, darling. Say it in French if you prefer."

"No. I will say it in English. I was wondering . . . after this weekend, when I go back to Menton . . . when will I see you again?"

"As soon as possible, sweetheart. I shall take my holidays in September and, I promise you faithfully, I shall come to Menton."

"You will want to see me again, John. This has made no difference to you?"

"It has made all the difference, Yvette." He raised her chin and looked into her eyes. "I'll want to see you more than ever."

"Oh, John." She gave a contented sigh. "I cannot believe it was only four days ago that I came to London. I feel a different person. I am a different person. And in just two days I must go back. What will we do for these days?"

"Well, I think we should start back tomorrow afternoon. I'm not too happy with the car. I'd prefer to take it easy and spend tomorrow night closer to London, perhaps in Oxfordshire. You'll be returning on Monday evening, I suppose."

"Could I not get a plane early on Tuesday morning? Early enough for you to get to the office afterwards?"

"I imagine so. Why?"

She ran a hand over his shoulder and pressed her cheek to his bare chest. "It would give us another night together," she said shyly.

PART FOUR

The mist was clearing slowly with the morning sun. Gradually the road ahead brightened, seeming to extend itself before my steady gaze.

How long had I been standing there, peering through the gloom, trying to penetrate the vaporous atmosphere with stinging eyes? I passed a hand over my hair and felt its coldness and dampness.

Suddenly, in the mist ahead, were twin small eyes of light and simultaneously I heard the engine sound of an approaching vehicle. It stopped about one hundred yards away and I could now identify it as a Mammoth tractor with Norman in the high driver's cab. I also noted, with pleased surprise, that Julie was in the seat beside Norman .

I walked towards them, smiling, waving a hand in greeting. Why, I wondered, didn't they acknowledge me? They simply sat there, gazing steadfastly ahead, stern almost antagonistic expressions on their faces, ignoring me.

Unexpectedly, with a grating of gears, the tractor moved into reverse and began to draw away from him. I broke into a run, calling out to them to stop. Were they deaf? Didn't they hear me? Whatever the case, the tractor remained as far away as ever, its occupants still seemingly unaware of me.

The road had been getting narrower, and now the tractor seemed to fill the entire width of track between the steep grass banks. The road surface was getting rougher and the tractor started bounding over the uneven stretches in an alarming manner. I ran faster, shouting, "You see, you see, your suspension is all wrong. Your tracks should oscillate separately." The blood was pounding in my head and my breath was being expelled in raucous gasps.

All at once I heard a sound in the road behind me and looked back. In the distance a car was approaching at great speed. Good, I thought, I'll stop the car and get a lift. Then I'll catch them up. I stood in the middle of the road, arms outstretched. The car was getting close now, but its speed had not slackened. What's the matter with everyone today, I wondered, are they all blind?

Suddenly the air was filled with the sound of the car's horn: the high-pitched scream of a soul in anguish. With a flood of panic I knew that the driver had no intention of stopping. I turned my head and found that the tractor had vanished. I would have to get out of the way. But where? How? The road was too narrow; the grass banks too steep. Only a hundred yards now separated me from the car and I started yelling frantically, waving my hands in a frenzy of despair.

The car horn sounded again, deafeningly, and as the moment of impact arrived I found myself rooted to the spot, a scream of terror in my throat, staring at the driver.

With sickening horror I saw that I myself was the driver.

Who was I killing, then? *Who was I killing*?

I screamed.

"Wake up. Wake up, John."

Someone was shaking me. I forced my eyes open, angrily, half my mind still there on the road, wanting to return.

"What is it?" My body was bathed in sweat, I was trembling.

"You were shouting. I think you were asleep. Were you dreaming?"

"Yes. No. I don't know. What was I shouting?"

"I'm not sure. It sounded like . . . mother."

"Mother," I repeated doubtfully. Then I shivered.

"John, you are wet all over. You had better towel yourself down. I fell asleep also and we have to leave now for my train."

"All right, darling."

I got off the bed, went to the sink, and ran a damp face flannel over my face, under my armpits, down my body. Then I rubbed myself fiercely with the coarse towel. I tried to remember what I had been dreaming, but it had already faded. There had been a road . . . and a car . . . and . . . I could not remember any more. Why would I have shouted 'mother' in my sleep? I felt weak.

I could not tell her anything now. I was not up to facing the inevitable scene which my words would provoke. I would tell her when she was on the train. That way there would be no time for recriminations.

We dressed and I took her to the Gare St. Lazare and saw her onto the platform where her suburban train was waiting. She leaned out of the carriage window, lowered her face so that I might kiss her. Her lips felt cold against mine, yet my face was burning.

I felt a tremble threatening. This was the moment to tell her. I could do it now and the story would be re-written; the record would spin to its end and a new one laid on the turntable.

I licked my lips and drew a breath, but the words wouldn't come. From along the platform came the sound of the guard's whistle. The train started to move forward slowly.

Tell her. Tell her now. Quickly. I walked beside the train, trying to speak, to explain, to break the spell of silence. Two short sentence were all that were needed.

"Goodnight, darling." She smiled. "I'll see you tomorrow evening."

No, Yvette, no, I wanted to shout. But I remained mute.

"Don't forget." She blew a kiss. "*Jardin des Tuileries*."

Suddenly I found my voice. "I'll be there," I shouted.

After all, I could always tell her tomorrow.

I listened to the wheels of the train moving away down the track, symbolising the wheels I had set in motion last week. God, yes, it was only one week ago . . .

CHAPTER SIXTEEN

John slit the envelope with an impatient hand. He was bitterly irritated, and it was only partly the effect of the drinks he had had last night, he told himself. He should have listened to Mattson. Matt had known. He had had the benefit of several years more experience than John. Since his departure it had taken John a matter of mere months to parallel the path of his predecessor.

He put the invoice to one side and turned his attention to the next envelope.

Yes, everything Matt had said had come to pass. The timber company had lost the United Swiss account and, barely one month later, Reid-Parry Enterprises had lost Graumann's agency business. Who the hell had it now? They'd certainly be cashing in on Mattson's years of effort and expertise. And the American Truck Company agency had gone for a Burton too, simultaneously with the withdrawal of the American Timber Company account from Alfred Reid Timbers. How long before Dumard, too, got fed up with them?

Speak of the devil!

He smoothed out the letter from Dumard Frères nervously. What had they got to say for themselves? Were they going to pay for the tractors or not?

He read the letter carefully, then read it again, trying to assess the implications of the complaint and the settlement proposed by the French company. It was going to be a difficult problem to solve; even worse than he had imagined when Dumard's cable had arrived last week. The best chance for a solution lay in a visit to Paris to discuss the matter with Dumard personally. Actually the real answer would be a visit to the Cameroons by one of Mammoth's technical wallahs, but Mammoth would hardly be likely to foot the bill, and he couldn't see Reid agreeing to pay it.

God, this constant effort to steer a course between the problems of his customers and the pig-headedness of his own Board. Well, they would just have to agree to send him to Paris.

The intercom buzzed. He lifted the receiver. Parry.

"Good morning, sir."

"Anything good in today, Graham?" His usual opening gambit.

"A few invoices. One small spares order. A letter from Dumard." Deliberately keeping that information back till last.

"Oh, yes." Parry's voice perked up." "Have they sorted out the snags on the tractors?"

"No, sir," John said wearily "They want a ten percent reduction on the price or they'll suspend payment of our draft."

There was silence at the other end, pregnant with Parry's unspoken thoughts, then he said, "You'd better come across here to discuss it."

For once Parry did not engage in delaying tactics when John entered the Room. With twelve thousand pounds at stake he was evidently of the opinion that time was money. He took the letter which John handed him and then threw it back across the desk. "It's in French," he snapped. "What does it say?"

John picked the letter up. "They say there are faults in both tractors. Neither of them has the separately oscillating tracks which are the special feature of the unit, and the reason they chose to buy it in the first place. They consider it will cost several thousand francs to have them put right, plus the loss of time before they can use them in their timber operations. Accordingly they ask for a ten percent reduction in the purchase price, and they suggest we will be able to recover the money from Mammoth under warranty."

"Hmmm. And what do Mammoth say."

"They don't know about it yet, sir. This is the first we've heard officially about the complaint. I haven't had a chance to discuss it with Mammoth."

"I see." Parry smiled. He had obviously decided on a change of tactics now that they matter was outside the realm of finance alone, but touched on technicalities. John knew exactly what was coming. "Well, Graham, what do you suggest?"

Dear God! For a moment he was tempted to play Parry's game, Parry's way; to force Parry to make the decisions. But that could result in a thorough balls-up, and he was uncomfortably aware of his responsibility to both Mammoth and Dumard.

He said, "I'll get on to Margolis at Mammoth and get his view. Then I think . . ." he paused in the act of suggesting to Parry that he, Graham, ought to go to Paris. Let's play it Parry's way, this time, he thought. ". . . I think you should go to Paris, sir, and have the matter out with Dumard."

It was laughable, ludicrous, but totally predictable. Parry's face turned a bright red. Suggesting he visit Paris was like asking a Trappist monk to give a lecture on contraception.

Parry cleared his throat. "I don't really see . . . I don't think . . ."

"It's the only way, sir. Time is money." Having launched himself into this gambit he was beginning to relish it, to enjoy Parry's discomfiture. He chose to misunderstand Parry's reluctance. "I can understand you not wanting to spend money on such a trip, but every day our draft is delayed will cost us interest. I'm sure a few pounds spent of a visit to Dumard will be more than justified."

"Yes, yes," Parry was playing with a paper knife, "I see that. But I don't think I'm the person. Furthermore I really can't spare the time away from the office." He pricked himself with the point of the paper knife, dropped it on the desk and began rubbing his finger. "No, I think perhaps you will have to go over there, Graham. It will involve technicalities, and you can speak their language. Yes, I think that's the answer."

There was almost a look of disappointment on his face, John felt, and keeping his own face straight he said, "As you say, sir. When do you think I should go?"

"When . . .?" Parry gave him a look of perplexed enquiry, as if he had suddenly realised what he had agreed to, but couldn't comprehend how he had been manoeuvred into that position.

"Yes . . . well . . . you will have to decide that yourself after you have had a word with Mammoth. It may depend on what they say. You had better speak to them right away."

Back in his own office, John asked Sally to get Margolis on the phone, and to put an outside line through to him while she was placing the call. He got out his diary and searched it for a telephone number, then he dialed the continental exchange and asked the operator the delay on a call to Menton in France. Learning that it would be no less than half an hour, he gave her the telephone number and replaced the receiver. Almost immediately the phone rang and he picked up the receiver again.

"Graham."

"Hello, John. This is your call. Dare I hope for another order?"

"Sorry. No can oblige, Victor. A complaint."

"Oh?" Victor Margolis's voice became wary. "What's up?"

"The two tractors we shipped to Douala last month. So far I've not received the precise details, but I gather they are having difficulties with the free track oscillation. According to the customer the tracks are not oscillating separately."

"While he was speaking a series of grunts at the other end suggested that Margolis was becoming agitated. Now her interjected, "That's nonsense, John, and you know it. All out tractors come off the same assembly line. How can one differ from the others? Let alone two."

"That's what I want to find out. You can imagine how important it is to us when I tell you they're asking for a ten percent price reduction."

"Balls!" Margolis exploded. "They're trying to pull a fast one. You shouldn't stand for it."

"All very well for you to say that, Victor. And you don't have to persuade *me*. But just remember that it's *our* money that's at stake. We've already paid you. . . Now just a minute," he hastily stopped Margolis's attempted interruption, "I'm not trying to get anything out of you for the moment except information. As a matter of fact I'm going to Paris to discuss the matter in person with their head office. All I want is to be sure I have all the technical data available to me when I get there."

"Sorry." He sounded sheepish. "These trumped-up claims always piss me off. We'll certainly give you all the help we can."

Of course they will, thought John, now it's no longer a question of money. He said, "Fine, Victor. How long will it take you to get everything off to me? I want to leave as soon as possible."

"I'll get Coulson, our head of engineering, to express something in the post to you today. You'll have it first thing in the morning at the latest." Margolis paused and then added, "Didn't we ship those two united PKD?"

"PKD?" John queried.

"You know. In partly knocked-down condition."

"Yes. We did. To save freight costs."

"Hmm. In that case they've probably made a simple error in re-assembly. That would explain the same fault in both units. I suggest you delay going over there until next week and, in the meantime, ask them to arrange for an immediate independent survey report. Then have their Paris office check the details against the track assembly instructions we will send you."

"That sounds a good idea. Thanks, Victor."

"Don't mention it. All part of the Mammoth service. When are you coming up to Wolverhampton again?"

John laughed. "I'll probably bring our invoice for the ten percent reduction up to you personally."

Margolis laughed back, but the laughter sounded strained. People find it hard to joke about things that are important to them, thought John.

"Seen our friend Mattson lately?" Margolis asked.

"No. Haven't seen him since he left us. He phoned once, about a month ago. Wanted to know how things were going. But apart from that . . . nothing."

"Oh." Victor seemed surprised. "I thought he was going to be in touch with you."

"Really?" It was John's turn to be surprised. "Have you heard from him?"

"Yes. He was up here a couple of weeks back."

"What's he doing now?"

"I don't know if he wants me to mention it." Margolis sounded apologetic.

"Christ, Victor, Matt and I are friends. You know that."

"Well . . . He's started his own business. He came up her to discuss placing some orders with us." Margolis grunted. "Uh, don't let on that I told you."

"Don't worry. He'll probably tell me himself – in his own good time."

They said goodbye. John replaced the phone and buzzed Parry on the intercom. He told the director he had spoken to Margolis, recounted what Mammoth proposed to do, and suggested that the following Tuesday would be a good time to see Dumard. That would give them eight days to fix the independent survey.

Parry thanked him, said he would let him know, and hung up. Five minutes later he called back and told John to go and see Reid.

John sent for Sally Carter. He explained that he was expecting a call from France and that it might come through while he was with Reid. If it did, she was to buzz him in Reid's office and say there was an urgent trunk call for him, without revealing the origin of the call. Did she understand? Yes, she confirmed, it was quite clear.

He went across to Reid's office.

For once the director was alone and John wondered momentarily if Parry's absence had any significance. Reid was examining a document on his desk, leaning forward from where his waist would be if he had one. He spoke without looking up.

"Understand you're off to Paris next week."

"Yes, sir."

"Going to see Dumard."

"Yes, sir."

"Trouble with a tractor."

"Yes, sir." No, sir. Three bags full, sir. John smiled inwardly.

"What do you propose to do about it?"

"Mr Parry knows all about it, sir."

"I know he does, Graham." Reid raised his voice and his head. He looked at John for the first time. "I want to know what *you* propose to do about it. Or haven't you given it any thought?"

There was no need for Reid to adopt that tone. He need not stand there and take it, John thought. But he knew he would.

"Margolis - Mammoth's export sales manager – is preparing a technical report for me to take to Paris. I think I'll be able to answer Dumard's questions. I'm also cabling him today to arrange an independent survey on site, and to have the report airmailed to his Paris office by next Tuesday when I shall be there."

"Twelve thousand pounds is a lot of money, Graham."

"I'm aware of that, sir."

"What's your friend Dumard playing at, boy?"

"I have no idea. I'm not aware he's playing at anything." He couldn't keep the asperity out of his voice. He refrained, with an effort, from pointing out that Dumard was not his friend.

Reid glared at him. Pressing his hands flat against the arms of his chair, giving a series of grunts, he pushed himself upright and waddled over to a small table on which stood a decanter and a glass. Nothing froglike about his walk, thought John, remembering Yvette's description.

"How far overdue is the payment now?" asked Reid, pouring liquid into the glass. It looked like water.

John calculated rapidly. "We shipped the units about eleven weeks ago . . say five weeks to reach Douala . . . that leaves six. We're supposed to be paid thirty days after arrival, so we should have been paid two weeks ago."

"Oh, excellent," Reid sneered. "They only ship timber against letters of credit, and get their money immediately. When we ship goods to them, they expect extended credit. Anything goes wrong and we can whistle for our money."

"It's hardly *anything*. They say they can't use the tractors. And twelve thousand's a lot of money for them, too."

Reid took a sip from the lass, then waddled back to his desk and dropped into his chair with a groan. "We don't need you to play devil's advocate, Graham." His tone had changed subtly; he was speaking almost gently. "You know as well as I do that in the case of a complaint you pay first and put in a claim afterwards. That's common business ethics. It's what we do regularly with timber. The trouble with these Frenchmen, they have no understanding of contractual obligations."

"Do you think you're being quite fair to them, Mr Reid?"

"Fair?" For a moment Reid seemed about to lose his temper. Then he smiled. "I keep forgetting he's a friend of yours. How is that charming young lady, by the way?"

Reid was altogether a different person when he smiled. It was almost seductive. John had to remind himself that this wily old bird was probably an expert at baiting traps. "Very well, sir, I believe."

"Good, good." Reid nodded. "Now look, Graham, I'm a lot older than you. You can take it from me the French have a different set of ethics from us. Probably comes from their different standard of morality. Just don't let Dumard put one over on you, boy."

John was finding conversation with Reid bewildering. he had never seen the old man in this vein before. His normally staccato, slightly imbecilic, form of speech had vanished and John wondered if it was adopted for Parry's benefit. Come to that, Reid's last remark would have more appropriately come from Parry.

"I won't, sir."

"That's it, Graham. Just remember who pays your salary."

"Yes, sir."

"Good. Now another thing. I don't want you to say anything to Dumard about the timber business."

"The timber business?"

"The timber business. *My* business." A hint of acrimony crept back into Reid's voice. "If Dumard tries to question you about our business next week, you know nothing. Understand? Nothing."

"Why should he question me about timber, sir?"

"Don't you understand English, boy?"

The sharpness of Reid's tone, the abrupt change from friendliness to anger, wrong-footed John He was finding it impossible to keep up with these mood swings. He stammered, "I. . . I don't follow you, sir."

"You don't have to, Graham. Just remember what I say. You do not discuss the timber business with Dumard. All right?"

"Yes sir, but if I might just . . ."

"That will be all, Graham. Drop in on Parry on your way back."

"Yes, sir, but there's . . ."

"THAT WILL BE ALL, GRAHAM."

John bit off an oath, turned his back on the director and left the room. He felt as if his emotions had been put through a wringer. That was a technique they used in brainwashing: friendly as pie one moment then, when you relaxed your defences, as rotten as hell. No wonder Parry was such a gutless specimen if he'd had to put up with that for more than thirty years.

He walked into Parry's office without knocking. Parry, as usual, kept on working, ignoring his presence. This time John did not feel like pandering to his superior's whim.

"Mr Reid asked me to see you."

Parry went on working. John approached him and put his palms on the desktop.

"I don't think you heard me. Is there something you need to tell me?"

Parry looked up slowly, his eyes narrowing ominously, "I'm busy, Graham."

"Yes, I see that. I've got work of my own to do. I'm anxious to get back to it."

Parry's eyes opened wide in surprise. John felt almost sorry for the man: bullied on all sides, first Reid and now Graham. Was it possible that Reid had torn him off a strip for agreeing that John visit Dumard?

His words almost confirmed the thought. "Did Mr Reid tell you not to discuss timber with Dumard?"

"Yes, Mr Parry. I don't know why he thought it necessary to tell me that. How can I discuss timber when I don't know the first thing about it?"

"Yours not to reason why, Graham. Just follow instructions. Dumard are behaving abominably and we're not going to put up with it."

"I don't see how you can say that. If the tractors don't work, they've got every justification for making a fuss."

"Oh, have they? Despite the fact that they haven't paid for them."

"That's another matter, of course. But I can't help feeling that this might have been avoided if I'd been allowed to make the overseas trip I wanted after Mattson left."

"Well you ought to be pleased now, Graham." Irony was thick in his voice. "You *are* going overseas, aren't you?"

"I want to go overseas to get business, not to collect debts."

"Hah!" Parry jeered. "Perhaps it's as well you not gone then, if we're not going to get paid for the business you get. Let us get one thing clear, Graham. While you work for us you will do things our way. If you don't like our way, the remedy's in your own hands."

"And what sort of a remedy would that be?" John swallowed hard. "I took this job, Mr Parry, because it was a challenge. And I think I've done pretty well at it. But I've reached the limits of what I can do behind a desk in a London office."

"Well, if you can't sell from the greatest metropolis in the world, what do you expect to do overseas?" asked Parry scathingly.

"You simply don't understand, sir. How much timber do you think your salesmen would sell if they didn't travel? In our case it's even more important. We're selling a service. Why should people trust us when they never see us?"

"Now you understand this, Graham. I'm quite satisfied with what we're doing. When I think you should go overseas, I'll tell you. In the meantime you will work my way, or you can clear out."

"If that's the way you want it, sir."

"That's the way I want it. And what I want you to do now is organise your office so that you can get over to Paris next week and clear up this mess of yours."

John was staggered. "Of *mine*?"

"You sold the tractors. You agreed the terms of payment."

"With your approval, Mr Parry."

Parry thumped the desk. "On your recommendation, Graham. On your recommendation. There's no point in prolonging this discussion. You know what you have to do?"

"Yes, sir. I know what I have to do." He walked to the door.

Parry called after him, "How long do you expect to be gone?"

John paused with his hand on the doorknob and turned to face Parry. "I shall fly over on Monday. I shall see Dumard on Tuesday. If there's any trouble I shall come straight back to London. But if all goes well and the money is paid, I shall take a few days holiday."

"Holiday?" Parry echoed bleakly.

"Yes, sir. I've had no holidays for two years. If I'm going to organise the office for my absence, I may as well profit by taking some of my overdue holiday now. I shall phone you from Paris and, unless there is anything that requires my urgent return, I'll probably take the rest of the week off."

He stared at Parris, silently begging him to make an issue of it. It would be the last straw. He would take no more of the little man's nonsense. He had had enough.

As though he had read his mind, Parry said quietly, "I think that's a good idea, Graham. You probably need a break."

Sally Carter met him in the passage as he was returning to his office.

"Oh, Mr Graham," she sad, "I've been trying to find you. Your call has come through."

"Thanks, Sally."

He hurried into his room and raised the receiver.

"Go ahead." Sally's voice. "You're through."

"*Je voudrais parler avec Mademoiselle Beaumont*," he said.

"*Elle-même à l'appareil.*"

"Yvette!"

"Is that you, John?" Wonder in her voice. "Where are you?"

"Listen, darling. I'm phoning from London, so I'll have to make this brief. I shall be in Paris next Monday and Tuesday. I can come to Menton, I think for a few days after that."

"Oh, darling. Is that all the time you can spare?"

"I don't know. I may be able to come again in September as we planned, but I'm still not sure." There was silence at the other end. "Yvette, are you still there?"

"Yes, John. I was thinking. Look, if I come to Paris we could have a whole week together."

"Why, yes. But can you. . .?"

"Yes. I can get away for a week. I'll stay with my aunt in Colombes. Write the number down." She dictated the telephone number and he jotted it on the corner of his desk blotter. "Have you got that, John?"

"Yes."

"Ring me when you get to Paris."

"Okay."

"And, John . . . I love you, darling."

"And I love you."

"Goodbye, darling."

"*Au 'voir, chérie.*"

He pushed his chair away from the desk and stretched out, feeling tension draining out of his shoulders. He had not been aware of being so tense. He also felt the relief of a sudden resolution and a spontaneous decision. The door opened and Sally came in.

"Oh, Mr Graham . . ."

He cut her short. "Sit down, Sally."

She sat dutifully in his visitors' chair, her big-boned body resting on about six inches of its forward edge.

"Make yourself comfortable."

She fidgeted back a few inches. He grinned at her.

"How do you like working here, Sally?"

"Very much, Mr Graham."

"How is Gladys getting on?"

She wrinkled her nose. The movement caused her spectacles to rest at an angle on the bridge of her nose, giving a peculiarly twisted look to her face. "She's very slow, Mr Graham. I think she'll master the work eventually, but it will take time."

"Good," he said. "You keep on training her. I'm very pleased with your own progress in shorthand."

Her face lit up with pleasure. Proudly she said, "I got my RSA certificate for 90 words a minute last week."

"That's fine, Sally. Just fine. You'll make someone a first-class secretary one day."

"Someone?" she queried uncertainly.

"Yes. I shall be leaving here shortly."

"Oh, Mr Graham." Her face seemed to crumple. "Have you found a better job?"

"No, Sally. I'm thinking of emigrating to France. I'm not sure yet. It depends on my visit next week, and whether or not I get married."

"Married," she repeated forlornly.

"Yes. If I do, then I will probably make my home in France."

"Oh, Mr Graham." A tear appeared behind the left spectacle lens and slowly worked its way down her cheek. He got up and went over to her, resting a hand on her shoulder.

"Now Sally, it's nothing to cry about. You should be happy for me."

"Oh, I am, I am. It's just that you've been so good to me . . . making me your secretary . . . giving me the chance to practise shorthand. What am I going to do when you leave?" She started sobbing in earnest.

"There, there." He began to regret the impulse that had caused him to confide in her ten seconds after he had himself reached a decision. He removed a handkerchief from his top pocket and handed it to her. "Now dry those tears and don't be so foolish. You're good enough to be anyone's secretary now. Just keep going after those RSA certificates."

She removed her glasses and dabbed at her eyes.

"And, Sally . . . don't tell anyone what I've said. Not yet."

"No, Mr Graham." She stood up and walked to the door, still clutching his handkerchief.

He called out as she stood in the doorway. "Er, Sally, did you have a reason for coming in here?"

She stared at him stupidly for a moment. Then she said, "Oh yes. A Mr Bernstein called while you were out. He wants you to call him back."

"Bernstein? Are you sure?"

"Yes. I wrote the name down. I think he's an American."

"Good Lord! Did you take his number?"

"Yes."

"Get him for me, will you, Sally."

"Yes, Mr Graham."

He sat behind his desk again. By all that was wonderful! Fancy Bernie being back in town. He was struck by the sudden awareness of an ache in his heart and of an emptiness in his life, the result of an absence for some time past, of any real friends about him, male or female, to whom he could unburden the worries and frustrations of his working life. It had been at its worst in the months since Matt left.

The phone rang. He picked it up. Sally's voice: "Mr Bernstein for you."

"Hello. Is that really you, Bernie?"

"No one but, feller. How's it going?" Raymond's voice, as warm and friendly as ever, had developed a real American accent, right out of the Bronx – or maybe it was Manhattan.

"Jesus, Bernie, you sound just like a bloody Yank."

"I hope you're smiling when you say that."

"Smiling?" John bubbled. "I'm laughing my blooming head off. God, it's good to hear from you. What are you doing back in London?"

"I've been transferred here for a while. Guess they figure the limeys need civilizing, and who better than their own house-trained limey to do the job. So, you're okay, huh?"

"Fan-bloody-tastic now I'm talking to you. But how are you? And how's Ruth?!

"You'll be able to find out for yourself, I hope. What're you doing tonight?"

"Nothing, as far as I know."

"Well, you're hereby invited to dinner – if you think you can face Ruth's cooking."

"What do you mean, Bernie? Ruth's cooking? Are you already installed? How long have you been back?"

"Oh, a couple of weeks. Meant to contact you earlier, but you know how it is. We had to settle down first, find a place to live, get straight. Anyway, you can ask all your questions later. We're in a maisonette in Finchley, not too far from you. Make a note of the address." Bernstein dictated it slowly.

"Got it," said John. "And I know where it is. What time?"

"Are you coming alone?"

"What do you mean?"

"I mean, like in: are you batching it, or do you have a gal to make up a foursome."

"Uh-uh. I don't even know anyone suitable at the moment."

A sympathetic murmur from Raymond. "Yeah. I heard about Julie. I'm sorry, John."

"You did?" John was amazed. "Who from?"

"Megan."

"Oh."

"Well, look, John, I'll get Ruth to invite a friend over. A girl named Barbara Hamilton. And, as you don't have to pick anyone up first, why not come right on over from the office? That way we'll have time for a drink or two and a chinwag before dinner."

"Sounds great, Bernie, but I'd rather go home first and shower and shave. I could be with you around seven, if that's all right."

"Sure."

"But about this Barbara woman . . . you don't have to invite her on my account. I should warn you, I'm a reformed character."

Raymond guffawed at the concept. "We'll invite her anyway. But watch yourself, feller, she a man-eater."

John laughed. "That should simplify Ruth's cooking arrangements."

CHAPTER SEVENTEEN

If there should be anywhere more unpleasant than a large city in the heat of midsummer, John Graham had yet to discover it. And of all cities he could imagine none more obviously designed to assist the discomforting efforts of the sun than London, where archaic convention allied to outmoded architecture performs feats of masochistic torture; where tradition demands that a businessman endure the heat in stoical silence and a coat and tie, while lack of air conditioning or even adequate ventilation intensify his suffering so that by the end of the working day, his shirt is sticking to his back, his scalp tingling, his palms clammy, his skin itching and his nerves jumping.

Leaving the office, crossing Moorgate, walking up Fore Street, the sun leaned a heavy hand on the back of his neck. For a moment, after seating himself behind the steering wheel of his car, John felt like a trussed chicken placed in the oven to roast. He rolled down both windows, loosened the two nuts above the windscreen, pushed back the hood, and thanked the extravagant whim that had caused him to part-exchange the Anglia for this 1949 Triumph Roadster 2000, despite the monthly repayments which the deal had demanded.

Five minutes later he felt reasonably cool, but a long crawl in frustratingly heavy traffic up Haverstock Hill frayed his temper and restored his discomfort. It was with relief bordering on rapture that he took a cool shower, shaved, and changed his clothing before leaving for the Bernsteins.

The address Raymond had given him was of a maisonette in the Swedish style, of which there were a great many in this district, all of the same mold: two storey houses that had been converted into two separate flats, the original front entrance leading to a ground floor flat, a side entrance leading to an upper floor flat. The Bernsteins were on the ground floor.

He paused a moment, his hand on the door-knocker, prolonging the thrill of anticipation at seeing his friend again, his mind rehearsing the wealth of news he had to impart: his commercial progress and frustrations, his decision to quit his job, his even more drastic decision to get married. What would Bernie make of all that?

He knocked. Footsteps sounded behind the door. The door opened.

And all his thoughts vanished like the fabled snows of yesteryear as he stared at the young woman who had opened the door. She was beautiful! No, she wasn't beautiful; she was striking! Yes, that was the word. He stared at the gently-waved ash-blond hair with its streak of silver forming an eye-catching parting down the centre of her head. He stared at the narrow, highly arched eyebrows, the slender nose with its slightly flared nostrils, at the generous mouth with long upper lip and full lower lip, at the healthy glow of her skin.

He stared for an infinity which lasted five seconds and then became aware she was laughing and holding out her hand, saying, "You must be John. Do come in. I'm Barbara."

He followed her into the house and she apologised on behalf of Ruth and Raymond. Ruth was busy in the kitchen, and Raymond was in his study completing a report for New York. They sat in armchairs, in the lounge section of a large lounge-diner, facing each other, and John realised that he had not spoken a word since she had opened the door to him. It had been years since he had felt similarly dumbstruck with the appearance of a woman. His memory shied away from the recollection which threatened and he pulled a packet of cigarettes from his pocket, offering her one, then a light, noticing with annoyance the slight nervous trembling of his hand. She sat back in her chair and puffed out smoke, smiling at him, completely at ease, as if she had not noticed his silence or had come to expect this wordless homage from men.

Then Raymond entered the room and John jumped to his feet with relief. "Really good to see you again, Bernie."

"I thought I heard you arrive, John." He glanced at Barbara. I see you two have already met. If you'd like, I'll disappear again."

John laughed. The spell had been broken.

Barbara said, "I know you two have a lot of catching up to do, so I'll give Ruth a hand in the kitchen."

John watched her leave the room, noting with approval the long, shapely legs and trim ankles, while Raymond regarded him with amusement.

"So, you're a reformed character, are you?"

John said, "Wow!" He could think of nothing else to say.

Raymond grinned. "Some dish, huh? How about a scotch?"

"Fine."

"On the rocks?"

"Please. And soda."

They sat down with their drinks and John said, "Now, what's all this about a transfer to London?"

"Quite straightforward, really. It's standard policy for the syndicate. I guess they figure they don't want correspondents with calluses on their backsides, so every two years they give us an overseas assignment and a chance to shake the dust from our pants. Last time they sent me to Rio. This time it's London."

"How long are you likely to be here?"

"Oh. . ." Raymond pursed his lips. "Anything from six to twelve months. We've taken this place on a renewable six months lease. What about you? How's the job?"

John scowled. "Driving me round the bend. I'm general manager now, which is a euphemism for a glorified office boy. The business is going rapidly down the drain and there's nothing I can do about it. The directors have the Victorian belief that British is automatically best, so we don't have to go out and hustle for business. We just sit on our rumps and wait for the order to come to us."

Raymond made a sympathetic sound. "And what would you like to do?"

"Well, for a start, the obvious thing of getting out of the office and touting for business."

"And they won't let you?"

"I'm off to Paris next week. To deal with a complaint. That's their idea of an overseas assignment."

"Have you told them how you feel about it?"

"Told them!" John snorted. "I've never stopped telling them. The managing director can't be told anything. He's a tyrant with more than a streak of idiocy. His partner is even worse: a slimy hypocrite who agrees with everything you say and does nothing about it. I think he just resents anyone else being successful. However," John sighed, "I shan't be there much longer."

"Oh? Got another job?"

"No. Not exactly. I . . ." John hesitated. For some reason he was reluctant to mention Yvette and the possibility of marriage. "I can find another job easily enough," he improvised hastily.

"Yeah, I guess so," Raymond agreed doubtfully. "Just don't rush into anything, John. I know how impetuous you can be."

"Only where women are concerned. And speaking of women . . . who the hell is she?"

"Barbara?"

"Who else?"

"Uh, we met her on the Elizabeth coming over. She'd been to New York for a holiday."

"Just like that, eh?"

"If you mean money, I guess she's no church mouse. But she's no poor little rich girl, either. She works for it."

"What does she do?"

"A whole variety of things in the health and beauty business. She's a qualified chiropodist and physiotherapist. She has a business in Mayfair with a small staff, specialising in home visits. Manicure, pedicure and massage in your own home. I gather that part of the reason for her New York trip was to study the possibility of opening a branch over there."

John whistled softly. "Quite a girl. How old is she?"

Raymond shrugged. "About thirty, I'd guess." He grinned. "So, you're impressed, huh?"

"And how! Though I doubt I've impressed her very much. I don't know what got into me. I was behaving like a love-struck adolescent."

Raymond laughed. "Don't let it bother you. You should have seen the pack of wolves howling at her on the boat. One snarl from Barbie and they were ready to leap from the nearest porthole. Not that she snarled very often. I gather from Ruth that she's a bit like you – in reverse, of course."

"What do you mean?"

"Well, it's not that she thinks of men all the time, but when she thinks she thinks of men."

"Charming."

They both laughed.

"Going to let us in on the joke?"

John jumped up. "Ruth! How wonderful to see you. You look terrific." He kissed her cheek, then held her away from him, studying her. "It must be the apron. How I yearn for domesticity."

"Thanks, John. You always manage to say the right thing. Why don't you give Ray a few lessons."

"Hell," John pulled a face. "Wouldn't you say he was past it?"

"You could be right at that. Notice he hasn't offered us a drink yet? No, never mind," pushing Raymond back into his armchair, "I'll help myself. You take sherry too, don't you, Barbara?"

Barbara nodded.

Ruth poured the drinks and then sat in Raymond's lap with an arm around his neck. "He's really a lamb," she announced, "and I wouldn't have him any other way." She nuzzled his neck.

John experienced a sense of what was not quite envy, more the vague disquiet which assailed him whenever he was made aware of the emotional security of others. He looked at Barbara, seated in another armchair, and found that her attention, too, was directed at the Bernsteins. He wondered what she was thinking. Could she also be envious of this so-obviously happy couple? At the moment she turned her head and looked directly into his eyes. For an instant he felt disturbed, as if she had caught him doing something wrong.

Then he laughed and gestured towards the Bernsteins. "Sickening, isn't it?"

Dinner *à l'américaine*, with corn-on-the-cob and large grilled sirloin steaks, was a merry affair made more diverting by Raymond's provision of cheap but effective red Burgundy and his amusing accounts of life and adventures in Brazil.

Then Raymond suggested they adjourn to the lounge area of the room while he dispensed liqueurs. John sat on a settee and Barbara sat beside him. In sitting down her hand touched his knee.

John grinned. "Not getting fresh, are you?"

She looked at him coldly. "When I want to make a pass at you, you won't have to ask, you'll know."

The Bernsteins started laughing and John joined in. Then he stopped, wondering whether she had meant it as a joke. Suddenly he felt like a small boy, trying to mix in adult company, finding himself way out of his depth.

Raymond handed John a drink and said, "You mustn't mind Barbie. She believes in speaking her mind. The prerogative of a successful businesswoman."

Barbara frowned. "Shit! It really makes me angry the way you men treat women in business as a big joke."

Raymond raised his hands in mock-horror. "Hold on. Who's joking?"

"No, I mean it. You seem to want a woman to do nothing more than look decorative and pander to your whims. When she's able to demonstrate that she has an intelligence at least the equal of your own, you either resent it or pigeon-hole her as a crank. When she's also attractive, you view her with pity."

"Whoa! Pardon me," said Raymond. "As you have now gathered, John, our Barbie's a very independent soul."

"There you go. Now you're patronising me."

John said, "Bernie told me about your work. I'm impressed. Is there really such a great demand for your services?"

"Oh yes. It took a long time before we got known, but now we have more work than we can cope with. You see most of our clients, once they are sold on our service, want regular visits, which means we are automatically assured of a reasonably full week's work. Then we also work for some of the smaller hotels in town who aren't large enough to employ a full-time manicurist or podiatrist, but who like to advertise the service as being available."

"And you've organised this entirely by yourself?"

"You see what I mean. If I had been a man you wouldn't have been a bit surprised. I don't care what you say, no matter how much you men insist that you approve the emancipation of women, you still retain a deep-rooted psychological prejudice against women in business."

"Oh, God," John moaned, "let's not get onto psychology. I can't think of any single subject that gives rise to more twaddle."

Raymond gave him a quick, puzzled glance. "What do you mean?"

"I mean that every Tom, Dick and Sigmund nowadays fancies himself as a parlour psychoanalyst. The parlour game of our times: probing one's psychological prejudices. It can't be done."

Ruth frowned. "Can you explain that remark, please."

"Hey now, I said I didn't want to talk about psychology."

"Please John, this is something Ray and I are always arguing about."

"Well, of course," said John, "it's far worse in your country, isn't it? If you haven't got a complex under analysis, I gather, you are out of fashion."

Raymond spluttered. Ruth spoke before he could open his mouth. "I agree entirely. A lot of my friends regard a visit to their analyst as important as a regular check-up by their dentist. I sometimes get the feeling they get more pleasure in baring their minds to a man, while lying on a couch, than they'd get in baring their bodies."

"Hell!" Raymond exploded. "Just because a bunch of dizzy dames, with more time and money than sense, want to hear a man talking about castration complexes and penis envy, hardly seems ground enough to condemn an advance in medicine as important as the discovery of vaccines. What about people suffering from physical disorders for no organic reason? What about the people who used to be regarded as malingerers until psychiatry was able to prove that their condition came from deep-seated hysteria? Tell me it's wrong that such people should receive treatment, and I'll think you've both escaped from the Dark Ages."

"It's not that," said John, patiently. "I quite agree that there are people seriously in need of help. Not simply people with a physical symptom resulting from a mental condition, but the seriously deranged, whose mental state may affect not only their social, business or domestic lives, but also the lives of others. Of course psychiatry is of benefit to these people.

"But I'm thinking of the vast majority of us; people with the minor complexes or repression or neuroses that are an inevitable – and, yes, normal! – part of modern life. In our case the remedy can be more dangerous than the disease – if it is a disease."

"So you feel that the cure should be reserved for a chosen few," said Bernstein caustically.

"No. I think there are a hell of a lot of people around who have very little wrong with them, but who imagine themselves to possess any number of complaints. And I think this is exaggerated by the spread of a popular and superficial knowledge of psychology. At one time an honest attempt at self-analysis could content itself with the acceptance of obvious motives and straightforward moral judgements. Nowadays we can draw on the writings of Freud, Adler, Jung, Horney, and instead of accepting the obvious we begin a process of increasing introspection."

"That's all very well, feller," said Bernstein. "I hope you won't take offence when I say that, to me, you are revealing a lot more about yourself than about your views. Y'know, this attack on psychiatry is itself so terribly emotional. You want to believe that psychiatry is a menace in order to help your own peace of mind – so you attack it."

"But don't you see, that's exactly what I have against psychiatry – the ability it has to explain any attack in its own terms. The psychiatrist can never lose.

"Let me tell you a story – a true story – about a friend of mine from college who became a visiting lecturer at Columbia University in your own New York. He was a brilliant student, with one big problem – a beastly temper. Not your usual, normal temper – if there is such a thing – but an anger inside him which was always looking for a reason to explode. It never held him back while he was in England, because his friends knew him and understood him; they knew his background – which I won't disclose here – and made allowances. Anyway . . . he met a girl in New York and fell in love. For a while, everything was okay; in the first flush of love, presumably he was able to hold himself in check. Eventually, however, he started to give in to his fits of anger. He told me they would argue over the most trivial things, mere disagreements, which always led to him losing his temper, and a big bust-up.

"She persuaded him to visit a shrink. For the best part of a year he was in analysis. Finally he was pronounced cured. Really cured. No more temper, no more fits of rage, no more angry outbursts. Cured." John paused for dramatic effect.

"So what are you trying to prove?" Raymond asked.

"Simply this. The girl left him. Couldn't stand him any longer. Found him too dull."

Ruth and Barbara laughed.

Raymond stared in stupefaction. "You made that story up, John."

John shook his head. "Word of honour, Bernie. It's the absolute truth, repeated just as it was told to me by my friend. And I believe him. I could see the change for myself. He'd become lethargic, lazy, content to let others make decision for him."

"Thank you for that story," said Ruth. "That's the sort of ammunition

I've needed. What have you got to say to that, Ray-man?"

"Just one thing. I don't see how John can know – how his friend can know – that he's not better off now. How can you know what really caused his fits of anger. They must have been a symptom of something far more serious. Okay, so in losing his lack of control, he's also lost some aspect of his personality, and he's also lost his girl friend. Maybe it's for the best. Perhaps he was in danger of losing far more."

"All right," John held up his hands in surrender. "You may have the last word. I told you I didn't want to start this discussion in the first place. I said you could find an answer for everything in psychological terms." He turned to Barbara. "You haven't said a word on the subject," he observed.

She regarded him coolly. He could have sworn there was a faint curl of scorn to her lips. "Frankly, it's not a subject that excites me. I've never felt the need for analysis and I doubt that I ever shall. I know what I want, I know how to get it, and I don't regard myself as having any inhibitions. I don't have to question my motives or desires or intentions. All I need, all I have ever wanted, I have admitted to myself, and I've just gone ahead and got it.

"As for your friend," she continued, "if he was so far from being a man that a woman could talk him into seeing a head doctor, he deserved to lose her."

She was not boasting. It was simply a statement of fact. John found it exciting and frightening, as if a veil had been lifted to reveal a monster. He could almost fill in what had been left unsaid: that she would get what she wanted no matter how hard, cruel, or selfish she had to be in the process. He was horrified, and yet drawn more closely to her as one is instinctively drawn towards strength as a refuge from one's own weaknesses.

"What is it?" asked Raymond.

"A Triumph Roadster," said John proudly.

"Heck, things must be going well for you financially."

"Let's not exaggerate. First of all it's five years old, and secondly I shall be two years older before it has been paid for."

"Even so," said Raymond. He called to the two women standing in the doorway. "Come and have a look at this."

Ruth and Barbara dutifully examined the long-bonneted black car. Raymond took John to one side, "I hope you didn't mind my suggesting you run Barbie home."

"I would have suggested it myself."

"Yeah," said Raymond dryly. "But I'm thinking of Julie. I don't want her to blame me for what may happen."

"Julie? What do you mean? Don't you know that Julie and I are finished?"

"No, I didn't know that."

"But . . . on the phone . . . you said you'd heard . . ."

"About her illness, that's all."

"Illness? What illness?"

"Oh, Jesus, feller. Don't you know?"

"Know what?"

"Gee, I'm sorry . . I thought . . ." Raymond took hold of John's arms. "She's in hospital in Cheltenham. Suspected breast cancer."

"God, no!" John closed his eyes, feeling suddenly sick.

"I'm sorry, John."

"Hey, you two," Ruth called. "Are you going to stand there gabbing all night?"

John opened the car door, passenger side, for Barbara to get in, then he got behind the wheel.

"Mind how you go now," Raymond smiled. "Don't do anything I wouldn't do."

"Well, he's left you plenty of scope," said Ruth dryly.

They drove off.

"Where to?" asked John.

"You're looking tired," Barbara answered enigmatically.

"No, I'm not tired. Just thoughtful."

"Well I live in Ambrose Mews, Mayfair. But if you're really not tired, could we go for a drive first. This car feels as if it could go fast. It might clear my head."

"Why not," he agreed. "It might do me a bit of good too. But you'll probably be disappointed with the speed. I've never had her over seventy-five."

"That'll do," she said.

They drove north, along the AI, and then turned off into the narrow Hertfordshire lanes, the twin beams of his headlights restricting their world to dark hedgerows and forbidding trees. The air was oppressive and sultry, carrying the scent of an impending storm. He drove at around sixty miles an hour on the straight stretches and slowed to under thirty on the bends. At Essendon he suggested they return to town.

"Do you think I might drive it back, John?"

He stopped the car in surprise. "Can you drive?"

She clicked her tongue impatiently. "Here we go again. I suppose you think that's another male prerogative."

"I'm sorry. I didn't mean it that way. Of course you may drive her." He got out of the car and walked around to the nearside, opening the door for her. He took the passenger seat while she sat behind the wheel.

"You'll have to show me how this funny little gear lever works." She was fiddling with the gear lever, unusually set on the right-hand side of the steering column.

He explained the gears to her.

"Right," she said. "Here we go."

The car jerked forward with an angry roar. The engine was complaining angrily at thirty before she changed into second gear. She changed gear very cleanly. Then they were sweeping around the bends at fifty and he was gripping the bottom of his seat with both hands. He looked at her, wanting to tell her to take it easy, but afraid she would take it as just another example of male prejudice. Her face was wild and excited, her hair blown up and back by the wind, looking like Medusa's serpents. Then they hit a straight stretch and he sensed rather than saw her feet press harder on the accelerator while, almost simultaneously, she released the accelerator, pressed down on the clutch, sent the engine into top gear, and gave it still more throttle. The needle was hovering around the eighty mark.

A sound halfway between a scream and a groan came from her throat and she looked at him. "This is wonderful!"

Her eyes returned to the road. She gasped. Before he could realise what had happened, she swung the car to the left and stamped on brake and clutch pedals in an emergency stop. Only the grip he had maintained on the bottom of the seat stopped him from being propelled into the windscreen. As it was he slid forward onto his knees and felt something jar into his chest. He was indistinctly aware of the screech of rubber on the road surface and the angrily insistent note of a car's horn passing them from the opposite direction.

He pulled himself back onto the seat, muttering a curse. Then he looked at her.

She had her head thrown back and was laughing. At first he thought it must be hysteria, then he saw that it was sheer, excited enjoyment.

"What happened?" he asked.

"I didn't see the bend in time." She laughed again. "Then I saw the car coming round it."

He looked through the windscreen. The car's headlights illuminated a sharp left-hand bend less than ten yards away. The nearside of the care was almost touching the hedgerow.

"My God. You might have killed us."

"Nonsense," she gurgled. "They missed us by miles."

"At least six inches," he grumbled. "I don't think it's a joking matter."

"Oh my goodness," she said angrily. "What's the matter with you? I suppose you want to take over again."

"No, that's all right. But for heaven's sake drive more slowly. This isn't a sports car, even if it may look like one."

She restarted the stalled engine with an annoyed grunt. "Suit yourself. All I can say is, if you're so scared of taking chances with the small things, how are you going to face up to the bigger things in life?"

She drove off. For the next ten minutes the car remained in second gear and maintained a sedate thirty-five miles an hour. Then she pulled into the side of the road and braked.

"I'm sorry." She put a hand on his arm. "That wasn't fair of me. It is your car and you have every right to be cross. Will you drive it again now?"

For the second time they changed places and, following her directions, he found himself outside her mews flat just as the storm broke. She got out of the car quickly.

"You'd better put the hood up before you get out," she said. "I'll leave the door open for you."

He experienced a moment of shock, a dim recollection playing at the fringe of his memory. Then he dismissed the groping thought in the sheer wonder of her incredible forthrightness. None of the silly game-playing, the fumbling in the front of the car, the hesitancy, the pretence, the playing to the rules of the game. Barbara made her own rules. Or, more precisely, she had no rules, merely a tacit acceptance of an inevitable situation. He would obviously angle for an invitation to her flat, so why waste time? Either she wanted him to come up, or she didn't. And, apparently, she did!

He finished tightening the hood nuts and wound up the side windows as the first heavy drops of rain fell, heralded by a flash of lightening. That, too, seemed to pluck a chord of memory as he dashed for the yellow and black street door. He closed the door behind him and mounted the short flight of stairs which led directly into a large room, brightly decorated and furnished in black and white.

"Where are you?" he called out.

"In the bathroom. Make yourself at home. You'll find drinks in the sideboard I'll be out in a minute."

He opened the sideboard doors. Sherry, port, Dubonnet – ugh! He looked around the big room. In one corner a divan with black and white check coverlet. One armchair. A low, long coffee table and two squat stools, leather upholstered. Reproduction paintings on the walls; Gauguin, Lautrec, Picasso. A bookcase. He studied the books. Three volumes of works by Freud. Was this the woman who felt no need for analysis? Ellis, Malinowski, Chesser. Ah, *that* side of Freud's works, of course. Olympia Press editions of Frank Harris and Henry Miller. He was beginning to understand what Bernie had meant.

"I suppose you've read them all."

He turned round. She was smiling at him. Dressed in a simple housecoat.

"No, not all." He smiled back.

"What, no drink?"

"I'm sorry. Sherry, port and Dubonnet are not my tipple."

"There's some beer in the fridge."

"I doesn't matter. I'm not very thirsty." He was lying. His mouth felt as dry as the proverbial birdcage.

"Well, in that case . . ." she paused, her lips smiling, her eyes mocking, "what are we waiting for?"

Slowly her fingers were undoing the buttons on the front of her housecoat. All the time her eyes were staring at him, taunting him, daring him to look away from her face and down at her body. He could feel a pulse pounding in his temples.

The he let his eyes drop. She stood proudly naked before him, aware of the beauty and magnetism of her body. Her breasts were small, taut, up-tilted, with large, erect brown nipples. Her body was perfectly formed, the reflected light from two floor lamps highlighting the curves, shadowing the hollows, a perfect triangle of fair hairs confirming her natural blondeness.

"Do you like it?" she asked mockingly.

"His tongue felt too large for his mouth. Mutely he nodded his head.

They made love on a sheepskin rug before the empty fireplace. And he had never known lovemaking such as this. She had an apparent orgasm as he was kissing her; at least, her body spasmed as though in orgasm. She had her second orgasm as he searched for and then located her clitoris. And this time there was no mistaking it. She became fiercely demanding, rolled over until she assumed the dominant role, and then reached for him, inserted his bursting penis into her vagina and commanded, fiercely, authoritatively, "Fuck me! Fuck me! Yes! Yes! Now! Now!" And with each demand she apparently had another climax. Her vociferous demands had the effect of inhibiting his own orgasm until, with unexpected empathy, she relaxed and led him slowly, tenderly yet painfully, patiently yet hungrily, step by step up to the summit of his own ecstatic experience. The groans and shuddering of his body were matched precisely by her own and, as they fell apart, he heaved a final sigh of utter, ecstatic weariness.

Now he knew, with startling clarity, what had caused him to refrain from mentioning Yvette to Bernstein. It had been an intuitive prescience of just this situation.

He leaned towards her, trapped a small, pear-shaped breast in his hand. She sighed.

"Darling," he said.

"Hmm?"

"It was wonderful. You are wonderful."

Her eyes were closed. Her lips were smiling.

"Darling." He nudged her. "Did you hear what I said?"

One eye opened and looked at him. "Yes. I heard. You're pretty wonderful yourself."

"Am I? Am I? What do you mean?" He was hungry for praise.

"I mean, it's not often it can be so good the first time."

He winced at this oblique reference to the many other times, to the many others who had preceded him, then cursed himself for a child. This was a woman, a grown woman. Had he expected a teen-age virgin?"

He pressed his lips to her ear. "Barbara, darling, do you believe in love at first sight?"

"Of course," she said, her voice tinkling with merriment. "It happens to me all the time."

Shortly afterwards she turned to him. "John," she whispered, "do you think . . . if I help you . . . you might . . .?"

"I can try," he said.

CHAPTER EIGHTEEN

He unfastened his seat belt, opened a packet of tax-free cigarettes, lit one, and sat back in his seat with a sigh of relief. For an hour or so he could relax and take pleasure in this feeling of earthly detachment; for sixty minutes he would be able to indulge the delight of suspension from terrestrial cares. And he was grateful for this removal from the source of those cares, for the opportunity to consider them impartially, as though the elevation were bestowing on him the omniscient vision of a deity.

Behind him lay London and ahead was Paris and it was astonishing to consider the ambivalence of his emotions in relation to each. The past days with Barbara had confirmed beyond all doubt that he was in love with her, and had gone a long way toward removing any doubts that she might share his feelings. Yesterday at the office, however, had merely served to confirm his certainty that the bigotry, lack of vision, and apparently hell-bent course of his superiors made his working conditions utterly untenable. It was as if the degree of frustration he experienced in the office increased in direct ratio to the amount of pleasure he derived from his private life.

By contrast his trip to Paris should have filled him with elation. Here was an opportunity to come to grips with a commercial problem, to handle it personally, to determine for himself whether he had the ability and acumen that he often secretly doubted. But waiting for him in the French capital would be Yvette, and the difficulty of explaining to her why it was now impossible for them to resume their intimate relationship. How could he tell her? What could he say?

There was no way to tell her that would not hurt her; no way to express his gratitude. And he was grateful. She had, after all, broken down his resistance, his blind, unreasoning refusal to commit himself to a significant relationship. If it hadn't been for Yvette he would never have committed his feelings for Barbara. Yvette had shown him how much he had been missing my selfishly compartmentalising his own ability to give.

How differently he would have felt had he been making this trip just one week earlier, he reflected with a bitterness that was markedly at variance with the love he felt for Barbara, the joy he derived from her company, the undiluted delight he got from their intimacy.

And how close they had been all week; how their spirits as well as their bodies had fused and blended and become as one. Intimacy, he now recognised, extended to more than the mere exercise of his genitals – it involved the whole of his being. It enshrouded him in a warmth of sentiment and a sense of compassion; it contained not merely desire but the wish to protect and to cherish and, yes, to pity. Barbara would be outraged, he imagined, if she realised that his feelings for her included pity. What, she would demand, gave him the idea that she needed pitying? But he knew her so well now that he was sure her confidence of manner and independence of spirit were but compensations for an early absence of affection, and he pitied her the possible circumstances which had robbed her of that affection.

Or was he over-simplifying things? So easy to do when you are in love.

"I beg your pardon?"

The woman sitting in front off him had turned in her seat and was fixing him with a coldly perplexed stare. With an effort he controlled the laughter that threatened to erupt as he realised he had spoken his last thought aloud.

"I said it's a pleasing view from above."

The woman turned away, with a doubtful look and a disapproving lift of her shoulder.

Yet the view was pleasant. The plane was flying above cotton-wool balls of cloud, the sky was deep blue, the sun shone fiercely, and there were occasional glimpses of sea below. Was it love, he wondered, which was heightening his powers of perception?

Certainly he had never felt clearer-headed nor clearer-sighted than the morning after the Bernsteins' dinner party, when he had driven Barbara to her place of work, had arranged to meet her again that evening, and had telephoned the office to say he would not be in until the afternoon. He could no longer remember the business appointment he had invented as his excuse, but he could clearly remember his thoughts, lying in bed at the flat, trying to assess the importance of what had happened to him during the preceding twelve hours.

It is a strange but presumably well-intentioned feature of the mind that it closes up in the face of the unpleasant, and memory hides itself behind a barred door when one tries to recall past upsets. Yet every now and then a shutter is lifted to reveal, in startling clarity, a long-forgotten experience which prompts the question: *My God, was that really me*?

So it had been with John that morning; as if a light had been switched on suddenly to illuminate a part of him he had previously ignored, or deliberately buried.

He had started thinking back over the years, trying to recall a succession of love affairs and short-lived episodes, trying to discover what it was that made Barbara so wonderfully different from anyone he had previously known. He had stumbled over the thought of Yvette, hesitated and by-passed consideration of Julie, and skipped quickly over the less important influences, recalling here a physical feature, there an amusing episode, elsewhere a scrap of conversation.

Then, with a feeling akin to horror, he had recalled Betty Lane, and that feeling of bitterness which had engulfed him after his discovery of her perfidy. Surely, he thought, surely I have not spent my life trying to strike back at Betty through all the women I have since met? But the more he thought about it, the more valid it seemed to be.

Yet even as honesty enables us to admit the validity of our self-analysis, it simultaneously seems to prohibit the logical conclusions of our admission. It is as if the kaleidoscope of our life is shaken and presents such a picture of impelling truth, such a dazzling display, as to completely divert our attention from its true meaning.

John Graham made his discovery and then deliberately thrust it into the recesses of his mind, replacing it by another recollection of the previous night's joys.

They had planned a picnic for the weekend. She had given him a list of the things he should buy and he had gone shopping on the Saturday morning and had added to her list all sorts of extra luxury items, while she hard-boiled eggs and made sandwiches. Then he had returned and they had prepared the picnic hamper.

They were on their hands and knees on the floor, packing and repacking the hamper, testing the various combinations which would allow the wicker basket to close, deciding at last that they could not get everything in. She had pressed the hamper lid down and there was the sound of cracking eggshells and she had cursed. He had looked at her and grinned, and she had looked back at him, her face flushed and irritated, and then she had grinned too. And then the coverlet was off the bed, lying on the floor, and he had eased his arm out from under her head and looked at his watch. It was three in the afternoon. And they had opened the hamper, broken open two cans of beer, and had taken their picnic sitting on the floor of her room, eating off the low coffee table. Then they had gone back to bed.

Last night, at some point during their lovemaking, he had looked at her. She was lying on her back, staring at the ceiling. "What are you thinking?" he asked. And then, when she did not reply, "You know I sometimes feel you are two different people."

Still she did not answer. Suddenly she turned on her side, away from him, and muttered, "Oh, go to sleep."

"I'm not sleepy," he said. "I don't want tonight to end. I don't want to have to leave you tomorrow."

She turned back to him. "Why on earth not?" she said sharply. "Okay, so Paris can be uncomfortably hot in August, but it's still a wonderful city – and to be able to go there with all expenses paid . . ."

"I agree. That makes it even more annoying. It's just the thought of leaving you and the worry about what I shall say to Yvette."

"That's the French woman you told me about."

"Yes. I don't know what to do about her. We've a sort of understanding and she will . . ." he groped for the words ". . . she'll probably expect me to sleep with her."

Barbara laughed. "Lucky you!"

"Do you mean," he demanded incredulously, "you wouldn't object?"

"Why should I object? You're a free agent. Anyway, why disappoint the lady when she's been looking forward to it."

He was bewildered. "But that's ridiculous. I mean, I don't want to sound conceited, but after all that we've been to each other these past days, do you mean to say I can make love to another woman – even assuming I wanted to – and it wouldn't upset you?"

She reached for one of his hands and held it. "You sweet, young innocent. I would have to be awfully naive to believe a man can only make love to one woman at a time – even if he believes himself to be in love with her. Sex is to be enjoyed in its own right – quite divorced from any complications of the heart. You go ahead, John. Make love to your Yvette. You won't be depriving me of anything and you may make her very happy."

He shuddered. "No. I don't think I could do that. I should feel ashamed and dirty."

Barbara laughed and said, "You can always take a bath afterwards."

"You know that's not what I meant," he said angrily.

But she merely laughed again.

They were circling Le Bourget airport, and there was Paris below, and then they were on the tarmac and, from the second his feet touched ground, the old magic was back. Through the customs' shed, onto the uncomfortable airport bus with its haphazard seating arrangement, along the suburban roads and through the tunnels, until finally they passed the Arc de Triomphe, crossed the Seine, and entered the bus depot at Les Invalides. And all the time his heart was echoing the words of a song he had first heard so many years earlier: "*Paris, tu n'as pas changé, mon vieux*."

He had one small piece of baggage only and decided to walk to his hotel, rather than take a taxi. He walked across the Seine to the Place de la Concorde, traffic as thick as ever despite the exodus of the Parisians during August, breathing in the atmosphere of this beloved city. He was vaguely disturbed, as though something were out of place, until he recalled that the sounding of klaxons had been made illegal since his last visit. He continued past the Place de la Madeleine, towards the Gare St Lazare, looking for the hotel where Dumard had booked him a room.

After checking into the hotel he phoned Dumard and confirmed their next day's appointment. Then he rang the Colombes number that Yvette had given him, cut short her excited questions, and arranged to meet her later in the hotel lounge.

That evening he spotted Yvette the moment he entered the lounge. She was sitting upright in a high-winged armchair, her legs demurely crossed, reading a copy of *Elle*. He was standing by her chair before she noticed him, and then she jumped to her feet with a cry of pleasure and clasped his hands in her own.

"John! I did not expect to see you yet."

"But, Yvette, I am the one staying at the hotel, and you are the one who is fifteen minutes early."

"I was so anxious to see you, you understand."

"Of course." He squeezed her hands. "Come, let's do our talking over a drink in the bar."

When they were seated and had ordered their drinks, he studied her more closely and was distressed to note worry lines around her eyes which had certainly not been there four months earlier. Her face, too, seemed subtly changed, gauntly shadowed. He commented on it.

"I know," she said. "That is why I am able to take this week's holiday although this is our busiest season. *Maman* insisted I need the rest."

"But why? Have you been ill?"

She shrugged. "Not exactly. A little run down. Working too hard."

"You look more than a little run down. Have you seen a doctor?"

"Of course."

He felt a vague anger, as if he were personally responsible for her health. "And what did he say?"

She shrugged again. "He told me I was suffering from nervous exhaustion . . . that I should take a holiday." She smiled. "That I should find myself a husband."

His anger promptly vanished and was replaced by embarrassment. She was making a joke, he realised, but he was unable to rise to it. Instead he said," Well, let's see if we can't speed your convalescence. The first thing I prescribe is a good dinner. Where would you like to eat?"

"Could we eat here? It hardly seems worth the effort to go elsewhere. Besides . . ." She hesitated.

"Besides – what?"

"Nothing. Do you object to eating here?"

"Not at all. I've no idea what the food is like, but no, as you wish."

John's disquiet increased throughout the dinner. This was not the way he had planned their reunion. Although *planned* was probably the wrong word, for he had made no plans except a determination to find the most opportune moment to break the news to Yvette of his newly-formed attachment in London, and to break it as quickly as possible. But looking at her face, at the evidence of her reduced health, he knew he could not tell her yet. Besides, his presence was clearly helping her. *Therapeutically*, he thought, was one of the ways Barbara had omitted form her suggestions as to how he might treat Yvette.

Yvette, unaware of this undercurrent of emotion in him, blithely continued to question him about his activities in London. How cheerfully he might have responded, how pleasantly he might be regarding this evening, were it not for his plaguing conscience. And how was the evening to end? What would Yvette expect of him? Foolish questions! It was evident what was in her mind when she suggested they eat in the hotel.

Over coffee he said, "I suppose you will have to get back to Colombes soon."

Her face dropped. "But, John, it is so early . . . and we haven't been alone yet."

He felt caught in a trap he had himself set. "I was only thinking of you . . . and your train. Of course, I don't want you to go yet."

"Well then," her face cleared, "there is no need to worry. My train does not leave until eleven-thirty."

"What would you like to do now? A walk? A cinema? Dancing?"

"Oh, John, darling John, what has happened to you? Is it that you fear I may no longer feel the same as in London? Come," she laid her hand upon his, "I am not too proud to suggest we go to your room."

The next morning the feeling of self-loathing manifested itself in a physical sickness that almost caused him to cancel his meeting with Dumard. He tried to avoid thinking about what had happened the night before, but the memories crowded back until his self-accusation and feeling of guilt became intolerable. He spent five minutes doubled over the wash basin in his hotel room, while his stomach spasmed.

Dear God, what was he going to do about Yvette? How was he to break the news to her now? Last night he had put off telling her from one minute to the next, right up to the moment her train had left Saint Lazare, deceiving himself with the thought that it would be easier next day. It wasn't at all easier; it was impossible. Why had he done it? Why hadn't he been honest with her? Why had he grabbed at the straw of her poor health as an excuse to postpone the inevitable?

Weak, weak, weak, an inner voice repeated; too weak to do the decent thing. Not at all, another voice responded, you didn't want to hurt her. Wasn't that the decent thing?

At ten-thirty he presented his business card to the receptionist at Dumard Frères and was immediately shown into the office of Henri Dumard. Short, plump, fiftyish, receding hairline and broad smile, Dumard stood up and walked around his desk to shake John's hand.

"Ah, Mr Graham, I 'ave been looking forward to this pleasure for a long time."

His English was slow and hesitant, the French accent very strong.

"I, too, Monsieur Dumard. I still have to thank you for your kind letter of introduction to Mr Reid."

"Ah, yes, I 'ad forgotten that. Claude asked me to do it for you." His face grew solemn. "You 'ave 'eard about Claude?" John nodded. "A tragedy. A veritable tragedy. But please be seated, Mr Graham, I beg you." Dumard resumed his seat across the desk, facing John, opened a case of small cigars and offered one to John.

As he gave John a light, Dumard said, "Ah, yes... Claude. He spoke about you often. He told me you speak excellent French and I 'ope you will excuse that I speak English with you, but I 'ave so rarely the occasion."

"Not at all," said John. "Your English is very good."

Dumard beamed. "You are too kind. I suppose you know France well?"

"Paris," John corrected. "Not France. I was here immediately after the war, with the British Army."

"*Tiens*!" Dumard clicked his tongue. "I suppose you find things greatly changed?"

"Not really. Of course on the surface there are changes: the luxuries in the shops, the food, the clothes. But *au fond* nothing has changed. For me, Monsieur Dumard, a country is but the spirit of its people, and the French spirit has always been indomitable."

John felt a bit ashamed of his own glibness, afraid he had overdone the saccharine sentiment, but Dumard clapped his hands with delight.

"Ah, you flatter us. I can see why Claude admired you so. Perhaps it is your knowledge of French which is, after all, the language of diplomacy, that enables you to be so diplomatic in your own tongue."

John acknowledged the compliment with a nod and wondered when they would get down to the real reason for his visit. This exchange of small talk was all very well, but it wouldn't get the draft paid. Perhaps Dumard was hoping that, by putting John at his ease in this way, he would become more receptive to any demands that might be made. Well, he could soon put a stop to that.

"To get to business, Monsieur Dumard. *A nos moutons*, I think you say." He felt pleased with his interjection of that piece of levity. "I have here some technical details from Mammoth. Presumably you have already received the survey report from Douala, so if you would like to go through this with me."

"Ah, yes, the tractors," said Dumard. "I think per'aps we let Champion 'ave the papers. He his our technical man. I ask myself, Mr Graham, if it will not trouble you to meet me for dinner this evening. That way I will 'ave the report of Champion when we meet."

Obviously, thought John, the old scoundrel was not technically equipped to study the documents, hence his delaying tactics.

He said, "By all means. I appreciate the invitation."

"Good, good. May I suggest that I call for you at eight o'clock at your 'otel?"

"That will be excellent."

Dumard accompanied him to the outside office door, shaking his hand three times en route, and John was left with the prospect of not only being able to conclude his business in the more congenial ambiance of a restaurant, but of having a legitimate reason for delaying his next meeting with Yvette. Not that it would help much, he told himself sourly, it was merely delaying the inevitable.

By the time they had reached the stage of coffee and liqueurs, he was on first name terms with Dumard, but they had still not discussed the commercial problem that had brought him to Paris. Dumard was a gourmet and refused to allow any diversion from his gastronomic pleasure, save that it referred to the food itself. By the end of dinner, having matched Dumard's appetite through four memorable courses, their digestion assisted by a *Mouton Cadet* of noble vintage, little could have been further from his thoughts than the independent oscillation of a Mammoth tractor. It was as well, therefore, that the subjected was broached by Dumard himself.

"*Voilà, jeune homme*," he began breezily. "Now that we 'ave taken care of the important matter, let us turn our minds to the more . . . 'ow do you say it? . . . *ennuyeux*?"

"Tiresome," John suggested.

"Tiresome." Dumard savoured the word almost as he had savoured his wine. He produced a cigar case and offered a cigar to John who shook his head and took a cigarette from the packet beside him on the table. Dumard made a performance of lighting his cigar and then said, "My man Champion 'as studied your material and indicates to me that the problem is solved."

John raised his eyebrows in astonishment. Surely there had not been time enough for the Mammoth report to have been studied adequately. Dumard must have sensed the unasked question for he continued, "The mistake was entirely our own. It did not take Champion long to spot our small error in re-assembly."

John made no effort to hide his disbelief. "Surely that came to light as soon as you got the survey report."

Dumard shrugged. "*Malheureusement*, that I cannot answer. Champion made no mention of it."

It was quite unsatisfactory, but the little Frenchman was evidently going to say no more on the subject.

"In that case," said John, "you no longer have reason to delay settlement of our draft."

Dumard raised his glass of Armagnac, cupped it in his palm, swirled it gently, inhaled its aroma, and then smiled at John as though inviting him to share a secret. "This was never in doubt, and you may assure Messieurs Reid and Parry that their money is quite safe. But tell me, my dear John, do you charge everybody five percent for your services?"

"Of course. Sometimes we charge more, where the account is not so valuable or where we consider the customer may not be quite so financially sound. You see, Henri, you were in danger of having your own charges raised." He accompanied the words with a grin.

The humour was apparently lost on Dumard. "Do you not think this charge excessive?" He waved his hands, cutting off John's attempted interruption. "After all, you are simply buying and shipping goods on our behalf."

"Surely that is not all, Henri. Don't we perform an essential service that deserves to be paid for? Remember, we pay for your goods and give you credit where often you would have to pay the manufacturer at the time of your order. Also we sometimes get you trade discounts which you might not get yourself, so that the goods may end up costing you less, even after our commission has been added. And don't forget that we also get you quicker deliveries. Why, I got a cable from you personally last month, thanking me for that recent air freight despatch of vital spares."

Dumard signalled the waiter to bring them two more brandies, then smiled knowingly at John. "Mon vieux, this you do not 'ave to tell me. 'ave I not been giving you my business for eight years? I know all the benefits. If I did not get the service, you would not get the business. I merely suggest that you are charging too much. Remember, not only do you charge us five percent for buying the goods, but you also get a five percent rebate on the freight when you ship the goods. And sometimes the freight is very considerable."

John sipped the fresh Armagnac that had been placed before him. "Henri, you are being unfair. You talk as if you have only now found out about the freight rebates, but you have known about them all along. When you first asked Reid to find the equipment and spares that you desperately needed, nothing was important except fulfilling your large timber contracts. The five percent buying commission was a drop in the ocean compared to the cost each day your production was held up. So were the freight rebates. So was the interest we charged on outstanding payments. Now you act as if this is something new."

Dumard scowled. "It is you who is being unfair. Eight years ago these things *were* unimportant, as you say. But things 'ave changed now. Our own business conditions 'ave changed. We can no longer sell our timber without effort. We 'ave to cut our prices to sell, and we 'ave to spend more money trying to get the business now there is so much competition. So why should you expect to get the same benefits? Do you know there are many companies who would like to do our buying for one half of what you charge us?"

John raised his brandy snifter while considering his answer. He felt disgusted. Everything Dumard had said was true. He himself had said it often enough to Parry, and Mattson had never ceased saying it. Why the hell was he expected to defend a system with which he disagreed? It was, in fact, indefensible. Perhaps he had had too much to drink, but all at once he found himself sick to death of mouthing the words of Reid and Parry. Anyway, it was not Reid and Parry who were giving Dumard his service, but he – John Graham. And Dumard was entitled to the truth.

"All right, Henri, I admit it. You're quite right. Our charge to you is excessive. Stupidly so. But I'm afraid I can do nothing about it. I'm only the general manager. You must talk to Mr Reid."

Dumard smiled delightedly. "For a moment, John, I feared you were no longer the honest man to whom I gave a reference many years ago. Really, we would not make so much fuss about the five percent if it was not for two other matters. In the first place we are angry because Mr Reid makes us pass to 'im the freight rebates on the timber we ship. What do you say to that?"

John shifted uncomfortably in his chair, Reid and Parry's warnings echoing in his head. "I regret, Henri, that I am not permitted to discuss the timber business. Even if I knew anything about it, which I don't"

"I think I 'ear the words of Mr Reid, n'est-ce pas?"

"Well . . ."

"Nevertheless, you will discuss it?"

John frowned, then thought: in for a penny . . . "Of course."

Dumard nodded with satisfaction. "You know we 'ave been Reid's biggest shippers of West African 'ardwoods since the War?"

"Yes."

"Ah-hah. And do you also know he has recently started importing a much inferior mark from Nigeria?"

"Not really. I do know his shipments from Nigeria have increased recently, just as our exports to his suppliers have also increased."

"*Voilà*. I must tell you, he has been offering this timber as an alternative to ours at a much lower price, with the result that our timber sales 'ave fallen and our prices 'ave been depressed. Yet he continues to overcharge for 'is services to us. You see our problem? What would you do?"

"I cannot answer that question. I have already said more than I should have said. From your point of view I imagine it doesn't seem very moral."

Dumard smiled. "Morality in business, *cher jeune homme*, ends where the profit motive begins. But in Mr Reid's case it is, I fear, 'ow do you say . . .

"Stillborn."

"Thank you. But do not concern yourself about anything you 'ave said. We 'ave already decided to use another timber broker. The question was: did we want you to continue to do our purchasing?"

"And the answer?"

"It is obvious, I fear. We shall 'ave to make other arrangements."

John pursed his lips in a soundless whistle. "Well, that settles it then. I doubt if I shall continue working for Reid-Parry Enterprises."

"If you are still worried about anything you said to me this evening, John, let me reassure you that I will say nothing to Mr Reid."

"Oh, I not worried about that, Henri. It's just that we've lost so much business lately that once your account goes I don't think there will be enough left to sustain my salary."

Dumard nodded gravely, letting the information sink in. "Well if ever I can 'elp you, John, please do not 'esitate . . ."

"Thank you. But tell me, did you really mean what you said about morality in business."

"It was a generalisation." Dumard spread his hands. "I suppose there are still some of us who believe we can make a profit without sacrificing our honour."

"But not Mr Reid," said John angrily.

"You are still a young man. You should not judge older men too harshly. The blacks and whites of our youth merge imperceptibly as we age. I am sure your Mr Reid does not regard himself as a dishonest man."

CHAPTER NINETEEN

The next morning, as his wakening consciousness filled with the memory of the past two days events, he knew what he had to do. Dumard had presented him with a solution to his problem. He could plead the gravity of the business situation as his excuse for an immediate return to London. There was no need to meet Yvette again. He could telephone her, explain the position, and catch an early plane back. Later he could write to her; it would be easier in a letter.

Immediately after breakfast he phoned her. He knew, before he had finished explaining, that she was going to be difficult. Her sharp intake of breath when he said he would have to return today, the sob in her voice when she asked why he couldn't simply phone his office, her gasp of dismay when he said he wouldn't even have time to see her before leaving.

"That's absurd. Even if you leave immediately you will not be in London until this afternoon. You will not go to the office until tomorrow morning."

"I suppose so," he admitted grudgingly.

"Then there is no reason why we should not meet first. You can take an evening plane."

"Yes," he agreed. At least he could avoid another night with her.

"Meet me at eleven o'clock in the Jardin des Tuilleries," she suggested. "By the pond near the Place de la Concorde."

A few minutes before eleven he arrived in the Tuilleries gardens and stood watching the children at play, rolling their hoops, sailing their small boats n the pond. A little girl was whimpering, her hoop having rolled into the pond. Her mother, or nanny, scolded her and then retrieved the hoop. Second later the child was screaming with joy. How wonderful was childhood, he thought, when everything was so simple, when pleasure was the normal state, pain merely transitory.

Then Yvette appeared and, after embracing, they sat on two metal chairs some distance from the pond, away from the noise of the children playing. They were silent and yet it was as if their silence had sound, as if each was conscious of the other's unspoken thoughts. Yvette was clearly distressed and her silence seemed to pose an accusation and a challenge, though he could not understand why this should be so.

In the end she spoke first. "What is troubling you, John?"

"Eh?" He was startled by the question, as if she had been looking into his mind, reading his thoughts. "Why should anything be troubling me?"

She stared at him, wide-eyed, nervously, her lower lip starting to tremble. Oh you damned fool, he thought, why don't you wake up and realise I'm no good for you, that I can only make you unhappy? Abruptly he felt his anger transfer from himself to her and he said, "You've only yourself to blame if you're feeling miserable. We could have said goodbye on the telephone."

His awareness of his lack of reason served to make him even more angry, but his words seemed to have a calming effect on Yvette.

"Something is troubling you," she insisted, "and it is not your business worries. What is wrong?"

"There's nothing wrong," he said irritably.

He might not have answered. She said, "Is it something I have done?"

"No, Yvette. You've done nothing."

"Then it must be another woman."

His anger vanished instantly and was replaced by a feeling of emotional numbness. How could she be so intuitive? A hasty denial rose to his lips, but he found himself unable to utter the one syllable that would set her mind at rest. She stared at him, mutely begging him to respond, her eyebrows drawn together as though she were suffering an unendurable pain.

Then she said softly, "I felt something the other night. You were . . . different. I thought it must be my imagination. Then yesterday . . . when you telephoned, you sounded . . . almost pleased that we would not be meeting. This morning I was sure . . ."

"I'm sorry."

He reached for her hand, but she pulled it away from him. "Tell me about it, John."

He started to speak, slowly at first, then more hurriedly, trying to get it over with as quickly as possible. Finally, in a torrent of words, he told her the whole story.

She looked dazed. "I can't believe it." She spoke the words to herself.

"I wasn't completely sure before I came to Paris, but now I'm certain. I shall ask her to marry me when I get back to London."

"But why? Why tell me now? Why not on Tuesday? Why try to act as if nothing had changed between us?"

"I didn't want to hurt you."

"Didn't want to hurt me!" she echoed, her voice shocked and

incredulous. "Didn't want to hurt me!" she repeated shrilly. "And what do you think you are doing now? My God, when I think of Tuesday night. Ugh!" She shuddered. "I feel dirty. Defiled. You must take me for a *putain*. No! With a *putain, c'est son métier*, she gets paid for it. What does make me, John? What is *my* job?"

"I . . . I . . ." he began, not knowing how to answer her. But she gave him no opportunity to continue.

"I no longer know what manner of man you are. I thought I knew you as well as it was possible to know anyone. Perhaps I did. But you have changed and now I do not recognise what I see. Go back to London – back to your woman. I only hope for her sake you treat her better than you have treated me."

"But Yvette," he protested. "The last thing I wanted to do was to hurt you. That's why I didn't want to tell you."

Her eyes flashed. "Oh, you make me feel sick. You say you did not want to hurt me, yet you allowed me to give myself to you – you took me – and it meant nothing to you. Less than nothing. You made love to me, thinking all the time of your woman in London."

"But it did mean something to me."

She slapped his face, and the shock of it, the realisation of how much she must be hurting to have done so, was more painful than the blow itself. For a moment, seeing her wild eyes and flushed cheeks, his face still smarting from the slap, he suffered with her, for her.

"How dare you!" she exclaimed. "You are not satisfied with having dishonoured my love, you now want to destroy my pride with your filthy deceit. I only hope you do not judge all Frenchwomen by me; you make me feel I have debased my nationality and my sex."

Her words echoed in the air around him and he seemed hardly aware that she had left. He was shaken and numb, and oblivious to his surroundings.

A hoop rolled over the dusty ground and came in contact with his leg, falling over, half-encircling his knees. His hand closed round the thin wooden band, gripped it more and more tightly as he continued to remember the look of anguish and pain on Yvette's face. Suddenly he thrust the hoop from him, sent it rolling towards the pond. The small boy who had been standing before him, head on one side, mutely begging him to return the hoop, gave a small scream and set off in pursuit.

He pressed the bell nervously. For a moment, a terrifying moment, he couldn't visualise her face and wondered if he had imagined his feelings for her. Had be built a fragile castle of desire from a few straws of memory?

Then the door opened and Barbara stood before him, looking exactly as he last remembered her, her cheeks flushed, her hair dishevelled. But there was a look of surprise on her face.

"Why John .. what are you doing back?"

He grinned. "I couldn't stay away from you." He moved to take her in his arms, but she pushed her hands against his chest and held him off.

"Why didn't you warn me you were coming?"

"I thought it would be a nice surprise." He took hold of her wrists. "Are we going to stand here chatting all evening, or am I invited in?"

"I'm sorry." She gave him a quick, flustered smile. "This is rude of me, isn't it? Of course you may come in, but not yet; the place is an absolute shambles."

He grinned again. "You forget. I'm used to it."

"No, John, really .. Go to the pub for a drink and give me half an hour to tidy up."

"Well, if I must, I must."

"I'm afraid you must. And stop pouting like a little boy who's lost his lollipop; mama will give it back soon."

He tried again to kiss her, and she pushed him away, laughing.

"Not now . . . later." She kissed a finger, pressed it to his lips, and closed the door.

In the pub, over a pint of draught ale, he reviewed their few moments conversation and was angry with himself for his childish reaction. What right had he to expect her to throw herself into his arms like a moonstruck adolescent. He had only been away two days and she had no reason to share his relief that the Paris episode was now behind him.

But the annoyance persisted and was made worse by the nagging suspicion that there was something not quite right about her reception of him, something he could not quite pinpoint.

He started thinking of how he would ask her to marry him, and the prospect served to cheer him up. Would he ask her before or after they had made love? The whisper of a smile creased his face at the thought, and then he shivered as he imagined himself, in the privacy of her room, holding her in his arms, pressing his lips to her throat . . .

He looked at the pub clock. Damn! Only ten minutes had passed. Should he go back now? She had surely had enough time to tidy up.

Oh, hell, she had said half an hour. He had better wait a bit longer. He would give it another ten minutes, and then saunter back.

But why should she want half an hour? She only had one room to tidy and it couldn't be that much of a shambles. Or if it were, what had she been doing to bring it to such a state? He was aware that he really knew very little about Barbara and her habits. In any case, it was absurd of him to imagine that she might not have had a full social life before he entered it. On the contrary it was precisely what he would have expected of her, and it was an unwarranted assumption on his part that should could drop everything the moment he turned up unexpectedly at her door.

For a moment the fringe of his memory brushed against the recollection of another time, another place, a similar situation, and then he let it go, and glanced at the clock. Twenty minutes had now passed since he had left her. Time to go back and dispel any remaining doubts. But that was stupid. There were no remaining doubts. He drained his glass and left the pub.

The tone of the doorbell had barely stopped reverberating when she opened the door to him. She was dressed in wine-coloured slacks and a navy blue sweater. Her hair was drawn back and tied with a ribbon behind her head. She took his arm and led him into the small hallway. "You're a naughty boy. I said half an hour, and you're five minutes early."

In the room he could not resist looking round for signs of disorder, but everything was spick and span. And then he looked at her and he could no longer contain his desire. He gathered her into his arms, his lips seeking hers. The warmth of her response and the marvel of her body in his arms, and he was once again trapped in the wonder of his feeling for her. After a moment she drew out of his embrace, led him to an armchair, and deposited herself in his lap. Then, with a natural, unhesitating movement, her arms were around his neck and they were once more kissing.

After a while she drew back and looked at him. "Now tell me, what are you doing back so unexpectedly and so soon?"

"I'd finished my business and I couldn't wait to get back to you."

"And what about your poor little mademoiselle? What's her name?"

"Yvette. Oh, that's didn't work out."

Barbara tweaked his ear and he yelped with only partly simulated pain. "What was that for?"

"For lying."

"What do you mean?"

"You're either lying now, or you were lying to me the other day." She took the lobe of his ear once again between thumb and forefinger. "Now come on, before I really hurt you. Did you or did you not take advantage of poor little Yvette?"

"All right, I give in. Just let go of my ear." She released it. "Yes, yes I did."

"And you still came back early?"

"I'm here, aren't I?"

"Hmm," she acknowledged doubtfully. But I don't know whether to be flattered or offended."

"What on earth do you mean?"

"I mean, dear round-heeled John, that if you're telling the truth, either your little Yvette suffered by comparison with me, or . . ." and she tweaked his ear again, but gently, ". . . or she rejected you and you hot-footed it back to my bed. Or could it be . . ." She paused.

"Could it be what? Go on. This is fascinating."

"No," She laughed. "You would hardly be so foolish."

"You'll leave me wondering all evening if you don't tell me."

"Well it just occurred to me that you might have told your French friend about me."

"I did."

"You *did*? What did you tell her?"

"Only that I love you."

"And was this before or after you had had your wicked way with her?"

He swallowed. "After."

"My God! I thought you said you were fond of the girl."

"I was. I *am*."

"Oh, John . . . I can't decide whether you're teasing me or just naive. Jesus, how that poor girl must have suffered." And she burst into laughter that set her whole body shaking against him.

He felt himself blushing, partly in shame, partly in anger. Was she deliberately taunting him, or was this merely another aspect of the hardness he had already suspected in her – a hardness which he had previously dismissed as a protective shell.

He tried to remain calm, but burst out angrily, "Don't worry. I shan't make you suffer that way."

She stopped laughing. "Oh I know you won't," she said coldly. "Neither you nor anyone else has the power to make me suffer – that way, or any other way." And then, as if to soften the words, she laughed again and said, "Tell me all about it."

"All about what?"

"Why all about you and Yvette, of course."

"But I've already told you."

"No, silly. I mean what you and she did together. And how."

He felt the heat of embarrassment creep up the back of his neck. "You can't be serious?"

She looked at him in surprise for a moment, was about to say something and checked herself. Then she bounded from his lap. "No, I'm not serious. How about a drink."

"Please. I need one."

"Whiskey?"

"You mean you've got some?"

She went to the sideboard, opened it, produced a bottle. "Satisfied?"

"Don't tell me you got that just for me. It's half-empty."

"Just for you? Of course not. I had some friends over last night." She poured out his drink, took the glass over to him, and sat down again in his lap. "Now tell me the truth. Why did you come back so soon?"

"But I have told you. How many times must I repeat it before you believe me. I wanted to see you again." He put his glass on the floor and held her hand. "Barbara, what you said last week . . .you did mean it, didn't you?"

"I'm not sure what you are thinking of, in particular, but I always mean what I say."

"Look," he said, "I know we haven't known each other very long, but you mean an awful lot to me. You see I . . . I've never felt quite this way about anyone before. It's more than just a casual affair, isn't it? I mean, for you as well as for me."

"Of course, darling." She kissed his forehead. "My affairs are never casual."

"No. Don't humour me. I'm being serious. We may have known each other only one week, but what I told you that first night was quite true. I did fall in love with you at first sight. It's never happened to me before. And you said it was different for you also. Did you mean that?"

"I told you. I always mean what I say."

He drew a relieved breath, pulled her head down to his, and kissed her.

"Let's do this properly," she said.

She got off his lap, led him over to the divan, pulled the coverlet from it in one swift, careless motion, letting it drop onto the floor. She lay down and pulled him down towards her.

"Undress me, John," she whispered. "And do it slowly."

Desire rose in him like the gently nurtured ember of an almost dead camp-fire gradually fanned back into life. He couldn't understand what was making it so difficult for him; his response to her had previously been immediate and overwhelming. He grunted and softly groaned with the impossible effort, while she lay outstretched and breathing heavily, her body twisting and shuddering and climaxing beneath his caressing fingers. Her frequent, effortless orgasms before had instantly aroused him, now they seemed to have no effect.

"I don't know what the matter is," he said in dismay. "You'll have to help me, darling."

"Damn you! Damn you!" she hissed. "I don't want it that way. I want *you* to do it, for God's sake!"

He could feel his jaws chomping from the strain of his exertions and then, for a while, it was a little better and he was able to penetrate her. He persisted with difficulty while she gasped and whined, squealed and writhed and shuddered, and finally her back arched and her fingernails scored his shoulders, and she sank back with the deeply expelled breath of ultimate completion.

He did not look at her. He could not speak to her. He turned his face away and buried it in the pillow, knowing that his frustration and shame had been evident to her. After a time he felt her leave the bed and heard the sound of water running in the bathroom. His body was sticky and sour-smelling where the sweat had dried on his chest and in his armpits; it mingled with the sweet-sour smell of their lovemaking and faintly sickened him.

When he heard her return to the room he picked his clothes off the floor and went into the bathroom, still too ashamed to look at her. He ran several inches of cold water into the bath and then sank into it, gasping with the shock. Quickly he soaped himself and then rinsed off the thin lather. He towelled himself dry, dressed, and went back into the room.

The divan-bed had been remade, the black and white check coverlet once more in place. Barbara was sitting in the solitary armchair, sipping a sherry. She had replaced her slacks, but remained bare above the waist. Her sharply pointing breasts were twin fingers of accusation and scorn; the corners of her mouth drooped in a sneer.

"You must have enjoyed yourself in Paris more than you confessed."

An angry denial sprang to his lips. And remained there. He stared at her, his hurt and humiliation reflected in his eyes.

She patted the side of her thigh. "Come and sit down here."

He sat on the floor beside her. Her fingers played with his hair.

"What was the matter with you?" Her voice sounded contrite, encouraging him to speak.

"I don't know," he said miserably. "It's not something I have ever experienced. Perhaps I was looking forward to it too much. Perhaps it was the reaction to what happened in Paris."

"Poor John," her voice crooned. "Was it really so bad over there?"

He nodded.

"And I haven't helped much, have I?"

"Oh Barbara," he said, looking up at her. "This reunion was going to be so different. There was so much I wanted to tell you."

"Such as?"

"Such as asking you to marry me."

Her eyes revealed a shock of disbelief.

"I know it sounds crazy," he went on hurriedly, "when we've known each other such a short time. But really, when you think that some people go through a lifetime without finding what we've found . . ."

She threw her head back and laughed, startling him. Her laughter grew louder, more uncontrollable; her body trembled and her breasts quivered. He jumped to his feet and stared at her in amazement.

"What's so damned funny?" He grasped her arms and shook her. "I said, what's so damned funny?"

Her laughter died down into a mild spluttering. "Oh, John, you're not serious."

"Of course I'm serious."

As the laughter threatened to erupt once more, he again shook her into passivity. "Stop that," she said sharply. "You're hurting me." Then as he stopped shaking her, "Why would you want to get married?"

"Why do you think. Because I love you. Because I can't imagine spending my life without you."

"And what can marriage give you that you're not getting already?"

He sighed. "You don't want to understand, do you? I'm not just talking about sex. It's you I want. All of you."

She shook her head sadly. "Nobody will ever have all of me. Nobody will ever own me."

"Who said anything about owning you. Hell, you know why people get married as well as I do. Anyway, I thought you loved me."

"Oh, but I do, I do. I never have sex with a man unless I love him. I love lots and lots of men."

His face reddened. "If you're saying that to make me angry, you're succeeding very well."

"I'm not trying to make you angry – just to make you see sense. Believe me I would be really happy if I thought that what we've shared – I'm not talking about what happened tonight – would continue for evermore. But it won't. I know myself too well. I'm surprised it's lasted as long as it has. Almost a record for me."

"What do you mean?"

"What I mean," she explained patiently, "is that marriage should mean more than what we've enjoyed together for a few days. And I'm afraid it wouldn't. Not for me. I couldn't even promise to be faithful, because I know damn well it's a promise I'd have no intention of keeping."

He rubbed his eyes with a tired gesture. "I think you're wrong, Barbara. And I think I was wrong to ask you so soon. I know what we mean to each other. In time you will come to know it too."

"Poor lamb," she said. "You still don't understand. I suppose I've been guilty of an error of judgement."

"And error of judgement?" he queried bemusedly.

"Yes. I'm afraid so. I assumed from what I'd heard about you that we were very much alike. I never dreamt you would get so serious. Look, John, why do you think I wouldn't allow you in here when you first arrived this evening?"

"You said it was because you wanted to tidy up."

"And that is true. But what I wanted to do was to change the sheets on the bed before you came in. I had a friend stay over last night. Do I have to spell it out for you?"

"No! No, you don't have to spell it out." He stumbled over to the divan and sat down heavily. "My God, my God . . ." and he buried his face in his hands, elbows on knees, trying to control the fit of trembling in his body.

CHAPTER TWENTY

For a long time he could not get to sleep.

It was not merely the scene he had played with Barbara which kept repeating itself in detail in his mind, nor the memory of his earlier episode with Yvette, the two intermingling and juxtaposing themselves in a ghastly retributional rhythm; it was not this alone which kept him awake. It was as though some earlier memory refused to be smothered, yet would not come close enough to the surface of his memory to bring relief.

Lying in bed, smoking cigarette after cigarette, reliving both experiences, searching for something deeper, vexing himself with possible explanations for Barbara's conduct and his own inner confusion, he was like a cat toying with a ball of string, giving it a life of its own, unwilling or unable to accept his own responsibility for its movements.

Finally he had fallen asleep, a restless, disturbed sleep, punctuated by a fitful, disturbing dream full of taunting shapes and mocking shadows. A dream of groping and seeking and stretching and striving for something always beyond his reach, something without form or substance. And then the running and stumbling and tripping down the long dark tunnel with the pinpoint of light at the other end, the light which always seemed to recede as he ran towards it.

He woke up damp and feverish, with a sense of utter deprivation. He washed his face in cold water, then took a shower, trying to sort his thoughts into some sort of order. Life had suddenly become a confusion of shattered ideals and forlorn ambitions. Everything he had wanted, everything he had sought and touched, all had turned to dross. He had wrecked friendships, he had broken hearts, he had destroyed trust – and none of it had been intended. He had always been motivated by the desire not to cause hurt to those who meant most to him. Where had he gone wrong? Wherein lay his mistake?

And now it was his turn to suffer. Perhaps there was some justice in it.

An hour later he walked into his office and found Mitchell sitting at his desk.

"What are you doing in here, Mitchell?"

Mitchell looked at him as though he had just returned from the grave. "Sorry, Mr Graham. I thought you were still in Paris."

"Well, as you can see, I'm not."

Mitchell got up from behind John's desk with a hesitant laugh. "But I thought . . thought you were going to phone in yesterday."

John slapped his forehead. "Christ, yes. I completely forgot about it. Did old man Parry say anything?"

"No." Mitchell frowned. "Only been over here once, he has. This morning it was. To say Dumard was settling the draft."

John felt his stomach muscles contract. "How the hell did he know that? What else did he say to you?"

"Nothing, really." Mitchell looked ill-at-ease. Or was that John's imagination?

"Come on, Mitchell. Out with it. He must have said something."

"Well, he asked if I'd heard from you, and . . ."

"And?"

"Nothing. I mean, that's all."

"Look here, Mitchell, it's obvious something's going on." Mitchell looked at him blankly. "Oh, hell, there's only one way to find out."

He depressed a key on the intercom and heard the click of the receiver being lifted at the other end. "Good morning, sir. Graham here."

"Graham! When did you get back?"

"Last night, sir. I thought I'd have time to phone you from London Airport, but we got in rather too late."

"Oh."

"Should I come over and see you, sir?"

"No, Graham. Wait in your office. Mr Reid will probably send for you shortly."

John turned back to Mitchell. "Haven't you any work to do?"

"Yes. Of course."

"Then why don't you go outside and do it," John snapped. Mitchell's face turned red as he went to the door. "And send Miss Carter in here."

Sally Carter's face beamed with pleased surprise when she entered. "Oh, Mr Graham, welcome back." She sat down, crossed her legs, tucked a kleenex tissue into her dress sleeve, and opened her notebook.

"Thank you, Sally. You won't need your book, I'm not going to dictate." She frowned in mild enquiry. "Did anything unusual happen in here this morning?"

"Unusual, Mr Graham?"

"You know . . . out of the ordinary."

She pursed her lips thoughtfully. "I don't think so. Mr Mitchell was opening the morning mail when I came in. Then he went into your office, and a few minutes later Mr Parry came over to see him. That was all until you sent for me."

"I see. Thank you, Sally."

As she left, the intercom buzzed. Reid wanted to see him immediately. He sensed the hostility and anger in the man's voice and, inside himself, a rebellion took place. He did not know what had happened, but he could guess that somehow Reid had already learned of Dumard's decision to take his business away, and Reid – being Reid – would now be looking for a scapegoat. Well it was not going to be John. He'd had enough of Reid's dictatorial brow-beating. He'd had it up to here. He'd been pushed around long enough, both inside and outside the office. It was time to assert himself.

Yet with each step he took along the corridor, his resolve grew weaker and more indecisive.

Parry shifted uncomfortably in his chair facing Reid as John entered the director's office; his eyes shifted too, and fixed themselves on a spot six inches above John's head. Reid wore anger on his face like a carnival mask. John stopped about a yard from Reid's desk and waited for one of the directors to speak.

It was Reid. "So you've decided to come back."

"Was there any doubt, Mr Reid?"

A look of surprise flashed across Reid's face and then was gone. John's reply was apparently not one he had anticipated.

"And what about the draft, Graham?"

"What *about* the draft, Mr Reid?" John echoed. "Mitchell told me you already know it's going to be paid."

It was Parry's turn to suffer one of Reid's looks, this time of sheer malevolence. He looked at John again.

"Yes, Graham, we know it's going to be paid. But wasn't it your place to tell us? As soon as you knew?"

"Possibly. But what was the rush? It would have been different if Dumard had refused to pay."

Reid toyed with a pencil, taking time out for thought. Evidently the interview was not proceeding according to plan.

"And what did Dumard say about the timber business?"

"Why should he have said anything?"

"Don't treat me like a bloody imbecile, Graham," Reid barked.

"What are you trying to suggest, Mr Reid?"

"I'm suggesting that you're a bloody liar, Graham, and a bloody traitor."

"I don't . . ."

"You'd better read this before you say any more." Reid thrust a telegram at him. John read it.

HAVE INSTRUCTED BANK TRANSFER DRAFT PROCEEDS STOP IN VIEW YOUR NIGERIAN COMMITMENTS HAVE SUSPENDED ALL TIMBER CONTRACTS PRESENTLY UNSHIPPED STOP LETTER FOLLOWS

Under different circumstances, John would have grinned. Dumard certainly didn't believe in wasting time. He said, "What has this got to do with me?"

"I'll tell you what it's got to do with you. Doesn't it strike you as funny that Dumard should take this step twenty-four hours after you've seen him? Doesn't that strike you as being a bit too much of a coincidence? Do you still insist that you didn't discuss timber with him?

John flared up inside. This discussion was making him sick. Reid must be completely round the bend if he thought John could possibly influence Dumard into taking this step.

"Of course we discussed timber. How could we talk about equipment for extracting timber without talking about timber? But how could I tell him anything he didn't already know? And what makes you think I could influence him? Of course, I don't expect you to understand that. You're too wrapped up in your own little world of petty tyranny and self-importance. Well, here's another little tit-bit for you. When you get Dumard's letter you'll find out that you've lost his buying agency business too. And now I suppose you'll want my resignation. I suppose you require the full period of notice?"

"No." Reid looked relieved, as though he had been waiting for John's outburst, and his voice was icy calm, which John found somehow more compelling than his habitual enraged roar. "No, I don't want your resignation. You're fired. As of ten minutes ago. Parry has already made out your salary cheque up to the end of next month. And that's more than you deserve."

"Well, in that case, there's nothing more to be said, is there?" He turned around and started walking towards the door.

"Now listen, Graham . . ."

"No, you listen, Mr Reid." John turned again to face him.

"GRAHAM!" Reid screamed, his face apoplectic. "Until you pick up your cheque you are still in my employ. You might have the grace to listen."

John ran a finger along the back of his shirt collar. "Go ahead."

"Thank you." Reid's voice dripped with sarcasm. "I know you think yourself the epitome of commercial ability. A pity I can't share your opinion. You know, the one thing I believed in was your integrity. But I was wrong. I don't think you lack aptitude or energy, but what you lack is more fundamental: a sense of duty, of allegiance to the people who pay your salary. How old are you, Graham?"

"Twenty-eight."

"How much have we been paying you?"

"Fourteen hundred."

Reid sniffed. "D'you know I was over forty before I earned that much. D'you know I started my working life selling newspapers on the streets of Manchester. I've built this business up with the sweat of my own hands, and no young upstart is going to tell me what I should or shouldn't do with my money. I know that in your book I'm a reactionary bastard. I know I could have spent money as you wanted and, maybe, increased your turnover. But what would that have meant to me and my family? Very little. The only benefit would have been to the Chancellor of the Exchequer. On the other hand, we might easily have lost money, and after fifty years of hard work I'm not prepared to take risks of that sort." He paused, suddenly a very old man. "All right, you can pass your stuff over to Mitchell, and then clear out."

John shook his head sadly. "You'll never understand, will you? You made your money in the days of the sellers' market, and you can't accept that times have changed. You'll lose this business and still won't understand. You'll go to your grave wondering where you went wrong, still not understanding.

"No," John cut off Reid's attempt to interrupt. "You've had your say, now let me finish. I must admit you are right in one respect. I have been lacking. It is your business and you have every right to say how it is run. My lack was in not seeing that earlier and leaving when Mattson left."

He was drunk.

He knew it the moment he entered the car and tried to fumble the ignition key into its lock. But he was sober enough to know that he was in no fit state to drive. He got out of the car and viciously slammed the door shut. Then he started walking to Moorgate Station.

It was those last few drinks in Shorts' that had done it. Up until then he had manage to retain some small measure of control. Or had he?

Hadn't he really set out to get drunk?

Yes, he was drunk. But he was not drunk enough, and with the City pubs now closed, he was unlikely to get drunk enough.

Oh, hell. What did he want? Did he really expect to find the answer refracted through the amber liquid? Or did he simply want to wallow in self-pity?

It had been all right while he had had that argument with Reid. It had temporarily driven all other thoughts out of his head. But then, when he had left the office, they had started crowding back in again, and now the drinks – too many and not enough – were making it worse.

In Moorgate Station he studied the underground plan. Where should be go now? There was that little drinking club behind Charing Cross Station. Or the Mandrake in Soho. Or he could go home. He had booze in the flat, and he could come back tomorrow for his car. But no! Drinking was not enough. He didn't want to be alone.

Unconsciously his eyes had been following the lines up to Belsize Park and, suddenly, at the top right-hand edge of his vision, he caught the name Finchley. Bernie. That was the answer. Good old Bernie. There was a good chance he would be home; it was certain he would have drinks in the house; and no doubt at all that he would provide a sympathetic ear and a broad pair of shoulders. And to hell with the risk – he *would* take the car.

The special god who watches over fools and drunken drivers – the two often synonymous – had certainly looked after him. As he pulled into the kerb outside Raymond's house, he could not remember a single moment of his drive there. His thoughts had been elsewhere than on the road during the entire journey. Yet he had arrived safely; he had undoubtedly taken all the correct turnings; he had without question stopped at all the red lights and halt signs. It had been instinctive. It had also been criminally insane.

He knocked at the door. He waited a full minute and knocked again. Bugger it, he thought, there's nobody home. In disgust he slammed the knocker down with his full force and turned back to the car. Behind him he heard the door open.

"John? What're you doin' here feller?"

He turned round again. "Bernie!" A sob of relief.

"Good God, man, what's the matter with you?"

John felt a smile of inanity appear on his face. "You could say I just a teeny, weeny bit drunk," he confessed. "Didn't think anyone was home."

"Ruth's out. I was working. I thought at first it was a door-to-door salesman. Come in."

"No." John articulated the word carefully, pursing his lips in an elongated circle. "Mustn't interrupt your work."

"Don't be a fool." Raymond grabbed his arm and urged him into the house. "You're in no fit state to drive. Don't know how you made it here. Now come in and sit down."

Raymond was right, John decided. He was drunker now than when he had left Shorts. He dropped heavily into an armchair.

"Can I get you something? Coffee? Alka Seltzer?"

"Scotch and soda."

"Don't you think you've had enough?"

John pouted. "Need another little drinkie. Please."

"Suit yourself." Raymond poured the drink. "Mind if I don't join you?"

"Mustn't be unfriendly, Bernie. Don't want to drink alone."

"Oh, hell . . ." Raymond poured a small amount of scotch into a glass, filled it up with soda water. "Now tell me what this is all about. You look pretty sick."

John swigged half his glass in one gulp. "Been sacked. No job, no references, no nothing."

"Suffering cats, feller, what's to worry about? You wanted to leave anyway."

"Not like this. Wanted to find another job first. Get married."

"Get what!" Raymond laughed. "Who'd have you?" John glowered at him. "Anyhow, my information is that you've spent all your spare time with Barbara. That's fine behaviour for someone wanting to get married." Raymond looked at John and gasped. "Jesus, guy, you don't mean it's Barbie you want to marry?"

John nodded glumly.

Raymond yelped. "Say, if that don't beat all. What's the matter with you? You in your right mind? I mean you didn't get a crack on the head recently, did you?"

"What's so crazy about wanting to marry Barbara?"

"Hey! Don't bit my head off. I didn't get you into this fix. And don't get me wrong. I'm fond of Barbie, so's Ruth. We've got nothing against her. But she's not the kind you marry. You must admit I gave you fair warning. Hell, you don't need me to spell it out, do you? She's a nympho. But you know that already, don't you?"

"Yes. I know that . . . now. Anyway, I can't marry her . . . she won't have me." He looked at his empty glass and held it out to Bernstein. "Give me another drink, Bernie. Not that it helps. Anyway, there's too much else involved. And I've never felt with anyone the way I feel with Barbara. Not just in bed. It's more than that. But . . . You know I've not got the best of reputations with women, but with Barbara . . . I was . . . I don't know how to put it . . . I wanted to let all my defences down. She gave me something I never had before."

"Nonsense," said Bernstein. "*You* gave *yourself* something you never had before. Barbie would have given you nothing. She's strictly a taker. Not that she would deliberately hurt someone else; she would assume they knew what she was and they were getting what they wanted. If your affair with Barbie has made you aware of a fundamental weakness in your other relationships, well . . . good for Barbie."

"Well, thanks for nothing. I get turned down by the only woman I've ever proposed to . . . I get sacked from my job . . . I destroy my friend's home and break the heart of the sweetest person on earth . . . But thanks anyway. You preach a good sermon."

Raymond stared at him in wonder. "What's all this about breaking hearts and destroying homes?"

"Did I say that?"

"You certainly did."

John put his glass on the floor and palmed his eyes, elbows resting on knees. His shoulders shook with quiet, drink-induced laughter, one stage removed from sobbing. "It's ironic," he muttered, "it really is. I suppose I've been doing my damndest not to think about it all day."

"Want to tell me about it?"

"Why not?" John looked up and laughed without humour. "It'll be fitting, I suppose. You were really in on it from the beginning."

Slowly, abashedly, he began telling Raymond the truth about his first visit to Paris. He told him about Yvette and Claude, about Betty and Norman and Julie, about his extended phase of dissipation and its culmination with Megan, about the gulf, the feeling of void, that replaced the dissolute gaiety. Then he described his feelings of sick shame at the awareness of his own immorality, and how first Yvette and finally Barbara had helped his recovery. But to what effect? For what good? He had behaved even more badly after he had believed himself cured than he had before.

Raymond listened in silence, then said gently, "My God, you are a chump. You prattle on about sex and morality as if one is the antithesis of the other. You seem to think overindulgence in sex is wicked. You've got morality on the brain, and you've probably spent the last ten years chastising yourself for your own wickedness."

"Don't, for heaven's sake, try to be kind to me. I have behaved wickedly. Otherwise I wouldn't feel the way I do."

"And how do you know how you feel . . . really feel, I mean? Aren't you the chap who was telling me the other day that it was impossible to know yourself? And if you can't know yourself, how are you going to know what's right and wrong for yourself?"

"Right's right and wrong's wrong," said John stubbornly.

"Really?" Raymond raised his eyebrows. "Just like that? And if you're a cannibal and it's right to eat the human flesh of another tribe, and your law allows it, and you've grown up believing it, and inside you're satisfied that it's right – does that make it right for everyone else? Including the people you eat?

"And if you're a German youth in the thirties, and you stone a man to death because he has side whiskers and wears a skull cap, and they've told you he's one of the filthy Jews who own all the wealth of the country, and start all the wars, and want to see you and your family starving, and everyone applauds your act and tells you that you're a splendid fellow and have done the right thing – does that make it right?

"No, John. There's no simple morality, and no simple right and wrong. The only criterion is how your actions are going to affect other people. If you live in society, that is. It's not what you do that's morally debilitating, it's the reaction you have to what you do.

"Look at it this way, John. You feel that you've behaved in a pretty rotten way to a number of people. All right, I'll agree with you that you have behaved pretty despicably to some of them, but I think it's your own shame and self-disgust that has caused you to behave that way. I know you don't like things put in psychoanalytical terms, but it's a common enough psychological pattern when you feel guilty of something to immerse yourself even further in the acts that disgust you."

"Preposterous!" John burst out. "If I feel guilty – and I do – it's the acts themselves I feel guilty of."

"You only think that . . ."

"I *know* that."

"Let me finish. You only think that because it's what you want to think."

"Balls! More parlour psychology."

"Call it what you like. You've got something on your mind. I don't know what it is, but it's there. You probably don't even know what it is yourself – not consciously. But whatever it is, it seems to put you in the position of constantly hurting people. I don't think you've set out deliberately to hurt anyone you've been fond of. I think you've just been terribly, terribly weak and have let yourself drift into situations where that has been the inevitable result."

"Thank you very much. You're doing a great job of white-washing."

"I'm not trying to whitewash you, John. I'm just trying to show you that you're not as black as you try to make yourself. For Christ's sake, you seem to think there's something disgusting and unclean about the numbers of women you and Norman fucked while you were living together. If you'd been born in a different society, or at a different time, you'd have accepted it as a normal part of your life to pay for a professional whenever you felt the need. Go to Amsterdam or Hamburg. Visit the red light districts. Do you think the only men who frequent them are immoral? Disgusting? Unclean? Are they hell! They're ordinary men, from all walks of life, who regard sex as a normal requirement of a healthy body. And they're prepared to pay for it. As for you, you've had it for free. Or perhaps, in a way, you've paid for it more than they have. Jesus, what crazy Puritanism."

"Do you really mean all that?"

"Well I'm not just talking to hear the sound of my own voice. And frankly, from what you've told me, I shouldn't be surprised if that early experience you had with that woman Betty hasn't affected you more than you've disclosed. In some crazy way you've probably confused it with guilt feelings about your mother's death. It seems to me that you gravitated towards Barbara because of certain real or imagined similarities between her and Betty. You think about it."

John thought. He wrinkled his brow and tried to force the remaining alcoholic cobwebs from his head. Bernie certainly seemed to have a valid point. Funny how hard it was to think about Betty after all this time. But there was certainly a similarity between Betty and Barbara – the similarity of control, and guidance, and force of character. Since Betty he had not been with another woman who had taken control of their relationship out of his hands – until he met Barbara.

"You may be right, Bernie. At least partly. But that can't excuse everything I've done . . . things I can never put right."

"None of us can ever put everything right – after the event. But, there are a few things it seems to me that you can do, and at very little cost – except to your ego. And I guess your ego could stand a few more jolts. You can apologise to your French friend Yvette. And you can get in touch with Norman and clear up any misunderstandings there. From what I gather, he could use some cheering up too. Megan has left him."

"Has she? How do you know?"

"Ruth saw her yesterday." Raymond's face clouded. "Unfortunately there's one person you won't be able to apologise to now."

John's face came up in sudden enquiry.

"I'm sorry, John, but Megan told Ruth that Julie died the other day. They tried to operate, but it was no good."

It was as if a black mist had dropped before John's eyes. Raymond was still talking, but John could not hear what he was saying. His body jerked with an uncontrollable fit of trembling and, for a moment, he feared he would faint. He was vaguely aware of Raymond's hands gripping his arms, shaking him, but the act had no significance. The whole of his conversation with Raymond vanished into a limbo of unimportance, and his head started thudding with the words: just like mother, just like mother.

In a drunken daze he felt himself get up from the chair and walk out of the room, out of the house. He started repeating the words aloud, over and over, while behind him someone was shouting at him. He didn't know who it was, or what they were shouting. He didn't care. Without thought, without awareness, without reflection, he climbed into the car and drove off. And he was two people. One of them was behind a steering wheel, dimly conscious of the road ahead; the other was in a hospital waiting room, sobbing, sobbing, sobbing, in an effort to wash away the stains of sin which refused to be cleansed.

CHAPTER TWENTYONE

He was back in the tunnel, the grimy, soot-filled tunnel, moving aimlessly, without apparent direction. And yet there was direction and he was following its course. But, with animal cunning, he was moving stealthily in a haphazard manner, so that the spot of light in the distance would not be aware of his progress, would not suddenly retreat.

And every now and then a portion of the tunnel would become abruptly illuminated, like the stations along an underground train line, but with quick sharp flashes, without continuity yet with peculiar vividness.

Like the moment he had sold the car. Where he had sold it, why he had sold it, he did not know. It had suddenly become important to have the money. Why he needed the money, what he had done with the money, he did not know either. He could merely recall a man in shirt sleeves and braces, checking the log book, phoning the finance company, while another man in soiled green overalls had probed and fumbled beneath the bonnet, and raced the engine. Then he had had difficulty in explaining why it was important to receive the money in cash and not by cheque. He had a faint recollection of a peculiar look in the man's eyes as he had counted out the pound notes and fivers, and of his own surprise that there was not more.

But it couldn't have been the money alone, for sometime after that he had gone to the bank to cash a cheque. Or had that been before he sold the car? There had been a faintly disgusted look on the bank-teller's face. He had tried to control the trembling of his hand while making out the cheque. He had gripped his right wrist with his left hand, and had sickly noticed the grubby knuckles and grimy nails.

Then there was the galling memory of being thrown out of a bar because he had been trying to pick a fight with someone on the next stool: a little man, with reddish plump cheeks, and a smile like Parry's. He couldn't remember where it was. He could only remember the surprise he had felt when the little man had slipped off the bar stool, a vague recollection of having contributed to the slip by an impatient dig in the chest, a dim feeling of revulsion that the little fellow was a good six inches smaller than himself, and the satisfyingly penitential pain of the bartender's blow in his belly to help him on his way through the door.

And waking one morning, or one afternoon, or one evening, and feeling the softness under his head. And turning his head painfully, opening one swollen lid, and seeing a great brown staring eye which slowly transformed itself into the hideous nipple and aureole of an ugly sagging breast. And half-recalling the gross and disgusting creature on the bar-stool next to his, and the drinks he had bought her, and leaving the bar together. He had closed his eye in shame and horror, and the next time he opened it he was alone in bed.

But even that had not been enough to bring him out of his alcoholic haze, out of the welter of self-pity. He continued moving through a foggy world of bars and brawls, and then even that became too much trouble. That must have been after he disposed of the car. He started calling at the off-licence whenever he awoke, feeling tears of anger smarting his eyes on the occasions when he arrived there to find it closed. The kindly *now then, sir* of the tall uniformed policeman the time he had kicked at the off-licence door in frustrated fury; the firm but gentle hand under his elbow, leading him away; the quiet but insistent *you'd better go home now, sir.*

Most of the time, though, the off-licence would be open, and he would grab his bottles and hurry back to the flat, sometimes remembering to buy a steak or a chop on the way, rarely troubling to eat it, never managing to finish it even on the few occasions that he cooked it.

And occasionally the voices would be stilled, and at those times the light at the end of the tunnel would glow with dazzling brightness, and it was almost as if a choir of angels were inviting him to join them on the outside in the sunshine's warmth.

At these times, aware of the dirt and squalor of his existence, he would ask himself when, how, *if* it was going to end. The smell of his unwashed body would temporarily over-ride the stench of undiscarded garbage; the food-congealed plates and dishes piling up in the kitchen; the dust everywhere; the empty bottles; the unopened letters pushed to one side behind the front door. Very occasionally he would be sickened and indulge in a frenzy of housework, and then return to the bottle.

Now count your dead, the mocking eyes said. And this time no important omissions; this time start right at the beginning; this time follow through to the acid end. Tote them up, enter them on the debit side of the ledger. Where's the credit entry? The red eyes scoffed. What's the balance carried forward? The denunciatory eyes taunted. Put them on the scales of justice. What goes on the side of mercy? Which way do the scales dip? The weary eyes sneered.

You know the answer, the eyes said. What are you waiting for? You know what you have to do. There's no other way out. The supreme penalty, and the only one fitting the crime. You owe it to them; you owe it to yourself. Your mother and Julie; Julie and your mother. A perfect circle. A just and fitting end. Nemesis.

The eyes came closer, red and black. Closer they came, and merged. One great red jeremiad, black centred, mocking him, deriding him, daring him. He rested his brow against the mirror and felt the coolness of the glass against the heat of his head. He drew back slowly and the eye-amoeba split and separated, the fissured ovals jeering at his weakness.

With slow inevitability his hand opened the medicine cabinet, removed the bottle of white tablets. They were all he had, and it would undoubtedly require a great many of them. But the bottle was almost full. Fitting, too, that they should have been left at the flat by Julie. He uncapped the bottle, shook out a tablet, placed it on his tongue, threw back his head, swallowed. His head came down, his lips twisted into a grimace or a smile, refuting the disbelief in the eyes, as he repeated the process. Slowly, carefully, again and again the bottle was shaken, the hand raised to mouth, the head thrown back. Again, and again, and again.

And then he gagged and choked and doubled over the sink, and vomited. Whiskey and wine and beer and aspirin tablets, and then he was clinging to the sink, retching, his eyes streaming. Even that you can't do right, he thought. But then you knew it wasn't going to work, didn't you? You knew you couldn't hold them down on top of that crazy mixture. You didn't want to die. You had no intention of dying.

And the red and streaming eyes assured him that he stood no chance of dying, but that life could be a living hell henceforth.

Stomach aching and twitching, he groped his way into the living room, found the half-bottle of whiskey, raised it to his lips, tilted it, gulped the fiery liquid. One, two, three swallows, and then he started to gag again. He made the sink just as the whiskey came back up. He tried again, more slowly this time. It stayed down for perhaps ten seconds longer, and then he was retching again.

In time he was able to hold it down and, after a while, the spasms in his stomach stopped.